THE LAST TEMPLAR

RAYMOND KHOURY

An Orion paperback

First published in Great Britain in 2005
by Ziji Publishing
distributed by Duckworth
This paperback edition published in 2006
by Orion Books Ltd,
Orion House, 5 Upper St Martin's Lane,
London WC2H 9EA

An Hachette UK company

A CIP catalogue record for this book
is available from the British Library.

Printed in Great Britain by
Clays Ltd, St Ives plc

The Orion Publishing Group's policy is to use papers
that are natural, renewable and recyclable products and
made from wood grown in sustainable forests. The logging
and manufacturing processes are expected to conform to
the environmental regulations of the country of origin.

For my parents

For my girls: Suellen, Mia, and Gracie

and

For my buddy
Adam B. Wachtel
(1959–2005)

You would have gotten such a kick out of this

It has served us well, this myth of Christ.
– Pope Leo X, 16th century

PROLOGUE

Acre, Latin Kingdom of Jerusalem, 1291

The Holy Land is lost.

That single thought kept assaulting Martin of Carmaux, its brutal finality more terrifying than the hordes of fighters swarming through the breach in the wall.

He fought to block the thought, to push it away.

Now was not the time to lament. He had work to do.

Men to kill.

His broadsword held high, he charged through the clouds of choking smoke and dust and plunged into the seething ranks of the enemy. They were everywhere, their scimitars and axes ripping into flesh, their warrior howls piercing the haunting, rhythmic beat of the kettle drummers outside the fortress walls.

With all of his strength, he brought down his sword, splitting one man's skull clear to the eyes, his blade springing free as he lunged at his next opponent. Flicking a quick glance to his right, he spotted Aimard of Villiers driving his sword into the chest of another attacker before moving on to his next opponent. Dazed by the wails of pain and the screams of rage around him, Martin felt someone clutch at his left hand and swiftly clubbed the offender away with the pommel of his sword before bringing down its blade, feeling it cut through muscle and bone. From the corner of his eye, he sensed something menacingly close to his right and instinctively swung his sword at it, slicing through the upper arm of another one of the invaders before slashing open his cheek and severing his tongue in one blow.

It had been hours since he or any of his comrades had known any respite. The Muslim onslaught had not only been ceaseless, it had also been far worse than anticipated. Arrows and projectiles of blazing pitch had rained down incessantly on the city for days, starting more fires than could be tackled at once, while the Sultan's men had dug holes beneath the great walls into which they had packed brushwood that was also set alight. In several places, these makeshift furnaces had cracked the walls that were now crumbling under a barrage of catapulted rocks. The Templars and the Hospitallers had managed, by sheer force of will, to repulse the assault on Saint Anthony's Gate before setting it on fire and retreating. The Accursed Tower, however, had lived up to its name, allowing the rampaging Saracens into the city and sealing its fate.

Gargling shrieks of agony receded into the confused uproar as Martin yanked his sword back and looked around desperately for any sign of hope, but there was no doubt in his mind. The Holy Land was indeed lost. With mounting dread, he realized that they would all be dead before the night was over. They were facing the largest army ever seen, and despite the fury and the passion coursing through his veins, his efforts, and those of his Brothers, were surely doomed to failure.

It wasn't long before his superiors realized it too. His heart sank as he heard the fateful horn calling on the surviving Knights of the Temple to abandon the city's defenses. His eyes, darting left and right in a confused frenzy, again found those of Aimard of Villiers. He saw in them the same agony, the same shame that was burning through him. Side by side, they fought their way through the scrambling mob and managed to make their way back to the relative safety of the Templar compound.

Martin followed the older knight as he stormed through the throngs of terrified civilians who had taken refuge behind the bourg's massive walls. The sight that greeted them in the great hall shocked him even more than the carnage he had witnessed outside. Lying on a rough refectory table was

William of Beaujeu, the Grand Master of the Knights of the Temple. Peter of Sevrey, the Marshal, stood at his side, along with two monks. The woeful looks on their faces left little room for doubt. As the two knights reached his side, Beaujeu's eyes opened and he raised his head slightly, the movement causing an involuntary groan of pain. Martin stared at him in stunned disbelief. The old man's skin was drained of all color, his eyes bloodshot. Martin's eyes raced down Beaujeu's body, struggling to make sense of the sight, and he spotted the feathered bolt sticking out of the side of his ribcage. The Grand Master held its shaft in the curve of his hand. With his other, he beckoned Aimard who approached him, knelt by his side and cupped his hand with both of his own.

'It is time,' the old man managed, his voice pained and weak, but clear. 'Go now. And may God be with you.'

The words drifted past Martin's ears. His attention was elsewhere, focused on something he'd noticed as soon as Beaujeu had opened his mouth. It was his tongue, which had turned black. Rage and hate swelled in Martin's throat as he recognized the effects of the poisoned bolt. This leader of men, the towering figure who had dominated every aspect of the young knight's life for as long as he could remember, was as good as dead.

He noticed Beaujeu lifting his gaze to Sevrey and nodding almost imperceptibly. The Marshal moved to the foot of the table and lifted a velvet cover to reveal a small, ornate chest. It was not more than three hands wide. Martin had never seen it before. He watched in rapt silence as Aimard rose to his feet and gazed solemnly at the chest, then looked back at Beaujeu. The old man held his gaze before closing his eyes again, his breathing taking on an ominous rasp. Aimard went up to Sevrey and hugged him, then lifted the small chest and, without so much as a backward glance, headed out. As he passed Martin, he simply said, 'Come.'

Martin hesitated and glanced at Beaujeu and at the Marshal, who nodded his head in confirmation. He hurried quickly after Aimard and soon realized that they weren't heading toward the enemy.

They were heading for the fortress's quay.

'Where are we going?' he called out.

Aimard didn't break his step. 'The *Falcon Temple* awaits us. Hurry.'

Martin stopped in his tracks, his mind reeling in confusion. *We're leaving?*

He had known Aimard of Villiers since the death of his own father, a knight himself, fifteen years earlier, when Martin was barely five years old. Ever since, Aimard had been his guardian, his mentor. His hero. They had fought many battles together and it was fitting, Martin believed, that they would stand side by side and die together when the end came. But not this. This was insane. This was... *desertion*.

Aimard stopped too, but only to grasp Martin's shoulder and push him into motion. 'Make haste,' he ordered.

'No,' Martin yelled, flicking Aimard's hand off him.

'Yes,' the older knight insisted tersely.

Martin felt nausea rising in his throat; his face clouded as he struggled for words. 'I will not desert our Brothers,' he stammered. 'Not now – not ever!'

Aimard heaved a ponderous sigh and glanced back at the besieged city. Blazing projectiles were arcing into the night sky and hurtling down into it from all sides. Still clutching the small chest, he turned and took a menacing step forward so that their faces were now inches apart, and Martin saw that his friend's eyes were wet with unshed tears. 'Do you think I want to abandon them?' he hissed, his voice slicing the air. 'Abandon our Master – in his final hour? You know me better than that.'

Martin's mind seethed with turmoil. 'Then... *why?*'

'What we have to do is far more important than killing a few more of those rabid dogs,' Aimard replied somberly. 'It's crucial to the survival of our Order. It's crucial if we are to make sure everything we've worked for doesn't die here as well. We have to go. Now.'

Martin opened his mouth to protest, but Aimard's expression was fiercely unequivocal. Martin bowed his head in curt, if unwilling, acquiescence and followed.

The only vessel remaining in the port was the *Falcon Temple*, the other galleys having sailed away before the Saracen assault had cut off the city's main harbor a week earlier. Already low in the water, it was being loaded by slaves, sergeant-brothers, and knights. Question after question tumbled through Martin's brain but he had no time to ask any of them. As they approached the quay, he could see the ship's master, an old sailor he knew only as Hugh and who, he also knew, was held in high regard by the Grand Master. The burly man was watching the feverish activity from the deck of his ship. Martin scanned the ship from the aftcastle at the stern, past its high mast and to the stem from which sprang the figurehead, a remarkably lifelike carving of a fierce bird of prey.

Without breaking step, Aimard's voice bellowed out to the ship's master. 'Are the water and provisions loaded?'

'They are.'

'Then abandon the rest and set sail at once.'

Within minutes, the gangplank was pulled in, the mooring ropes cast off, and the *Falcon Temple* was pulled away from the dockside by oarsmen in the ship's longboat. Before long, the overseer had called out and the banks of galley slaves had dipped their oars into the dark water. Martin watched as the oarsmen scrambled up onto the deck then hauled the longboat up and made it secure. To the rhythmic beat of a deep gong and the grunts of over a hundred and fifty chained rowers, the ship gathered speed and cleared the great wall of the Templar compound.

As it moved into open water, arrows rained down on it while the sea around it erupted with huge, sizzling explosions of white foam as the Sultan's crossbows and catapults were trained on the escaping galley. It was soon beyond their range, and Martin stood up, glancing back at the receding landscape. Hordes of Saracens lined the city's ramparts, howling and jeering at the ship like caged animals. Behind them, an inferno raged, resounding with the shouts and screams of men, women and children, all against the incessant rolling thunder of the drums of war.

Slowly, the ship gathered speed, aided by the offshore wind, its banks of oars rising and falling like wings skimming the darkening waters. On the distant horizon, the sky had turned black and threatening.

It was over.

His hands still shaking and his heart leaden, Martin of Carmaux slowly and reluctantly turned his back on the land of his birth and stared ahead at the storm that awaited them.

CHAPTER 1

At first, no one noticed the four horsemen as they emerged out of the darkness of Central Park.

Instead, all eyes were focused four blocks south of there where, under a barrage of flashbulbs and television lights, a steady stream of limos decanted elegantly attired celebrities and lesser mortals onto the curb outside the Metropolitan Museum of Art.

It was one of those mammoth events that no other city could pull off quite as well as New York, least of all when the hosting venue happened to be the Met. Spectacularly lit up and with searchlight beams swirling across the black April sky above it, the sprawling building was like an irresistible beacon in the heart of the city, beckoning its guests through the austere columns of its neoclassical facade, over which floated a banner which read:

TREASURES OF THE VATICAN

There had been talk of postponing the event, or even canceling it altogether. Yet again, recent intelligence reports had prompted the government to raise the national terror alert level to orange. Across the country, state and local authorities had stepped up security measures, and although New York City had been at orange since 9/11, additional precautions were taken. National Guard troops were posted at subways and bridges, while police officers were working twelve-hour shifts.

The exhibition, given its subject matter, was deemed to be particularly at risk. Despite all this, strong wills had prevailed and the museum's board had voted to stick to its plans. The show would go on, further testimony to the city's unbreakable spirit.

A young woman with impeccable hair and brightly enameled teeth stood with her back to the museum, taking her third shot at getting her intro right. Having failed at studiously knowledgeable and blasé, the reporter was going for earnest this time as she stared into the lens.

'I can't remember the last time the Met hosted such a star-studded party, certainly nothing since the Mayan show and that's going back a few years,' she announced as a chubby, middle-aged man stepped out of a limo with a tall, angular woman in a blue evening dress a size too tight and a generation too young for her. 'And there's the Mayor and his lovely wife,' the reporter gushed, 'our very own royal family and fashionably late, of course.'

Going on in earnest, she adopted a more serious look and added, 'Many of the artifacts on display here tonight have never been seen by the public before, anywhere. They've been locked away in the vaults of the Vatican for hundreds of years and –'

Just then, a sudden surge of whistles and cheers from the crowd distracted her. Her voice trailing off, she glanced away from the camera, her eyes drifting toward the growing commotion.

And that was when she saw the horsemen.

The horses were superb specimens: imperious grays and chestnuts, with flowing, black tails and manes. But it was their riders that had roused the crowd.

The four men, riding abreast, were all dressed in identical medieval armor. They had visored helmets, chain mail vests, flanged plate leggings over black jerkins and quilted hose. They looked as though they had just beamed in through a time travel portal. Further dramatizing the effect, long scabbarded broadswords hung from their waists. Most striking of all, they wore long white mantles over their armor, each bearing a splayed, blood-red cross.

The horses were now moving at a gentle trot.

The crowd went wild with excitement as the knights advanced slowly, staring ahead, oblivious to the hoopla around them.

'Well, what do we have here? It looks like the Met and the Vatican have pulled out all the stops tonight, and aren't they magnificent,' the reporter enthused, settling now for plain old showbiz. 'Just listen to that crowd!'

The horses reached the curb outside the museum, and then they did something curious.

They didn't stop there.

Instead, they turned slowly until they were facing the museum.

Without missing a step, the riders gently coaxed their mounts up and onto the sidewalk. Continuing the advance slowly, the four knights guided the horses onto the paved piazza.

Side by side, they ceremoniously climbed up the cascading steps, heading unerringly for the museum's entrance.

CHAPTER 2

'Mom, I've really gotta go,' Kim pleaded.

Tess Chaykin looked at her daughter with an annoyed frown on her face. The three of them – Tess, her mother Eileen, and Kim – had only just walked into the museum, and Tess had hoped to take a quick look around the crowded exhibits before the speeches, the schmoozing and the rest of the unavoidable formalities took over. But that would now have to wait. Kim was doing what every nine-year-old inevitably did in these occasions, which was to hold off until the least convenient time had arrived before announcing her desperate need for a rest room.

'Kim, honestly.' The grand hall was teeming with people. Navigating through them to escort her daughter to the ladies' wasn't a prospect Tess relished right now.

Tess's mother, who wasn't doing much to hide the small pleasure she was finding in this, stepped in. 'I'll take her. You go on ahead.' Then, with a knowing grin, she added, 'Much as I enjoy watching you get your payback.'

Tess flashed her a grimace, then looked at her daughter and smiled, shaking her head. The little face and its glinting green eyes never failed to charm its way out of any situation.

'I'll meet you in the main hall.' She raised a stern finger at Kim. 'Stay close to Nana. I don't want to lose you in this circus.'

Kim groaned and rolled her eyes. Tess watched them disappear into the melee before turning and heading in.

The huge foyer of the museum, the Great Hall, was already crowded with gray-haired men and vertiginously glamorous women. Black ties and evening gowns were de rigueur and, as she looked around, Tess felt self-conscious. She fretted that she stood out as much for her understated elegance as for her discomfort at being perceived as part of the 'in' crowd all around her, a crowd she firmly had no interest in.

What Tess didn't realize was that what people noticed about her had nothing to do with her being understated in the precise, seamed black dress that floated a few inches above her knees, nor with her discomfort at attending platitude-intensive events like this one. People just noticed her, period. They always had. And who could blame them. The seductive mass of curls framing the warm green eyes that radiated intelligence usually triggered it. The healthy, thirty-six-year-old frame that moved in relaxed, fluid strides confirmed it, and the fact that she was totally oblivious to her charms sealed it. It was too bad she'd always fallen for the wrong guys. She'd even ended up marrying the last of that contemptible bunch, a mistake she had recently undone.

She advanced into the main room, the buzz of conversation echoing off the walls around her in a dull roar that made individual words impossible to determine. Acoustics, it seemed, had not been a prime consideration of the museum's design. She could hear traces of chamber music, and tracked it to an all-female string quartet tucked away in a corner and sawing away energetically but almost inaudibly at their instruments. Nodding furtively at the smiling faces in the crowd, she made her way past Lila Wallace's ever-present displays of fresh flowers and the niche where Andrea della Robbia's sublime blue-and-white glazed terracotta *Madonna and Child* stood gracefully watching over the throng. Tonight though, they had company, as this was only one of many depictions of Jesus Christ and the Virgin Mary that now adorned the museum.

Almost all of the exhibits were displayed in glass cabinets, and it was clear from even a cursory glance that many of those exhibits were enormously valuable. Even for someone with Tess's lack of religious conviction, they were impressive, even stirring, and as she glided past the grand staircase and into the exhibition hall, her heart raced ahead with the rising swell of anticipation.

There were ornate alabaster altar pieces from Burgundy, with vivid scenes from the life of Saint Martin. Crucifixes by the score, most of them of solid gold and heavily encrusted with precious stones; one of them, a twelfth-century cross, consisted of more than a hundred figures carved out of a walrus tusk. There were elaborate marble statuettes and carved wooden reliquaries; even emptied of their original contents, these chests were superb examples of the meticulous work of medieval craftsmen. A glorious brass eagle lectern proudly held its own next to a superlative six foot painted Spanish Easter candlestick, which had been prized away from the pope's own apartments.

As Tess took in the various displays, she couldn't help but feel recurring pangs of disappointment. The objects before her were of a quality she would have never dared hope for during her years out in the field. True, they had been good, challenging years, rewarding to a certain extent. They had given her a chance to travel the world and immerse herself in diverse and fascinating cultures. Some of the curiosities she had unearthed were on display in a few museums scattered around the globe, but nothing she'd found was noteworthy enough to grace, say, the Sackler Wing of Egyptian Art or the Rockefeller Wing of Primitive Art. *Maybe... maybe if I'd stuck with it a little bit longer*. She shook the thought away. She knew that that life was over now, at least for the foreseeable future. She would have to make do with enjoying these marvelous glimpses into the past from the remote, passive viewpoint of a grateful observer.

And a marvelous glimpse it was. Hosting the show had been a truly remarkable coup for the Met, because almost none of the items sent over from Rome had ever been previously exhibited.

Not that it was all gleaming gold and glittering jewels.

In a cabinet facing her now was a seemingly mundane

object. It was a mechanical device of some sort, about the size of an old typewriter, boxlike and made of copper. It had numerous buttons on its top face, as well as interlocking gears and levers protruding from its sides. It seemed out of place amidst all this opulence.

Tess brushed aside her hair as she leaned forward to take a closer look. She was reaching for her catalogue when, above her own blurred reflection in the glass of the cabinet, another loomed into view as someone came up behind her.

'If you're still looking for the Holy Grail, I'm going to have to disappoint you. It ain't here,' a gravelly voice said to her. And although it had been years since she'd heard it, she recognized it even before she turned.

'Clive.' She turned, taking in the sight of her former colleague. 'How the hell are you? You look great.' Which wasn't exactly true; even though he was barely into his fifties, Clive Edmondson looked positively ancient.

'Thanks. How about you?'

'I'm good,' she nodded. 'So how's the grave-robbing business these days?'

Edmondson showed her the backs of his hands. 'The manicure bills are killing me. Other than that, same old same old. Literally,' he chuckled. 'I hear you joined the Manoukian.'

'Yeah.'

'And?'

'Oh, it's great,' Tess told him. That wasn't true either. Joining the prestigious Manoukian Institute had been a big coup for her, but as far as the actual experience of working there went, things weren't all that good. But those things you kept to yourself, especially in the surprisingly gossipy and backstabbing world that archaeology could be. Seeking an impersonal remark, she said, 'You know, I really miss being out there with you guys.'

His faint smile told her he wasn't buying that. 'You're not missing much. We haven't hit the headlines yet.'

'It's not that, it's just...' She turned, glancing at the sea of displays around them. 'Any one of these would have been great. Any one.' She looked at him, suddenly melancholic. 'How come we never found anything this good?'

'Hey, I'm still hoping. You're the one who traded in the camels for a desk,' he quipped. 'Not to mention the flies, the sand, the heat, the food if you can call it that...'

'Oh my God, the food,' Tess laughed. 'Come to think of it, I'm not so sure I really miss it anymore.'

'You can always come back, you know.'

She winced. It was something she often thought about. 'I don't think so. Not for a while, anyway.'

Edmondson found a grin that seemed more than a little strained. 'We'll always have a shovel with your name on it, you know that,' he said, sounding anything but hopeful. An awkward silence settled between them. 'Listen,' he added, 'they've set up a bar over in the Egyptian Room, and from the looks of it, they've got someone who knows how to mix a decent cocktail. Let me buy you a drink.'

'You go ahead, I'll catch up with you later,' she said. 'I'm waiting for Kim and my mom.'

'They're here?'

'Yeah.'

He held up his palms. 'Whoa. Three generations of Chaykins – that should be interesting.'

'You've been warned.'

'Duly noted.' Edmondson nodded as he ventured into the crowd. 'I'll catch you later. Don't disappear on me.'

Outside, the air around the piazza was electric. The cameraman jostled to get into a clean shot as the claps and whoops of delight from the elated crowd drowned out his reporter's efforts at commentating. It got even noisier when the crowd spotted a short, heavy-set man in a brown security guard uniform leave his position and hurry over to the advancing horsemen.

From the corner of his eye, the cameraman could tell something wasn't exactly going according to plan. The guard's purposeful stride and his body language clearly indicated a difference of opinion.

The guard raised his hands in a stopping motion as he reached the horses, blocking their procession. The knights reined in their horses, which snorted and stamped, obviously uncomfortable at being kept stationary on the steps.

An argument seemed to be under way. A one-sided one, the cameraman observed, as the horsemen weren't reacting to the guard's ranting in any discernible way.

And then one of them finally did something.

Slowly, milking the moment for all its theatricality, the knight closest to the guard, a bear of a man, unsheathed his broadsword and raised it high above his head, provoking another barrage of popping flashbulbs and yet more applause.

He held it there, with both hands, still staring straight ahead. Unflinching.

Although he had one eye glued to his viewfinder, the cameraman's other eye was picking up peripheral images and he was suddenly aware of something else happening. Hurriedly, he zoomed in on the guard's face. *What was that look? Embarrassment? Consternation?*

Then he realized what it was.

Fear.

The crowd was now in a frenzy, clapping and cheering wildly. Instinctively, the cameraman zoomed out a touch, broadening his view to take in the horseman.

Just then, the knight suddenly brought down his broadsword in a quick, sweeping arc, its blade glittering terrifyingly in the flashing artificial light before striking the guard just below the ear, the power and velocity of the blow great enough for it to shear straight through flesh, gristle and bone.

From the onlookers came a huge collective gasp which turned into penetrating screams of horror that rang through the night. Loudest of all was the shriek of the reporter who clutched at the cameraman's arm, causing his picture to judder before he elbowed her away and kept on shooting.

The guard's head fell forward and began to bounce hideously down the museum's steps, unspooling a splattered, red trail all the way down behind it. And after what seemed like an eternity, his decapitated body slumped sideways, collapsing onto itself while spouting a small geyser of blood.

Screaming teenagers were stumbling and falling in their panic to escape the scene, while others, further back and unaware of exactly what was happening but knowing that something big was taking place, pushed forward. In seconds there was a terrified tangle of bodies, the air ringing with screams and cries of pain and fear.

The other three horses were now stamping their hooves, jinking sideways on the steps. Then one of the knights yelled, 'Go, go, go!'

The executioner spurred his mount forward, charging at the wide-open doorways to the museum. The others bolted and followed close behind.

CHAPTER 3

In the Great Hall, Tess heard the screams from outside and quickly realized there was something very, very wrong. She turned in time to see the first horse burst through the door, shattering glass and splintering timber inward as the Great Hall erupted into chaos. The smooth, polished, immaculate gathering disintegrated into a snarling atavistic pack as men and women shoved and screamed their way out of the path of the charging horses.

Three of the horsemen rampaged through the crowd, swords crashing through display cabinets, trampling on broken glass and shattered timber and damaged and destroyed exhibits.

Tess was thrown aside as scores of guests tried desperately to escape through the doors and into the street. Her eyes darted around the hall. *Kim, Mom – Where are they?* She looked around, but couldn't see them anywhere. To her far right, the horses wheeled and turned, obliterating more displays in their path. Guests were sent flying into cabinets and against walls, their pained grunts and shrieks echoing in the vast room. Tess glimpsed Clive Edmondson among them as he was knocked violently sideways when one of the horses suddenly reared backward.

The horses were snorting, nostrils flared, foam spilling from around the bits in their mouths. Their riders were reaching down and snatching up glittering objects from the broken cabinets before stuffing them into sacks hooked onto their saddles. At the doors, the crowd trying to get out made it impossible for the police to get in, helpless against the weight of the terrified mob.

One of the horses swung around, its flank sending a statue of the Virgin Mary reeling over to smash onto the floor. The horse's hooves pounded down onto it, crushing the Madonna's praying hands. Ripped from its mounting by the fleeing guests, a beautiful tapestry was trampled underfoot by both people and animals. Thousands of painstaking stitches, shredded in seconds. A display case toppled, a white and gold miter bursting through the breaking glass to be kicked aside in the mad scramble. A matching robe drifted, magic carpet-like, until it, too, was stamped upon.

Hurriedly getting out of the way of the horses, Tess looked down the corridor where, partway along, she could see the fourth horseman and beyond him, way back at the far end of the corridor, yet more people scattering into other parts of the museum. She searched for her mom and her daughter again. *Where the hell are they? Are they alright?* She strained to pick out their faces from the blur of the crowd, but there was still no sign of them.

Hearing a commanding shout, Tess spun around to see that the police officers had finally made it through the fleeing mob. Weapons drawn and shouting above the mayhem, they were closing in on one of the three horsemen who, from beneath his robe, pulled out a small, vicious looking gun. Instinctively, Tess dropped to the floor and covered her head, but not before witnessing the man loose a burst of bullets, moving the gun from side to side, spraying the hall. A dozen people went down, including all of the policemen, the broken glass and smashed cases around them now splattered with blood.

Still crouched on the floor, her heart pounding its way out of her chest, and trying to keep as still as she could even though something inside was screaming at her to run, Tess saw that two of the other horsemen were now also brandishing automatic weapons like the one their murderous consort was carrying. Bullets ricocheted off the museum walls, adding to the noise and to the panic. One of the horses reared suddenly and its rider's hands flailed, the gun in one of them sending a fusillade of bullets up one wall and onto the ceiling, shattering ornate plaster moldings that came showering down onto the heads of the crouching, screaming guests.

Risking a glance from behind her cabinet, Tess's mind raced as she evaluated routes of escape. Seeing a doorway to another gallery three rows of exhibits beyond to her right, Tess willed her legs forward and scurried toward it.

She had just reached the second row when she spotted the fourth knight headed straight toward her. She ducked, darting quick glances as she watched him weave his mount among the rows of still undamaged cabinets, apparently uninvolved and unconcerned with the mayhem his three companions were wreaking.

She could almost feel the breath venting from his snorting horse as the knight suddenly reined to a stop, barely six feet away from her. Tess crouched low, hugging the display for dear life, urging her beating heart to quieten. Her eyes drifted up and she spotted the knight, reflected in the glass displays around her, imperious in his chain mail and his white mantle, staring down at one cabinet in particular.

It was the one Tess had been looking at when Clive Edmondson had approached her.

Tess watched in quiet terror as the knight drew his sword, swung it up and brought it thundering down onto the cabinet, smashing it to bits and sending shards of glass spewing onto the floor around her. Then, sliding his sword back into its scabbard, he reached down from the saddle and lifted out the strange box, the contraption of buttons, gears and levers, and held it up for a moment.

Tess could barely breathe and yet, against all rational survival instincts she believed she possessed, she desperately needed to see what was happening. Unable to resist, she leaned out from behind the display case, one eye barely clearing the edge of the cabinet.

The man stared at the device, reverently it seemed, for a moment, before mouthing a few words, almost to himself.

'*Veritas vos libera –*'

Tess stared, entranced by this seemingly most private of rituals, when another burst of gunfire snapped both her and the knight out of their reverie.

He wheeled his horse around and for an instant, his eyes, though shadowed beneath the visor of his helmet, met Tess's. Her heart stopped as she crouched there, utterly and helplessly frozen. Then the horse was coming her way, straight at her –

– before brushing past, and as it did so she heard the man yelling to the other three horsemen, 'Let's go!'

Tess rose to see that the big horseman who had started the shooting was herding a small group into a corner by the main staircase. She recognized the Archbishop of New York, as well as the Mayor and his wife. The leader of the knights nodded his head and the big man forced his mount through the knot of distraught guests, grabbed the struggling woman and lifted her up onto his horse. He jammed his gun into the side of her head and she went still, her mouth open in a silent scream.

Helpless, angry and afraid, Tess watched as the four horsemen moved toward the doorway. The lead knight, the only one without a gun, she noticed, was also the only one without a bulging sack tied to his pommel. And as the horsemen charged away through the galleries of the museum, Tess stood up and rushed though the debris to find her mother and her young daughter.

The knights stormed out through the doors of the museum and into the glare of the television floodlights. Despite the sobbing of the frightened and the moaning of the injured, it was suddenly a lot quieter and from around them came shouts; men's voices, police mostly, with random words identifiable here and there: '... hold your fire!' '... hostage!' '... don't shoot!'

And then the four horsemen were charging down the steps

and up the avenue, the knight with the hostage protectively bringing up the rear. Their movements were brisk but not urgent, contemptuous of the approaching police sirens sawing at the night, and in moments they had disappeared back into the marled darkness of Central Park.

CHAPTER 4

At the edge of the museum's steps, Sean Reilly stood carefully outside the yellow and black crime scene tape. He ran a hand over his short brown hair as he looked down at the outline of where the headless body had lain. He let his eyes drift down lower, following the trail of blood splatters to where a basketball-sized mark noted the position of the head.

Nick Aparo walked over and peered around his partner's shoulder. Round faced, balding, and ten years older than Reilly's thirty-eight, he was average height, average build, average looking. You could forget what he looked like while you were still talking to him, a useful quality for an agent and one he had exploited very successfully during the years Reilly had known him. Like Reilly, he wore a loose-fitting dark blue windbreaker over his charcoal suit with big white letters, FBI, printed on the back. Right now, his mouth was twisted in distaste.

'I don't think the coroner's gonna have too much trouble figuring that one out,' he observed.

Reilly nodded. He couldn't take his eyes off the markings of where the head had lain, the pool of blood leading down from it dark now. Why was it, he wondered, that being shot or stabbed to death didn't seem quite as bad as having your head chopped off? It occurred to him that official execution by beheading was standard procedure in some parts of the world. Parts of the world that had spawned many of the terrorists whose intentions had the country gripped by heightened alert levels; terrorists whose trails consumed all of his days and more than a few of his nights.

He turned to Aparo. 'What's the word on the mayor's wife?' He knew she had been dumped unceremoniously in the middle of the park, along with the horses.

'She's just shaken,' Aparo answered. 'She's got more bruises to her ego than to her butt.'

'Good thing there's an election coming. It'd be a shame to see a good bruising go to waste.' Reilly looked around, his mind still coming to terms with the shock of what had taken place right where he was standing. 'Still nothing from the roadblocks?'

Roadblocks had been set up at a ten block radius and at all bridges and tunnels leading in and out of Manhattan.

'Nope. These guys knew what they were doing. They weren't waiting around for a cab.'

Reilly nodded. Professionals. Well organized.

Great.

As if amateurs couldn't do as much damage these days. All it took was a couple of flying lessons or a truckload of fertilizer, along with a suicidal, psychotic disposition – none of which were exactly in short supply.

He surveyed the ravaged scene in silence. As he did, he felt an upwelling of utter frustration and anger. The randomness of these deadly acts of madness, and their infuriating propensity to catch everyone off guard, never ceased to amaze him. Still, something about this particular crime scene seemed odd – even distracting. He realized he felt a strange detachment, standing there. It was all somehow too outlandish to take in, after the grim and potentially disastrous scenarios he and his colleagues had been trying to second-guess for the last few years. He felt as if he were stuck outside the big tent, distracted away from the main event by some freakish sideshow. And yet in a disturbing way, and much to his annoyance, he felt somewhat grateful for it.

As Special Agent in Charge heading up the field office's Domestic Terrorism unit, he had suspected the raid would end up in his corner from the moment he'd gotten the call. Not that he minded the mind-boggling job of coordinating the work of dozens of agents and police officers, as well as the analysts, lab technicians, psychologists, photographers, and countless others. It was what he always wanted to do.

He had always felt he could make a difference.

No, make that *known*. And *would*.

The feeling had crystallized during his years at Notre Dame's law school. Reilly felt there were a lot of things that were wrong in this world – his father's death, when he was only ten, was painful proof of that – and he wanted to help make it a better place, at least for other people, if not for himself. The feeling became inescapable the day when, working on a paper involving a case of race crime, he attended a white supremacist rally in Terre Haute. The event had affected Reilly deeply. He felt he had been witnessing evil, and he felt a pressing need to understand it more if he was going to help fight it.

His first plan didn't work out quite as well as he'd hoped. In a youthful burst of idealism, he had decided to become a Navy pilot. The idea of helping rid the world of evil from the cockpit of a silver Tomcat sounded perfect. Fortunately, he turned out to be just the kind of recruit the Navy was looking for. Unfortunately, they had something else in mind. They had more than enough Top Gun wannabes, and what they needed were lawyers. The recruiters did their best to get him to join the Judge Advocate General Corps and Reilly flirted with the idea for a while, but ultimately decided against it and went back to focus on passing the Indiana bar exam.

It was a chance meeting in a secondhand bookstore that diverted his path again, this time for good. That was where he met a retired FBI agent who was only too happy to talk to him about the Bureau and encourage him to apply, which he did as soon as he passed the bar. His mother wasn't too thrilled with the idea of his spending seven years in college to end up as what she called 'a glorified cop', but Reilly knew it was right for him.

He was barely a year into his rookie stint in the Chicago office, logging some street duty on robbery and drug trafficking squads, when on the twenty-sixth of February, 1993, every-thing changed. That was the day a bomb exploded in the car park underneath the World Trade Center, killing six people and injuring over a thousand. The conspirators had actually planned to topple one of the towers onto the other while simultaneously releasing a cloud of cyanide gas. Only financial limitations had prevented them from achieving their objective; they simply ran out of money. They didn't have enough gas canisters for the bomb that, apart from being too meager to fulfill its nefarious purpose, was also placed alongside the wrong column, one that wasn't of criti-cal structural importance.

The attack, although a failure, was nevertheless a serious wake-up call. It demonstrated that a small group of unsophisti-cated, low-level terrorists, with very little funding or resources, could cause a huge amount of damage. Intelligence agencies scrambled to re-allocate their resources to meet this new threat.

And so less than a year after joining the Bureau, Reilly found himself working out of the Bureau's New York City field office. The office had long had the reputation of being the worst place to work because of the high cost of living, the traffic problems, and the need to live quite a way out of the city if one wanted anything more spacious than a broom closet. But given that the city had always generated more action than anywhere else in the country, it was the dream posting of most new, and naïve, special agents. Reilly was such an agent when he'd been assigned to the city.

He wasn't new, or naïve, anymore.

As he looked around, Reilly knew the chaos surrounding him was going to monopolize his life for the foreseeable future. He made a mental note to call Father Bragg in the morning and let him know he wouldn't be able to make soft-ball practice. He felt bad about that; he hated to disappoint the kids, and if there was one thing he tried not to allow his work to trespass, it was those Sundays in the park. He'd probably be in the park this Sunday, only it would be for other, less congenial reasons.

'You want to have a look inside?' Aparo asked.

'Yeah,' Reilly shrugged, casting one last sweeping look at the surreal scene around him.

CHAPTER 5

As he and Aparo stepped carefully over the scattered debris, Reilly's gaze took in the devastation inside the museum.

Priceless relics lay strewn everywhere, most of them damaged beyond repair. No yellow and black tape in here. The whole building was a crime scene. The floor of the museum's Great Hall was an ugly still life of destruction: chips of marble, slivers of glass, smears of blood, all of it grist to the crime scene investigators' mill. Any of it capable of providing a clue; then again, all of it could fail to offer a single damn thing.

As he glanced briefly at the dozen or so white-suited CSIs who were working their way systematically through the debris and who, on this occasion, were joined by agents from the ERT – the FBI's Evidence Response Team – Reilly mentally checked off what they knew. Four horsemen. Five dead bodies. Three cops, one guard, and one civilian. Another four cops and over a dozen civilians with bullet wounds, two of them critical. A couple of dozen cut by flying glass, and twice that number bruised and banged about. And enough cases of shock to keep rotating teams of counselors busy for months.

Across the lobby, Assistant Director in Charge Tom Jansson was talking with the rail-thin Captain of Detectives from the Nineteenth Precinct. They were arguing over jurisdiction, but it was a moot point. The Vatican connection and the distinct possibility that what had happened here involved terrorists meant that overall command of the investigation was promptly transferred from the NYPD to the FBI. The sweetener was that years earlier, an understanding had been reached between the two organizations. When any arrest was to take place, the NYPD would publicly take credit for the collar, regardless of who actually made it happen. The

FBI would only get its share of the plaudits once the case went to court, ostensibly for helping secure the conviction. Still, egos often came in the way of sensible cooperation, which seemed to be the case tonight.

Aparo called over a man Reilly didn't recognize, and introduced him as Detective Steve Buchinski.

'Steve's happy to help us out while the dick measuring contest's sorted out,' Aparo said, nodding over to the ongoing debate between their superiors.

'Just let me know what you need,' Buchinski said. 'I'm as keen as you are to nail the sons of bitches that did this.'

That was a good start, Reilly thought gratefully, smiling at the blunt-featured cop. 'Eyes and ears on the street. That's what we need right now,' he said. 'You guys have the man-power and the networks.'

'We're already running it down. I'll borrow a few more shields from the CPP, that shouldn't be a problem,' Buchinski promised. The precinct adjoining the Nineteenth was Central Park; horseback patrols were a daily feature of their work. Reilly wondered briefly if there might be a link and made a mental note to check on that later.

'We could also use some extra bodies for the follow-up interviews,' Reilly told the cop.

'Yeah, we're up to our eyeballs in witnesses,' Aparo added, motioning up at the main staircase. Most of the offices above were being used as makeshift processing rooms.

Reilly looked over and spotted Agent Amelia Gaines coming down the stairs from the gallery. Jansson had put the striking, ambitious redhead in charge of interviewing witnesses. Which made sense, since everybody loved talking to Amelia Gaines. Following her was a blonde who was carrying a small replica of herself. Her daughter, Reilly guessed. The child looked like she was fast asleep.

Reilly looked again at the blonde's face. Usually, Amelia's alluring presence made other women pale into insignificance.

Not this one.

Even in her current state, something about her was simply mesmeric. Her eyes connected briefly with his before looking down to the clutter under her feet. Whoever she was, she was seriously shaken.

Reilly watched as she headed for the door, picking her way through the debris with unease. Another woman, older, but with a vague physical resemblance, was close behind. Together, they walked out of the museum.

Reilly turned, refocusing. 'The first sort through's always a huge waste of time, but we've still got to go through the motions and talk to everybody. Can't afford not to.'

'Probably more of a waste of time in this case. The whole damn thing's on tape.' Buchinski pointed at a video camera, then another. Part of the museum's security system. 'To say nothing of all the footage from the TV crews outside.'

Reilly knew from experience that high security was all very well for high-tech crimes, but no one had allowed for low-tech raiders on horseback. 'Great,' he nodded. 'I'll get the popcorn.'

CHAPTER 6

From his seat at a large mahogany table, Cardinal Mauro Brugnone glanced around the high-ceilinged room that was located close to the heart of the Vatican, studying his fellow cardinals. Although, as the only cardinal-bishop present, Brugnone outranked the others, he deliberately avoided sitting at the head of the table. He liked to maintain an air of democracy here, even though he knew that they would all defer to him. He knew it and accepted it, not with pride, but through pragmatism. Committees without leaders never achieved anything.

This unfortunate situation, however, neither called for a leader nor a committee. It was something Brugnone would have to deal with himself. That much was clear to him from the moment he had seen the news footage that had been broadcast around the world.

His eyes eventually settled on Cardinal Pasquale Rienzi. Although he was the youngest of them all and only a cardinal-deacon, Rienzi was Brugnone's closest confidant. Like the others seated at the table, Rienzi was speechlessly engrossed in the report before him. He looked up and caught Brugnone's eye. The young man, pale and earnest as always, promptly coughed gently.

'How could something like this happen?' one man asked. 'In the heart of New York City? At the Metropolitan Museum...' He shook his head in disbelief.

How foolishly otherworldly, Brugnone thought. Anything could happen in New York City. Hadn't the destruction of the World Trade Center proved that?

'At least the Archbishop wasn't harmed,' another cardinal stated somberly.

'It seems the robbers escaped. They don't yet know who

is behind this... abomination?' another voice asked.

'It's a land of criminals. Lunatics inspired by their amoral television programs and sadistic video games,' another answered. 'Their prisons ran out of room years ago.'

'But why dress as they did? Red crosses on white mantles... They were masquerading as Templars?' asked the cardinal who had spoken first.

There it is, Brugnone thought.

That was what had set off his alarm bells. Why, indeed, were the perpetrators dressed as Knights Templar? Could it be simply a matter of the robbers seeking a disguise and fastening onto whatever happened to be available? Or did the apparel of the four horsemen have a deeper, and possibly more disturbing, significance?

'What is a multigeared rotor encoder?'

Brugnone looked up sharply. The question had been asked by the oldest cardinal there. 'A multi...?' Brugnone asked.

The old man was peering short-sightedly at the circulated document. '"Exhibit 129,"' the old man read out. '"Sixteenth century. A multigeared rotor encoder. Reference number VNS 1098." I've never heard of it. What is it?'

Brugnone feigned studying the document in his hands, a copy of an email, which contained a provisional list of items stolen during the raid. Again, he felt a shiver – the same shiver he felt the first time he spotted it on the list. He kept his face impassive. Without raising his head, he flicked a quick glance around the table at the others. No one else was reacting. Why should they? It was far from common knowledge.

Sliding the paper away, he leaned back in his chair. 'Whatever it is,' he stated flatly, 'those gangsters have taken it.' Glancing at Rienzi, he inclined his head slightly. 'Perhaps you will undertake to keep us informed. Make contact with the police and ask for us to be kept abreast of their investigation.'

'The FBI,' Rienzi corrected, 'not the police.'

Brugnone raised an eyebrow.

'The American government is taking this very seriously,' Rienzi affirmed.

'And so they should,' the oldest cardinal snapped from across the table. Brugnone was pleased to see that this elder appeared to have forgotten about the machine.

'Quite,' Rienzi continued. 'I've been assured that everything that can be done, will be done.'

Brugnone nodded, then motioned to Rienzi to continue with the meeting, his gesture implying, *wind it up*.

People always had deferred to Mauro Brugnone. Probably, he knew, because the way he looked suggested a man of great physical strength. If it were not for his vestments, he knew that he looked like the burly, heavy-shouldered Calabrian farmer he would have been had the Church not called him more than half a century ago. His rough-hewn appearance, and the matching manner he had cultivated over the years, first disarmed others into thinking he was just a simple man of God. That, he was, but because of his standing in the Church, many proceeded to another assumption: that he was a manipulator and a schemer. He was not, but he'd never bothered to disabuse them. It sometimes paid to keep people guessing even though, in a way, that was in itself a form of manipulation.

Ten minutes later, Rienzi did as he asked.

As the other cardinals filed from the room, Brugnone left the meeting room by another door and walked along a corridor to a stairwell that took him out of the building and into a secluded courtyard. He made his way down a sheltered brick pathway, across the Belvedere courtyard and past the celebrated statue of Apollo, and into the buildings that housed part of the Vatican's enormous library, the *Archivio Segreto Vaticano* – the secret archive.

The archive wasn't, in actual fact, particularly secret. A major part of it was officially opened to visiting scholars and researchers in 1998 who could, in theory at least, access its tightly controlled contents. Among the notorious documents known to be stored in its forty miles of shelf space were the handwritten proceedings of Galileo's trial and a petition from King Henry VIII seeking an annulment to his first marriage.

No outsiders, however, were ever allowed where Brugnone was headed.

Without bothering to acknowledge any of the staff or scholars working in its dusty halls, he quietly made his way deeper into the vast, dark repository. He headed down a narrow, circular stairwell and reached a small anteroom where a Swiss Guard stood by an immaculately carved oak door. A curt nod from the elderly cardinal was all that was needed for the guard to enter the combination into a keypad and unlock the door for him. The deadbolt snapped open, echoing up the hollowness of the limestone stairs. Without any further acknowledgement, Brugnone slipped into the barrel-vaulted crypt, the door creaking shut behind him.

Making sure he was alone in the cavernous chamber, his eyes adjusting to the dim lighting, he made his way to the records area. The crypt seemed to hum with silence. It was a curious effect that Brugnone had once found disconcerting until he had learned that, just beyond the limits of his hearing, there really was a hum, emanating from a highly sophisticated climate control system that maintained constant temperature and humidity. He could feel his veins tighten in the controlled, dry air as he consulted a file cabinet. He really didn't like it down here, but this visit was unavoidable. His fingers trembled as they flicked through the rows of index cards. What Brugnone was looking for wasn't listed in any of the various known indexes and inventories of the archive's collections, not even in the *Schedario Garampi*, the monumental card-file of almost a million cards listing virtually everything held in the archive up to the eighteenth century. But Brugnone knew where to look. His mentor had seen to that, shortly before his death.

His eyes fell on the card he was looking for, and he pulled it out of its drawer.

With a deepening sense of foreboding, Brugnone trawled through the stacks of folios and books. Reams of tattered red ribbon, bound around official documents and thought to be the origin of the term red tape, dangled in deathly silence from every shelf. His fingers froze when he finally spotted the one he was looking for.

With great discomfort, he lifted down a large and very old leather-bound volume, which he placed on a plain wood table.

Sitting down, Brugnone flicked over the thick, richly illustrated pages, their crackling loud in the stillness. Even in this controlled environment, the pages had suffered the ravages of time. The vellum pages were eroded, and iron in the ink had turned corrosive, creating tiny slashes which had now replaced some of the artist's graceful strokes.

Brugnone felt his pulse quicken. He knew he was near. As he turned the page, he felt his throat tighten as the information he was seeking appeared before him.

He looked at the illustration. It depicted a complex arrangement of interlocking gears and levers. Glancing at his copy of the email, he nodded to himself.

Brugnone felt a headache forming at the back of his eyes. He rubbed them, then stared again at the drawing before him. He was quietly furious. *By what delinquency had this been allowed to happen?* He knew the device should never have left the Vatican, and was immediately irritated with himself. He rarely wasted time in stating or thinking the obvious, and it was a measure of his concern that he did so now. Concern was not the right word. This discovery had come as a deep shock. Anyone would be shocked, anyone who knew the significance of the ancient device. Fortunately, there were very few, even here in the Vatican, who did know the legendary purpose of this particular machine.

We brought it upon ourselves. It happened because we were too careful not to draw attention to it.

Suddenly drained, Brugnone pushed himself upright. Before he moved to return the book to its place on the shelf, he placed the file card that he had carried with him from the cabinet randomly inside it. It would not do to have anyone else stumble across this.

Brugnone sighed, feeling every one of his seventy years. He knew the threat wasn't from a curious academic or from some ruthlessly determined collector. Whoever was behind this knew exactly what he was looking for. And he had to be stopped before his ill-gotten gain could unveil its secrets.

CHAPTER 7

Four thousand miles away, another man had the exact opposite in mind.

After closing and locking the door behind him, he picked up the intricate machine from where he had placed it on the top step. Then he moved slowly down into the cellar, his movements careful. The machine wasn't too heavy, but he was anxious not to drop it.

Not now.

Not after fate had interceded to bring it within reach, and certainly not after all that it had taken to seize it.

The underground chamber, although lit by the flickering glow of dozens of candles, was too spacious for the yellow light to reach into every recess. It remained as gloomy as it was cold and damp. He no longer noticed. He had spent so long here that he had grown accustomed to it, never felt any discomfort. It was as close to being a home as anything could be.

Home.

A distant memory.

Another life.

Placing the machine on a sagging wooden table, he went over to a corner of the cellar and rummaged through a pile of boxes and old cardboard files. He took the one he needed to the table, opened it, and gently withdrew a folder from it. From the folder, he pulled out several sheets of thick paper that he arranged neatly beside the machine. Then he sat down and looked from the documents to the geared device and back again, relishing the moment.

To himself, he murmured, 'At last.' His voice was soft, but cracked from too little use.

Picking up a pencil, he turned his full attention to the first of the documents. He looked at the first line of faded writing, then reached for the buttons on the top casing of the machine and began the next, crucial stage in his personal odyssey.

An odyssey, the end result of which he knew would rock the world.

CHAPTER 8

After finally succumbing to sleep barely five hours earlier, Tess was now awake again and eager to start work on something that had been bugging her ever since those few minutes at the Met, before Clive Edmondson had spoken to her and all hell had broken loose. And she would get to it, just as soon as her mother and Kim were out of the house.

Tess's mother Eileen had moved in with them at the two story house on a quiet, tree-lined street in Mamaroneck soon after her archaeologist husband, Oliver Chaykin, had died three years ago. Even though she was the one who had suggested it, Tess hadn't been too sure of the arrangement. But the house did have three bedrooms and reasonably ample space for all of them, which made things easier. Ultimately, it had worked out all right even if, as she sometimes guiltily recognized, the advantages seemed more skewed her way. Like Eileen baby-sitting when Tess wanted to be out evenings, driving Kim to school when she needed her to, and like right now, when taking Kim out on a doughnut run would help get the girl's mind off the previous night's events and probably do her a world of good.

'We're going,' Eileen called out. 'You sure you don't need anything?'

Tess came into the hallway to see them off. 'Just make sure you save me a couple.'

Just then, the phone rang. Tess didn't look like she was in any rush to answer it. Eileen looked at her. 'You gonna get that?'

'I'll let the answering machine pick it up,' Tess shrugged.

'You're gonna have to talk to him, sooner or later.'

Tess made a face. 'Yeah, well, later's always better where Doug's concerned.'

She could guess the reason for the calls her ex-husband had left on her voice mail. Doug Merritt was a news anchor at a network affiliate in Los Angeles, and he was totally absorbed in his job. His one-track mind would have linked the raid on the Met with the fact that Tess spent a lot of time there and would definitely have contacts. Contacts that he might use to get an inside track on what had become the biggest news story of the year.

The last thing she needed right now was for him to know that not only was she there, but that Kim was there with her. Ammo he wouldn't hesitate to use against her at the first opportunity.

Kim.

Tess thought again about what her daughter had experienced last night, even from the relative shelter of the museum's rest rooms, and how it would need to be addressed. The delay in the reaction, and the odds were there would be one, would give her time to better prepare for how to deal with it. It wasn't something she was looking forward to. She hated herself for having dragged her there, even though blaming herself was far from reasonable.

She looked at Kim, grateful again for the fact that she was standing there before her, in one piece. Kim grimaced at the attention.

'Mom. Would you quit it already.'

'What?'

'That pathetic look,' Kim protested. 'I'm okay, alright? It's no biggie. I mean, you're the one who watches movies through your fingers.'

Tess nodded. 'Okay. I'll see you later.'

She watched them drive off, and walked in to the kitchen counter where the answering machine was blinking, showing four messages. Tess scowled at the device. *The nerve of that creep.* Six months ago, Doug had remarried. His new wife was a twenty-something, surgically enhanced junior executive at the network. This change in his status would lead, Tess knew, to his angling for a review of his visitation rights. Not that he missed, loved or even particularly cared for Kim; it was simply a matter of ego, and of malice. The man was a spiteful prick, and Tess knew she'd have to keep fighting the occasional bursts of fatherly concern until his nubile young plaything got herself pregnant. Then, with a bit of luck, he'd lose the pettiness and leave them alone.

Tess poured herself a cup of coffee, black, and headed for her study.

Switching on her laptop, she grabbed her phone and managed to track down Clive Edmondson to the New York-Presbyterian Hospital on East 68th Street. She rang the hospital and was told he was not in a critical condition but would be there for a few more days.

Poor Clive. She made a note of visiting hours.

Opening the catalogue of the ill-fated exhibition, she leafed through it until she found a description of the device taken by the fourth horseman.

It was called a multigeared rotor encoder.

The description told her that it was a cryptographic device and was dated as sixteenth century. Old and interesting, perhaps, but not something that qualified as what one would normally term a 'treasure' of the Vatican.

By now, the computer had run through its usual booting up routine and she opened up a research database and keyed in 'cryptography' and 'cryptology'. The links were to websites that were mostly technical and dealt with modern cryptography as related to computer codes and encrypted electronic transmissions. Trawling through the hits, she eventually came across a site that covered the history of cryptography.

Surfing through the site, she found a page that displayed some early encoding tools. The first one featured was the Wheatstone cipher device from the nineteenth century. It consisted of two concentric rings, an outer one with the twenty-six letters of the alphabet plus a blank, and an inner one having just the alphabet itself. Two hands, like those of a clock, were used to substitute letters from the outer ring for coded letters from the inner one. The person receiving the coded message needed to have an identical device, and had to know the setting of the two hands. A few years after the Wheatstone was in general use, the French came up with a cylindrical cryptograph, which had twenty discs with letters on their outer rims, all arranged on a central shaft, further complicating any attempts at deciphering a coded message.

Scrolling down, her eyes fell on a picture of a device that looked vaguely similar to the one she had seen at the museum.

She read the caption underneath it and froze.

It was described as 'the Converter', an early rotor encoder, and had been used by the US Army in the 1940s.

For a second, it felt as if her heart had stopped. She just stared at the words.

1940s was 'early'?

Intrigued, she read through the article. Rotor encoders were strictly a twentieth century invention. Leaning back in her chair, Tess rubbed her forehead, scrolled back up to the first illustration on the screen, and then re-read its description. Not the same by any means, but pretty damn close. And way more advanced than the single wheel ciphers.

If the US government thought that its device was early, then there was little wonder the Vatican was eager to show off one of its own devices; one which appeared to pre-date the army's by some four hundred years.

Still, this bothered Tess.

Of all the glittering prizes he could have taken, the fourth horseman had zeroed in on this arcane device. Why? Sure, people collected the weirdest things, but this was pretty extreme. She wondered whether or not he might have made a mistake. No, she dismissed that thought – he had seemed very deliberate in his choice.

Not only that, but he took nothing else. It was all he wanted.

She thought about Amelia Gaines, the woman who looked more like someone out of a shampoo commercial than an agent of the FBI. Tess was pretty certain that the investigators wanted facts, not speculation, but even so, after a quick moment's thought, she went into her bedroom, found the evening bag she'd carried last night, and pulled out the card given to her by Gaines.

She placed the card on her desk, and flashed back to the moment the fourth horseman had picked up the encoder. The way that he had picked it up, held it and whispered something to it.

He had seemed almost... *reverent*.

What was it he had said? Tess had been too distraught at the Met to make a big deal out of it, but all of a sudden, it was all she could think of. She focused on that moment, pushing everything else out of her consciousness, reliving the scene with the horseman lifting the encoder. And saying... what? Think, damn it.

Like she had told Amelia Gaines, she was pretty sure the first word was Veritas... but then what? Veritas? Veritas *something*...

Veritas vos? Somehow, that seemed vaguely familiar. She trawled her memory for the words, but it was no use. The horseman's words had been cut off by the gunfire that erupted behind him.

Tess decided she would have to go with what she had. She turned to her computer and selected the most powerful meta-search engine from her links toolbar. She entered 'Veritas vos' and got over 22,000 hits. Not that it really mattered. The very first one was enough.

There it was. Calling out to her.

'*Veritas vos liberabit.*'

The truth will set you free.

She stared at it. The truth will set you free.

Great.

Her masterful detective work had uncovered one of the most trite and overused soundbites of our time.

CHAPTER 9

Gus Waldron emerged from the West 23rd Street station and headed south.

He hated this part of town. He wasn't a big fan of gentrification. Far from it. On his own turf, the fact that he was the size of a small building kept him safe. Here, his size only made him stand out among the fancy piss-ants scurrying along the sidewalks in their designer outfits and two hundred dollar haircuts.

Hunching his shoulders, he knocked a few inches off his height. Even then, big as he was, it didn't help much and neither did the long black shapeless coat he wore. But he could do nothing about that; he needed the coat to conceal what he was carrying.

He turned up 22nd Street, heading west. His destination was a block away from the Empire Diner, located in the center of a small row of art galleries.

As he walked past, he noted that most of the galleries had just one or maybe two pictures in their windows. Some of the pictures didn't even have frames for chrissakes, and none that he could see had a price tag.

How were you supposed to know if it was any fucking good if you didn't know what it fucking cost?

His destination was now two doors away. To outward appearances, Lucien Boussard's place looked like a slick up-market antiques gallery. In fact, it was that and a whole lot more. Fakes and pieces of dubious origin infected the few genuine, unsullied objects. Not that any of his neighbors suspected as much, for Lucien had the style, the accent and the manners to fit in seamlessly.

Very cautious now, eyes alert for anything or anyone that didn't look right, Gus walked past the gallery, counted off twenty-five paces, then stopped and turned around. He made as if to cross the street, still couldn't see anything that seemed out of place, and went back and was inside the gallery, his movements quick and light for a man his size. And why shouldn't they be? In thirty fights he had never once been hit hard enough to go down. Except when he was supposed to.

Inside the gallery, he kept one hand in his pocket, wrapped around the butt of a Beretta 92FS. It wasn't his handgun of choice, but he'd had a couple of misfires with the .45 ACP, and after the big night, it wasn't smart to carry the Cobray. He took a quick look around. No tourists, nor any other customers for that matter. Just the gallery's owner.

Gus didn't like many people but even if he had, he would not have liked Lucien Boussard. He was a smarmy little shit. Narrow face and shoulders to match, he wore his long hair pulled back into a ponytail.

Fucking French fag.

As Gus came in, Lucien looked up from behind a small spindly-legged table where he sat working and faked an elated smile, a feeble attempt to hide the fact that he had instantly started sweating and twitching. That was possibly the one thing that Gus did like about Lucien. He was always on edge, as if he thought Gus might at any moment decide to harm him. The greasy little fuck was right about that.

'Gus!' It came out like *'Gueusse'*, which only made him hate Lucien even more, every damn time he heard it.

Turning his back to him, Gus set the lock on the door, then walked over to the table. 'Anyone out back?' he grunted.

Lucien shook his head rapidly from side to side. *'Mais non, mais non, voyons,* there is no one here but me.' He also had an annoying habit of repeating his faggoty French expressions several times. Maybe they all did that.

'I wasn't expecting you, you didn't say –'

'Shut the fuck up,' Gus spat back. 'I've got something for you.' He grinned. 'Something special.'

From beneath his coat, Gus pulled out a paper sack and laid it on the table. He glanced back at the door to make sure they were out of any passerby's sight line, and took something out of the sack. It was wrapped in newspaper. He started to unwrap it, looking up at Lucien as he did.

Lucien's mouth opened and his eyes suddenly flared wider as Gus finally brought out the object. It was an elaborate, jewel-encrusted gold cross, around a foot and a half long, breathtaking in its detail.

Gus set it down onto the open newspaper. He heard the hiss as Lucien sucked in his breath.

'*Mon dieu, mon dieu.*' The Frenchman dragged his eyes up to Gus's and all at once the sweat was popping across his narrow forehead. 'Jesus, Gus.'

Well, he had that right.

He looked down again and, following his example, Gus looked and saw that the newspaper was open at a photo spread of the museum.

'This is from the...'

'Yeah,' Gus smirked. 'It's something, isn't it? One of a kind.'

Lucien's mouth was twitching. '*Non mais, il est complètement taré, ce mec.* Come on, Gus, I can't touch this.'

It wasn't as if Gus wanted Lucien to touch it, he just needed him to sell it. And he couldn't exactly wait for a bidding war either. For the past six months, Gus had had a seriously bad run at the track. He had been in the hole before, but never like this; and he had never before been in the hole to the people who were now holding his markers. Throughout pretty much all of his life, since the day he grew taller and heavier than his old man and had beaten the crap out of the drunken bully, people had been afraid of Gus. But right now, for the first time since he was fourteen years old, he knew what it meant to be afraid. The men who held the markers for his gambling debts were in a different league from anyone else he had ever known. They would kill him as readily and as easily as he would step on a roach.

Ironically, the track had also provided him with a way out. It was how he'd met the guy who got him in on the museum job. And now here he was, even though he'd been given clear instructions not to attempt to sell any of his hoard for at least six months.

The hell with that. He needed money and he needed it now.

'Look, don't worry about where it's from, alright,' Gus ordered Lucien. 'You just work out where it's going and for how much.'

Lucien looked like he was about to have a seizure. '*Non mais*... listen to me, *Gueusse*, this is not possible. It's not possible at all. It's too hot to touch right now, it would be crazy to –'

Gus seized Lucien around the throat and dragged him halfway across the table, which rocked precariously. He thrust his face within an inch of Lucien's. 'I don't care if it's thermo-fucking-nuclear,' he hissed. 'People collect this shit and you know where to find them.'

'It's too soon,' Lucien's voice squeaked from the pressure around his throat.

Gus let go and the Frenchman dropped back into his seat. 'Don't talk to me like I'm some kind of retard,' he barked. 'It's always gonna be too soon for this shit, there's never gonna be a right time. So it might as well be now. Besides, you know there's people who'll buy this because of what it is and where it came from. Sick fucks who'll pay a small fortune to be able to jerk off at the idea of having it locked up in their safe. All you have to do is find me one of them and find him fast. And don't even think of trying to dick me on the price. You get ten percent, and ten percent of priceless is nothing to piss on, is it?'

Lucien swallowed, rubbing his neck, then pulled out a taupe silk handkerchief and wiped his face. His eyes darted around the room nervously, his mind clearly taking another tack now. He looked up at Gus and said, 'Twenty.'

Gus looked at him, bemused. 'Lucien,' – he always said it like 'loo-*shin*', just to annoy him – 'you're not growing balls on me all of a sudden now, are you?'

'I am serious. For something like this, it has to be twenty percent. *Au moins.* I will be taking a big risk on this.'

Gus reached out again but this time Lucien was too fast, sliding his chair back so that his neck was out of reach. Instead, Gus calmly took out the Beretta and moved closer, jamming it into Lucien's crotch. 'I don't know what you've been snorting, but I'm not really in a negotiating mood here, princess. I've made you a generous offer and all you do is try and take advantage of the situation. I'm disappointed, man.'

'No, look, Gus...'

Gus raised his hand and shrugged. 'I don't know if you caught the best part on TV that night. Outside. With the guard. It was something. And I've still got the blade, you know, and, let me tell ya, I'm kinda getting into that whole Conan shit, you know what I'm saying?'

For a moment, while he let Lucien sweat it, Gus was thinking hard. He knew that if he had all the time in the world, Lucien's fear of him would work in his favor. But he didn't have all the time in the world. The cross was worth a small fortune, maybe even seven figures, but right now he would take what he could get and be happy about it. The up-front cash he had made by signing on for the museum raid had bought him time; now he needed to get those leeches off his back.

'I'll tell you what,' he told Lucien. 'Make this worth my while, and I'll go to fifteen.'

He saw a flicker in Lucien's weasel eyes. He was hooked.

Lucien opened a drawer and pulled out a small digital camera. He looked up at Gus.

'I need to –'

Gus nodded. 'Knock yourself out.'

Lucien took a couple of pictures of the cross, clearly doing a mental run through his client list already.

'I'll make some calls,' Lucien said. 'Give me a few days.'

No good. Gus needed the money and the freedom it would give him. He also needed to get out of town for a while until the dust settled around the museum job. All of these things he needed now.

'Uh-uh. It's got to be quick. A couple of days, max.'

Once again, he could see something working away behind Lucien's eyes. Probably trying to figure how he could work a deal with a buyer, a fat fee for promising to barter the seller down, even though the seller had already agreed. The slimy little shit. Gus decided that a few months from now, when the time was right, he would really enjoy paying Lucien another visit.

'Come back at six, tomorrow,' Lucien said. 'No promises, but I'll do my best.'

'I know you will.' Gus picked up the cross, grabbed a cleaning rag that was lying on Lucien's desk and wrapped it around the jeweled relic before placing it carefully into one of the inside pockets of his coat. He then put the gun into another. 'Tomorrow,' he said to Lucien, and grinned humorlessly before he went out into the street.

Lucien was still shaking as he watched the big man walk all the way to the corner and disappear from sight.

CHAPTER 10

'You know, I could've done without this right now,' Jansson growled as Reilly dropped into a chair across from his boss. Already seated at the table in the Assistant Director in Charge's office at Federal Plaza were Aparo and Amelia Gaines, as well as Roger Blackburn, who ran the violent crimes/major offenders task force, and two of Blackburn's ASACs.

The complex of four government buildings in lower Manhattan was just a few blocks away from Ground Zero. It housed twenty-five thousand government employees, and was also home to the New York field office of the FBI. Sitting there, Reilly was relieved to be away from the incessant noise in the main work area. In fact, the comparative tranquility of his boss's private office was just about the only thing about Jansson's job that was even remotely tempting.

As ADIC of the New York field office, Jansson had been shouldering a huge burden over the last few years. All five areas of major concern to the Bureau – drugs and organized crime, violent crime and major offenders, financial crime, foreign counterintelligence, and the latest black sheep of that odious herd, domestic terrorism – were firing on all cylinders. Jansson certainly seemed built for the task: the man had the imposing bulk of the former football player he was, although beneath his gray hair, his solid face had a detached, distant expression. This didn't throw the people working under him for long, as they quickly learned that one thing, beyond the proverbial death and taxes, was certain: if Jansson was on your side, you could count on him to bulldoze anything that came in your path. If, however, you made the mistake of crossing him, leaving the country was definitely worth considering.

With Jansson being so close to retirement, Reilly could understand why his boss didn't particularly appreciate having his last few months in office complicated by something as high profile as METRAID – the robbery's imaginative new case name. The media had, quite rightly, pounced on the story. This wasn't a routine armed robbery. It was a full-blown raid. Automatic machinegun fire had raked New York's A-list. The mayor's wife was taken hostage. A man was executed in plain sight; not just shot, but beheaded, and not in a walled courtyard in some Middle Eastern dictatorship, but here, in Manhattan, on Fifth Avenue.

On live television.

Reilly looked from Jansson to the flag and the Bureau insignia on the wall behind him, then back again as the ADIC rested his elbows on his desk and sucked in a barrelful of air.

'I'll make sure I tell those bastards how inconsiderate they've been when we book 'em,' Reilly offered.

'You do that,' Jansson said as he leaned forward, his intense glare sweeping across the faces of his assembled team. 'I don't need to tell you the amount of calls I've gotten on this or from how high up they've come. Tell me where we are and where we're going with it.'

Reilly glanced at the others, and took the lead.

'Preliminary forensics don't point us in any particular direction. Those guys didn't leave much behind besides shell casings and the horses. The ERT guys are pulling their hair out at having so little to go on.'

'For once,' Aparo chimed in.

'Anyway, the casings tell us they were packing M11/9 Cobrays and Micro Uzis. Rog, you guys are looking into that, right?'

Blackburn cleared his throat. He was a force of nature who had recently pulled off the dismantling of the biggest heroin distribution network in Harlem, resulting in over two hundred arrests. 'Garden variety, obviously. We're going through the motions, but I wouldn't hold my breath. Not on something like this. Can't imagine these boys just bought them off the Web.'

Jansson nodded. 'What about the horses?'

Reilly picked up. 'So far, nothing. Grey and chestnut geldings, pretty common. We're cross-checking them against records of missing horses and chasing down the saddles' points of origin, but again...'

'No brands or chips?'

With over fifty thousand horses stolen each year across the country, the use of identification marks on horses was becoming more and more prevalent. The most popular method was freeze branding, which involved the use of a super cold branding iron to alter the color pigment producing cells, resulting in white hair growing at the brand site, instead of colored hair. The other, less common, method involved using a hypodermic needle to inject a tiny microchip with an identification number programmed into it under the skin of the animal.

'No chips,' Reilly replied, 'but we're having them scanned again. The chips are so tiny that unless you know exactly where they are, it's not an easy find. Added to the fact that they're usually hidden in less obvious areas to make sure they're still there if and when a stolen horse is recovered. On the plus side, they did have freeze brands, but they've been branded over and are now unreadable. The lab boys think they may be able to get something by separating the different passes to bring up the original mark.'

'What about the outfits and the medieval hardware?' Jansson turned to Amelia Gaines, who had been following up that line of investigation.

'That's going to take more time,' she said. 'The typical sources for that type of kit are small specialists scattered across the country, especially when it comes to broadswords that are the real thing, not just party props. I think we'll get something here.'

'So these guys just disappeared into thin air, is that it?' Jansson was clearly losing patience.

'They must have had cars waiting. There are two exits out of the park not far from where they dumped the horses. We're canvassing for witnesses, but so far, nothing,' Aparo confirmed. 'Four guys, splitting up, walking out of the park, that time of the evening. It's easy to go unnoticed.'

Jansson sat back, nodding quietly, his mind collating the disparate chunks of information and ordering his thoughts. 'Who do we like for this? Anyone have a favorite yet?'

Reilly glanced around the table before chiming in. 'This one's more complicated. The first thing that pops to mind is a shopping list.'

Art thefts, especially when the objects were well known, were often either stolen to order or pre-sold to collectors who wanted to own things even if they could never allow them to be seen by anyone else. But from the moment he had arrived at the museum, Reilly had pushed this angle to the back of his thinking. Shopping lists almost always went to smart thieves. Riding horseback along Fifth Avenue wasn't the action of smart people. Neither was the mayhem, and least of all the execution.

'I think we're all on the same page on this,' he continued. 'The profilers' prelims also concur. There's more behind this than just grabbing some priceless relics. You want to get the pieces, you choose a quiet, rainy Wednesday morning, get in before the crowds, pull out your Uzis and grab what you want. Lower visibility, lower risk. Instead, these guys chose the busiest, most heavily guarded moment possible to stage their heist. It's almost like they wanted to taunt us, to embarrass us. Sure, they got the booty, but I think they were also out to make a statement.'

'What kind of statement?' Jansson asked.

Reilly shrugged. 'We're working on it.'

The ADIC turned to Blackburn. 'You guys agree?'

Blackburn nodded. 'Put it this way. Whoever these guys are, they're heroes on the street. They've taken what all these coked-out jackasses fantasize about when they're plugged into their Playstations and actually gone out and done it. I'm just hoping they don't start a trend here. But, yeah, I think there's more going on with these guys than cold efficiency.'

Jansson glanced back at Reilly. 'So it looks like it's your baby after all.'

Reilly looked at him and quietly nodded. Baby wasn't exactly the first word that sprung into his mind. It was more like a two thousand pound gorilla and, he mused, it was indeed all his.

The meeting was interrupted by the arrival of a slim, unassuming man wearing a brown tweed suit over a clerical collar. Jansson got out of his chair and offered his huge paw to shake the man's hand.

'Monsignor, glad you could make it. Please, have a seat. Everybody, this is Monsignor De Angelis. I promised the Archbishop we'd let him sit in and help out in any way.'

Jansson proceeded to introduce De Angelis to the assembled agents. It was highly unusual to allow outsiders in on a meeting as sensitive as this, but the apostolic nuncio, the Vatican's ambassador to the US, had made enough well-placed phone calls to allow it.

The man was in his late forties, Reilly guessed. He had neatly trimmed dark hair that receded in perfect arcs at the temples, with flecks of silver around the ears. His steel-rimmed spectacles were slightly smudged, and his manner was affable and quietly unobtrusive as he acknowledged the agents' names and positions.

'Please, don't let me interrupt,' he said as he sat down.

Jansson shook his head slightly, dismissing the thought. 'The evidence isn't pointing us anywhere yet, Father. Without wanting to prejudice the matter – and I need to stress that this is purely an airing of ideas and gut feelings at this point – we were kicking around our thoughts about possible candidates for the raid.'

'I understand,' De Angelis replied.

Jansson turned to Reilly who, although uncomfortable with the idea, continued. He knew he had to bring the monsignor up to speed.

'We were just saying that this is clearly more than just a museum robbery. The way it was carried off, the timing, everything indicated more at play here than a simple armed heist.'

De Angelis pursed his lips, absorbing the implications of what was said. 'I see.'

'The knee-jerk reaction,' Reilly continued, 'is to point to Muslim fundamentalists, but in this case I'm pretty sure it's way off the mark.'

'Why do you think that?' De Angelis asked. 'As unfortunate as it may be, they do seem to hate us. I'm sure you remember the uproar when the museum in Baghdad was looted. The claims of double standards, the blame, the anger... That didn't go down too well in the area.'

'Believe me, this doesn't fit their M.O. – in fact, it's nowhere close. Their attacks are typically overt; they like to take credit for their actions and they usually favor the kamikaze route. Besides, it would be anathema for any Muslim fundamentalist to wear an outfit with a cross on it.' Reilly looked at De Angelis, who seemed to agree. 'Of course, we'll look at it. We have to. But I'd put my money on another bunch.'

'A bubba job.' Jansson was using the politically incorrect shorthand for redneck bombers.

'Much more likely in my opinion,' Reilly nodded with a shrug of familiarity. Individual 'lone wolf' extremists and violent homegrown radicals were as much a part of his daily life as were foreign terrorists.

De Angelis looked lost. '*Bubba?*'

'Local terrorists, Father. Groups with ludicrous names like The Order or The Silent Brotherhood, mostly operating under an ideology of hate called the Christian Identity, which, I know, is a pretty strange perversion of the term...'

The monsignor shifted uncomfortably. 'I thought these people are all fanatical Christians.'

'They are. But remember this is the Vatican we're talking about – the Catholic Church. And these guys, they're not fans of Rome, Father. Their twisted churches – none of which is even remotely Catholic, by the way – aren't recognized by the Vatican. Your people actually make it pretty clear they don't want to have anything to do with them, and with good reason. What they all have in common, apart from blaming all their troubles on blacks and Jews and homosexuals, is a hatred for organized government, ours in particular, yours by association. They think we're the great Satan – which, oddly enough, is the same terminology Khomeini coined for us and which is still echoing around the Muslim world today. Remember, these guys bombed the federal building in Oklahoma City. Christians. Americans. And there are a lot of them around. We just picked up a guy in Philadelphia who we've been after for a long time, he's part of an Aryan Nations spin-off group, the Church of the Sons of Yahweh. Now this guy was previously Aryan Nations minister for Islamic liaison. In that role, he's admitted to trying to form alliances with anti-American Muslim extremists after the 9/11 attacks.'

'The enemy of my enemy,' De Angelis mused.

'Exactly,' Reilly agreed. 'These guys have a seriously deranged view of the world, Father. We just need to try and understand what insane mission statement they've now come up with.'

There was a brief silence in the room after Reilly finished. Jansson took over, 'Okay, so you're going to run with this.'

Reilly nodded, unfazed. 'Yep.'

Jansson turned to Blackburn. 'Rog, you're still gonna look at the straight robbery angle?'

'Absolutely. We've got to cover both until something breaks that points us one way or the other.'

'Okay, good. Father,' he said, now turning to De Angelis,

'it would really help us if you could get us a list of what was stolen, as detailed as you can. Color photographs, weight, dimensions, anything you have. We need to get some alerts set up.'

'Of course.'

'On that point, Father,' Reilly interjected, 'one of the horsemen seemed only interested in one thing: this,' he said, as he pulled out a blow-up of a vidcap from the museum's security cameras. It showed the fourth horseman holding the encoder. He handed it to the monsignor. 'The exhibition's catalogue lists it as a multigeared rotor encoder,' he said, then asked, 'any idea why one would take that, given all the gold and jewels around?'

De Angelis adjusted his glasses as he studied the photograph, then shook his head. 'I'm sorry, I don't know much about this... machine. I can only imagine it to have value as an engineering curiosity. Everybody likes to flaunt their brilliance once in a while, even, it seems, my brothers who selected what should be included in the exhibit.'

'Well, perhaps you could check with them. They might have ideas, I don't know, collectors who may have previously approached them about it.'

'I'll look into it.'

Jansson looked around. Everyone was set. 'Okay, folks,' he said, arranging his papers. 'Let's put these freaks out of business.'

As the others walked out of the room, De Angelis edged over to Reilly and shook his hand. 'Thank you, Agent Reilly. I feel we are in good hands.'

'We'll get them, Father. Something always gives.'

The monsignor's eyes were locked on his, studying him. 'You can call me Michael.'

'I'll stick to "father" if that's alright. Kind of a tough habit to break.'

De Angelis looked surprised. 'You're Catholic?'

Reilly nodded.

'Practicing?' De Angelis looked down in sudden embarrassment. 'Forgive me, I shouldn't be so inquisitive. I suppose some of my habits are equally hard to break.'

'No problem. And yes, I'm in the fold.'

De Angelis seemed quietly pleased. 'You know, in many ways our work is not too dissimilar. We both help people come to terms with their sins.'

Reilly smiled. 'Maybe, but... I'm not sure you get exposed to the same caliber of sinners we get around here.'

'Yes, it is worrying... things are not well out there.' He paused, then looked up at Reilly. 'Which makes our work all the more valuable.'

The monsignor saw Jansson looking his way; he seemed to be calling him over. 'I have full confidence in you, Agent Reilly. I'm sure you'll find them,' the man in the collar said before walking off.

Reilly watched him go, then picked up the vidcap from the desk. As he was tucking it back into his file, he glanced at it again. In a corner of the photograph, which was grainy from the low resolution of the museum's surveillance cameras, he could clearly make out a figure crouching low behind a cabinet, peeking out in terror at the horseman and the device. He knew from the videotape that it was the blonde woman he had spotted leaving the museum that night. He thought of the ordeal she'd been through, of how terrified she must have been, and felt drawn to her. He hoped she was all right.

He filed the photograph back in its folder. As he left the room, he couldn't help but think of the word Jansson had used.

Freaks.

The thought was not at all reassuring.

Figuring out the motives when sane people committed crimes was hard enough. Getting inside the minds of the insane was often impossible.

CHAPTER 11

Clive Edmondson was pale, but he didn't seem to be in too much pain, which surprised Tess as she watched him lying there in his hospital bed.

She knew that one of the horses had backed into him, driving him to the floor, and that in the ensuing panic, he'd had three ribs broken. Their location was too close to the lungs for comfort, and given Clive's age, his general health, and his fondness for strenuous activities, the doctors at the New York Presbyterian Hospital had decided to keep him under observation for a few days.

'They've got me on a really nice cocktail of stuff,' he told her, glancing up at the IV pouch that was dangling from its stand. 'I can't feel a thing.'

'Not exactly the kind of cocktail you were going for, was it?' she quipped.

'I've had better.'

As he chuckled, she looked at him, wondering whether or not to bring up the more pressing reason for her visit. 'You up to talking about something?'

'Sure. As long as it doesn't involve going over what happened yet again. That's all everyone around here wants to hear about,' he sighed. 'Understandable, I guess, but...'

'Well, it's... related,' Tess admitted sheepishly.

Clive looked at her, and smiled. 'What's on your mind?'

Tess hesitated, then decided to dive in. 'When we were chatting at the museum, did you happen to notice what I was looking at?'

He shook his head. 'No.'

'It was a machine, some kind of box with buttons and levers coming out of it. The catalogue calls it a multigeared rotor encoder.'

His forehead creased in thought for a moment. 'No, I didn't notice it.' Of course, he wouldn't have. Not with her there. 'Why?'

'One of the horsemen took it. He didn't take anything else.'

'So?'

'So don't you think it's strange? That of all the priceless stuff that was there, he only took that contraption. And not only that, but when he grabbed it, it was like it was part of some ritual for him, he seemed totally consumed by the moment.'

'Okay, well, he's obviously a really keen collector of arcane encoding machines. Get Interpol on the horn. The Enigma box is probably next on his list.' He cast her a wry look. 'People collect worse things.'

'I'm serious,' she protested. 'He even said something. When he held it up. "*Veritas vos liberabit.*"'

Clive looked at her. '*Veritas vos liberabit?*'

'I think so. I'm pretty sure that was it.'

Clive thought about it for a moment, then smiled. 'Okay. You don't just have yourself a hardcore collector of coding machines. You've got one that went to Johns Hopkins. That ought to narrow down the search.'

'Johns Hopkins?'

'Yep.'

'What are you talking about?' She was utterly lost.

'It's the university's motto. *Veritas vos liberabit.* The truth will set you free. Trust me, I ought to know. I went there. It's even on that awful song of ours, you know, The Johns Hopkins Ode.' He started singing: '*Let knowledge grow from more to more, and scholars versed in deepest lore...*' Clive was watching Tess, enjoying her bewildered look.

'You think...?' Then she noticed his look. She knew that self satisfied grin. 'You're messing with me, aren't you?'

Clive nodded guiltily. 'Well, it's either that or he's a disgruntled ex-CIA agent. You do know it's the first thing you

59

see when you step into their building at Langley.' Heading off her question, he added, 'Tom Clancy. Major fan, what can I say.'

Tess shook her head, annoyed at being so gullible. Then Clive surprised her.

'You're not far off, though. It fits.'

'What do you mean?' She noted that Clive's face was now serious.

'What were the knights wearing?'

'What do you mean, what were they wearing?'

'I asked you first.'

She wasn't with him. 'They were in standard issue medieval outfits. Wire mesh, mantles, helmets.'

'And...?' He teased. 'Anything more specific?'

She knew Clive was baiting her. She tried to recall the terrifying sight of the knights rampaging in the museum. 'No...?'

'White mantles with red crosses. Blood red crosses.'

She grimaced, still not with him. 'Crusaders.'

Clive wasn't done yet. 'Getting warmer. Come on, Tess. Nothing special about their crosses? A red cross on the left shoulder, another on the chest? Anything?'

And it hit her. 'Templars.'

'Final answer?'

Her mind was racing. It still didn't explain the significance. 'You're absolutely right, they were dressed as Templars. But that doesn't necessarily mean anything. It's the generic Crusader look, isn't it? For all we know, they just copied the first image of a crusader knight they happened to come across, and the odds are it would be a Templar, they've got the most coverage.'

'I thought so too. I didn't attach any significance to it at first. The Templars are by far the most famous, or rather infamous, group of knights associated with the Crusades. But then, your little Latin catchphrase... that changes things.'

Tess stared at Clive, desperate to know what he was talking about. He stayed quiet. It was driving her nuts. '... *Because – ?!*'

'*Veritas vos liberabit*, remember? It also happens to be a marking on a castle in the Languedoc, in the south of France.' He paused. 'A Templar castle.'

CHAPTER 12

'What castle?' Tess was breathless.

'The Chateau de Blanchefort. In the Languedoc. The marking's right there in plain sight, carved into the porch lintel above the castle's entrance. *Veritas vos liberabit*. The truth will set you free.' The phrase seemed to inspire a whole stream of recollections in Edmondson.

Tess frowned. Something was bothering her. 'Weren't the Templars dissolved –' then cringing at her unfortunate choice of words, '– disbanded in the thirteen hundreds?'

'1314.'

'Well then it doesn't match. The catalogue says the encoder's from the sixteenth century.'

Edmondson mulled it over. 'Well, maybe they've got their dates wrong. The fourteenth century wasn't exactly the Vatican's proudest moment. Far from it. In 1305, the pope, Clement V, who was already little more than a puppet of the French king, Philip IV, had to suffer the indignity of being forced to leave the Vatican and move the seat of the Holy See to Avignon – where he was kept on an even tighter leash, especially when it came to helping King Philip bring down the Templars. In fact, the Papacy was under complete French control for seventy years – it's referred to as the Babylonian Captivity. It lasted until Pope Gregory XI found the guts to make a break, drawn back to Rome by the mystic Catherine of Siena – but that's another story. What I mean is that if this decoder of yours was from the fourteenth century –'

'– the odds are it didn't even originate in Rome,' Tess chimed in. 'Especially not if it's Templar.'

Edmondson smiled. 'Exactly.'

Tess hesitated. 'Do you think I'm onto something or am I clutching at straws here?'

'No, I think there could definitely be something there. But... Templars aren't exactly within your area of expertise, are they?'

'Only by a couple of thousand years, give or take a continent.' She grinned. Her expertise was in Assyrian history. The Templars were way off her radar.

'You need to talk to a Templar geek. The ones I know of that are knowledgeable enough to be of use to you are Marty Falkner, William Vance and Jeb Simmons. Falkner must be eighty-something by now and probably a bit of a handful to deal with. Vance I haven't come across for ages, but I know Simmons is around –'

'*Bill* Vance?'

'Yes. You know him?'

William Vance had dropped in on one of her father's digs while she was there. It was around ten years ago, she remembered. She'd been working with her father in northeastern Turkey, as close as the military would allow them to get to Mount Ararat. She recalled how, rarely for her father, Oliver Chaykin had treated Vance as an equal. She could visualize him clearly. A tall, handsome man, maybe fifteen years her senior.

Vance had been charming, and very helpful and encouraging to her. It had been a rotten time for her. Lousy conditions in the field. Uncomfortably pregnant. And yet, although he barely knew her, Vance had seemed to sense her unhappiness and discomfort and had treated her so kindly that he made her feel good when she felt awful, attractive when she knew she looked terrible. And there had never been the slightest hint that he had an ulterior motive. She felt mildly embarrassed now to think that she had been a little bit disappointed at his obviously platonic attitude toward her, because she had been rather attracted to him. And, toward the end of his brief stay at the camp, she had sensed that maybe, just maybe, he had started to feel the same way about her, though just how attractive a seven-month pregnant woman

63

could be was, in her mind, highly questionable.

'I met him once, with my dad.' She paused. 'But I thought his specialty was Phoenician history.'

'It is, but you know how it is with the Templars. It's like archaeological porn, it's virtually academic suicide to be interested in them. It's gotten to the point where no one wants it known that they take the subject seriously. Too many crackpots obsessed with all kinds of conspiracy theories about their history. You know what Umberto Eco said, right?'

'No.'

'"A sure sign of a lunatic is that sooner or later, he brings up the Templars."'

'I'm struggling to take that as a compliment here.'

'Look, I'm on your side on this. They're eminently worthy of academic research.' Edmondson shrugged. 'But like I said, I haven't heard from Vance in years. Last I know he was at Columbia, but if I were you I'd go for Simmons, I can hook you up with him pretty easily.'

'Okay, great.' Tess smiled.

A nurse popped her head around the door. 'Tests. Five minutes.'

'Wonderful,' Clive groaned.

'Will you let me know?' Tess asked.

'You bet. And when I'm out of here, how about I buy you dinner and you can tell me how it's panning out?'

She remembered the last time she'd had dinner with Edmondson. In Egypt, after they'd dived together on a Phoenician shipwreck off Alexandria. He'd got drunk on arak, made a half-hearted pass which she had gently rebuffed, and then he'd fallen asleep in the restaurant.

'Sure,' she said, thinking that she had lots of time in which to come up with excuses and then felt guilty at her unkind thought.

CHAPTER 13

Lucien Boussard paced cautiously across the floor of his gallery.

He reached the window and peered out from behind a fake *Ormulu* clock. He stayed there for several minutes, thinking hard. Part of his brain registered that the clock was in need of cleaning and he carried it back to the table and stood it on the newspaper.

The one with the pictures of the Met raid, staring up at him.

He ran his finger over the photographs, smoothing the newspaper's folds.

There's no way I'm getting involved in this.

But he couldn't simply do nothing. Gus would kill him for doing nothing just as easily as he would kill him for doing something wrong.

There was only one way out and he'd already been thinking about it while Gus was standing there, in his gallery, threatening him. Turning Gus in, especially knowing what he had done at the museum, was dangerous. But given Gus's swordplay outside the museum, Lucien felt reasonably sure he would be safe. There was no way the big man would be coming out of prison to take revenge on him one day. If they didn't change the law and give him the needle, Gus was looking at life without parole. Had to be.

Just as important, Lucien had problems of his own. He had a cop on his back. A relentless *salopard* who'd been after him for years and was showing no signs of going away or even easing off. All because of a Dogon statuette from Mali that turned out to be more recent than Lucien had said it was and that was, consequently, worth a fraction of what he'd sold it for. Its septuagenarian buyer had, luckily for Lucien, died of a heart attack before the lawyers got their act together. Lucien had wormed his way out of a very tight spot, but Detective Steve Buchinski didn't let go of it. It was almost like a personal crusade. Lucien had tried feeding the cop a few tips but they hadn't been enough. Nothing would ever be enough.

But this was different. Feed him Gus Waldron and maybe, just maybe, the leech would let go.

He looked at his watch. It was half past one.

Sliding open a drawer, Lucien rummaged through a box of cards until he found the one he wanted. Then he reached for the phone and dialed.

CHAPTER 14

Poised outside the heavy, paneled door to a fifth floor apartment on Central Park West, the leader of the FBI tactical unit held up one hand, all fingers splayed, and glanced at his team. His number two reached out a cautious arm and waited. On the opposite side of the hallway, another man brought a pump action shotgun up to his shoulder. The fourth man in the team flicked the safety off a stun grenade. The remaining pair who completed the unit gently eased the safety catches on their Heckler & Koch MP5 machine guns.

'Go!'

The agent nearest the door rapped firmly with his fist and yelled, 'FBI. Open up!'

The reaction was virtually instantaneous. Gunshots ripped out through the door, spitting splinters of teak across the hallway.

The FBI shotgunner returned the compliment, racking his weapon in a blur of action, blasting away until he had torn several head-sized holes through the door panel. Even with the earplugs she wore, Amelia Gaines felt the jarring shock waves in the confined space.

More shots erupted from inside, splintering the door jambs and punching through the plasterboards across the hallway. The fourth man moved forward, flicking the stun grenade through the opening blown in the door. Then the shotgun took out the rest of the central door panel and moments later the two men with the H&Ks were inside.

A momentary pause. Echoing silence. A single shot. Another pause. A voice called out, 'Clear!' More 'Clears' followed. Then a casual voice said, 'Okay, party's over.'

Amelia followed the others into the apartment. It made the word plush sound cheap. Everything about it reeked of money. But as Amelia and the unit leader checked the place out it quickly became apparent that this particular reek was of drugs.

The occupants, four men, were swiftly identified as Colombian drug traffickers. One of them had a serious gunshot wound in his upper body. Elsewhere in the apartment, they found a small horde of drugs, a pile of cash, and enough leads to keep the DEA happy for months.

The tip off, an anonymous phone call, had spoken of money to burn, weapons and several men speaking in a foreign language. All of that was right. But none of it had anything to do with the museum raid.

Another disappointment.

It wouldn't be the last.

Disheartened, Amelia looked around the apartment as the other Colombians were handcuffed and led out. She compared this place with her own apartment. Hers was pretty nice. Tasteful, classy, if she said so herself. But this one was simply stunning. It had everything, including a great view of the park. As she looked around, she decided that overstated opulence was not her style and she didn't envy any of it. Except maybe the view.

She stood at the window for a moment, looking down into the park. She could see two people riding horses along a track. Even at this range, she could see that both the riders were women. One of them was having trouble; her horse looked to be high-spirited or maybe it had been spooked by the two roller-blading youths gliding by.

Amelia took another look around the apartment, then left it to the tactical unit leader to wrap things up, and headed for the office to deliver her somber report to Reilly.

Reilly had been busy scheduling a succession of low-key visits to mosques and other gathering points for the city's Muslims. After a brief preliminary discussion with Jansson on the politics of this side of the investigation, Reilly had decided that these visits would all be exactly that. Simple visits, by no more than two agents or cops, one of whom was, as often as possible, Muslim. Not the merest hint of them being raids. Cooperation was what they sought and, mostly, cooperation was what they got.

Computers at the FBI offices at Federal Plaza had been spilling out data nonstop, adding to the rising tidal wave of information coming in from the NYPD, Immigration and Homeland Security. Databases that had mushroomed after Oklahoma City were awash with names of homegrown radicals and extremists; those following 9/11 were overflowing with names of Muslims of many nationalities. Reilly knew that most of them were on those lists not because they were suspected by the authorities of terrorist or criminal acts or tendencies, but simply because of their religion. It made him uneasy; it also made for a lot of unnecessary work, sifting out the few possibles from the many who were innocent of everything except their beliefs.

He still felt the bubba route was the way to go on this, but one thing was missing. The specific grudge, the link between a group of heavily armed fanatics and the Roman Catholic Church. To that end, a team of agents was scouring manifestos and databases for the elusive common thread.

He took in the open floor, absorbing the ordered chaos of agents working their phones and their computers before making his way to his desk. As he reached it, he spotted Amelia Gaines coming toward him from across the room.

'You got a minute?'

Everyone always had a minute for Amelia Gaines. 'What's up?'

'You know that apartment we hit this morning?'

'Yeah, I heard,' he said cheerlessly. 'Still, it did buy us some brownie points with the DEA, which isn't a bad thing.'

Amelia shrugged the notion away. 'When I was in there, I was looking out the window, into the park. A couple of people were out riding. One of them was having some trouble

69

with her horse and it got me thinking.'

Reilly pushed a chair over to her and she sat down. She was a breath of fresh air in the male-dominated Bureau, where the percentage of female recruits had only recently risen to the lofty height of ten percent. The Bureau's recruiters made no secret of their wish for more female applicants, but few applied. In fact, only one female agent had ever reached the rank of SAC, earning herself the mocking nickname *Queen Bee* in the process.

Reilly had worked with Amelia a lot over the last months. Amelia was a particularly useful asset when it came to dealing with Middle Eastern suspects. They loved her red locks and freckled skin, and a well-timed smile or a strategic flash of skin often got more results than weeks of surveillance. Although no one at the Bureau went out of their way to hide their attraction to her, Amelia hadn't incited any cases of sexual harassment; not that it was easy to imagine anyone victimizing her. She was raised in a military family where she had four brothers, she was a karate black belt at the age of sixteen, and she was an expert markswoman. She could pretty much take care of herself in any situation.

Once, less than a year ago, they had been alone at a coffee shop and Reilly had come close to inviting her out to dinner. He had decided against it, knowing that there was a good chance, in his hopeful mind anyway, that it wouldn't end with dinner. Relationships with co-workers were never easy; at the Bureau, he knew, they simply didn't stand a chance.

'Keep going,' he now said to her.

'Those horsemen at the museum. Watching the videos, it's pretty obvious that those guys weren't just riding the horses, they were skillfully controlling them. Riding them up the steps, for instance. Easy for Hollywood stuntmen, but in real life that's a pretty hard thing to do.'

She sounded as if she knew; she also sounded uneasy.

Amelia saw his glance and smiled tightly. 'I can ride,' she confirmed.

He immediately realized she was onto something. The connection with horses glared at him. He'd had an inkling in the first few hours when he'd thought of how Central Park Precinct officers used horses but he hadn't developed the thought. Had he done so, they might've been onto this sooner.

'You want to look into stunt men with rap sheets?'

'For a start. But it's not just the horsemen. It's the horses themselves.' Amelia moved a touch closer. 'From what we heard and what we've seen on the videos, people were screaming and shouting and there was all that gunfire. And yet those horses weren't panicking.'

Amelia stopped, looking across to where Aparo was picking up a phone call, as if unwilling to add her next thought.

Reilly knew where she was going. He made the uncomfortable connection for her. 'Cop horses.'

'Right.'

Dammit. He didn't like this any more than she did. Cop horses could mean cops. And nobody liked to contemplate the possibility of the involvement of other law enforcement officers.

'It's all yours,' he said. 'But go easy.'

She didn't have time to answer. Aparo was rushing over.

'That was Steve. We've got something. Looks like the real deal this time.'

CHAPTER 15

As he turned into 22nd street, Gus Waldron began feeling jittery. Okay, so he'd had the jumps since Saturday night, but this was different. He recognized the signs. He did a lot of things on instinct. Betting on the horses was one of them. The results? Lousy. But other things he did instinctively sometimes worked out for the best, so he always paid attention.

Now he saw that there was a reason for his jitters. A car, plain and ordinary. Too plain, too ordinary. Two men, looking carefully at nothing in particular. *Cops. What else could they be?*

He counted off the steps and stopped to look in a window. Reflected in it, he saw another car nosing around the corner. Just as unremarkable, and as he risked a quick glance over his shoulder he saw that two men were in this one as well.

He was boxed in.

Gus immediately thought of Lucien. He flashed on any number of gruesome ways he would end the miserable French prick's life.

He reached the gallery and suddenly dived for its door, storming in fast and rushing across the floor to where a startled Lucien was now rising out of his chair. Gus kicked the table aside, sending the big ugly clock and a can of cleaning fluid crashing to the floor, and smacked Lucien hard across the ear.

'You ratted me out to the cops, didn't you?'

'No, *Gueusse –*'

As Gus raised his hand to hit him again, he saw that Lucien twisted his head, his eyes popping as he looked toward the rear of the gallery. *So the cops were out back too –* then Gus realized that he could smell something, gasoline maybe. The can he had knocked off the table was leaking onto the floor.

Snatching up the can, Gus pulled Lucien off the floor and thrust him ahead toward the door, where he kicked him behind the knees, sending the skinny weasel down again. Keeping him down with his boot, he tipped the can over Lucien's head.

'You know better than to mess with me, you little shit,' he barked as he kept on pouring.

'Please!' The Frenchman sputtered, his eyes burning from the liquid when, too fast for the terrified man to resist, Gus yanked open the door, picked Lucien up by the scruff of his neck, pulled out a Zippo, ignited the fuel, and booted the gallery owner into the street.

Flames flared blue and yellow around Lucien's head and shoulders as he stumbled across the sidewalk, his screams mingling with yells from shocked onlookers and a sudden blare of car horns. Gus emerged close behind him, eyes darting left and right, fixed like a hawk on the four men, two at each end of the block, rushing out of their cars now and with guns, and all more concerned with the burning man than with him.

Which was exactly what he needed.

Reilly knew they'd been spotted as soon as he saw the man bolt off the street and dive into the gallery. Yelling, 'He's made us. We have a go, I repeat, we have a go!' into the mike tucked into his sleeve, he chambered a round into his Browning Hi-Power handgun and scrambled out of his car, with Aparo emerging from the passenger side.

He was still behind the car's door when he saw a man stagger out of the gallery. Reilly wasn't sure he was seeing straight. The man's head seemed to be on fire.

As Lucien staggered along the street, his hair and shirt ablaze, Gus followed him out, keeping close enough so that the cops wouldn't risk shooting.

Or so he hoped.

To make them think twice about getting too close, he loosed off shots in both directions. The Beretta was fucking useless for this kind of action, but it sent the four men diving for cover.

Windshields shattered and screams of panic echoed in the street as the sidewalks emptied.

Reilly saw him raise his handgun in time to duck behind his car's door. The shots thundered in the street, two bullets crunching their way into a brick wall behind Reilly, a third lodging into the left headlight of his Chrysler in an explosion of chrome and glass. Darting a glance to his right, Reilly spotted four bystanders crouching behind a parked Mercedes, clearly terrified out of their wits. Reilly could tell they were looking to make a run for it, which was not a good idea. They were safer behind the car. One of them looked his way. Reilly made an up-and-down gesture with an open palm, yelling, 'Get down! Don't move!' The nervous man nodded his shocked acceptance and curled away, out of sight.

Reilly turned, leaned out and tried to squeeze off a shot, but the man he knew as 'Gus' had crept up right behind the gallery owner. He was too close to him. Reilly couldn't get a clear shot. More urgently, he couldn't do anything about the gallery owner who had now fallen to his knees, his cries of agony reverberating across the now deserted street.

Just then, Gus moved away from the burning man, firing a couple of rounds in the direction of the other agents. Time seemed to slow down as Reilly saw the opportunity and grabbed it. He held his breath and popped up from behind the car door, cradling his Hi-Power in a two-handed, straight-armed stance, and in a split second he lined up the front post and the rear notch on the gun and pulled the trigger in a smooth, even motion, using steadily increasing force. The bullet thundered out of the Browning's barrel. A red splatter burst out from Gus's thigh.

Reilly scrambled to his feet to rush to the burning man, but fate cut short any heroic plans the agent was formulating when a delivery van chose that moment to come lumbering into the street.

Lucien was rolling around, arms flailing, desperately trying to quash the flames. Gus knew he had to make a run for it when something hit him in his left thigh, sending him staggering sideways. He felt the area of the wound, his hand coming up dripping with blood.

Sonofabitch. The cops had got lucky.

Then he saw the van and, blasting away at both sets of cops, he used it as cover and made his move. He limped around the corner and now it was his turn to get lucky. A cab had pulled over, dropping off a fare, a Japanese business-man in a pale suit. Gus shouldered the man aside, snatched open the door, reached in and dragged the driver out onto the street. Scrambling behind the wheel, he put it in gear, and then felt something hit him on the side of the head. It was the driver, out to reclaim his car, yelling in some unin-telligible language. *The dumb fuck.* Gus shoved the muzzle of the Beretta out the window, squeezed the trigger and popped a bullet into the man's furious red face. Then he was away, hurtling down the street.

CHAPTER 16

Flooring the black department Chrysler, Reilly ramped it over the sidewalk and past the delivery truck, catching a glimpse of a cluster of people leaning over the dead cab driver.

On the radio, Aparo was talking and listening as Buchinski was organizing back up and roadblocks. Too bad this had been rushed. They should have had the street totally sealed off, but then, like Buchinski had said, they might have scared away the big man before he even reached the gallery if the normally busy street had been unnaturally quiet. He thought about the blazing figure he had seen stagger from the shop, and the cab driver blown backward from a head shot. *Maybe it would have been better if scaring off the suspect was all that we'd done.*

He glanced in his rear view mirror, wondering if Buchinski was with them.

No. They were on their own.

'Watch the road!'

His attention snatched back by Aparo's interjection, Reilly jinked the Chrysler through a chicane-like cluster of cars and trucks, most of them already blaring angry horns at the cab that had flashed past them. Now the cab spun into an alley. Reilly followed through a swirling cloud of trash, trying but failing to get his bearings.

'Where the hell are we?' Reilly yelled.

'Heading toward the river.'

A big help that was.

As the cab burst from the alley, it pulled a screaming right and moments later Reilly did the same.

Cars thundered past, seemingly heading in all directions. There was no sign of the cab.

It was gone.

Reilly darted looks left and right while trying to avoid the rushing traffic.

'There,' Aparo yelled, pointing.

Reilly rapiered a look, hit the handbrake and hung a tyre-smoking left into another alley and there was the cab. He floored the gas pedal as they bounced down the narrow street, swiping past garbage dumpsters, which sent sparks flying down the side of the car.

This time, when they came out into a street it was crowded with parked cars and he heard the screech of metal on metal as the cab ripped fenders and hubcaps from other vehicles, the impacts fleeting, but enough to slow the cab's progress.

Another right turn and this time Reilly could see signs announcing the Lincoln Tunnel. More to the point, they were closing in on the cab. From the corner of his eye he saw that Aparo had his gun on his lap.

'Don't risk it,' Reilly said. 'You might get lucky and hit him.'

Causing the cab to crash at that speed on this street could be a disaster.

Then the cab turned again, scattering pedestrians who were ambling over a pedestrian crossing.

Reilly saw something emerge from the driver's window of the cab. Couldn't be a gun. A man would have to be stupid to drive and shoot at the same time. Stupid or certifiable.

Sure enough, a flash and smoke blossomed.

'Hang on,' Reilly said.

Swinging the wheel, he swerved the Chrysler into a lumbering fishtail, spotted a gap where a building had been torn down and drove into it, ripping through chain link fencing and raising a cloud of dust.

Seconds later, the Chrysler was spinning out of the vacant lot and once again on the trail of the taxi. So far as Reilly could see, the driver's arm and gun were no longer sticking out of the window.

Aparo yelled, 'Watch it!'

77

A woman walking a black terrier tripped, cannoning into a delivery man wheeling a stack of beer crates that tumbled into the Chrysler's path. Reilly jerked the wheel, narrowly avoiding the people, but not the crates, one of which bounced up and over the hood, smashing into the windshield which held but was now spiderwebbed all over.

'I can't see a thing!' Reilly shouted. Aparo, using the butt of his gun, pounded the windscreen and on the third blow it busted out and flipped up, flying over the car and spinning to a rest on the roof of a parked car.

Screwing up his eyes against the buffeting wind, Reilly could see a no-entry sign where the street narrowed abruptly. Would the man risk it? If he met something, he'd be a goner. Spotting an opening on the right, maybe fifty yards short of the no-entry, Reilly guessed that's where the cab would go. He urged more power out of his car, hoping he might push the other driver into overcooking the turn. The Chrysler charged closer to the cab.

He almost succeeded. The cab screeched into the opening, its rear fishtailing wide to the left, lighting up the tyres as it smashed into the brickwork on the corner of a building.

As Reilly followed into the new street, Aparo muttered, 'Oh shit,' as they both saw a kid on a skateboard gliding across the roadway ahead of the cab. The boy had earphones on and was totally oblivious to the approaching storm.

Instinctively, Reilly slowed, but there was no corresponding flash of braking lights from the cab, which was charging straight at the kid.

He's gonna hit him. He's gonna obliterate him.

Reilly jammed the horn, willing it to cut through the boy's private concert. The cab got closer. Then the boy nonchalantly glanced to his left, saw the cab mere feet away, and dove away in time as the cab bulldozed through, chewing up the skateboard as it streaked ahead.

As they passed the stunned boy, Reilly realized that the street ahead was relatively quiet. No moving vehicles. No pedestrians. If he was going to try something, now was the time to do it. *Before this thing turns really ugly.*

He floored it again and gained on the cab. He saw smoke coming from its rear left wheel and guessed that the side-swipe of the wall had jammed the bodywork onto the tyre.

Aparo noticed how close they now were. 'What're you doing?'

Reilly rammed the Chrysler into the cab's rear end, the repercussion of the jolt cannoning through his neck and shoulders.

Boom. Once.

Twice.

He dropped back, floored it, and rammed him a third time.

This time, the cab went into a helpless spin before lurching over the sidewalk, catapulting onto its side and scraping through a storefront window. As he stood on the brakes and the Chrysler screeched to a halt, Reilly looked over and saw the back of the cab, still on its side, sticking out of what he now saw was a musical instrument store.

As the Chrysler stopped, Reilly and Aparo scrambled out. Aparo already had his gun out and Reilly was reaching for his but soon realized that it wasn't needed.

The driver had flown through the front windshield and was lying face down amidst broken glass, surrounded by bent and twisted musical instruments. Pages of sheet music fluttered to a rest on his inert body.

Cautiously, Reilly poked the toe of his shoe under the driver's body and rolled him onto his back. He was clearly unconscious, but he was breathing, his face slashed to bloody ribbons. With the movement, the man's arms spread sideways. A gun slid loosely from one hand. As Reilly nudged it away with his foot, he spotted something else.

From under the man's coat poked a jeweled gold cross.

CHAPTER 17

Only a few messages awaited Tess when she walked into her office at the Manoukian Archaeological Institute on Lexington and 79th. Predictably, half of them were from her ex-husband, Doug; the other half, almost as predictably, were from Leo Guiragossian, the head of the Manoukian Institute. Guiragossian never made any secret of the fact that he tolerated Tess only because having Oliver Chaykin's daughter at the Institute was very useful when it came to fundraising. She disliked the balding creep, but she needed the job, and with current budget restraints sparking rumors of staff cuts, now was not the time to act the way she would like to act toward him.

She tossed all the messages into the wastebasket, ignoring the rolled eyes of Lizzie Harding, the demure and motherly secretary she shared with three other researchers. Both Leo and Doug would want the same thing from her: the gory details of Saturday night's events. Her boss's reasons for wanting to know, out of morbid curiosity, were, in a way, slightly less irksome than Doug's self-serving ones.

Tess kept her computer and telephone positioned so that, with a slight turn of her head, she could look out into the paved garden that lay behind the brownstone. The house had been lovingly restored years before her time by the Institute's founder, an Armenian shipping magnate. A massive weeping willow dominated the garden, its elegant foliage cascading down to shelter a bench as well as scores of pigeons and sparrows.

Tess turned her attention back to her desk and fished out the number Clive Edmondson had given her for Jeb Simmons. She dialed it and got his answering machine. She hung up and tried the other number she had for him. His secretary at the History Department at Brown University informed her that Simmons was away on a dig in the Negev desert for three months, but could be reached if it was important. Tess said she'd call back and hung up.

Recalling her conversation with Edmondson, Tess decided to try another tack. She checked the online Yellow Pages, clicked on the dial icon and got through to the switchboard at Columbia University.

'Professor William Vance,' she said to the reedy voice that answered.

'One moment, please,' the woman said. After a momentary pause, she was told, 'I'm sorry, I don't show anyone listed by that name.'

She expected as much. 'Can you connect me with the History Department?' A couple of clicks and buzzes and she was speaking to another woman. This one seemed to know who Tess was talking about.

'Sure, I remember Bill Vance. He left us... ooh, it must be five or six years ago.'

Tess felt a surge of anticipation. 'Do you know where I can reach him?'

'I'm afraid I don't, I believe he retired. I'm sorry.'

Still, Tess was hopeful. 'Could you do me a favor?' she persisted. 'I really need to talk to him. I'm with the Manoukian Institute, and we met years ago on a dig. Perhaps you could ask around, see if any of his colleagues at the department know where he can be reached?'

The woman was only too happy to help. Tess gave her her name and contact numbers, thanked her and clicked off. She mused on it for a moment, then went back online and did a white pages search for William Vance. She started in the New York area, but got no hits. One of the disadvantages of cellphone proliferation, most of which weren't listed. She tried Connecticut. No hits either. She widened the search nationwide but this time there were just too many matches. She then entered his name into her search engine and got hundreds of hits, but a quick trawl through them didn't reveal any that pointed to his current affiliation.

She sat there, thinking for a moment. In the garden, the pigeons were gone and the sparrows had doubled their presence and were squabbling among themselves. She swung her chair around, letting her eyes range over her bookshelves. An idea struck her and she redialed Columbia University, this time asking to be connected to the library. After identifying herself to the man who answered, she told him she was looking for any research papers or publications they had that were written by Vance. She spelled the name for him and pointed out that she was particularly interested in anything that dealt with the Crusades, knowing Vance probably wouldn't have written papers dealing specifically with the Templars.

'Sure, hold on a moment,' the librarian told her, and disappeared. After a few moments, he came back. 'I just called up everything that we have by William Vance.' He read out the titles of the papers and articles Vance had written that seemed to fulfill Tess's requirements.

'Any chance you can send me copies of them?'

'Not a problem. We'll have to charge you though.'

Tess gave him her office address and made sure he billed her in her own name. Right now was not a good time to upset the budget watchers at the Institute. She hung up, and felt strangely elated. It brought back memories of the field and of the excitement, particularly at the beginning of a dig, when everything was possible.

But this wasn't a dig.

What are you doing? You're an archaeologist. This isn't detective amateur hour. Call the FBI, tell them what you're thinking, and let them follow it up. Tess wondered if not telling them what she was working on was in any way hindering their progress. Then she dismissed the thought. They'd probably laugh her out of the building. Still. Detectives and archaeologists. They weren't that different, were they? They both uncovered what happened in the past. Okay, so two days ago wasn't really a timeframe archaeologists usually focused on.

It didn't matter.

She couldn't help herself. She was way too intrigued by it all. She was there, after all. She was there and she'd made the connection. And most of all, she really, really missed a bit of excitement in her life. She went back online and dove back into her research into the Knights Templar. She glanced up and noticed Lizzie, the secretary, looking at her curiously. Tess smiled at her. She liked Lizzie, and occasionally confided in her over personal matters. But, having already talked with Edmondson, she wasn't about to confide in anyone else. Not about this.

Not to anyone.

CHAPTER 18

Neither Reilly nor Aparo had been hurt, just a few seatbelt bruises and a couple of minor lesions from windshield debris. They had trailed the speeding ambulance carrying Gus Waldron up the FDR drive to the New York Presbyterian hospital. Once Waldron was in the operating room, a black nurse with a short temper persuaded them to let her check them over. When they finally relented, she cleaned and bandaged their cuts, more brusquely than they would have liked, and they were free to go.

According to the doctors in the ER, their man was unlikely to be in any condition to talk to them for at least a couple of days, maybe more. His wounds were extensive. All they could do was wait for him to be fit for questioning while hoping the agents and detectives now looking into the wounded raider's life got a handle on where he'd been holed up since the robbery.

Aparo told Reilly he'd call it a day and head home to his wife who had, in her mid-forties, managed to become pregnant with their third child. Reilly decided to stick around and wait until the raider came out of surgery before heading home. Although he was both physically and mentally exhausted by the events of the day, he was never in that much of a rush to go back to the solitude of his apartment. Living alone in a city teeming with life did that to you.

Wandering in search of a hot cup of coffee, Reilly stepped into an elevator to find a familiar face staring back at him. There was no mistaking those green eyes. She gave him a brief, cordial nod before turning away. He could see she was preoccupied with something and looked elsewhere, his gaze settling on the doors of the elevator as they slid shut.

Reilly was surprised to find that the confines of the small

elevator cabin made her proximity unnerving. As the elevator hummed its way down, he glanced over and saw her acknowledge him again. He hazarded something that was trying to be a smile, a quasi-smile, and was surprised to see a look of recognition crossing her face.

'You were there, weren't you? At the museum, the night of...' she ventured.

'Yes, sort of. I came in later.' He paused, thinking he was being too coy. 'I'm with the FBI.' He hated the way that must have sounded, although there was no simpler way of putting it.

'Oh.'

There was an uncomfortable pause before they spoke at the same time, her 'How is the –' colliding with his 'So are you –'. They both stopped and smiled mid-sentence.

'I'm sorry,' Reilly offered. 'You were saying?'

'I was just going to ask how the investigation was going, but then I don't suppose it's something you can discuss freely.'

'Not really.' *That sounded way too self-aggrandizing,* Reilly thought, quickly catching it up with, 'But it's not like there's that much to tell anyway. Why are you here?'

'I was just visiting a friend. He was hurt that night.'

'Is he okay?'

'Yeah, he'll be fine.'

The elevator pinged, having reached the ground level. As he watched her walk out, she turned, seeming to make her mind up about bringing something up.

'I've been meaning to contact your office again. Agent Gaines gave me her card that night.'

'Amelia. We work together. I'm Reilly. Sean Reilly.' He extended his hand.

Tess took it and told him her name.

'Is it anything I can help you with?' he asked.

'Well, it's just... she said to call if I thought of anything, and, well, there's this one thing I've been thinking about. It's actually something my friend who's here has been helping me with. But then I'm sure you guys have already looked into it.'

'Not necessarily. And believe me, we're always open to new leads. What is it?'

'It's that whole Templar thing.'

Reilly clearly didn't know what she was talking about. 'What Templar thing?'

'You know, the outfits they were wearing, the decoder they took. And the Latin saying one of the horsemen said when he grabbed it.'

Reilly looked at her, perplexed. 'Do you have time for a cup of coffee?'

CHAPTER 19

The café on the ground level of the hospital was almost empty. After they had brought their coffees to a table, Tess was surprised when the first thing Reilly did was ask if it was her daughter who'd been with her at the museum.

'Yes, she was,' she smiled. 'Her name's Kim.'

'She looks like you.'

She was immediately disappointed. Even though she'd only glimpsed him fleetingly at the Met, and only actually met him minutes earlier, something about him felt comfortable. *God, I've really got to get my male sensors recalibrated.* She cringed as she waited for the inevitable guy-on-the-make's traditional compliment. You don't look old enough; I thought you were sisters; whatever. But he surprised her again when he asked, 'Where was she when it all happened?'

'Kim? My mom had taken her to the ladies' room. While they were in there, she heard the uproar and decided to stay put.'

'So they missed the bad part.'

Tess nodded, curious as to his interest. 'Neither of them saw anything.'

'What about afterward?'

'I went to find them and made sure we stayed away until the ambulances were gone,' she told him, still unsure about where he was going with this.

'So she didn't see any of the wounded or...'

'No, just the damage in the Great Hall.'

He nodded. 'Good. But she obviously knows what happened.'

'She's nine, Agent Reilly. She's everyone's new best friend at school right now, they all want to know what it was like to be there.'

'I can imagine. Still, you should really keep an eye on her. Even without actually witnessing it, something like this can have after-effects, especially on someone that young. Could be just nightmares, could be more. Just keep an eye out, that's all. You never know.'

Tess was totally thrown by his interest in Kim. She dazedly nodded, 'Sure.'

Reilly sat back. 'How about you? You were right in the thick of it.'

Tess was intrigued. 'How'd you know that?'

'Security cameras. I saw you on the tape.' He wasn't sure about whether or not that sounded mildly perverted. He hoped it didn't, but he couldn't tell from her look. 'You okay?'

'Yeah.' Tess flashed back to the horsemen trashing the museum and firing their guns, and to the fourth horseman grabbing the encoder inches away from her, his horse literally breathing down her neck. It wasn't a sight she'd ever forget, nor would the fear she felt soon dissipate. She tried not to show it. 'It was pretty intense, but... somehow it was so surreal that, I don't know, maybe I've tucked it away under the fiction section of my memory bank.'

'Just as well.' He hesitated. 'I'm sorry to be nosy, it's just that I've been around circumstances like this and it's not always easy to deal with.'

She looked at him, brightening. 'I understand. And I do appreciate your concern,' she said, mildly curious to note that while she was usually defensive when anyone talked to her about Kim, she did not take exception to this man. His concern appeared to be genuine.

'So,' he said. 'What's all this stuff about Templars?'

She edged closer, surprised. 'You guys aren't looking into any kind of Templar angle?'

'Not that I'm aware of.'

Tess felt deflated. 'See, I knew it was nothing.'

'Just tell me what you're thinking.'

'What do you know about them?'

'Not much,' he confessed.

'Well, the good news is you're not a lunatic.' She smiled before quickly regretting her comment, which he didn't get, and moving on. 'Okay. Let's see... 1118. The First Crusade is over, and the Holy Land is back in Christian hands. Baldwin II is the King of Jerusalem, people across Europe are jubilant and pilgrims are flocking to see what all the fuss was about. What the pilgrims often didn't know was that they were venturing into dangerous territory. Once they'd "liberated" the Holy Land, the crusading knights considered their vows fulfilled and were went back to their homes in Europe, taking their plundered riches with them and leaving the area precariously surrounded by hostile Islamic states. The Turks and the Muslims who had lost much of their lands to the Christian armies weren't about to forgive and forget, and a lot of the pilgrims heading there never made it to Jerusalem. They were attacked and robbed, and often killed. Arab bandits were a constant threat to travelers, which kind of defeated the purpose of the Crusade in the first place.'

Tess told Reilly how in a single incident that year, marauding Saracens ambushed and killed over three hundred pilgrims on the dangerous roads between the port city of Jaffa, where they landed on the coast of Palestine, and the holy city of Jerusalem. Bands of fighters soon became a fixture outside the walls of the city itself. And that's when the Templars first made their appearance. Nine pious knights led by Hughes de Payens arrived at Baldwin's palace in Jerusalem and offered their humble services to the king. They announced that they had taken the three solemn vows of chastity, poverty and obedience, but had added a fourth: a perpetual vow to protect the pilgrims on their journey from the coast to the city. Given the situation, the knights' arrival was very timely. The crusading state was in desperate need of trained fighters.

King Baldwin was very impressed by the religious knights' dedication and gave them quarters in the eastern part of his palace, which stood on the site once occupied by King Solomon's Temple. They became known as *The Order of the Poor Knights of Christ and the Temple of Solomon* – or, more simply, the Knights Templar.

Tess leaned in. 'The religious significance of the site Baldwin gave the burgeoning order is key,' she explained. Solomon had built the first temple in 950 BC. His father David had started the work following God's command, building a temple to house the Ark of the Covenant, a portable shrine that contained the tablets of stone which were engraved with the commandments God gave Moses. The glorious reign of Solomon came to a close with his death, when eastern nations moved in and conquered the Jewish lands. The Temple itself was destroyed in 586 BC by the invading Chaldeans, who proceeded to take the Jews back to Babylon as slaves. More than five hundred years later, the Temple was rebuilt by Herod in an attempt to ingratiate himself with his Jewish subjects and demonstrate to them that their king, despite his Arab origins, was a devout follower of his adopted religion. It would be his crowning achievement: prominently dominating the Kidron valley, the new Temple was a magnificent and elaborate building of a far grander design than its predecessor. Its inner sanctum, reached by two huge golden doors, housed the Holy of Holies, which was accessible only to the Jewish High Priest.

After Herod's death, the Jewish rebelliousness was rekindled and by 66 AD, the insurgents were back in control of Palestine. The Roman Emperor Vespasian dispatched his son Titus to put down the rebellion. After fierce fighting for over six months, Jerusalem finally fell to the Roman legions in 70 AD. Titus commanded that the city, whose population was by now totally annihilated, be razed. And so, 'the most wonderful edifice ever seen or heard of', as it was described at the time by the historian Josephus, was lost again.

A second Jewish rebellion, less than a hundred years

later, was also crushed by the Romans. This time, all Jews were banned from Jerusalem and sanctuaries to Zeus and to the Roman god-emperor Hadrian were built on the Temple Mount. Six hundred years later, the site would see the building of another holy shrine: with the rise of Islam and the conquering of Jerusalem by the Arabs, the location of the holiest site of Judaism was to be redefined as the place from which the prophet Mohammed's horse ascended to heaven. And so in 691 AD, the Dome of the Rock was built on the site by the Caliph Abd El-Malik. It has remained a shrine to Islam ever since, except for the period during which the Crusaders controlled the Holy Land when the Dome of the Rock was converted into a Christian Church called the *Templum Domini*, the 'Temple of our Lord', and when the Al-Aqsa mosque, built in the same compound, was turned into the headquarters of the burgeoning Knights Templar.

The heroic idea of nine brave knights valiantly defending the vulnerable pilgrims quickly captured people's imaginations across Europe. Many soon regarded the Templars with a romantic reverence and offered themselves as new recruits. Nobles across Europe also paid generously to support them, showering them with gifts of money and land. This was all helped greatly by the fact that they were given papal blessings, a rare occurrence that meant a great deal at a time when all kings and all nations looked to the papacy as the ultimate authority in Christendom. And so the Order grew, slowly at first, then much more rapidly. They were highly trained as fighters, and as their successes in the field mounted, their activities widened. From their original mission of protecting the pilgrims, they gradually came to be regarded as the military defenders of the Holy Land.

In less than a hundred years, the Templars became one of the wealthiest and most influential bodies in Europe, second only to the papacy itself, owning huge tracts of land in England, Scotland, France, Spain, Portugal, Germany, and Austria. And with such an extensive network of territories and castles, they soon established themselves as the world's first international bankers, arranging credit facilities for bankrupt royals across Europe, safeguarding the pilgrims' funds, and effectively inventing the concept of the traveler's cheque. Money in those days was just gold or silver, which was simply worth what it weighed. Instead of taking it with them and risk getting robbed, the pilgrims could deposit their money at a Templar house or castle anywhere in Europe, where they would be given a coded note for it. Once they reached their destination, they would go to the local Templar house, present the note, which would be decoded using their tightly guarded encryption practices, and draw that amount of money there.

Tess looked at Reilly to make sure he was still with her. 'What started off as a small team of nine well-intentioned noblemen dedicated to defending the Holy Land from the Saracens quickly became the most powerful and most secretive organization of its time, rivaling the Vatican in terms of wealth and influence.'

'Then it all went wrong for them, didn't it,' Reilly asked.

'Yes. In a big way. The Muslim armies finally recaptured the Holy Land in the thirteenth century and sent the crusaders packing, this time for good. There were no further Crusades. The Templars were the last to leave, after their defeat at Acre in 1291. When they got back to Europe, their whole *raison d'être* was gone. There were no pilgrims to escort, no Holy Land to defend. They had no home, no enemy, and no cause. And they didn't have too many friends either. All that power and wealth had gone to their heads, the poor soldiers of Christ weren't so poor anymore and had grown arrogant and greedy. And many royals, the King of France in particular, owed them a lot of money.'

'And they came crashing down to earth.'

'Crashed and burned,' Tess nodded. 'Literally.' Tess took a sip from her coffee and told Reilly how a whispers campaign had started about the Templars, no doubt facilitated by the ritualistic secrecy with which the Order had conducted its initiation rites over the years. Soon, a shocking and outrageous litany of heresy charges was leveled at them.

'What happened then?'

'Friday the thirteenth,' Tess answered wryly. 'The original version.'

CHAPTER 20

Paris, France – March 1314

Slowly, Jacques de Molay's consciousness returned.

How long had it been this time? An hour? Two? The Grand Master knew it couldn't possibly have been any longer than that. A few hours of unconsciousness would be a luxury that they would never allow.

As the mists receded from his mind, he felt the usual stirrings of pain and, as usual, he banished them. The mind was a strange and powerful thing, and after all these years of imprisonment and torture, he had learned to use it like a weapon. A defensive weapon, but a weapon nevertheless, one with which he could counter at least some of what his enemies tried to accomplish.

They could break his body, and they had, but his spirit and his mind, though damaged, were still his own.

As were his beliefs.

Opening his eyes, he saw that nothing had changed, although there was a curious difference he didn't recognize at first. The walls of the cellar were still covered with a green slime that leaked onto the roughly cobbled floor, a floor that was almost level from the accumulation of dust, dried blood, and excrement on it. How much of the filth had come from his own body? A lot of it, he feared. After all, he had been here for... he concentrated his mind. *Six years? Seven?* Ample time in which to wreck his body.

Bones had been broken, allowed to reset crudely, then broken again. Joints had been wrenched apart, tendons severed. He knew that he couldn't do anything meaningful with his hands and arms, nor could he walk. But they couldn't stop the movement of his mind. That was free to roam, to leave these dark, miserable dungeons beneath the streets of Paris and travel... *anywhere.*

So, where would he go today? To the rolling farmlands of Central France? To the foothills of the Alps? To the seashore, or beyond, back to his beloved *Outremer?*

I wonder, he thought, and not for the first time, *if I'm insane? Probably,* he decided. To suffer everything the torturers who ruled this underground hellhole had inflicted on him, there was no way he could have retained his sanity.

He concentrated a little harder on the time he had spent here. Now he had it. It was six and a half years since the night that the king's men had overrun the Paris Temple.

His Paris Temple.

It was on a Friday, he remembered. October 13, 1307. He'd been asleep, as had most of his fellow knights, when dozens of seneschals had stormed the preceptory at first light. The Knights Templar should have been better prepared. For months, he'd known that the venal king and his lackeys were trying to find a way to overturn the power of the Templars. That morning, they had finally summoned up the courage and the excuse. They had also found the stomach for a fight, and although the knights didn't surrender easily, the king's men had surprise and numbers on their side and it wasn't long before the knights were overpowered.

They had stood back helplessly and watched as the Temple was ransacked. All the Grand Master could do was hope that the king and his henchmen would fail to grasp the significance of the loot that they carried away, or be so consumed by greed for the gold and jewels they couldn't find that they would fail to notice those seemingly worthless objects that were in fact of immeasurable value. Then silence had fallen until slowly and with surprising courtesy, de Molay and his fellow knights were herded into wagons to be carried to their fate.

Now, as de Molay remembered that silence, he realized that this was what was different about today.

It was quiet.

Usually, the dungeon was a noisy place: chains clattering, racks and wheels creaking, braziers hissing, along with the endless screams of the torturers' victims.

Not today, though.

Then the Grand Master heard a sound. Footsteps, approaching. At first, he thought it was Gaspard Chaix, the chief of the torturers, but that ogre's footsteps were unlike these; his were heavy and menacing. It wasn't anyone of his crew of shambling animals either. No, there were many men coming, moving quickly along the tunnel and then they were in the chamber where de Molay hung in chains. Through swollen, bloodshot eyes, he saw half a dozen brightly-dressed men standing before him. And at their center, of all people, was the king himself.

Slender and imposing, King Philippe IV stood a full head taller than the group of fawning sycophants clustered around him. In spite of his parlous state, de Molay was as always struck by the outward appearance of the ruler of France. How could a man of such physical grace be so thoroughly evil? With youthful features belying his forty-six years, Philippe le Bel was light skinned and had long blond hair. He looked the very picture of a nobleman, yet for almost a decade, driven by an insatiable greed for wealth and power matched only by his vulgar profligacy, he had wreaked calculated death and destruction, inflicting torment upon all those who stood in his way or even merely displeased him.

The Knights Templar had done more than merely displease him.

De Molay heard more footsteps coming along the tunnel. Hesitant, nervous steps heralded the arrival in the chamber of a slight figure dressed in a cowled gray robe. The man's foot slipped and he stumbled awkwardly on the uneven floor. The cowl fell away and de Molay recognized the pope. It was a long time since he had seen Clement and, in the intervening period, the man's face had altered. Deeply etched lines turned down the corners of his mouth as if he suffered some continual internal discomfort, while his eyes had sunk deep into dark hollows.

The king and the pope. Together.

This couldn't be good.

The king's gaze was fixed on de Molay, but the broken man wasn't interested in him right now. His eyes were locked on the diminutive man in the cape who stood there fidgeting nervously, avoiding his look. De Molay wondered at the pope's reticence. Was it because the man's deception and his subtle manipulation of the king had precipitated the fall of the Knights Templar? Or was it that he simply couldn't bear to see the grievously misshapen limbs, the rank open sores, or the unhealed flesh of putrefying wounds?

The king stepped closer. 'Nothing?' he snarled at a man hovering beyond the edge of the group. The man stepped forward, and de Molay saw that it was indeed Gaspard Chaix, the torturer, his eyes downcast, his head shaking from side to side.

'Nothing,' the stubbly man replied.

'Damn him to hell,' the king burst out with a voice that was filled with the undercurrent of fury that consumed him.

You've already done that, de Molay thought. He saw Gaspard look his way, the eyes, beneath thick brows, dead as the stones that made up the floor. The king moved forward, peering closely at de Molay, a handkerchief held against his nose to protect him from a stench that the Grand Master knew to be there but had long ago ceased to notice.

The king's whispery voice sliced the stale air. 'Talk, damn you. Where is the treasure?'

'There is no treasure,' de Molay simply replied, his voice barely audible even to himself.

'Why must you be so stubborn?' the king rasped. 'What end does it serve? Your Brothers have revealed all; your sordid initiation ceremonies, your humble Knights of the Cross denying the divinity of Christ, spitting on the Cross, even urinating on it. They've admitted... *everything.*'

Slowly, de Molay licked at his cracked lips with a swollen tongue. 'Under torture such as this,' he managed, 'they would confess to killing God himself.'

Philippe inched closer to him. 'The Holy Inquisition will prevail,' he said indignantly. 'That much should be obvious to a man of your intellect. Just give me what I want and I'll spare your life.'

'There is no treasure,' de Molay repeated with the tone of a man resigned to never convincing those who heard him. For a long time, de Molay had sensed that Gaspard Chaix believed him, even though he had never faltered in his brutal assaults upon his victim's flesh. He also knew that the pope believed him, but the head of the Church wasn't about to let the king in on his little secret. The king, on the other hand, needed the riches he knew the Knights Templar had amassed over the past two hundred years, and his needs overwhelmed the conclusion any sane man would have reached at seeing the broken man hanging from the wall before him.

'It's useless.' The king turned away, still angry but now apparently as resigned as his victim. 'The treasure must have been spirited away that first night.'

De Molay watched the pope, whose face was still turned away. *The man's moves were brilliantly executed,* he thought. The Grand Master felt a perverse satisfaction in knowing it. And it stoked his determination even more, for the wily man's actions only confirmed the nobility of the Templars' goal.

The king looked coldly at the heavyset torturer. 'How many of them still live within these walls?'

De Molay's entire body went rigid. For the first time, he was going to learn of the fate of his Brothers from the Paris Temple. Gaspard Chaix told the king that, apart from the Grand Master himself, only his deputy, Geoffroi de Charnay, survived.

The old Templar shut his eyes, his consciousness flooded

in a tangle of horrific images. *All gone*, he thought. *And yet we came so close. If only...* If only word had come, all those years ago, from the *Falcon Temple*, from Aimard and his men.

But nothing had.

The *Falcon Temple* – and its precious cargo – had simply vanished.

The king turned and took one final look at the broken man. 'End it,' he ordered.

The torturer shuffled closer. 'When, Your Majesty?'

'Tomorrow morning,' the king said, the prospect perversely brightening his spirits.

Hearing the words, de Molay felt something spread over him that he didn't recognize at first. It was a feeling he hadn't experienced in many years.

Relief.

Through hooded eyes, he glanced toward the pope and saw his stifled delight.

'What about their possessions?' the pope asked, his voice quavering. By now, de Molay knew, all that would remain was anything that couldn't be sold to help pay off the king's debts. 'The books, papers, artifacts. They belong to the Church.'

'Then take them.' The king waved a dismissive hand before casting one last seething glance at de Molay and storming out of the chamber, his entourage trailing hurriedly after him.

For the briefest of instants, the eyes of the pope and de Molay met before Clement could turn and rush from the chamber. In that brief space of time, de Molay had read the pope's mind, confirming the small man for what he was: a scheming opportunist who had manipulated the greedy king for his own ends. For the Church's ends.

A scheming manipulator who had bested him.

But de Molay couldn't give him the satisfaction of believing it. He seized the opportunity and rallied himself, summoning all of his strength and channeling it into a glare of confident defiance that he beamed at his nemesis. For a fleeting second, a look of fear crossed the pope's weathered features before he composed his face into a stern gaze and lifted up his cowl.

The Grand Master's cracked lips curled into what would have once been a smile. He knew he'd succeeded in sowing doubt in the small man's mind.

A victory of sorts.

The pope wouldn't sleep well tonight.

You may have won this battle, de Molay thought. *But our war is far from over.* And with that thought, he closed his eyes and awaited his approaching death.

CHAPTER 21

Reilly did his best to avoid appearing conflicted. Much as he was enjoying sitting there with Tess, he couldn't see the relevance of everything she'd just told him. A bunch of selfless knights grow into a medieval superpower only to get their wings clipped and disappear ignominiously into the annals of history. What did that have to do with a gang of armed robbers trashing a museum seven hundred years later?

'You think the guys at the museum were wearing Templar outfits?' he asked.

'Yes. The Templars wore simple clothing, very different from the gaudy outfits other knights wore back then. Remember, they were religious monks, committed to poverty. The white robes symbolized the purity of life that was expected of them, and the red crosses, the color of blood, advertised their special relationship with the Church.'

'Okay, but if you asked me to draw a knight, I'd probably come up with something that looks pretty close to that without consciously thinking about the Templars. It's a pretty iconic look, isn't it?'

Tess nodded. 'Look, on its own, I agree, it's not conclusive. But then there's the encoder.'

'This is the object the fourth horseman took. The one you were next to.'

Tess moved in a bit closer, seeming more driven now. 'Yes. I looked it up. It's far more advanced than anything that appeared for hundreds of years. I mean this thing is revolutionary. And the Templars were known to be masters of encryption. Codes were the backbone of their whole banking system. When the pilgrims traveling to the Holy Land deposited money with them, the receipts they were given were written in code, which could only be deciphered by Templars. That way, no one could forge a deposit note and cheat them. They were pioneers in this field and somehow, this encoder fits their sophisticated, secretive methods.'

'But why would a Templar encoder be part of the Vatican's treasures?'

'Because the Vatican and the King of France both conspired to bring down the Order. They were both after its wealth. It's easy to imagine that whatever the Templars had in their preceptories ended up either at the Louvre or in the Vatican.'

Reilly looked uncertain. 'You mentioned something about a Latin saying?'

Tess visibly rallied herself. 'That's what got me started. The fourth horseman, the one who took the encoder. When he had it in his hands, it was like this big religious moment for him. Like he was in a trance. And as he held it, he said something in Latin. I think he said "*Veritas vos liberabit*".'

She waited to see if Reilly knew what it meant. His quizzical look indicated he didn't. 'It means "the truth will set you free." I looked into it, and although it's a very widely used saying, it also happens to be a marking on a Templar castle in the south of France.'

Tess could see that he was pondering what she'd just told him, but wasn't sure how to read him. She fidgeted with her cup, downing the last of her coffee which had by now gone cold, then decided to keep going.

'I know it probably doesn't sound like much, but that's only until you start to understand the level of interest that the Templars inspire in people. Their origins, their activities and beliefs, and their violent demise are all shrouded in mystery. They have a huge following. You wouldn't believe the amount of books and material I found about them, and I've only scratched the surface. It's just phenomenal. And here's the thing. What usually triggers off the conjecture is that their fabulous wealth was never recovered.'

'I thought that was why the King of France rounded them up,' Reilly observed.

'It's what he was after. But he never found it. No one ever did. No gold, no jewels. Nothing. And yet the Templars were known to have a phenomenal treasure trove. One historian claims the Templars discovered 148 tons of gold and silver in and around Jerusalem when they first got there, even before the donations from across Europe started pouring in.'

'And no one knows what happened to it?'

'There are widely accepted claims that the night before the Templars were all arrested, twenty-four knights rode out of the Paris preceptory with several wagonloads of crates and escaped to the Atlantic port of La Rochelle. They're supposed to have sailed away on board eighteen galleys, never to be seen again.'

Reilly pondered the information. 'So you're saying the museum's raiders were really after the encoder, in order to use it to somehow help them find the Templars' treasure?'

'Maybe. The question is, what was that treasure? Was it gold coins and jewelry, or something else, something more esoteric, something that,' she hesitated, 'requires a slightly bigger leap of faith.' She waited to see how that sat with him.

Reilly flashed her a comforting grin. 'I'm still here, aren't I?'

She leaned forward and lowered her voice unconsciously. 'A lot of these theories claim that the Templars were part of an age-old conspiracy to discover and guard some arcane knowledge. It could be a lot of things. They were said to be the custodians of many holy relics – there's a French historian who even thinks they had the embalmed head of Jesus – but one theory I kept coming across and that seemed to hold more water than the others was that it has to do with the Holy Grail – which as you probably know isn't necessarily an actual cup or some kind of physical "chalice" that Jesus supposedly drank from at the last supper, but could well be a metaphorical reference to a secret concerning the real events surrounding His death and the survival of His bloodline into medieval times.'

'Jesus's *bloodline*?'

'Heretical as it may seem, this line of thought – and it's a very popular one, believe me – claims Jesus and Mary Magdalene had a child – maybe, probably more than one – that was raised in secret and hidden from the Romans, and that Jesus's bloodline has been a closely guarded secret for the last two thousand years, with all kinds of shadowy societies protecting His descendants and passing on their secret to a select group of "illuminati". Da Vinci, Isaac Newton, Victor Hugo, pretty much any illustrious name over the centuries – they're all supposed to have been part of this secret cabal of the holy bloodline's protectors.' Tess paused and watched for Reilly's reaction. 'I know it sounds ludicrous, but it's a popular story, a lot of people have worked on researching it, and we're not just talking about fiction bestsellers either, we're talking serious scholars and academics as well.'

She studied Reilly, wondering what he must be thinking. *If I had him with the treasure bit, I've definitely blown it now.* Leaning back, she had to admit it sounded more and more preposterous now, hearing herself verbalize it out loud.

Reilly seemed to think about it for a moment, then a faint smile crossed his lips. 'Jesus's bloodline, huh? If He did have a kid or two, and assuming they then had children of their own, and so on... after two thousand years – which is, what, something like seventy or eighty generations later – it's exponential, there'd be thousands of them, the planet would be crawling with His descendants, wouldn't it?' He chuckled. 'People really take this stuff seriously?'

'Absolutely. The Templars' missing treasure is one of the great unsolved mysteries of all time. It's easy to see why people are drawn to it. The premise itself has a great hook: nine knights show up in Jerusalem, claiming to want to defend thousands of pilgrims. Just nine of them. Seems pretty ambitious by any standard outside of *The Magnificent Seven*, don't you think? On hearing this, King Baldwin gives them a prime slice of Jerusalem real estate, the Temple Mount, the site of the second Temple of Solomon that was destroyed by Titus's legions in 70 AD, its treasure plundered and brought back to Rome. So here's the big what if: what if the Temple's priests hid something there when they knew the Romans were about to pounce, something the Romans didn't find.'

'But the Templars did.'

She nodded. 'Perfect fodder for myths. It stays buried there for a thousand years, and then they dig it up. Then there's the so-called "Copper Scroll" they found in Qumran.'

'The Dead Sea Scrolls are part of this too?'

Slow down, Tess. But she couldn't help herself, and kept plowing on. 'One of the scrolls specifically mentions huge quantities of gold and other valuables buried under the Temple itself, supposedly in twenty-four hoards. But it also mentions a treasure of an unspecified kind. What was it? We don't know. It could be anything.'

'Okay, so where does the Turin Shroud figure into all this?' Reilly mused.

For a fleeting moment, an irritated look crossed her fine features before she composed her face into a gracious smile. 'You're not buying into any of this, are you?'

Reilly raised his hands, looking slightly contrite. 'No, look, I'm sorry. Please, keep going.'

Tess collected her thoughts. 'These nine ordinary knights are given part of a royal palace with stables that were apparently big enough to accommodate two thousand horses. Why was Baldwin so generous toward them?'

'I don't know, maybe he was a forward thinker. Maybe he was blown away by their dedication.'

'But that's the thing,' she argued, undeterred. 'They hadn't done anything yet. They get given this huge base to work from, and what do our magnificent nine do? Do they go out and perform all sorts of heroic deeds and make sure the pilgrims get to their destinations, like they're supposed to? No. They spend their first nine years in the temple. They don't leave it. They don't go out, they don't take on any new recruits. They just stay locked up there. *For nine years.'*

'They either turned agoraphobic, or...'

'Or it was one big scam. The most widely accepted theory – and personally, I think it makes sense – is they were digging. Looking for something buried there.'

'Something the priests hid from Titus's legionnaires a thousand years earlier.'

She sensed that she was finally getting through to him, and her eyes were ablaze with conviction 'Exactly. The fact is that they lie low for nine years, then all of a sudden they burst onto the scene and start growing in stature and wealth at a dizzying rate, with the Vatican backing them whole-heartedly. Maybe they found something there, something buried under the Temple that made it all possible. Something that made the Vatican bend over backward to keep them happy – and evidence of Jesus having fathered a child or two would certainly fit the bill.'

Reilly's face clouded over. 'Hold on, you think they were blackmailing the Vatican? I thought they were soldiers of Christ? Doesn't it make more sense that they found something that really pleased the Vatican, and the pope decided to reward them for their discovery?'

Her face scrunched inward. 'If that was the case, wouldn't they have announced it to the world?' She eased back, seeming a bit lost as well. 'I know, I'm still missing a piece to this puzzle. They did go on to fight for Christianity for two hundred years. But you've got to admit, it's pretty intriguing.' She paused, studying him. 'So do you think there's anything in it?'

Reilly weighed the information she'd so eagerly laid out for him. Regardless of how ridiculous it all sounded, he couldn't simply dismiss it entirely. The attack at the Met was clearly symptomatic of something frighteningly warped; there was more behind its extreme staging than a simple heist, that much everyone agreed on. He knew how radical extremists latched onto some mythology, some core belief, and how they made it theirs; how gradually that mythology got twisted and distorted until its devotees completely lost touch with reality and went off the deep end. Could this be the link he was looking for? The Templar legends certainly seemed rife with distortion. Was someone out there so infatuated with the terrible fate of the Templars that they identified with them to the point of dressing up like them, taking revenge on the Vatican on their behalf, and perhaps even trying to recover their legendary treasure?

Reilly's eyes settled on her. 'Do I think the Templars were the keepers of some big secret – good or bad – relating to the early days of the Church? I have no idea.'

Tess glanced away, trying to smother any visible signs of her dismay, when Reilly leaned in and continued. 'Do I think there's a possible link between the Templars and what happened at the Met?' He let it hang for a moment, nodding almost imperceptibly, before a faint smile crossed his lips. 'I definitely think it's worth looking into.'

CHAPTER 22

Gus Waldron was definitely not having one of his best days.

He remembered waking up a while ago. How long, he couldn't tell. Hours, minutes – and then he'd drifted off again. Now he was back, a little more alert.

He knew he was in bad shape. He winced as he remembered the crash. His body felt like it had taken more pounding than a veal chop at Cipriani's. And the irritating, incessant beeps from the monitors around him weren't helping either.

He knew he was in a hospital – the beeping and the ambient noise were clear indications of that. He had to rely on his hearing, as he couldn't see a goddamn thing. His eyes stung like hell. When he tried to move, he couldn't. There was something around his chest. *They've got me strapped to the bed.* Not real tight, though. So the strap was there for hospital reasons, not cop reasons. Good. His hands moved over his face, feeling bandages and finding other things. They had him stuck full of tubes.

There was no point in fighting it, not right now. He had to know how bad he was hurt, and he would definitely need his eyes back if he was to get out of there. So until he knew the score, he would try to cut a deal with the cops. But what did he have to offer? He needed something big, because they wouldn't like the fact that he'd chopped the head off that fucking guard. He really shouldn't have done that. It was just that, riding up there, dressed like Prince fucking Valiant, he had gotten to wondering what it would be like to take a swing at some guy. And it had felt real good; there was no denying it.

What he could do was rat out Branko Petrovic. He was already pissed off at that dick for not telling him the name of the guy who had hired *him*, rambling on about how cool it was, this idea of blind cells. Now he saw why. He'd been hired by Petrovic, who'd been hired by someone else, who'd been hired by some other asshole. Who could tell how many blind fucking cells there were before you reached the guy the cops were out to nail?

The hospital sounds rose slightly for a moment, then fell again. The door must have opened and closed. He heard footsteps, squeaky on the floor, as someone approached his bed. Then whoever it was lifted Gus's hand, fingertips resting on the inside of his wrist. Some doctor or nurse taking his pulse. No, a doctor. The fingers felt rougher, stronger than a nurse's would. At least the kind of nurse he would fantasize about.

He needed to know how badly hurt he was. 'Who's that? Doc?'

Whoever was there didn't answer. Now the fingers were lifting the bandages where they went around his head and over his ears.

Gus opened his mouth to ask a question but as he did so he felt a strong hand clamp down over his mouth and immediately there came a searingly painful jab in his neck. His whole body jerked against the restraint.

The hand covered his mouth tightly, turning Gus's shouts into a muffled whine. There was a hot feeling spreading inside his neck, around his throat. Then, slowly, the hand pressing down on his mouth released its hold.

A man's voice, very soft, whispered close to his ear. He could feel his hot breath on him.

'The doctors won't allow anyone to question you for a while. But I can't wait that long. I need to know who hired you.'

What the fuck...?

Gus tried to sit up but the strap held his body and a hand pressed against his head kept him in place.

'Answer the question,' the voice said.

Who was that? It couldn't be a cop. Some shithead trying

to cut himself in on some of the stuff he'd taken from the museum? But then why ask about who'd hired him?

'Answer me.' The voice was still very quiet, but sharper now.

'Fuck you,' Gus said.

Except that, he didn't say it. Not really. His mouth formed the words, and he heard them in his head. But no sound came out.

Where's my fucking voice gone?

'Ah,' the voice whispered. 'That's the Lidocaine's effect. Just a small dose. Enough to numb your vocal cords. It's annoying in that you can't talk. The upside of it is that, well, you can't scream either.'

Scream?

The fingers that had felt so gently for his pulse landed on his left hip, right where the cop's bullet struck. They rested there for a moment before suddenly bursting alive and pressing in. Hard.

Pain seared through his body like he was being branded from the inside, and he screamed.

Silently.

Blackness threatened to overwhelm his brain before the pain receded slightly and saliva pooled at the back of his throat. He thought he was about to throw up. Then the man's hands touched him again and he flinched, only this time the touch was gentle.

'Are you right- or left-handed?' the soft voice asked.

Gus was now sweating profusely. *Right- or left-handed? What the fuck difference does that make?* He lifted his right hand feebly, and soon felt something being placed between his fingers. A pencil.

'Just write the names down for me,' the voice told him, guiding the pencil toward what felt like a notepad.

His eyes bandaged shut and his voice gone, Gus felt completely cut off from the world and alone, more so than he'd ever imagined. *Where is everybody? Where are the doctors, the nurses, the fucking cops, for Chrissake?*

The fingers seized the flesh around his wound and squeezed again, this time harder and for longer. An excruciating pain shot through him. Every nerve in his body seemed to ignite as he bucked against the strap, screaming in silent agony.

'This doesn't have to take all night,' the man stated calmly. 'Just give me the names.'

There was only one name he could write. Which he did.

'Branko... Petrovic?' the man asked softly.

Gus nodded hurriedly.

'And the others?'

Gus shook his head as best he could. *That's all I know, for fuck's sake.*

The fingers again.

Pressing in, harder, deeper. Squeezing.

The pain.

The silent screams.

Jesus fucking Christ. Gus lost track of time. He managed to write the name of a place where Branko worked. Other than that, all that he could do was shake his head and mouth, *No*.

Over and over and over again.

Eventually, thankfully, he felt the pencil being taken away from him. At last the man believed that he was telling the truth.

Now, Gus could hear small sounds he did not recognize, then he again felt the man's fingers lift the edge of the bandage in the same place. He cringed, but this time he hardly felt the needle prick.

'Here's some more painkiller for you,' the man whispered. 'It'll ease the pain that you're feeling and help you sleep.'

Gus felt a slow, rising wave of dark weariness flow through his head and start down his body and with it came relief that the ordeal, the pain, was over. Then a terrifying realization descended on him: that the sleep into which he was helplessly plunging was one from which he would never awaken.

Desperate now, he tried to move but couldn't, and after a moment it seemed as though he didn't want to move. He relaxed. Wherever he was going, it just had to be a better place than the sewer in which he had spent his entire miserable life.

CHAPTER 23

Reilly climbed out of bed, pulled on a T-shirt and looked out the window from his fourth-floor apartment. Outside, the streets were deathly quiet. The city that never sleeps only seemed to apply to him.

He often didn't sleep well, for a number of reasons. One was simply his inability to let go. It was a problem he'd had more and more frequently over the last few years, this incessant mulling over leads and data relating to whatever case he was working on. He didn't really have a problem falling asleep. Sheer exhaustion usually took care of that. But then he'd hit that dreaded four a.m. threshold and suddenly find himself wide awake, his brain churning away, sorting and analyzing, searching for the missing kernel of information that might save lives.

Sometimes, the workload was sufficiently intense to monopolize his thoughts. Occasionally though, his mind would segue into personal issues, straying into even darker territory than the underworld of his investigations, and unpleasant anxiety attacks would worm their way to the surface and take over.

A lot of it had to do with what happened to his dad, how he'd shot himself when Reilly was ten, how the young boy had come home from school and wandered into the study that day and found his father there, sitting in his favorite armchair as he always did except this time, the back of his head was missing.

Either way, what followed was always a hugely frustrating couple of hours for him. Too tired to get out of bed and use the time to do something useful, but too wired to get back to sleep, he'd just lie there in the dark, his mind taking him to all kinds of desolate places. And he'd wait. Sleep usually came mercifully at around six or so, little comfort given that he'd have to be up again an hour later to go to work.

That night, the four a.m. wake up came courtesy of a call from the night duty officer. It informed him that the man he'd chased across the streets of lower Manhattan had passed away. The duty officer mentioned something about internal bleeding, heart failure, and unsuccessful efforts to resuscitate the dead man. Reilly had spent the next two hours, as was customary, reviewing the case, one which had now lost its most promising and only real lead given that he didn't think Lucien Broussard would be able to tell them much, if and when he was actually able to speak again. But thinking about the case soon merged with other thoughts that were swirling around in his mind after leaving the hospital earlier that night. Thoughts mostly relating to Tess Chaykin.

Looking out the window, he thought about how the first thing he'd noticed about her when they'd sat down at the café was that she wasn't wearing a wedding band, or any rings for that matter. Noticing things like that played an important role in his professional life. It was an instinctive attention to detail that came with years on the job.

Only this wasn't work, and Tess wasn't a suspect.

'His name was Gus Waldron.'

Reilly listened intently, cradling a hot mug of coffee, as Aparo scoured the rap sheet with practiced eyes, cutting to the chase for the benefit of the assembled core team of federal agents.

'Clearly a pillar of the community who'll be sorely missed,' Aparo continued. 'Professional boxer, minor leagues, a wild man in and out of the ring, banned from fights in three states. Four counts of assault and armed robbery, both here and in Jersey. Couple of stints at Rikers –' he looked up and said pointedly, '– including a cruise on the *Vernon Bain*.' The *Vernon C. Bain*, named after a well-liked warden who died in a car accident, was an eight hundred bed barge that housed medium to maximum security inmates. 'Suspected of two homicides, both beatings. No indictments there. Compulsive gambler. Been running a losing streak for half his life.' Aparo looked up. 'That's about it.'

'Sounds like a guy who's always in need of a fast buck,' Jansson observed. 'Who does he hang out with?'

Aparo flicked a page and went down the list of Waldron's known associates. 'Josh Schlattmann, died last year... Reza Fardousi, a three hundred-pound sack of shit – doubt any horse in the country could carry him.' His eyes scanned the names, editing the no-hopes. 'Lonnie Morris, a small-time dealer currently on parole and living with and working for, if you believe this, his grandmother who has a flower shop in Queens.' Then Aparo looked up again, this time with an expression on his face that Reilly knew spelled trouble. 'Branko Petrovic,' he stated unhappily. 'An ex-cop. And get this. He was with the NYPD's mounted division.' He looked up at them. 'Retired. And not by choice, if you get my drift.'

Amelia Gaines flicked a knowing glance at Reilly, then volunteered the question. 'What'd he do?'

'Theft. Dipped his hand into the cookie jar at the precinct after a dope bust,' Aparo said. 'Doesn't look like he did any time. Discharged, loss of pension rights.'

Reilly frowned, not exactly pleased at the prospect. 'Let's talk to him. Find out how he makes a living these days.'

CHAPTER 24

No matter how hard he tried, Branko Petrovic couldn't keep his mind on his work. Not that his job at the stables needed his undivided attention. Most days, he watered and fed the horses and shoveled horseshit on autopilot, keeping his stocky body hard and fit. His brain was left free to work out angles, calculate odds, make plans. Usually, that was.

Today was different.

It had been his idea to hire Gus Waldron. He'd been asked to find someone big and tough who could ride a horse, so he'd thought of Gus. Okay, so he knew that Gus could be a wild man at times, but he didn't expect him to go lopping off someone's head with a sword. *Christ, even the fucking Colombians didn't pull stunts like that.* Not in public anyway.

Something felt wrong. He'd tried calling Gus that morning and didn't get an answer. He fingered an old scar on his forehead, feeling the ache that always came back when things went wrong. Don't do anything that attracts attention, he'd been told, ordered even, and that's what he'd told Gus. A lot of fucking use that had been. Right now, attracting attention was the least of his worries.

A sudden panic surged over him. He had to get the hell out of Dodge while he still could.

He rushed across the stables and opened up one of the stalls where a frisky two-year-old flicked her tail at him. In a corner was a crimped-top tub packed with animal feed. Opening it, he thrust his hands inside, raking away the pellets, and pulled out a sack. He weighed it momentarily, then reached into it and pulled out a glimmering golden statuette of a rearing horse, gaudily encrusted with diamonds and rubies. He stared at it for a moment, then rummaged further and dug out a pendant of emeralds set in silver. The contents of the sack were nothing short of life changing. Carefully fenced, provided he took his time and did it carefully, he knew that the jeweled pieces in there were enough to buy him the condo down on the Gulf that he'd always promised himself and that, ever since he'd been dumped off the force, had looked as though it would never happen – and a whole lot more.

Closing the gate on the filly, he headed down the walkway between the stalls and was almost at the door when he heard one of the horses snicker and stomp restlessly, alarmed. Another horse followed suit, then another. Turning, he looked down the walkway, seeing nothing but hearing the racket as all the horses in the stable block had now joined in.

Then he saw it.

A tendril of smoke, drifting out of an empty stall at the farthermost end.

The nearest extinguisher was halfway along the walkway and when he reached it, he dropped the sack, yanked the cylinder out of its clamp, and headed for the empty stall. By now, the smoke was more than merely tendrils. Pulling open the gate, he saw that the fire was seated in a pile of straw in one corner. He pulled the pin off and squeezed the handle, quickly putting the fire out, when it suddenly occurred to him that he'd only finished working in that stall less than an hour earlier. There had been no pile, just the raked, level carpet of straw he'd spread himself.

Hastily, Branko stepped out of the stall, watchful now. No point in listening. Trying to hear anything but the frantic neighing of the horses, some of them also lashing out at the sides and gates of their stalls, was impossible.

He started back along the walkway, then saw more smoke, this time at the other end of the block. *Dammit.* There was someone in there with him. Then he remembered the sack. He had to go get it. His whole life's plans depended on it.

Dumping the extinguisher, he ran for the sack, snatched it up, then stopped short.

The horses.

He couldn't just run for it; he had to do something about them.

Slamming open the bolt on the nearest stall, he leaped back as the horse cannoned out through the gate. Then the next bolt. Another horse shot out like a bullet, its hooves deafening in the enclosed space. There were only three more horses to release when an iron-hard forearm locked around his throat.

'Don't struggle,' a voice said quietly, lips close to Branko's ear. 'I don't want to have to cripple you.'

Branko froze. The grip was firm, professional. He didn't doubt for a moment that the man was deadly serious.

He was quickly dragged back toward the stable door where he felt the man's other hand at his wrist, then the bite of a hard plastic strip against his skin and, in a move faster than he could have managed on his best day on the force, his hand was cuffed to the stable's huge sliding door. The man switched arms around his neck, repeated the procedure, and now Branko was spread-eagled across the doorway.

The three horses still trapped in their stalls were now whinnying and bucking wildly, kicking at the wooden partitions as the flames licked their way closer.

The man ducked beneath Branko's right arm and as he straightened up, he took Branko's hand in his and quickly and without apparent effort, broke his thumb.

Branko screamed in pain, lashing out with both legs, but the man stepped swiftly aside. 'What do you want?' the ex-cop yelped.

'Names,' the man said, his voice almost lost beneath the clamor of the horses. 'And make it quick. We don't have that much time.'

'What names?'

Branko saw a sudden flare of anger cross the man's face as he reached out and grabbed his left hand. He didn't go for a finger this time. He also grabbed his arm and, with a sudden twist of ferocious intensity, snapped Branko's wrist. The excruciating pain shot straight through him, making him momentarily black out, his howl echoing above the furor of the frenzied horses.

He looked up to see the man standing impassively, watching him through the thickening smoke.

'Names of friends. Friends you visit museums with.'

Branko coughed, peering desperately over the man's shoulder to where flames were now cracking as the timber rails caught fire. He couldn't string this out. 'Gus,' he blurted out frantically. 'Gus and Mitch. That's all I know.'

'Mitch who?'

Branko couldn't say the words fast enough. 'Adeson. Mitch Adeson. That's all I know, I swear to God.'

'Mitch Adeson.'

'That's it. That's how it was done. It's like a chain of command, blind cells, you know?'

The man studied him carefully, then nodded. 'I know.'

Thank God, the sick fuck believes me. 'Now get me out of these fucking cuffs,' he pleaded. 'Come on!'

'Where can I find this Mitch Adeson?' the man asked. He listened intently as Branko spluttered out what he knew, then nodded and said, 'There was a fourth man with you. Describe him to me.'

'I didn't see his face, he had a ski mask on, he never took the damn thing off. He had it on under the armor and the rest of that shit.'

Again the man nodded. 'Okay,' he murmured. Then he turned and walked away.

'Hey! HEY!' Branko yelled after him.

But the man didn't turn. He proceeded down toward the far end, pausing only to pick up the sack containing the stolen relics from the museum.

'You can't leave me here,' Branko pleaded.

Then he realized what the man was doing. He was releasing the last of the horses.

Branko screamed as the panic-stricken dappled filly led the other two horses out of their stalls. And then they were thundering toward him at a headlong gallop, eyes wild, nostrils flared, the flames behind them making them look like they were coming at him straight out of the mouth of Hell.

And he was strapped across their only escape route.

CHAPTER 25

'So tell me more about this chick.'

Reilly groaned at the question. From the moment he'd mentioned his conversation with Tess to his partner, he knew this was a conversation he'd have to suffer. 'This chick?' he deadpanned.

He and Aparo were headed east, through the choked streets of Queens. Apart from its color, the Pontiac they had been allocated was a virtual clone of the Chrysler they had wrecked in nailing Gus Waldron. Aparo made a face as he edged the car cautiously around a stationary truck with a steaming radiator, its driver uselessly kicking a front tyre.

'I'm sorry. Miss Chaykin.'

Reilly did his best not to appear nonplussed. 'There's nothing to tell.'

'Come on.' Aparo knew his partner better than anyone; not that he had much competition. Reilly wasn't one to let people get close.

'What do you want from me?'

'She approached you. Out of the blue. Just like that, she remembered you from the museum, from a quick eyeball from all the way across the hall, after everything she'd been through that night?'

'What can I say?' Reilly kept his eyes firmly on the road. 'The lady's got a photographic memory.'

'Photographic memory, my ass,' Aparo scoffed. 'This babe's on the prowl.'

Reilly rolled his eyes. 'She's not on the prowl. She's just... curious.'

'So she's got a photographic memory and an inquisitive mind. And she's a total hottie. But you didn't notice any of that. Nah. You were only thinking about the case.'

Reilly shrugged. 'Okay, so maybe I noticed a little.'

'Thank God. He breathes. He's alive,' he mocked in a tone straight out of an old Frankenstein movie. 'You do know she's single, right?'

'I kind of noticed.' Reilly had tried not to make a big deal out of it. Earlier that morning, he had read the statement Tess had given to Amelia Gaines at the museum, just before he had asked a research analyst to look for any reference to the Knights Templar in the bulging files they kept on extremist groups around the country.

Aparo eyed him. He knew him so well, he could read him at fifty paces. And he loved needling him. 'I don't know, but a babe like that makes a pass at me, I'd be all over her in a heartbeat.'

'You're married.'

'Yeah, well, I can dream, can't I?'

They were off the Long Island Expressway now and would soon be out of Queens. The address on Petrovic's file was out of date, but his old landlord there said he knew where Petrovic worked. The stables were somewhere around here and Reilly checked a street map, gave Aparo directions, then, knowing that his partner would never let go, he reluctantly picked up the thread. 'Besides, she didn't make a pass,' he protested.

'Sure she didn't. She's just a concerned citizen looking out for the rest of us.' He shook his head. 'I don't get it. You're single. You're not butt-ugly. You don't have any offensive aromas I'm aware of. And yet... See, we married guys, we need buddies like you, we need to live vicariously through you and, well, you're really letting the team down.'

Reilly couldn't argue with that. It had been a long while since he'd spent any meaningful time with a woman and, even though he wouldn't dream of mentioning it to his partner, he couldn't begin to deny the attraction he had felt toward Tess. But he knew that, like Amelia Gaines, Tess Chaykin didn't seem to be the kind of woman who would take kindly to being treated casually, which was just as well, given that he wasn't exactly the casual kind either. And therein lay the paradox at the heart of his loneliness. If a woman didn't completely enthrall him, he wasn't interested. And if she had that special quality that got him going, what happened to his father would soon become an issue for him; his fears would inevitably kick in at some point and deny the relationship any chance of blossoming.

You've got to let go. It doesn't have to happen to you too.

Looking ahead now, Reilly spotted some smoke and with it, the flashing lights of two fire trucks. He glanced at Aparo and reached for the flasher, slapping it on the roof as his partner hit the siren and floored the gas pedal. They were soon weaving in and out traffic, barreling their way through the nose-to-tail barrage of cars and trucks.

As they turned into the stable's parking lot, Reilly could see that in addition to the fire trucks, there were a couple of black and whites and an ambulance. Parking well clear of the exit, they left the car and walked over toward the scene, badging up as they went. One of the uniforms started toward them, arms spread wide, then saw the badges and let them through.

Although the fire was almost out, the smell of burnt wood hung heavily in the air. Three or four people, stable staff by the look of them, were stumbling around in the drifting smoke, trying to control frightened horses amidst the tangle of fire hoses that snaked across the ground. A man in a charcoal raincoat was standing with a grim expression on his face, watching them approach.

Reilly introduced himself and Aparo. The cop, a sergeant by the name of Milligan, didn't look thrilled. 'Don't tell me,' he said sardonically, 'you just happened to be in the neighborhood.'

Reilly nodded toward the charred stables. 'Branko Petrovic,' he simply stated.

Milligan shrugged and led the way into the stable, where a pair of paramedics were crouched over a body. Propped nearby was a lightweight stretcher.

Reilly glanced at it, then at Milligan who got the message: this had to be treated as a crime scene with a suspicious death. 'What do we know?' he asked.

Milligan leaned over the body that lay blackened and crumpled amidst splintered pieces of wood. 'You tell me. I thought this was gonna be an easy one.'

Reilly looked over Milligan's shoulder. It was hard to tell what was smoke-blackened flesh from what was blood mixed with soot and water from the fire hoses. Another gruesome detail added to the macabre setting: the man's left arm was lying there by the body, no longer attached to the torso. Reilly frowned. Whatever it was, the mess that had once been Branko Petrovic was barely identifiable as human.

'How can you be so sure it's him?' he asked.

Milligan reached down, pointing a finger at the side of the dead man's forehead. Reilly could see an indentation that, even among all the other damage, was clearly not recent. 'He got clipped by a horse, years ago. On the force. Used to be proud of it, surviving a kick in the head.'

As Reilly crouched down for a closer look, he noticed one of the paramedics, a dark-haired girl in her twenties. She seemed eager to chime in. Reilly met her eyes for a moment. 'You got something for us?'

She smiled and held up Petrovic's left wrist. 'Don't tell the M.E. I jumped the gun on this, but someone didn't like this guy. His other wrist's scorched through, but see this one here?' She was pointing at the detached arm. 'The contusions on it are still visible. He was tied up.' She pointed up at the doorway. 'I'd say he had one hand tied to each side. Like he was crucified across the doorway.'

Aparo grimaced at the imagery. 'You mean someone let the horses stampede over him?'

'Or through him,' Reilly added.

She nodded. Reilly thanked her and her partner before walking away with Milligan and Aparo.

'Why were you guys looking at Petrovic?' Milligan asked.

Reilly was studying the horses. 'Before we go there, you got any reasons to think someone might want him dead?'

Milligan inclined his head toward the smoldering stable block. 'Not particularly. I mean, you know how it is with these places. Wise guys like their horses, and given Petrovic's past ... But no, nothing specific. What's your take?'

He listened intently as Reilly filled him in on the link between Gus Waldron and Branko Petrovic, and their link to the raid at the Met.

'I'll ask for all this to be prioritized,' Milligan told Reilly. 'Get the crime scene guys over, ask the fire chief to run the arson tests today, push the autopsy to the top of the file.'

As Reilly and Aparo reached their car, a fine drizzle had started to fall.

'Someone's tying up loose ends,' Aparo said.

'Looks that way. We're gonna need to get the M.E. to take a closer look at Waldron.'

'If that's what this is, we need to find the other two horsemen before whoever's doing this gets to them.'

Reilly looked up at the darkening sky before turning to his partner. 'Two horsemen, or just one,' he countered, 'if the last of the four is the one doing the killing.'

CHAPTER 26

His eyes stinging from the strain of many hours spent poring over the ancient manuscripts, he removed his glasses and rubbed his eyes gently with a wet towel.

How long had it been? Was it morning? Night? He had lost all track of time since returning here after his mounted foray into the Metropolitan Museum of Art.

Of course, the media, that pack of dysfunctional, semi-literate creatures, were probably referring to it as a robbery or a heist. None of them, nor even anyone in higher places, would ever understand his way of thinking of it as an exercise in practical research. But that was what it was. And the time was not too far off when the whole world would know Saturday night's incident for what it really was: the first move in something that would irrevocably alter how many of them looked at their world. A move that would, one day soon, remove the scales from their eyes and open up their petty minds to something far beyond their feeble imaginings.

And I'm almost there. Not long to go now.

Turning, he looked at the wall behind him on which hung a calendar. Although the time of day was unimportant to him, dates always had significance.

One such date was circled with red.

Glancing again at the results of his work with the multi-geared rotor encoder, he re-read one passage that had troubled him from the moment he had decoded it.

Very puzzling, he mused. Then he smiled, realizing that, unconsciously, he had used the exact right word. It had not been enough for this manuscript to be set in code; before encoding, this particular passage had first been designed as a puzzle.

He felt a flood of admiration for the man who had written this document.

Then he frowned. He had to solve it speedily. So far as he knew, his tracks were thoroughly covered, but he wouldn't be so foolish as to underestimate the enemy. Unfortunately, in order to work out the puzzle, he needed a library. That meant he would have to leave the security of his home and venture above ground.

He thought for a moment, then decided with reasonable certainty that it was evening. He would visit the library. Carefully. Just in case anyone had made a connection and alerted those working there to report people asking for materials of a certain nature.

Then he smiled to himself. *Now you're being paranoid.* They weren't that clever.

After the library, he would return here, hopefully with the solution in hand, and then complete the decoding of the remaining passages.

He glanced again at the calendar with its encircled date.

A date seared into his memory forever.

A date he could never forget.

He had a small but important, and painful, duty to perform. After that, all being well, and with the manuscript fully decoded, he would fulfill the destiny that had been unfairly thrust upon him.

CHAPTER 27

Monsignor De Angelis sat on the hard rattan chair in his bedroom on the top floor of the austere Oliver Street hostel where the diocese had arranged for him to stay while he was in New York. It wasn't all bad. The hostel was practically located for him, being only a few blocks east of Federal Plaza. And from its upper floors, the view of the Brooklyn Bridge couldn't fail but inspire romanticized visions of the city in the hearts of the purists who normally occupied these rooms. But the view was wasted on him.

He wasn't exactly in a purist frame of mind right now.

He checked the time, then flicked open his cellphone and dialed Rome. Cardinal Rienzi answered, balked a little about disturbing Cardinal Brugnone, then acquiesced, as De Angelis knew he would.

'Tell me you have some good news, Michael,' Brugnone said, clearing his throat.

'The FBI people are making progress. Some of the stolen objects have been recovered.'

'That's encouraging.'

'Yes, it is. The Bureau and the NYPD are keeping to their word and devoting a lot of resources to this case.'

'What of the robbers? Have they arrested any others?'

'No, Your Eminence,' De Angelis replied. 'The man they had in custody passed away before they could question him. A second gang member also died, in a fire. I spoke to the agent overseeing the case earlier today. They're still waiting for results of forensic tests, but he believes the man may have been murdered.'

'Murdered. How terrible,' Brugnone sighed, 'and how tragic. Their greed is consuming them. They're fighting over the spoils.'

The Monsignor shrugged. 'It seems that way, yes.'

Brugnone paused. 'Of course, there is another possibility, Michael.'

'It has occurred to me.'

'Our man could be cleaning out his house.'

De Angelis nodded imperceptibly, to himself. 'I suspect that to be the case.'

'This is not good. Once he's the only one left, he'll be even more difficult to find.'

'Everyone makes mistakes, Your Eminence. And when he does, I'll make sure we don't miss it.'

De Angelis could hear the cardinal shuffling around uneasily in his seat. 'I'm not comfortable with these developments. Isn't there anything you can do to expedite matters?'

'Not without what the FBI would deem to be unwarranted interference.'

Brugnone was silent for a moment, then he said, 'Well, for the moment do not upset them. But you must ensure that we are kept fully abreast of the investigation.'

'I'll do my best.'

Brugnone's voice took on a more ominous tone. 'You understand how important this is, Michael. It's imperative that we recover *everything* before any irreparable damage is done.'

De Angelis knew exactly what the cardinal's stress on the word 'everything' meant. 'Of course, Your Eminence,' he said. 'I understand perfectly.'

After he had hung up, De Angelis remained seated for some minutes, thinking. Then he knelt beside the bed to pray; not for divine intervention, but that personal weakness might not cause him to fail.

There was far too much at stake.

CHAPTER 28

When the printouts from Columbia came through to Tess's office that afternoon, they appeared to be disappointingly thin. A quick skim confirmed the disappointment. Tess couldn't find anything that was of use. From what Clive Edmondson had told her, she was not expecting anything on the Knights Templar. It wasn't William Vance's official area of expertise. Mostly, he had concentrated on Phoenician history up to the third century before Christ. The link, though, was a natural one and seemed promising: the great Phoenician ports of Sidon and Tyre became, a thousand years later, formidable Templar strongholds. It was as if one had to peel through layers of Crusader and Templar history to get a peek at Phoenician life.

Furthermore, nowhere in his published papers that were sent to her was there any mention of the subjects of cryptography and cryptology.

She felt deflated. All the reading and research she'd done at the library, and now Vance's papers – none of it had helped her get any closer to figuring this out.

She decided to do one last trawl online, and the same several hundred hits came up again when she entered Vance's name into her search engine. This time, though, she decided to take her time and study them more carefully.

She had run through a couple of dozen sites when she came across a site that only mentioned Vance in passing, and in an unashamedly mocking tone. The article, a transcript of a speech given by a French historian at the Université de Nantes almost ten years ago, was a scathing review of what its author considered less than worthy ideas that were, in his view, muddying the waters for more serious academics.

The mention of Vance came two thirds of the way into his

presentation. In it, the historian mentioned in passing how he had even heard the ridiculous notion, from Vance, that Hughes de Payens may have been a Cathar, simply because the man's family tree indicated that he was originally from the Languedoc.

Tess reread the passage. *The founder of the Templars, a Cathar?* It was an absurd suggestion. Templarism and Catharism were as contradictory as could be. For two hundred years, the Templars had been the unflinching defenders of the Church. Catharism, on the other hand, was a Gnostic movement.

Still, there was something intriguing about the suggestion.

Catharism had originated in the middle of the tenth century, taking its name from the Greek *katharos,* meaning 'the pure ones'. It was based on the notion that the world was evil, and that souls would be continually reborn – and could even pass through animals, which was why the Cathars were vegetarians – until they escaped the material world and reached a spiritual heaven.

Everything the Cathars believed in was anathema to the Church. They were dualists who believed that, in addition to a merciful and good God, there had to be an equally powerful but evil God to explain the horrors that plagued the world. The benevolent God created the heavens and the human soul; the evil God entrapped that soul in the human body. In the Vatican's eyes, the Cathars had sacrilegiously elevated Satan to God's equal. Following this belief, the Cathars considered all material goods evil, which led them to reject the trappings of wealth and of power that had undeniably corrupted the medieval Roman Catholic Church.

More worryingly for the Church, they were also Gnostics. Gnosticism – which, like Cathar, is derived from a Greek word, *gnosis,* meaning higher knowledge, or insight – is the belief that man can come into direct and intimate contact with God without the need for a priest or a church. Believing in direct personal contact with God freed the Cathars of all moral prohibition or religious obligations. Besides having no use for lavish churches and oppressive ceremonies, they had no use for priests either. Religious ceremonies were simply performed in homes, or in fields. And if that wasn't enough, women were treated as equals and were allowed to become *'parfaits,'* the closest thing the Cathari faith had to a priest; since physical form was irrelevant to them, the soul residing within a human body could just as easily be male or female, regardless of outward appearance.

As the belief caught on and spread across the south of France and northern Italy, the Vatican got increasingly worried and ultimately decided that this heresy could no longer be tolerated. It didn't only threaten the Catholic Church; it also threatened the basis of the feudal system in Europe, as the Cathars believed oaths were a sin, given that they attached one to the material – hence evil – world. This gravely undermined the concept of pledges of allegiance between serfs and their lords. The pope had no trouble enlisting the support of the French nobility to put down this threat. In 1209, an army of crusaders descended on the Languedoc, and over the next thirty-five years, proceeded to massacre over thirty thousand men, women, and children. It was said that blood flowed ankle deep in the churches where some of the fleeing villagers had taken refuge, and that when one of the pope's soldiers complained about not knowing whether he was killing heretics or Christian believers, he was simply told to 'Kill them all; God will know his own.'

It simply doesn't make sense. The Templars went to the Holy Land to escort the pilgrims – the Christian pilgrims. They were the Vatican's storm troopers, its staunchest supporters. The Cathars, on the other hand, were the Church's enemies.

Tess was surprised that someone as learned as Vance would advance such a wild proposition, especially when it was based on the flimsy premise of one man's provenance. She wondered if she was barking up the wrong tree, but what she really needed, Tess knew, was to talk to him in person. Regardless of such an academic faux pas, if there were a connection between the Templars and the robbery, he would probably nail it in a flash.

She dialed Columbia University again and soon got through to the History Department. After reminding the secretary of their previous conversation, she asked her if she'd had any luck in finding anyone at the department who knew how to reach William Vance. The woman said she'd asked a couple of professors who taught there at the same time as Vance, but they'd lost touch with him after he'd left.

'I see,' Tess said wistfully. She didn't know where else to turn.

The woman picked up on her dismay. 'I know you need to reach him, but maybe he doesn't want to be reached. Sometimes, people prefer not to be reminded of, you know... painful times.'

Tess snapped to attention. '"Painful times?"'

'Of course. And after what he went through... it was all so sad. He loved her very much, you know.'

Tess's mind was racing, trying to think of whether or not she had missed something. 'I'm sorry, I'm not sure I know what you're referring to. Did Professor Vance lose someone?'

'Oh, I thought you knew. It was his wife. She fell ill and passed away.'

This was all news to her. None of the sites she'd looked at mentioned it, but then, they were purely academic and didn't delve into personal matters. 'When did this happen?'

'It's been a few years now, five or six years ago? Let's see... I remember it was in the spring. The Professor took a sabbatical that summer and never came back.'

Tess thanked the woman and hung up. She wondered if she should forget about Vance and concentrate on getting in touch with Simmons. Still, she was intrigued. She went online again and clicked onto the *New York Times*'s website. She selected the advanced search function, and was relieved to find that the archive went back to 1996. She entered 'William Vance', ticked the obituary section, and got a hit.

The brief article announced the death of his wife, Martha. It only mentioned complications after a brief illness, but gave no more details. Casually, Tess noticed where interment had been scheduled to take place: the Green-Wood cemetery, in Brooklyn. She wondered if Vance was paying for the upkeep of the grave. If he was, it was likely that the cemetery would have a record of his current address.

She thought about calling the cemetery herself, then decided against it. They probably wouldn't release such information to her anyway. Reluctantly, she found the card Reilly had given her and called his office. Told that Reilly was in a meeting, Tess hesitated about telling the agent on the line anything, and decided she'd wait to speak to Reilly in person.

Glancing back at her screen, her eyes fell on the obituary, and suddenly, a flash of excitement struck her.

The secretary was right about Martha Vance's death having occurred in the spring.

It had happened exactly five years ago tomorrow.

CHAPTER 29

'The autopsy confirms Waldron was also murdered,' Reilly stated as he looked around at the others seated at the table in the Bureau's viewing room. The only outsider present was Monsignor De Angelis. 'We found traces of Lidocaine in his blood. It's an anesthetic, and it wasn't administered by anyone looking after him at the hospital. The high dose triggered his heart failure. The interesting part is that there are also needle marks on his neck. The drug was used to numb his vocal cords, so he couldn't call for help.'

The monsignor stiffened a little at Reilly's report, seeming equally appalled. Also there were the main players in the METRAID investigation: Jansson, Buchinski, Amelia Gaines, Aparo, Blackburn and two of his ASACs, as well as a young techie who was manning the A/V commands. The report wasn't particularly reassuring.

'We also found freezebranding equipment at the stables,' Reilly continued, 'which Petrovic could have used to disguise the markings on the horses they used in the raid. All of which means one of two things. Either whoever's behind this is having his foot soldiers wiped out, or one of the gang's decided to keep it all for himself. Either way, we've got one, and potentially two, more horsemen looking like possible targets. And whoever's doing this isn't exactly a slacker.'

De Angelis turned to Reilly. 'You didn't recover any of our missing pieces from the stables?'

'I'm afraid not, Father. They're being murdered because of them.'

De Angelis took off his glasses and cleaned the lenses with his sleeve. 'And what about those extremist groups you were interested in. Have you had any luck with your inquiries there?'

'Not as yet. We're looking at a couple of them in particular, groups that have recently voiced anger at the Church for the way it's been critical of them. They're both in the midwest, so our field offices there are pursuing it. They don't have a conclusive link yet, just a lot of threats.'

De Angelis put on his glasses again, frowning. His disquiet was obvious, but he tried not to show it. 'I suppose we just have to wait and see.'

Reilly looked around the table. He knew they weren't making any great progress in getting to the bottom of the case. So far, they were reacting to events, rather than initiating them.

'You want to mention that Templar thing?' Aparo asked.

De Angelis turned to Aparo, whose gaze led him to Reilly. 'Templars?'

Reilly hadn't expected his partner to bring it up. He tried to downplay it as best he could. 'It's just a thread we're following.'

De Angelis's quizzical look prodded him on.

'One of the witnesses at the Met, an archaeologist... she felt there may be a link between the Templars and the raid.'

'Because of the red crosses on the knights' mantles?'

At least it's not that far off the chart, Reilly thought. 'Yes, that and other details. The knight who took the encoder said something in Latin which is apparently a marking on a Templar castle in France.'

De Angelis studied Reilly with the hint of a bemused smile. 'And this archaeologist, she thinks the raid on the museum was the work of a religious order that ceased to exist almost seven hundred years ago?'

Reilly felt all the eyes in the room boring into him. 'Not exactly. It's just that given their history and their cult status, the Templars could conceivably be the inspiration for a bunch of religious fanatics who idolize them and who may be acting out some kind of revenge or revival fantasy.'

De Angelis nodded to himself, pensively. He seemed

rather disappointed as he stood up and gathered his papers. 'Yes, well, that sounds very promising. I wish you continued luck with your investigation, Agent Reilly. Gentlemen, Agent Gaines,' he said as he glanced at Jansson before leaving the room quietly, leaving Reilly with the uncomfortable feeling that the Templars' lunatic stigma didn't only apply to academics.

CHAPTER 30

Mitch Adeson knew that if he had to stay holed up in this dump much longer, he would go stir crazy. But it would be just as crazy to stay in his own place, and the streets there were likely to be more dangerous. At least here, in his dad's apartment in Queens, he was safe.

First Gus, then Branko. Mitch was smart, but even if he'd been as dumb as Gus Waldron, he would've figured out that someone had a list, and that it was a racing certainty that not only was he on it, he was next in line.

It was time to move on to safer pastures.

He looked across the room at his deaf and barely continent father who was doing what he always did: staring at the fuzzy picture on the TV, tuned as always to an endless succession of trashy talk shows at which he constantly spewed abuse.

Mitch would have liked to check up on the guy who'd hired him. He had wondered if that man was the one to look out for, then decided he couldn't be. He'd handled himself well enough on a horse, but he wasn't someone who could've killed Branko, and he sure as hell couldn't have laid a glove on the mountain that was Gus Waldron. It had to be someone higher up the food chain. And to get to whoever it was and beat him to the punch, Mitch knew he had to go through the guy who'd originally approached him, the one who'd first told him about this crazy scheme. The only problem was, he had no way of contacting him. He didn't even know the man's name.

He heard his father break wind. Christ, he thought, *I can't just sit here. I need to do something.*

Daylight or not, he had to make a move. He told his father that he would be back in a few hours. The old man ignored him but then, as Mitch pulled on a coat and crossed to the door, he groaned out, 'Beer and cigarettes.'

It wasn't far short of being the longest sentence his father had spoken to him since the early hours of Sunday morning when he had gone there straight from Central Park, after they had stripped off the armor and gone their separate ways. It had been his job to stow the props in a panel truck that he had dropped off in a lock-up garage two blocks away from his own place. The rent was paid in advance for a year, and until then, he wouldn't go near it.

He went out of the apartment and down the stairs where, after taking his time checking for anything suspicious, he stepped into the darkening street and headed for the subway.

It was raining by the time Mitch moved cautiously through the alley at the back of the grimy seven-story building in Astoria that housed his apartment. He had a paper sack with a Coors six-pack and a carton of Winstons for his old man under his arm, and he was soaked. He hadn't intended on going near his own place for a while yet, but he had decided to take the risk to get some of his gear if he was going to pull a disappearing act.

He stood motionless in the alley for a couple of minutes before reaching up and pulling down on the balanced girder of the fire escape. He always kept it oiled, just in case, and it was pleasingly silent as it slid down. He hurried upward, casting nervous glances at the alley below. Outside his bedroom window, he stood the paper sack on the ladder and raked with his fingers into the gap between the escape and the wall, easing out the steel strip he kept there. Moments later, he had jimmied the window latch and was climbing inside.

He didn't put on a light, feeling his way around the familiar room instead. He dragged an old duffel from the shelf of the closet, then felt his way around the back and pulled out four cartons of shells that he piled into the bag. He then went into the bathroom and fished out a nylon bag from the water tank. In it was a big oilskin-wrapped package, which he opened and from which he took out the Kimber .45 and the small Bersa 9mm. He checked them, loaded the Bersa, which he stowed in his belt, and put the Kimber in with the shells. He grabbed some clothes and a favorite pair of work boots. That would do.

He climbed out the bedroom window, closed it behind him, shifted the duffel onto his shoulder, and reached down for the paper sack.

It was gone.

For an instant, Mitch froze, then carefully eased out his gun. He stared down into the alley. He couldn't see any movement. In weather like this, not even the cats were on the prowl, and from this height, the rats were invisible.

Who had taken the sack? Kids? Had to be. If someone was after him, they wouldn't dick around with a six-pack and a carton of smokes, but he wasn't in the mood for testing theories. He decided to go up onto the roof from where he could step across to another building and work his way down to street level a hundred yards away. He'd done it before, but not with the rooftops wet with rain.

He began to climb slowly and silently upward until he reached the roof. He was nipping around a ventilation shaft housing when his foot slid on one of the dozen or so lengths of tubular steel scaffolding left there by a careless maintenance crew. It sent him flying forward to land, face down, in a pool of rainwater. Scrambling back to his feet, he raced for the thigh-high parapet. Reaching it, he swung one leg up, then felt a sharp pain as someone suddenly kicked him behind the knee on his other leg, which promptly gave way.

He dived for his gun but the man grabbed his arm and twisted it. The gun flew from his hand and he heard it clatter down the sloping roof. He jerked against the grip with all his strength, felt himself break away from the man and experienced a moment of elation before he overbalanced and went over the far side of the parapet.

Fingers desperately grasping for anything within reach, he managed to latch on to the rough stone capping with both hands. Then his attacker clasped his arms, just above the wrists, holding on and preventing him from slipping away to certain death. Mitch stared upward, saw the man's face, and didn't recognize him.

Whatever the guy wanted, he decided, he could gladly have.

'Pull me up,' he wheezed out. 'Pull me up!'

The man slowly did what he asked, until Mitch was sprawled, face down, half on and half off the capstone. He felt the man release one of his arms, then he saw something reflecting the light. For an instant, Mitch thought it was a knife, then he realized what it was: a hypodermic needle.

He didn't know what the hell this meant, and tried to squirm free, but before he could move, he felt a sudden sharp pain in the taut muscles that stretched up from his shoulder toward his skull.

The man had just jabbed the needle into his neck.

CHAPTER 31

As he stared at the vidcap print before him in the privacy of his room, De Angelis fingered the golden, diamond- and ruby-encrusted statuette of a rearing horse.

Privately, he thought the antique was quite vulgar. He knew it was a gift from the Russian Orthodox Church to the Holy Father on the occasion of a papal audience in the late nineteenth century, and he also knew that it was priceless. Vulgar and ugly, but nevertheless priceless.

He studied the image more closely. It was the one Reilly had given him at their first meeting, when the agent had inquired about the importance of the multigeared encoder. The sight was still one that made his heart race. Even this grainy print managed to reawaken in him the sheer exhilaration he felt when he first witnessed the moment on the surveillance footage he'd been shown at Federal Plaza.

Knights in shining armor pillaging a Manhattan museum in the twenty-first century.

Such audacity, he thought. *Truly remarkable.*

The picture showed the rider, who De Angelis now knew to be the fourth horseman, holding up the encoder. He stared at the man's helmet, trying to burrow through the ink and the paper and into the horseman's thoughts. The image was a three-quarters view, taken from the rear left side. Smashed display cabinets lay all around the knight. And in the top left corner on the shot, peeking out from behind a cabinet, was a woman's face.

A female archaeologist who overheard the fourth horseman say something in Latin, De Angelis thought. She had to be close enough to hear him, and, staring at the picture, he knew it had to be her.

He focused on her face: taut with fear, frozen. Absolutely terrified.

It had to be her.

He set the picture and the jeweled horse down on his bed next to the pendant, which he now picked up. It was made of rubies and set in silver, a gift from the Nizam of Hyderabad. Worth a prince's ransom, which is what it once had been. As he twirled it, he scowled at the dead end he had reached.

His quarry had covered his tracks well; he would have expected no less from a man of such daring. The gang leader's minions, the desperate lowlifes that De Angelis had found, questioned, and dispatched with such ease, had proven useless.

The man himself still eluded him.

He needed a fresh tack. A divine intervention of sorts.

And now this. An annoyance.

A distraction.

He looked at her face again. He picked up his cellphone and hit a speed dial key. Two short rings later, a gravelly, hoarse voice answered.

'Who's this?'

'Just how many people have you given this number to, exactly?' the monsignor fired back tersely.

The man exhaled audibly. 'Good to hear from you, sir.'

De Angelis knew the man would now be putting out a cigarette butt while instinctively reaching for a fresh replacement. He had always found the habit repugnant, but the man's other talents more than made up for it.

'I need your help on something.' As he said it, he frowned. He had hoped he wouldn't need to involve anyone else. He stared at Tess's face again. 'I need you to access the FBI's database on METRAID,' then added, 'discreetly.'

The man's answer came quickly.

'Not a problem. It's one of the perks of the war on terror. We're all in a caring, sharing mode. Just tell me what you need.'

CHAPTER 32

Veering away from one of the many winding roads of the cemetery, Tess was now walking along a gravel path.

It was just past eight in the morning. The spring bulbs were in bloom all around the headstones, and the neatly clipped grass around her was wet from last night's rain. The small rise in air temperature had generated a coiling mist that shrouded the tombstones and trees.

Overhead, a lone monk parakeet flew by, breaking the serene setting with a haunting call. Despite the temperature rise and the cover of her coat, Tess shivered a little as she went deeper into the cemetery. Walking through a burial ground was uncomfortable at the best of times, and being here today made her think of her father and of how long it had been since she had visited his grave.

She stopped and checked the map she had printed out in the kiosk at the huge, gothic entrance. She thought she was headed in the right direction, but now she wasn't that sure anymore. The cemetery was spread out over more than four hundred acres, and it was easy to get lost, especially as she wasn't driving. She had taken the R from midtown to the 25th Street station in Brooklyn, walked a block east, and entered the cemetery from its main gate.

She looked around, trying to get her bearings, and wondered if coming here had been such a good idea after all. It was practically a lose-lose situation. If Vance was here, she'd be barging in on a hugely private moment. And if he wasn't here, then her trip would have been a waste of time.

She pushed her doubts to the back of her mind and kept on walking. She was now in what was obviously an older part of the cemetery. As she passed an elaborate tomb topped by a reclining granite angel, she heard a sound off to one side. Startled, she peered into the mist. She could see nothing except the dark, shifting shapes of the trees. Uneasy now, she walked at a slightly brisker pace, realizing that she was plunging even deeper into the recesses of the cemetery.

Checking the map quickly, she saw that she must now be close. Convinced of her current location, she decided to take a short cut across a small knoll, and hurried over the slippery grass. She stumbled on a moldy stone surround, her fingers clutching at a crumbling marker to save herself from falling.

And then she saw him.

He was about fifty yards away, alone, standing solemnly in front of a small headstone. A bouquet of carnations, dark red and cream colored, lay before it. His head was bowed. A lone gray Volvo was parked on the drive nearby.

Tess waited a moment before deciding to approach him. She walked toward him slowly, quietly, and glanced at the headstone, spotting the words 'Vance' and 'Martha' on it. He still hadn't turned when she got to within ten feet of him, even though they were the only ones around.

'Professor Vance,' she said hesitantly.

He stood rigid for a moment before slowly turning to face her.

She was standing before a changed man.

His hair was thick and silvery gray, his face gaunt. Although he was still slender and tall, the athletic build had receded, even displaying a slight stoop. His hands were in his coat pockets, and he wore a dark overcoat, its collar turned up. Tess noticed that it was threadbare at the cuffs and had a couple of stains on it. In fact, she was embarrassed to notice, his whole appearance was rather shabby. Whatever it was he did now, it was clearly several rungs below the position he had once enjoyed. Had she passed him in the street today, a decade after she last saw him, she doubted that she would have recognized him, but here, under the circumstances, she had no doubt.

He looked at her, his expression cautious.

'I'm really very sorry to intrude,' she stumbled, 'I hope you'll forgive me. I know this is an extremely personal moment for you and believe me, if there was any other way to contact you...' She stopped, noting that his face seemed to brighten ever so slightly with what seemed like recognition.

'Tess. Tess Chaykin. Oliver's daughter.'

She breathed in deeply and let out a low sigh of relief. As his face relaxed, his piercing gray eyes brightened, and she saw hints of the charismatic force he had been when they'd last met, all those years ago. There was clearly nothing wrong with his memory, because he said, 'Now I know why you look different. You were pregnant when we met. I remember thinking that the Turkish wilderness wasn't a good place for you then.'

'Yes.' She relaxed. 'I have a daughter. Kim.'

'She must be...' He was working out how long it had been.

'She's nine,' she offered helpfully, then her eyes darted away in embarrassment. 'I'm sorry, I... I really shouldn't be here.'

She felt a sudden urge to retreat and slip away when she noticed that his smile faded. His whole face seemed to darken as he glanced toward the headstone. His voice soft, he said, 'My daughter Annie would have been five years old today.'

Daughter? Tess looked at him, thrown, and turned to the headstone. It was elegant in its simplicity, white, with the inscription carved out in letters that were maybe two inches high:

MARTHA & ANNIE
VANCE
May their smiles brighten up
A better world than this

She didn't understand at first. Then it hit her.

His wife must have died in childbirth.

Tess felt her face flush, deeply embarrassed now at her thoughtlessness in tracking this man down to his wife and daughter's graveside. She looked up at Vance and saw that he was looking at her, the sadness etching deep lines into his face. Her heart sank. 'I'm so sorry,' she mumbled, 'I didn't know.'

'We had already chosen names, you see. Matthew if it had been a boy, and Annie, of course. We chose them the night we were married.'

'What... how did they...' She couldn't finish her question.

'It happened just over halfway into her pregnancy. She'd been under close observation from the start. She was – well, we both were – rather old to be having our first child. And her family had a history of high blood pressure. Anyway, she developed something called pre-eclampsia. They don't know why it happens. I was told it was pretty common, but it can be devastating. Which it was in Martha's case.' He stopped and took a deep breath, looking away. It was clearly painful for him to talk about it, and Tess wanted him to stop, she wanted the earth to open up and swallow her and avoid having him relive it through her selfish presence. But it was too late.

'The doctors said there was nothing they could do,' he continued mournfully. 'They told us Martha would have to have an abortion. Annie was too young to have any hope of surviving in an incubator, and Martha's chances of surviving the pregnancy herself were getting slimmer with each passing day.'

'The abortion didn't...'

His gaze turned inward. 'Normally, it wouldn't even have been an option for us. But this was different. Martha's life was at risk. So we did what we'd always done.' His expression hardened perceptibly. 'We asked our parish priest, Father McKay, what we should do.'

Tess cringed as she guessed what had happened.

Vance's face tightened up. 'His position, the Church's

position, was very clear. He said it would be murder. Not just any murder, you understand, but the most heinous of all murders. An unspeakable crime. Oh, he was very eloquent about it. He said we'd be violating the written word of God. "Thou shalt not kill." He said this was a human life we were talking about. We'd be killing a human being at the very beginning of its life, the most innocent murder victim possible. A victim who doesn't understand, a victim who can't argue, who can't plead for its life. He asked us if we would do it if we could hear its cries, if we could see its tears. And if that wasn't enough, his closing argument clinched it. "If you had a one year old baby, would you kill it, would you sacrifice it to save your own life? No. Of course you wouldn't. What if it was one month old? What if it was just one day old? When does the clock really start ticking for a life?"' He paused, shaking his head at the memory. 'We heeded his advice. No abortion. We put our faith in God.'

Vance looked at the grave, a cocktail of grief and anger visibly swirling in his veins. 'Martha held on until she went into convulsions. She died of a brain hemorrhage. And Annie, well... her little lungs never even got a chance to breathe our filthy air.'

'I'm so, so sorry.' Tess could barely speak. But it didn't really matter. Vance seemed to be in a world of his own. As she looked into his eyes, she could see that any sadness had now been overwhelmed by a fury that was rising from deep within.

'We were fools to put their lives in the hands of those ignorant, arrogant charlatans. It won't happen again. Not to anyone. I'll make sure of that.' He gazed at the emptiness around them. 'The world has changed a lot in a thousand years. Life's not about the will of God or about the malice of the devil. It's about scientific fact. And it's time people understand that.'

And in that instant, Tess knew.

Her blood froze as it hit her with absolute certainty.

He was the man in the museum. William Vance was the fourth horseman.

Images raced through her mind of the panic at the museum, the knights charging, the gunfire, the mayhem and the screams.

'*Veritas vos liberabit.*' The words just stumbled out of her mouth.

He looked at her, his gray eyes boring into her with rage and realization.

'Exactly.'

She had to get away, but her legs had turned to lead. She was utterly rigid, and in that moment, she thought of Reilly.

'I'm sorry, I shouldn't have come here,' was all she could say. She thought of the museum again, about the fact that people had died because of what this man had done. She looked around, hoping to see other mourners, or any of the tourists or bird-watchers who frequented the cemetery, but it was way too early for that. They were alone.

'I'm glad you did. I do appreciate the company, and you, of all people, should appreciate what I'm trying to do.'

'Please, I... I was only trying to...' She managed to will her legs back to life, and hesitantly took a few steps backward, darting nervous glances around, desperately trying to figure out an escape route. And at that moment, her cellphone rang.

Her eyes turned to saucers as she looked at Vance and, still stumbling backward, with Vance advancing slowly toward her, she held out one hand as her other hand dove into the bag for the phone, which was still ringing.

'Please,' she pleaded.

'Don't,' he said. And that's when she realized he was holding some kind of gun in his hand. It looked like a toy gun, with yellow stripes on its short, squared off barrel. And before she could move or cry out, her fingers grasping at the cellphone in her bag, she watched him pull the trigger, and two probes came flying out through the air. They struck her chest, and she felt burning waves of unbearable pain.

Instantly, her legs buckled; then she was paralyzed, help-less.

Falling to the ground.

Spinning into unconsciousness.

From behind a nearby tree, a tall man whose dark clothing reeked of stale cigarettes felt a surge of adrenaline as he saw Tess get hit and fall to the ground. Spitting out a wad of Nicorette gum, he pulled out his cellphone and hit a speed dial button, his other hand diving for the Heckler & Koch USP compact in the holster behind his back.

De Angelis was quick to answer. 'What's going on?'

'I'm still at the cemetery. The girl –' Joe Plunkett paused, watching her as she lay there on the wet grass. 'She met up with some guy, and he's just zapped her with a taser.'

'What?'

'I'm telling you, she's down for the count. What do you want me to do? You want me to take him out?' His mind was already laying out a plan of action. The taser wouldn't be a threat. He wasn't sure about whether or not the silver-haired man standing over the girl had any other weapon on him, but it wouldn't matter either way; he'd be able to overwhelm him before the man had a chance to react, especially since the older man seemed to be out here on his own.

Plunkett waited for the order. His heart was already priming itself for the rush, and he could practically hear De Angelis's mind whirring away. Then the monsignor spoke with a calm, subdued voice.

'No. Do nothing. She doesn't matter anymore. He's now your priority. Stay with him and make sure you don't lose him. I'm on my way.'

CHAPTER 33

A gale of dread blew through Reilly as he listened, his ear glued to his phone. 'Tess? Tess!' His calls remained unanswered, and then the line abruptly cut off.

He immediately hit the redial button, but after four rings, her recorded voice came up and asked him to leave a message. Another redial produced the same result.

Something's wrong. Something's very wrong.

He'd seen that Tess had called, but she hadn't left a message and had already left the office by the time he'd tried calling her back. He wasn't sure about how far he wanted to push her Templar angle anyway. He had felt awkward, almost embarrassed to have brought it up at the meeting with the rest of the team and the monsignor. Still, he had called her office bright and early and spoken to Lizzie Harding, her secretary, who had told him Tess hadn't come in that morning. 'She called to say she might be coming in late,' was how she'd put it.

'How late?'

'She didn't say.'

When he had asked for her cellphone number, he was told they didn't give out personal information, but he decided it was about time he had the number and the Institute's position was quickly reversed once he explained that he was with the FBI.

After three rings, her cellphone had clicked through but she hadn't said anything. He had only heard a shuffling noise, like when someone accidentally triggers a speed-dialed call from a cellphone in their handbag or pocket; but then he had heard her say 'Please,' in a tone that was disturbing. She had sounded scared. Like someone pleading. And then there was a succession of noises he was racing to make sense of:

a sharp crack, then a couple of small thumps, what sounded like a brief, muffled cry of pain and a much louder thump. He had shouted 'Tess' into the phone again, but didn't get an answer, and then the line went dead.

Staring at his phone now, his heart was pounding. He really didn't like the way that 'Please' had sounded.

Something was definitely, horribly wrong.

His mind racing, he dialed the Institute again and got through to Lizzie.

'It's Agent Reilly again. I need to know where Tess –' He quickly corrected himself, '– where Miss Chaykin is. It's urgent.'

'I don't know where she is. She didn't say where she was going. All she said was that she'd be coming in late.'

'I need you to have a look at her diary, check her email. Does she keep an electronic calendar, maybe a program that's in sync with her PDA? There's got to be something there.'

'Just give me a minute,' she said, sounding edgy.

Reilly could see his partner now looking at him with concern.

'What's going on?' Aparo asked.

Reilly cupped the mouthpiece with one hand and scribbled down Tess's cellphone number for Aparo with the other. 'It's Tess. Something's happened. Get a fix on her cell.'

Across the East River, a gray Volvo was slowly making its way up the Brooklyn-Queens Expressway, heading toward the Brooklyn Bridge.

Three cars behind the Volvo and keeping a discreet distance was a gunmetal gray Ford sedan, driven by a man who had the nasty habit of flicking cigarettes butts out the car window while they were still alight.

To his left and across the river, the spires of the Lower East Side beckoned.

As he had guessed, the Volvo was soon on the bridge and heading into Manhattan.

CHAPTER 34

Even before she opened her eyes, Tess was aware of the smell of incense. When she did open them, she saw what appeared to be hundreds of candles, their yellow flames throwing a soft, glowing light around the room she was in.

She was lying on a carpet of some kind, an old kilim. It felt rough and worn to her fingers. Suddenly, her encounter with Bill Vance flooded back and she felt a chill of fear. But he wasn't there. She was alone.

Sitting up, she felt dizzy, but forced herself to rise unsteadily to her feet. She felt a sharp pain in her chest, and another in her left side. She glanced down, feeling around, trying to remember what had happened.

He shot me. I can't believe he actually shot me.

But I'm not dead... ?

She examined her clothes, actually looking for telltale entry points, wondering why she was still breathing. Then she noticed the two spots where she'd been hit, the two places where her clothes were punctured, the edges of the holes slightly frayed and burnt. And then it slowly came back to her, the image of Vance and the gun he'd been holding. She realized he hadn't meant to kill her, only to incapacitate her, and that the gun he'd shot her with must have been some kind of stun gun.

Not that that was a particularly comforting thought either.

Looking around through eyes that were still hazy, she guessed that she was in a cellar. Bare walls, paved floor, low-vaulted ceiling carried on elaborate pillars. No windows. No doors. In one corner was a wooden staircase leading upward into a darkness that wasn't reached by the light from the candles, most of which stood on shapeless masses of melted wax.

She slowly realized that the place was more than a cellar. Someone lived here. Against one wall was a cot, with an old wooden box for a bedside table. It was crammed with books and papers. At the opposite end of the space stood a long table. Before it, tilted slightly as though it had seen many years of service, stood a large swivel office chair. The table was piled with more books and papers at each end and there, centrally placed and surrounded by yet more candles, sat the encoder from the Met.

Even in the darkness of the candlelit chamber, it shined with an otherworldly presence. It seemed to be in better condition than she remembered it.

Tess spotted her bag on the table, her wallet lying open beside it, and she suddenly remembered her cellphone. Vaguely, she recalled hearing its ringtone before blacking out. She remembered feeling her way around the phone while it was still ringing, and was sure she'd managed to hit a button, establishing the connection. She took a step to grab her bag but before she could get to it, a sudden noise spun her around. She realized that it came from the top of the stairs: a door opening, then closing with a metallic clunk. Then footsteps were coming down the steps and a pair of legs appeared, a man's. He was wearing a long overcoat.

Hastily, she stepped back as he came into view. Vance was looking her way and smiled warmly, and for an instant she wondered if she were imagining what he had done to knock her out.

He moved toward her, carrying a large, plastic bottle of water.

'I'm really sorry, Tess,' he said apologetically. 'But I didn't have much choice.'

Taking a glass from among the books on the table, he poured some water and handed it to her. Then he searched his pockets until he found a foil strip of tablets. 'Here. These are strong painkillers. Take one and drink as much water as you can. It'll help with the headache.'

She glanced at the foil and recognized the brand. The strip looked untouched.

'It's just Voltarol. Go on, take it. You'll feel better.'

She hesitated for a moment, then snapped a tablet out of the foil wrap and swallowed it with a gulp of water. He refilled her glass and she greedily drank that down, too. Still stunned by what had happened to her, she stared at Vance, her eyes striving to focus in the light of the candles. 'Where are we? What is this place?'

His face took on a saddened, almost confused look. 'I guess you could say it's home.'

'Home? You don't actually live here, do you?'

He didn't answer.

Tess was having trouble making sense of what was going on. 'What do you want from me?'

Vance was scrutinizing her. 'You came looking for me.'

'I came looking for you to help me figure something out,' she snapped angrily. 'I didn't expect you to shoot me and kidnap me like this.'

'Calm down, Tess. No one's been kidnapped.'

'Oh? So I suppose I'm free to leave.'

Vance looked away, thinking. Then he turned to face her. 'You may not want to leave. Once you've heard my side of the story.'

'Believe me, I'd just as soon get the hell out of here.'

'Well... maybe you're right.' He seemed lost, even ashamed. 'Maybe it is a little more complicated than that.'

Tess felt the anger in her giving way to caution. *What are you doing? Don't antagonize him. Can't you see he's lost it? He's unstable. He's into beheading people. Just stay calm.* She didn't know where to look or what to say. Glancing again toward the encoder, Tess spotted an opening in the wall against which the table stood. It was small, square, and shuttered. She felt a surge of hope, which just as quickly faded as she realized he wouldn't have left an escape route uncovered. *He might be unhinged, but he isn't stupid.*

Her eyes were drawn to the encoder again. That's what it was all about. She felt she needed to know more. She willed herself to calm down, then asked, 'It's Templar, isn't it?'

'Yes... And to think I'd been to the Vatican library several times, and all the time it must have been sitting there in some vault, gathering dust. I don't think they even realized what they had.'

'And after all these years, it still works?'

'It needed some cleaning up and some oiling, but yes, it still works. Perfectly. The Templars were meticulous craftsmen.'

Tess studied the device. She noticed that on the table beside it were numerous sheets of paper. Old documents, like sheets from a manuscript. She looked at Vance, who was watching her. It seemed to her like he was almost enjoying her confusion.

'Why are you doing this?' she finally asked. 'Why did you need it so badly?'

'It all started in France, quite a few years ago.' He cast a wistful glance at the old documents sitting by the encoder, his mind drifting. 'In fact, it was shortly after Martha and Annie died,' he said somberly. 'I'd left the university, I was... confused, and angry. I had to get away from it all. I ended up in the south of France, in the Languedoc. I'd been there before, on walking trips with Martha. It's beautiful down there. You can easily imagine what it must have been like back then. They have a very rich history, though a lot of it is rather bloody... Anyway, while I was there, I came across a story that just stayed with me. A story that had taken place several hundred years ago. It was about a young priest who was called in to a dying old man's deathbed, to give him the last rites and hear his confession. The old man was believed to have been one of the last surviving Templars. The priest went in, even though the man wasn't part of his congregation and hadn't asked, in fact had even refused, at first, to see him. Finally, he relented, and legend has it that when the priest came out, he was white with shock. Not just his face, but even his hair had turned white. They say he never smiled again after that day. And years later, just before he eventually died, he let the truth slip. It turned out that the Templar had told him his story, and had shown him some papers. Something that literally shocked the life out of him. And that was it. I couldn't shake that story, I couldn't get away from the image of this priest's hair turning white, just from spending a few minutes with a dying old man. From that point onward, finding out what this manuscript was, or where it might be, became –'

An obsession, Tess thought.

'– a mission, of sorts.' Vance smiled lightly, his mind clearly conjuring up images of distant, cloistered libraries. 'I don't know how many dusty archives I've rooted through, in museums, churches and monasteries all across France, even across the Pyrenees in the north of Spain.' He paused, then reached out a hand and rested it on the papers that sat beside the encoder. 'And then one day, I found something. In a Templar castle.'

A castle with an inscription on its portal. Tess felt light headed. She thought of the Latin words she had heard him say, about the Latin saying Clive had told her was carved into the lintel at the Chateau de Blanchefort, and took another look at the papers. She could see that they were ancient, handwritten documents. 'You found the actual manuscript?' she asked, surprised at feeling some of the thrill she knew Vance must have experienced. Then a flash of enlightenment struck her. 'But they were coded. That's why you needed the encoder.'

He nodded slowly, affirming her guess. 'Yes. It was so frustrating. For years, I knew I was sitting on something important, I knew I had the right papers, but I couldn't read them. Simple substitution or skipping codes didn't work, but then I knew they were more clever than that. I uncovered arcane references to Templar coding devices, but couldn't find any of the machines anywhere. It really seemed hopeless. All of their possessions had been destroyed when they were rounded up in 1307. And then fate intervened and brought up this little jewel from the bowels of the Vatican where it had been sitting all those years, hidden away long ago and all but forgotten.'

'And now you can read them.'

He patted the sheets. 'Like the morning paper.'

Tess looked at the documents. She chided herself for the feeling of wild excitement that was coursing through her, and had to remind herself that lives had been lost and that this man was quite possibly deranged and, given recent events, undoubtedly dangerous. The discovery he was working on was potentially a big one, bigger than anything she'd ever had the chance to uncover, but it was drenched in innocent blood, and she couldn't allow herself to forget that. It also had a darkness to it, something deeply unsettling about its history that she couldn't dismiss.

She studied Vance, who again seemed lost in his own thoughts. 'What are you hoping to find?'

'Something that's been lost for too long.' His eyes were narrow and intense. 'Something that'll make things right.'

Something worth killing for, she wanted to add, but decided against it. Instead, she remembered what she had read, about Vance's suggestion that the founder of the Templars was a Cathar. Vance had just told her that he'd found the letter in the Languedoc – where he had suggested, much to the affront of the French historian whose article she'd read, that Hughes de Payens's family came from. She wanted to know more about that, but before she could speak up, she heard a jarring noise from above, like a brick scraping against a stone floor.

Abruptly, Vance jumped to his feet. 'Stay here,' he ordered.

Her eyes darted up to ceiling, looking for its source. 'What is it?'

'Just stay here,' he insisted as he moved urgently. He went behind the table and pulled out the taser he had used on her, then decided against it and discarded it. He then rummaged through a pouch and pulled out another gun, this one a more traditional handgun, and awkwardly chambered a round as he hurried to the steps.

He climbed them briskly and, when his legs were out of view, she heard the metallic thud as he closed and locked the door behind him.

CHAPTER 35

De Angelis cursed to himself the instant his foot nudged the charred piece of timber off its sitting and disturbed the settlement of debris around him. Moving stealthily through the burnt-out church wasn't easy; scorched rafters and chunks of broken stone from the collapsed roof littered the dark, damp space around him.

He'd been initially surprised to find that this wreck was where Plunkett had trailed Tess and her silver-haired abductor. Skulking through the silent, ghostly remains of the Church of the Ascension, he now realized it was a perfect spot for someone who wanted to work undisturbed; someone whose dedication went beyond simple matters of personal comfort. One more confirmation, not that he needed it, that the man he was after knew exactly what it was he had taken from the Met that night.

De Angelis had entered the church from a side entrance; less than forty minutes earlier, Plunkett had observed a blind-folded Tess Chaykin being helped out of the back of the gray Volvo and led through the same entrance by her abductor. She had seemed barely conscious and needed the man's assistance to take the few steps into the doorway, her arm looped over his shoulder.

The small church was on West 114th Street, tucked in between two rows of brownstones with a narrow alleyway running alongside its east facade, which was where the Volvo and the sedan were now parked. The church had suffered a major fire in the recent past, and its reconstruction was evidently not on the cards yet. A large panel out front displayed the progress of the fundraising efforts for the rebuilding, in the form of a six-foot high thermometer which was graduated in the hundreds of thousands of dollars needed to bring the church back to its former glory, and which currently stood at only one third full.

The monsignor had made his way through a narrow passage and into the nave. Rows of columns divided it into two side aisles and a center section, which was strewn with mounds of half burnt pews. All around him, the stucco had been burnt off the walls, exposing the brick masonry which was blackened and occasionally holed. Below the ceiling, the few remaining plaster arches that spanned from the exterior walls to the columns were unrecognizable, charred and deformed by the flames. Only a hollow ring remained where the stained glass window had proudly stood over the church's entrance, its wide opening now boarded up.

He had crept along the edge of the nave, past the melted brass gates of the altar, and had climbed carefully up the steps and onto the sanctuary. The scorched remains of a large canopied pulpit loomed to his right. All around him, the church was silent, with only the occasional noise from the street wafting in through one of the many cavities in its exposed shell. He had surmised that whoever had taken the girl must be using the back rooms. With Plunkett outside keeping watch, he now slipped quietly past the remnants of the altar and into the passage behind the sanctuary, slowly twirling a silencer onto the nozzle of his Sig Sauer handgun.

And that was when his foot nudged the debris.

The noise echoed around him in the darkened hallway. He froze, listening carefully, alert to any disturbance he may have triggered. Squinting, he could barely make out a door at the far end of the passage, when suddenly, from beyond the door, he heard a muffled thud, then faint footsteps coming closer. Swiftly, De Angelis stepped aside, hugging the wall, raising his handgun. Footsteps approached the hall, the door handle rattled, but instead of the door opening outward, toward him, it opened inward and all that he saw was a dark space. He was the one in the light.

Too late and too dangerous to retreat, which was not, anyway, in his nature, he hurled himself forward into the darkness.

Gripping his gun with tight fingers, Vance stared through the doorway at the man who had trespassed into his sanctuary. He didn't recognize him. He glimpsed what he thought was a clerical collar. It made him hesitate.

Then the man was leaping forward and Vance tried hastily to use his gun, but before he could pull its trigger, the stranger was on him, knocking him to the floor, the handgun slipping from his hand. The passageway was narrow and low and Vance used the wall to thrust himself upward but the man was much stronger and down he went again. This time, he brought his knee up sharply, heard a satisfactory grunt of pain. Another gun, his attacker's, clattered noisily across the floor. But once again his attacker recovered quickly, swinging a fist hard against his head.

The blow hurt Vance but didn't daze him. More important, it jarred him into a fury. Twice in one day, first by Tess Chaykin, now by this stranger, his endeavor was being jeopardized. He used his knee again, then his fist, then a barrage of punches. His blows were unschooled, but they were fired by his anger. Nothing and no one had the right to come between him and his goal.

The intruder blocked his blows expertly and backed off, but as he did so he stumbled over some planks of wood. Vance, seeing his opportunity, kicked out, connecting savagely with the man's knee. Snatching up his gun, he leveled it and squeezed the trigger. The stranger was fast, though, throwing himself sideways as the bullets flew out. By the strained cry that followed, Vance thought one of them may have struck its intended target, but he couldn't be sure. The man was still moving, staggering backward into the sanctuary.

Vance hesitated for just a moment.

Should he follow, find out who the man was and finish

him off? Then he heard some noise coming from the far corner of the church. The man wasn't alone.

He decided it was best to escape. Turning, he hurried back to the trapdoor that shielded his cellar.

CHAPTER 36

Tess heard a loud gunshot, which was followed by what sounded like an angry cry. Someone was hurt. Then footsteps were rushing back toward the trapdoor. She wasn't sure if it was Vance or someone else, but she wasn't about to just stand there and wait to find out.

She dived across the chamber, grabbed her bag off the table, and pulled out her cellphone. In the faint glimmer of the candles, the LED screen lit up like a flashlight, only to inform her there was no signal in the cellar. It didn't really matter; she didn't know the FBI's number by heart, and while dialing 911 was an option, she knew it would take too long to explain what was happening. Besides, she didn't have a clue where she was.

Help, I'm in a cellar somewhere in the city.
I think.
Perfect.

Still dazed, and with her heart thumping loudly in her ears, she darted nervous glances around the chamber, then remembered the shuttered opening she'd spotted by the table. On impulse, she cleared some of the clutter off its surface, scrambled up onto the table and pulled wearily at the planks of wood covering the cavity, trying to loosen them. They wouldn't give. She pounded at them helplessly, but they held tight. Then she heard a sound as the cellar door opened. Turning, she saw legs beginning to descend. She recognized the shoes. It was Vance.

Her eyes quickly scanned the room and settled on the taser Vance had discarded. It was lying there on the corner of the table nearest to her, behind a stack of books. She grabbed it and leveled it at him, her hands shaking as his face emerged from the darkness, his eyes staring calmly into hers.

'Stay away from me!' she yelled at him.

'Tess, please,' he shot back with an urgent, calming gesture, 'we need to get out of here.'

'We? What are you talking about? Just stay away from me.'

He was still moving toward her. 'Tess, put the gun down.'

Panicking now, she pulled the trigger – but nothing happened. He was now less than ten feet away. She turned the gun, glaring at it, her eyes straining to figure out if she had missed something. He was moving faster now, coming at her. Fiddling desperately with the gun, she finally spotted the small safety and flipped it up. A small red light flashed at the back of the gun. She raised it up again and saw that she had also somehow activated its laser, which was beaming a tiny red mark onto Vance's chest. The dot danced left and right, mirroring her trembling hands. He was very close now. Pulse racing, she shut her eyes and pulled the trigger, which felt more like a rubber-coated button than what she imagined was the cold steel of a handgun's trigger. The taser came to life with a loud pop, and Tess shrieked as the two metal probes and their stainless steel barbs came blasting out of its front, trailing thin wires behind them.

The first probe just missed its mark, flying past his chest and disappearing into the darkness, but the second bit into his left thigh. Fifty thousand volts of electricity seared into him for five seconds, overriding his central nervous system and triggering incontrollable contractions in his muscles. He jerked and arched upward as the burning spasms erupted through his body, and his legs gave way. He collapsed on himself, helpless, his face contorted with pain.

Tess was momentarily confused by the cloud of tiny confetti-like ID disks that exploded out of the cartridge as she fired the gun, but the groans of Vance, lying there writhing in pain, soon whipped her back to her immediate predicament. She thought of stepping past him and heading up the stairs, but wasn't too keen on getting any closer to him. She also wasn't sure who Vance had confronted up there and was too scared to find out. She turned again to the shuttered opening and kicked and pulled at the panels until at last one of them loosened. She yanked it off, used it to jimmy the others loose, and looked in through the hole she'd made.

Beyond stretched a dark tunnel.

With nowhere else to go, she started to climb through the opening, then looked back, saw that Vance was still writhing in pain, and saw the encoder and the sheets, the manuscript, lying there, within reach.

They were beckoning her, too enticing to resist.

Surprising herself, she climbed back in and snatched the pile of documents, stuffing them into her bag. Something else caught her attention: her wallet, lying among the pile of clutter she'd rashly thrown off the table. She took a step to retrieve it when, from the corner of her eye, she saw Vance stir. She hesitated for a nanosecond before deciding she had taken enough of a risk as it was and had to get out of there now. She spun on her heels, clambered back into the tunnel, and hurried forward into the darkness.

Crouched low, her head brushing the top of the tunnel, she was perhaps thirty yards in when it opened up into a wider and higher shaft. She had a sudden, disconcerting flashback to an old Mexican catacomb she had visited as a student. The air smelled even damper in here and looking down she saw the reason. A narrow stream of black water flowed down the center. Tess stumbled along its edge, her feet slipping on the damp, worn stonework. The bitingly cold water swirled over the tops of her shoes. Then the stream ended, the water cascading down maybe five or six or more feet into another, still bigger tunnel.

Glancing back, Tess listened. Was that just water she heard, or was it something else? Then a harrowing shout echoed in the darkness.

'Tess!'

Vance's voice bellowed from behind. He was back on his feet and coming after her.

Taking a breath, she lowered herself over the ledge until her arms were at full stretch, water pouring into one sleeve of her coat, soaking her clothing and her body. Now, thankfully, the outstretched toes of her shoes touched solid floor and she let go. Turning, she saw that this time, the stream of water was deeper and wider. A filthy sludge was being carried along on its surface from which rose a smell so foul that she knew she was in a sewer. After a couple of attempts to walk along the edge, she gave up. The curve was too steep, the surface too slippery. Instead, closing her mind to what she knew the water carried in its oily grasp, she went down the center, the water now almost to her knees.

From the corners of her eyes she suddenly glimpsed movement and color and turned her head. Small specks of reddish light gleamed in the darkness, moving, and she heard a chittering noise.

Rats were scurrying along the edges of the stream of sewage.

'Tess!'

Vance's voice thundered along the damp tunnel, bouncing off the walls, seeming to come from all sides at once.

A few more yards, and she realized that ahead of her, the darkness wasn't quite as intense. Stumbling awkwardly, she kept on moving as fast as she dared. No way could she risk falling face down into this. When, at last, she reached the source of the light, it was coming in from above. From a sidewalk grille. She could hear people up above. Edging closer, she could actually see them, walking twenty feet overhead.

She felt a surge of hope and started yelling. 'Help! Help me! Down here! Help!' but no one seemed to hear her, and if they did, they simply ignored her cries. *Of course they're ignoring you. What did you expect? This is New York City. Taking deranged cries from the sewers seriously was the last thing any-*

one from around here would do.

Tess realized that her shouts were echoing down the tunnel ahead of her and behind her. She listened. Some sounds were closing in on her. Sloshing sounds, and heavy splashes. She wasn't about to stand there and wait for him to reach her. She set off again, completely heedless now of the water and the filth, and almost at once reached a fork in the tunnel.

One passageway was wider, but it was darker and looked wetter. Easier to hide in? Maybe. She chose that one. Barely fifty feet in and it looked as though she had made the wrong choice. There, in front of her, was a blank brick wall.

It was a dead end.

CHAPTER 37

After he had repelled the intruder in the crypt, Vance had planned on using the tunnels as his escape route from the cellar, taking with him the encoder and the still incompletely decoded manuscript. But all he now had, clasped firmly in his arms, was the intricate machine. The papers were gone. He felt a cold fury envelop him and shouted out her name, his angry cry bellowing across the damp walls that engulfed him.

He had no quarrel with Tess Chaykin. He remembered that he had liked her once, back when he was still capable of liking people, and he should have had no reason to dislike her now. Indeed, it had even crossed his mind to invite her to join his... crusade.

But she had stolen the papers, his papers, and that infuriated him.

Hoisting the encoder into a more comfortable position, he continued after Tess. If he didn't reach her soon, she might stumble onto one or another of several escape hatches from this tortuous maze.

He couldn't allow that to happen.

Again he felt his rage rising but fought it back. He couldn't risk moving or acting rashly.

Not now.

And especially not down here.

Tess had turned from the dead end and was planning to go back the way that she had come when she saw an iron door encased in a side wall. She grabbed its rusted handle and pulled. It wasn't locked, but it was jammed. With a despairing heave, she forced the door open and saw a staircase spiraling downward. Deeper and darker did not seem like a wise move, but she didn't have much choice.

Tentatively, feeling the angled rungs before putting her weight on them, Tess worked her way down the staircase and found herself in yet another tunnel. *How many tunnels were there down here, for God's sake?* At least this one was even bigger than before and, even better, it was dry. For the time being. Whatever it was, at least it wasn't a sewer.

She didn't know which way to run. She chose to go left. Ahead, she saw a glimmer of light. Moving, yellow light. *More candles?*

Hesitantly, she edged forward.

The light went out.

Tess froze. Then she realized it wasn't out; someone had stepped in front of it.

There were still noises behind her. Whoever was standing there ahead of her couldn't possibly be Vance. Or could it? Maybe he knew his way around these tunnels. He said he'd been living down here. Still, she forced herself forward and could now see not one but two figures a few yards along the tunnel. She didn't think either of them was Vance. Men or women, though, she had no idea, but down here, neither one was likely to be good news.

'Hey, baby,' a hoarse voice called out. 'You lost?'

Instantly deciding that hesitation would be bad for her health, Tess picked up her pace, awkward in the near-total darkness.

'Looks like your lucky day, man,' another voice said, this one high-pitched.

They didn't sound particularly friendly.

Tess kept going. Behind her came a louder noise. Her heart jumped. She was close to the two figures now. Their faces were still masked by the darkness. In the dim candle-light behind them, she could make out a clutter of cardboard boxes, rolls of what looked to be carpet, bundles of rags.

Tess thought fast. 'There are cops coming,' Tess snapped as she approached them.

'What the fuck do they want?' one of them grumbled.

As Tess pushed past the two men, one of them reached out and grabbed at her coat.

'Hey, come on, doll –'

Instinctively, Tess swung around, slamming the inside of her clenched fist across the side of the man's head. He stumbled back with a startled yelp. The one with the high-pitched voice was about to try his luck, but must have seen something in Tess's eyes, glinting in the yellow light, and backed off.

Tess turned away and put as much distance as she could between herself and the two bums. She ran, tired now, gasping for breath, the bleakness of the stygian underworld now starting to overwhelm her.

She reached another fork in the tunnel. She had no clue as to which way to go. This time, she went right. Stumbling a few more yards, she saw a recess in the wall, a grille that opened when she pushed on it. Another runged ladder going down. She needed to go up, not down. But she had to get away from Vance and decided to go for it, hoping he wouldn't follow.

Now she was in a much bigger tunnel, this one dry again, with straight walls. It was much darker here, and she advanced cautiously, running a hand along the wall for guidance. She couldn't hear Vance's footsteps or shouts anymore. She breathed out. *Great. Now what?* Then after what was probably less than a minute but seemed like an eternity, she heard a sound behind her. Not rats this time, and not a human pursuer. What she heard was the rumble of a train.

Shit. I'm in the subway.

A faint, flickering light was bouncing off the walls as the screeching train approached. It lit up the rails on the ground. She ran, desperately trying to keep the live rail in sight, hoping she wouldn't hit it. The train was closing in fast, its rhythmic clatter bouncing off the tunnel walls. It had almost reached her when, cast into relief by the train's headlights, she saw a slim cavity in the wall and threw herself into it. As she squeezed into the curving space, the train hurtled past, only inches from her trembling body. Heart racing, her arms curled around her face defensively, her eyes shut tight but still aware of the strobing light as the train flashed by, she waited. The hot, sooty air pushed against her, covering every inch of her body, snaking into her mouth and nostrils. She backed herself even tighter against the wall. The noise was deafening, overwhelming all her other senses. She kept her eyes shut and, as the lights were finally past her, a wailing squeal sheared the air as the train's sparking brakes bit into the wheels. Her heartbeat still throbbing in her ears, she felt a surge of relief.

A station. I must be near a station.

Tess drew on her last reserves of energy and stumbled the final, desperate few yards. As the train moved off again, she came out into the bright light and dragged herself up onto the platform. The last few passengers were disappearing up the stairs. If anyone saw her, they didn't react.

For a moment, Tess remained there, alone, on her hands and knees at the edge of the platform, her heart still racing with fear and exhaustion. Then, wet and filthy and still shaking, she pushed herself upright.

Wearily and on rubbery legs, she followed the others up into civilization.

CHAPTER 38

Wrapped in a blanket and cradling a huge mug of hot coffee, Tess sat in Reilly's car across the street from the subway station on 103rd and shivered. The cold had thoroughly penetrated her soaked clothing. From the waist down, she was frozen, and the rest of her didn't feel any better.

He'd offered to take her to a hospital or straight home, but Tess had insisted that she wasn't hurt and didn't need to go home just yet. She felt she had to fill him in on her findings first.

As she watched teams of police officers entering the station, she told him about her run-in with Vance. How Clive had suggested she consult the professor, how she'd actually met Vance years ago, how she'd taken a chance at the cemetery, hoping he could help her find a connection to what had happened at the Met. She went over what Vance had said, about his wife dying in childbirth and about how he blamed their priest for it, and about how he had said he wanted to 'make things right', which seemed to intrigue Reilly. She told him the story about the dying Templar and the priest whose hair had turned white, and explained how Vance had shot her, how she'd found herself in the cellar; how they were interrupted by someone, the gunfight she'd overheard, and finally how she had escaped.

As she talked, she envisioned the search parties fanning out into the various tunnels, looking for him in that underground nightmare, although she knew the odds were he'd be long gone. Thinking about the tunnels again made her shudder. It wasn't somewhere she was keen to revisit, and she hoped she wouldn't be asked to do so. She had never been as scared in her life. At least, not since the raid on the

Met, which was less than a week ago. She was on a roll, a pretty unpleasant one at that.

When she finished, Reilly was shaking his head.

'What?' she asked.

He was just eyeing her silently.

'Why are you looking at me like that?' she insisted.

''Cause you're nuts, you know that?'

She exhaled wearily. 'Why?'

'Come on, Tess. You're not supposed to be running around chasing clues and trying to solve this thing on your own. Hell, you're not even supposed to be trying to solve it, period. That's my job.'

Tess managed a grin. 'You're worried I'm going to make you all look bad, is that it?'

Reilly was having none of it. 'I'm serious. You could have been badly hurt. Or worse. You don't get it, do you? People have died because of this thing. It's not a joke. I mean, for God's sake, you've got a daughter to think of.'

Tess stiffened visibly at his mention of Kim. 'Hey, I thought I was meeting a history professor for a little academic chit chat over a cup of coffee, all right? I didn't expect him to zap me with his –' Her mind went blank.

'Taser.'

Whatever. '– His taser, stuff me in the back of his car, and chase me through rat-infested sewers. He's a history professor, for God's sake. They're supposed to be mild-mannered, pipe-smoking introverts, not –'

'Psychos?'

Tess frowned and looked away. Somehow, she didn't think the term was appropriate, despite everything that had happened. 'I'm not sure I'd go that far, but... he's definitely not in good shape.' She felt a tinge of empathy for the professor, which threw her, and she heard herself saying, 'He needs help.'

Reilly studied her, pausing for a moment. 'Okay, we'll need to do a proper, in-depth debriefing as soon as you're comfortable, but right now, I need to make sure we find where he took you. You have no idea where you were being held, where that cellar is?'

Tess shook her head. 'No, I told you. When I came to in the car, I was blindfolded, and getting out of there was just one big, dark maze of tunnels. But it can't be that far from here. I mean, I walked it.'

'How many blocks, if you had to guess.'

'I don't know... five?'

'Okay. Let's get some maps and see if we can find this dungeon of yours.'

Reilly was about to walk off when Tess reached out and stopped him. 'There's something else, something I didn't tell you.'

'Why am I not surprised?' he chastised. 'What is it?'

Tess reached into her bag and pulled out the roll of sheets she'd taken from Vance's desk. She spread them out for Reilly to see and now, in the light, she could see them properly for the first time. The documents, ancient vellum scrolls, were beautiful despite having no illustrations on them; they were just simply and oddly packed, virtually edge to edge, with a continuous stream of impeccably drafted letters. There were no breaks, no spaces between words or paragraphs.

Reilly scrutinized the sheets in stunned silence, then turned to her. She grinned, her smile lighting up a face smeared with the grime of the tunnels. 'They're Vance's,' she told him. 'The Templar manuscripts, from the Languedoc. But here's the thing. I can recognize Latin, and none of this makes sense. It's gibberish. That's why he needs the encoder. They're the key to what this is all about.'

His expression clouded over. 'But these pages, they're useless without the encoder.'

Tess had a self-satisfied glint in her eye. 'True, but... the encoder is also pointless without them.'

It was a moment she would always enjoy remembering: watching Reilly all conflicted and speechless. She knew he had to be delighted, but she also knew it was probably killing him that he couldn't show it. The last thing he wanted to do was encourage her recklessness. Instead, he just stared at her before climbing out of the car and calling over one of the other agents and asking for the papers to be photographed immediately. Moments later, an agent hurried over with a large camera, and Reilly handed him the sheets.

Tess watched as the photographer spread them out on the car's trunk and got to work. She then turned to see Reilly pick up a small two-way radio and get updated on the situation in the tunnels. There was something attractive about the urgency with which he went about his work. As she watched him mumbling cryptically into the radio, he glanced over at her, and she thought she spied a faint smile there.

'I need to go down there,' he told her after he signed off. 'They've found your two friends.'

'What about Vance?'

'No sign of him.' He clearly wasn't happy with that. 'I'll get someone to take you home.'

'No hurry,' she told him. Which wasn't true. She was desperate to get out of her filthy, wet clothes and stand under the shower for hours, but not before the photographer was finished. She was even more desperate to take a look at the documents that had started all this.

Reilly walked away, leaving her in his car. She watched him chat to a couple of other agents before they all headed toward the station entrance.

Abruptly, her thoughts were interrupted by her cellphone. The caller ID displayed her home number.

'Tess, dear, it's me.' It was Eileen.

'Mom. I'm sorry, I should have called you.'

'Called me? Why? Is anything wrong?'

Tess breathed out with relief. There was no reason for her mother to be worried about her. The FBI would have been careful not to alarm her if they'd called to find out where Tess was. 'No, of course not. What's up?'

'I was just wondering what time you'd be home. Your friend's already here.'

Tess felt a sudden chill shoot up her spine. 'My friend?'

'Yes,' her mother chirped. 'He's such a lovely man. Here, have a word with him, dear. And don't be too late. I've asked him to stay for dinner.'

Tess heard the phone changing hands, and then a newly familiar voice came on.

'Tess, darling. It's Bill. Bill Vance.'

CHAPTER 39

Tess froze in her seat, a knot the size of a fist forming in her throat. He was there, in her very own house. With her mother. And – *Kim?*

She turned away from the car door, clasping the phone tightly.

'What are you –'

'I thought you'd be here already,' he interjected calmly. 'I didn't get the time wrong, did I? Your message said it was rather urgent.'

Message? Tess's mind was racing. *He's in my house and he's playing games.* An anger swelled inside her. 'If you hurt them, I swear –'

'No, no, no,' he interrupted, 'it's not a problem. But I really can't stay too long. Much as I'd love to take up your lovely mother's invitation and have dinner with you all, I have to get back up to Connecticut. You said you had something for me. Something you wanted me to have a look at.'

Of course. The papers. He wants his papers back. She realized he didn't want to cause her mom or Kim any distress. He was posing as a friend, and was acting accordingly. Her mother wouldn't know anything was wrong. *Good. Let's keep it that way.*

'Tess?' he asked with disturbing serenity. 'Are you still there?'

'Yes. You want me to bring you the documents.'

'That would be great.'

Her mind flashed on her wallet, lying among the clutter on the floor of Vance's cellar, and she chided herself for not retrieving it. She looked out the car window nervously. Only the photographer was near, still taking pictures of the documents. Feeling a constriction in her chest, Tess took a deep breath and turned away from the photographer. 'I'm on my way. Please, don't do anything –'

'Of course not,' he chortled. 'I'll wait for you then. Is anyone else joining us?'

Tess frowned. 'No.'

'Perfect.' He paused for a moment. Tess wondered what he was doing. 'It'll be nice to spend some time and get to know them a bit better,' he continued. 'Kim is such a delightful little girl.'

So she was there after all. *That bastard*. He lost his daughter, now he's threatening mine.

'I'll come alone, don't worry,' Tess said firmly.

'Don't be long.'

She heard the phone click off, and for a moment she continued to hold the cellphone to her ear, running through the conversation again, trying to come to terms with what was happening.

She had a huge decision to make. *Do I tell Reilly?* She knew the answer to that: of course. Anyone who'd ever watched a TV show knew that, regardless of whatever a kidnapper said, you called the cops. You always called the cops. But that was TV, and this was real life. This was about her family, in the hands of a demolished man. Much as she wanted to tell Reilly, she didn't want to risk triggering some kind of hostage situation. Not given the state of mind Vance was in.

Grasping at straws, she tried to convince herself he wouldn't hurt them. He hadn't hurt her, had he? He was even apologetic about what he'd done to her. But now, she had crossed him, and she had his documents, the ones that were crucial to his mission. The documents, as Reilly had rightly put it, that people had died for.

She couldn't risk it. Her family was in harm's way.

She sneaked another look at the photographer. He was done. Still holding the cellphone to her ear, she edged toward him. 'Yes,' she said loudly, into the dead line. 'He's just finished photographing them.' She nodded to the photographer, dredging up a smile. 'Sure, I'll bring them right over,' she continued. 'You go ahead and start setting up the equipment.'

Clicking the phone shut, she addressed the photographer. 'Are you sure they'll come out?'

Her question surprised him. 'I hope so. It's what I'm paid for.'

She rolled up the papers as he reflexively moved away from them. 'I've got to race these over to the lab.' There was always a lab involved. She just hoped it sounded remotely credible. She glanced at the camera and added, 'Reilly wants those shots developed fast. Can you do that for him?'

'Sure, it's not a problem – given that they're digital,' he deadpanned.

Tess grimaced at her error as she walked as confidently as she could back to Reilly's car, resisting the urge to run. When she got to the driver's door, she glanced inside and saw that the key was still there, where she had seen Reilly leave it. She got in and flicked the ignition.

She scanned the faces at the scene, searching for Reilly, hoping not to see him. He wasn't around, nor was his partner. She nursed the car out of its double-parked spot and, slowly, navigated through the other sedans and police cars, inching forward, smiling sheepishly at the couple of officers who waved her through, hoping the sheer terror inside her wasn't breaking through to the surface.

Once she was clear, she pulled away, checking the rearview mirror, and, moments later, she was speeding up the street, headed for Westchester.

CHAPTER 40

As she pulled into the driveway outside her house, Tess misjudged the curb and hit it hard before squealing to a halt.

Sitting there, paralyzed with fear, she looked at her hands. They were trembling, and her breath was coming short and fast. She struggled to compose herself. She had to be calm about this. *Come on, Tess. Keep it together.* If she could just manage that, maybe, just maybe, she and Vance could each get what they wanted.

She got out of the car and suddenly regretted her decision not to tell Reilly about what had happened. She would have still been able to come here, while he set up... what? A SWAT team, men with guns and megaphones all around the house, bellowing 'Come out with your hands up'? Hours of fraught hostage negotiations before the inevitable and highly risky – however minutely planned – assault? Her imagination was getting the better of her. She tried to stay focused on the reality around her. No, maybe her choice had been the right one after all.

In any case, it was too late now.

She was here.

Walking up to the door, she suddenly hesitated. She could imagine what had happened here. Vance would have rung the bell, spoken with Eileen. A few words about Oliver Chaykin, about Tess, and Eileen would have been completely disarmed, and probably charmed too.

If only she had told Reilly.

Sliding her key into the lock, she opened the door and walked into the living room. The scene that greeted her was surreal. Vance was there, sitting with her mother on the sofa, chatting amiably, sipping a cup of tea. Tess could hear music coming from Kim's room. Her daughter was upstairs.

Eileen's mouth dropped when she saw the disheveled state her daughter was in. She jumped out of her seat. 'Oh my God, Tess, what happened to you?'

'Are you alright?' Vance stood up, sounding genuinely surprised.

He has the nerve to ask that. Tess stared at him, doing her utmost to keep her rage, which had by now overwhelmed any feelings of fear that she had, under control.

'I'm fine.' She managed to find a smile. 'There was a leak in the street outside the office and this truck drove straight through the puddle just as I was standing there, and, well... You don't want to know.'

Eileen took hold of her daughter's arm. 'You've got to get changed, dear, you'll catch cold.' She turned to Vance. 'You'll excuse us, won't you, Bill?'

Tess stared at Vance. He was just standing there, radiating warmth and concern.

'Actually, I'm afraid I really should be going.' His eyes bored into Tess's. 'If you want to give me those papers, I'll be on my way. Besides, I'm sure the last thing you want is a guest in the house right now.'

Tess stood there, glaring at him. The silence was deafening. Eileen looked at Vance, then at Tess, who could tell her mother was clearly sensing something uncomfortable in the room. She quickly snapped out of it and smiled at Vance.

'Of course. I have them right here.' She reached into her bag and pulled out the manuscripts. She handed them to him. He reached out to take them, and for a few seconds, they were both holding on to them.

'Thanks. I'll get to work on them as soon as I can.'

Tess forced another smile. 'That would be great.'

Vance turned to Eileen. He took her hand and cupped it in his. 'It's been a pleasure.'

Eileen relaxed and blushed, her face beaming from the compliment. Tess felt hugely relieved that Eileen was spared the truth of who Vance really was. For now, at least. She turned back to Vance. She couldn't read his look. He was studying her.

'I should be going.' He nodded at Tess. 'Thanks again.'

'Don't mention it.'

He stopped at the door and turned to Tess.

'I'll see you soon.' And with that, he walked out the door.

Tess left Eileen and stood at the door, watching him drive off. Eileen joined her.

'He's such a nice man. Why didn't you tell me you knew him? He told me he's worked with Oliver.'

'Come on, Mom,' Tess said in a low voice, as she quietly shut the door.

Her hands were still shaking.

CHAPTER 41

In the long mirror in her bathroom, Tess finally saw herself. She'd never been as dirty, bedraggled, or pale. Even though tremors of tension still pulsed through her legs, she resisted the urge to sit down. After all that had happened today, if she did sit down, she knew she probably wouldn't be able to get up again for a while. She also knew the day wasn't over yet. Reilly was on his way. He had called shortly after Vance had left and he was now rushing over. Even though he sounded reasonably calm, she knew he was furious with her. She would have some serious explaining to do.

Again.

Only this time would be a bit more difficult. She would have to tell Reilly why she didn't trust in him enough to ask for his help.

She stared at the stranger in the mirror. The confident, lively blonde was gone. In her place was a wreck, both physically and mentally. Self-doubt was besieging her mind. She thought back to the day's events, questioning her every move and kicking herself for putting her mother and daughter in danger.

It's not a game, Tess. You've got to stop doing this. You've got to stop now.

As she got undressed, she felt the onset of tears. She had resisted it when she went to hug Kim after Vance had left. She had resisted the nervous tears of laughter when Kim had pushed her back, saying 'Ew, Mom, you stink. You need a shower big time.' She resisted it on the phone with Reilly, all the while making sure her mom and Kim didn't overhear her conversation with him. Thinking about it, she couldn't remember the last time she had cried, but right now, she couldn't help it. She felt awful, shivering as much from the fear as from the 'what if' worst case scenarios she was imagining.

Apart from sluicing off the dirt and the smell, she used the time in the shower to make some decisions. Among them was that she owed Kim and Eileen something else.

Safety.

An idea came to her.

Wearing only a bathrobe and with her hair still dripping, Tess found Eileen in the kitchen. 'I've been thinking about our plans to stay with Aunt Hazel this summer,' Tess said without preamble. Hazel was her mother's sister. She lived on a small ranch just outside Prescott, Arizona, alone except for a few dozen assorted animals.

'What about it?'

Tess pressed on without missing a beat. 'I think we should go there now, for Easter.'

'Why on earth...' Her mother broke off, then said 'Tess, what aren't you telling me?'

'Nothing,' Tess lied, flashing back to the other man who had come looking for Vance in the cellar, the gunshot, and his anguished cry.

'But –'

Again, Tess interrupted her mother. 'We all need a break. Look, I'll come too, okay? It'll take me a few days to clear my calendar and arrange it with the office. But I want you and Kim to go tomorrow.'

'Tomorrow?'

'Why not? You've been dying to go, and Kim can just start her Easter vacation a few days early. I'll book some flights, be easier this way, we'll miss the Easter rush,' Tess insisted.

'Tess.' Her mother's tone was angry and firm. 'What's this all about?'

Tess smiled nervously at her mother's annoyance. She would apologize later. 'It's important, Mom,' she said quietly.

Eileen studied her. She had always been able to read her daughter, and today was no exception. 'What's going on? Are you in danger? I want an honest answer, now. Are you?'

She couldn't lie about this. 'I don't think so. What I do know is that in Arizona,' she said evasively, 'there'll be absolutely nothing to worry about.'

Her mother frowned. It obviously wasn't the answer she was hoping for. 'Well then come with us tomorrow.'

'I can't.' Her look and her tone left no room for argument.

Eileen breathed in deep, studying her. 'Tess –'

'I can't, mom.'

Eileen nodded unhappily. 'But you'll follow us there. You promise.'

'I promise. I'll be with you in a couple of days.'

All at once, she felt an overflowing sense of relief.

Then the doorbell rang.

'You should have told me, Tess. You should have told me.' Reilly was livid. 'We could have picked him up after he'd left the house, we could have put a tail on him, there's a number of ways we could have handled this.' He shook his head. 'We could have had him and put an end to this thing.'

They talked in her backyard, away from her mom and from Kim. She had asked him to be discreet and not show up with guns blazing, assuring him that they were all safe. With Aparo keeping an eye out front and waiting for the local PD squad car to show up, Reilly had quickly ascertained that the situation was, as she had said, under control and that the danger had indeed passed.

She was wearing a white toweling bathrobe, her long hair darker from being wet, her legs bare beneath the robe. Sitting under a large mallow tree, and despite the frustration and anger she could see she had caused in Reilly, she felt oddly calm. His presence had a lot to do with it. Twice in the same day, she had felt threatened in a way she had never experienced before, and twice he had been there for her.

She glanced away, collecting her thoughts, letting his own turmoil settle a bit, before glancing up at him. 'I'm sorry, I really am... I just didn't know what else to do. I guess I wasn't thinking straight. I had all these visions of SWAT teams and hostage negotiators and...'

'– and you panicked. I understand that, it's perfectly normal. I mean, the guy was threatening your daughter, your mom, but still...' He breathed out in frustration, shaking his head again.

'I know. You're right. I'm sorry.'

He looked at her.

He hated the fact that she'd been in danger, hated that her daughter had been too. And he also knew he couldn't blame her. She wasn't an FBI agent; she was an archaeologist and a mother. He couldn't expect her to think the same way he did, to respond to such an extreme situation coldly and rationally. Not when her daughter was concerned. Not after the day she'd had.

After a long moment, he spoke. 'Look, you did what you thought was best for your family, and no one can blame you for that. I would have probably done the same thing. The main thing is you're all safe. That's all that really matters.'

Tess's face brightened. She nodded, somewhat guiltily, flashing back to Vance, standing there in her living room. 'Still... I gave him back his papers.'

'And we still have the copies,' Reilly reminded her, his expression softening somewhat, before glancing at his watch. 'Alright. I'm sure you want to get some rest, so I'll get out of your hair. I'll have a squad car keep an eye on the house. Just make sure you lock up after I leave.'

'I'll be fine.' She was suddenly aware of how vulnerable she was. How vulnerable they all were. 'I don't have anything else he needs.'

'You sure about that?' He was only half joking.

'Scout's honor.'

There it was again. He really knew how to make her relax.

'Okay. If you're up to it,' he said, 'I'd really like you to come downtown in the morning. I think it would be really useful to go over everything again in detail with the rest of the team, get all our ducks in a row.'

'Not a problem. Just let me get Mom and Kim on a plane first.'

'Good. I'll see you tomorrow.'

Her eyes met his. 'Yeah.' She got up to walk him back to the house.

He had taken a few steps when he stopped and turned to her. 'You know, there's one thing I didn't get a chance to ask you back in the city.'

'What's that?'

'Why'd you take them?' He paused. 'The documents. I mean, you must have been desperate to get out of there... and yet you put that thought on hold long enough to grab the papers.'

She wasn't sure what had gone on in her mind. It all seemed a blur. 'I don't know,' she managed. 'They were just lying there.'

'I know, but still... I guess I'm just surprised, that's all. I would have thought the only thing on your mind would have been to get the hell out of there as fast as possible.'

Tess glanced away. She knew what he was getting at.

'Are you gonna be able to let go of this thing,' he insisted, 'or am I gonna have to lock you up for your own safety?' He was dead serious. 'How important is this for you, Tess?'

She half smiled. 'This thing, it's... there's something about it. That manuscript, its whole history... I feel I need to be there, I need to find out what it's all really about. You've got to understand something,' she pressed. 'Archaeology, it's... it's not the most generous of careers. Not everybody gets a Tutankhamen or a Troy. Fourteen years I was out there, digging and shoveling in the most godforsaken, mosquito infested corners of this planet, and all the time I kept hoping that I'd get a shot at something like this, not just obscure little pieces of pottery or a partially preserved mosaic, but something big, you know? It's every archaeologist's dream.

The real deal, one for the history books, something I could take Kim to see at the Met one day and point to proudly and say, "I discovered that".' She paused, watching for his reaction. 'This must be more than just a routine case for you too, isn't it?'

He took in what she said before lightening up. 'Nah, we get wackos on horses trashing museums every week. That's what I hate about this job. The routine. It's a killer.' His face turned serious again. 'Tess, you keep forgetting something here. This isn't just some academic challenge, it's not just about the manuscript and what it means... it's a murder investigation where a lot of people have died.'

'I know.'

'Let's get them behind bars first. Then you can figure out what they were after. Come in tomorrow. Walk us through what you know, then let us get on with it. If we need help, you'll be the first to know. And, I don't know, if you want some kind of exclusive deal should anything –'

'No, it's not like that. It's just...' She realized that nothing she said would make him change his mind.

'You're gonna have to let go of it, Tess. Please. I need you to let go of it.'

She was moved by the way he said it.

'Will you do that?' he continued. 'It's really not a game I want you playing at right now.'

'I'll try,' she nodded.

He studied her, then let out a small chortle and shook his head.

They both knew she had no choice in the matter.

She was into it hook, line and sinker.

CHAPTER 42

Shifting in his chair in the stark, glass-fronted conference room at Federal Plaza, De Angelis studied Tess Chaykin carefully. A very smart lady, he thought. That much was obvious. Of more concern was that it appeared she was also fearless. It was an intriguing yet potentially dangerous combination. But played correctly, it could also prove to be very useful. She seemed to know which questions to ask and what leads to follow.

Glancing at the others around the table, De Angelis listened to her account of her abduction and her subsequent escape. Discreetly, he gently massaged the place where Vance's bullet had grazed his leg. It stung with a burning twinge, especially when he walked, but the painkillers he was taking dampened the sensation to a point where he hoped any hint of a limp wouldn't be noticeable.

Her words made him flash back to the confrontation with Vance in the darkened crypt. He felt an anger swell inside him. He chided himself for the way he had allowed Vance to slip away. A feeble, tortured history professor, at that. *Inexcusable.* He wouldn't let it happen again. Thinking about it, it occurred to him that, had he succeeded against Vance, he might have had to deal with her too, which would have been messy. He had nothing against her, at least not yet. Not as long as her motives didn't prove antagonistic to his mission.

He needed to understand her better. *Why is she doing this? What is she really after,* he wondered. He would have to look into her background and, more importantly, her position concerning certain issues of paramount importance.

As she finished her story, De Angelis noted something else too. It was the way that Reilly was looking at her. There was something there, he mused. *Interesting.* The agent clearly saw her as something more than an aid to the investigation. Not surprising on Reilly's part, but was it reciprocated?

He definitely needed to keep a close eye on her.

When Tess was done, Reilly stepped in, calling up an image of the ruins of the church from his laptop. It popped up on the large flat panel facing the conference table. 'That's where he was holding you,' he told her. 'The Church of the Ascension.'

Tess looked surprised. 'It's burnt down.'

'Yeah, they're still working on raising the funds to rebuild it.'

'The smell, the dampness... it definitely fits, but...' She seemed thrown. 'He was living in the cellar of a burnt down church.' She paused, trying to correlate the picture in front of her with her recollection of Vance and what he had said. She looked at Reilly. 'But he hated the Church.'

'This wasn't just any church. It burnt down five years ago. Arson investigators didn't find anything suspicious at the time, even though the parish priest died in the blaze.'

She thought back, conjuring up the name of the priest Vance had mentioned. 'Father McKay?'

'Yes.'

Reilly looked at her. It was obvious they'd reached the same conclusion.

'The priest Vance blamed for the death of his wife.' Her imagination was galloping ahead now, and the images it was kicking up were horrific ones.

'And the dates match. The fire happened three weeks after he buried her.' He turned to Jansson. 'We're going to have to get that case reopened.'

Jansson nodded. Reilly turned to Tess, who seemed lost in thought.

'What is it?'

'I don't know,' she said as if emerging from a fog. 'It's just difficult thinking about him in such contradictory terms.

191

He's this charming, erudite professor on the one hand, and then the polar opposite, someone who's capable of such violence...'

Aparo stepped in. 'Unfortunately, it's not uncommon. It's like the quiet, friendly neighbor with body parts in his freezer. They're usually much more dangerous than the guys busting up bars every night.'

Reilly took over again. 'We need to understand what he's after, or what he thinks he's after. Tess, you were the first to see the link between Vance and the Templars, and if you can take us through what you know so far, maybe we can figure out what his next move's likely to be.'

'Where do you want me to start?'

Reilly shrugged. 'The beginning?'

'It's a long story.'

'Well keep us up at ten thousand feet. Anything looks interesting, we'll go into more detail.'

She briefly marshaled her thoughts before she began.

She told them about the Templars' origins, about the nine knights showing up in Jerusalem; about their nine years in seclusion at the Temple, the theories about them digging something up in that time; about their subsequent, somewhat inexplicable rapid rise to power; about their victories in battle, and their ultimate defeat at Acre. She walked them through the Templars' return to Europe, their power and their arrogance, and how it all grated on the king of France and on his submissive pope, and about their ultimate downfall.

'With the support of his lackey, Pope Clement V, the king starts a wave of persecutions, rounds up the Templars, accuses them of heresy. Within a few years, they're wiped out. Mostly meeting extremely painful deaths.'

Aparo looked confused. 'Hold on, heresy? How could they justify it? I thought these guys were the defenders of the Cross, the pope's chosen ones.'

'These were extremely religious times we're talking about,' Tess continued. 'The devil was very much alive in people's minds at the time.' She paused and glanced around the table. The silence egged her on. 'Claims were made that when knights were received into the order, they did so by spitting and even urinating on the Cross, and by denying Jesus Christ. And that wasn't all they were accused of. There were also claims that they worshipped a strange demon called Baphomet and that they engaged in sodomy. Basically, the usual claims of occult worship the Vatican wheeled out whenever it wanted to get rid of any competition in the religious sweepstakes.'

She flicked a glance at De Angelis. He kept his expression benignly interested, but said nothing.

'During the course of these final years,' Tess continued, 'they confessed to a lot of these accusations, but their confessions hold as much water as those made during the Spanish Inquisition. The threat of having a red-hot spike inserted into you is enough to make anyone admit to anything. Especially when all around you, the threat is being carried out on your friends.'

De Angelis took off his glasses and wiped them on the sleeve of his jacket, then replaced them and nodded somberly at Tess. It was very clear where her sympathies lay.

Tess flipped the papers back into the folder. 'Hundreds of Knights Templar all across France were rounded up and put through this charade. When there was no retaliation, dozens of bishops and abbots jumped on the bandwagon, and pretty soon the Knights Templar were on the run. Only here's the thing: their treasure was never found.' She told them about the stories of caskets of gold and jewels being hidden in caves or in lakes all across Europe, and about the Templars' ships fleeing from the port of La Rochelle the night before that fateful Friday the thirteenth.

'Is that what this is all about?' Jansson held up his copy of the coded manuscript. 'A lost treasure?'

'Nice to see some good old-fashioned greed making a comeback,' Aparo snorted. 'Makes a change from the misguided wackos we're usually hunting down.'

De Angelis leaned forward, clearing his throat and glancing at Jansson. 'Their treasure was never recovered, that much is generally accepted.'

Jansson tapped his fingers on the papers. 'So this manuscript could be some kind of treasure map that Vance is now able to read.'

'That doesn't make sense,' Tess interjected, suddenly feeling out of place as the faces around the table turned to face her. She turned to Reilly, before continuing, propped up by what she read as a supportive look. 'If Vance was after money, there was a lot more he could have taken from the Met.'

'True,' Aparo answered, 'but the stuff on show would be virtually impossible to sell. And from what you've told us, the treasure of the Templars has got to be worth a lot more than what was on show, plus it can be sold freely without fear of prosecution since it won't have been stolen, just found.'

The agents were nodding in agreement, but De Angelis noted that Tess looked doubtful, although she appeared to be wary of expressing her thoughts. 'You don't appear to be too convinced, Miss Chaykin.'

She grimaced with unease. 'It's clear Vance wanted the encoder to be able to read the manuscript he found.'

'The key to the treasure's location,' Jansson confirmed, half questioning.

'Probably,' she said, turning to him. 'But it depends on how you define treasure.'

'What else could it be?' De Angelis was hoping to see if she had gained any intimation from Vance.

She shook her head. 'I'm not sure.'

That was good, if she was telling the truth, De Angelis thought.

He hoped she was.

But then she dashed that hope and continued. 'Vance seemed to be after something else than just money. It's like he's possessed, he's a man on a mission.' She walked them through the more esoteric theories of the Templar treasure, including the notion of their being part of some cabal guarding Jesus's bloodline. She glanced at De Angelis as she was saying it. He was staring at her blankly, giving nothing away.

Once she'd finished, he waded in. 'Putting all the entertaining conjecture aside,' he said as he flashed her a slightly condescending smile, 'you're saying he's a man who's out for revenge, a man on a personal crusade of sorts.'

'Yes.'

'Well,' De Angelis continued with the calm, soothing manner of a worldly college professor, 'money, especially a lot of it, can be a phenomenal tool. Crusades, whether in the twelfth century or today, cost a lot of money, don't they?' He looked around the table.

Tess didn't answer.

The question hung briefly until Reilly stepped in. 'What I don't get is this. We know Vance blames the priest and, by inference, the Church for his wife's death.'

'His wife and daughter,' Tess corrected him.

'Right. And now he's got hold of this manuscript that he says was, I don't know, scary enough to turn a priest's hair white within minutes of being told about it. And we all seem to agree that this manuscript, which is written in code, is a Templar document, right?'

'What's your point?' Jansson interjected.

'I thought the Templars and the Church were on the same side. I mean, the way I understand it, these guys were the defenders of the Church. They fought bloody wars in the name of the Vatican for over two hundred years. I can imagine their descendants being ticked off at the Church for what happened to them, but the theories you're talking about,' he said as he looked at Tess, 'are about something they supposedly discovered two hundred years before they were persecuted. Why would they have anything in their possession, from day one, that would worry the Church?'

'It could help explain why they were burnt at the stake,' Amelia Gaines offered.

'Two hundred years later? And there's another thing,' Reilly continued, turning to Tess now. 'These guys went from defending the Cross to desecrating it. Why would they do that? Their initiation ceremonies just don't make sense.'

'Well, that's what they were accused of,' Tess said. 'Doesn't mean they actually did these things. It was a standard accusation at the time. The king used the very same charges a few years earlier to get rid of a previous pope, Boniface VIII.'

'Okay, but it still doesn't make sense,' Reilly went on. 'Why would they spend all that time fighting for the Church if they were hiding some secret that the Vatican didn't want exposed?'

De Angelis finally rejoined the discussion in his usual dulcet tone. 'If I may... I think that if you're going to entertain such flights of fancy, you might as well consider another possibility that hasn't yet been discussed.'

The gathered group turned to face him. He paused, letting the anticipation build before proceeding calmly.

'The whole conjecture about our Lord's bloodline comes up every few years and never fails to generate interest, whether it's in the realm of fiction or in the halls of academia. The Holy Grail, the San Graal or the Sang Real, call it what you will. But, as Miss Chaykin has very articulately explained,' he pointed out, nodding graciously at her, 'a lot of what happened to the Templars can simply be explained by that most basic of human traits, namely,' turning now to glance at Aparo, 'greed. Not only had they gotten too powerful, but without the defense of the Holy Land to keep them occupied, they were now back in Europe – mostly in France – and they were armed, they were powerful, and they were very, very wealthy. The king of France felt threatened, and rightfully so. Being virtually bankrupt and heavily indebted to them, he desperately coveted their wealth. He was a loathsome man by any account; I would be inclined to agree with Miss Chaykin on the whole affair of their arrest. I wouldn't read too much into their accusations. They were undoubtedly innocent, true believers, and Soldiers of Christ to the death. But the accusations gave the king the excuse to get rid of them, and by doing so, he killed two birds with one stone. He got rid of his rivals and got hold of their treasure. Or at least tried to, given that it was never found.'

'This is physical treasure we're talking about now, not some kind of "esoteric knowledge?"' Jansson asked.

'Well, I like to think so, but then I've never been blessed with a great sense of fantasy, although I do understand the appeal of all the colorful, alternative conspiracy theories. But the physical and the esoteric could be related in another way. You see, a lot of the interest in the Templars stems from the fact that no one can unequivocally explain how they got to be so rich and so powerful in such a short time. I believe it's simply the result of the abundance of donations they received once their mission was widely publicized. But then, who knows? Perhaps they did find some buried secret that made them incredibly wealthy in record time. But what was it? Was it related to the mythical descendants of Christ, proof that our Lord fathered a child or two a thousand years earlier...' he scoffed lightly, 'or was it something much less controversial, but potentially far more lucrative?'

He waited, making sure they were all still following his line of thought.

'I'm talking about the secrets of alchemy, about the formula to turn ordinary metals,' he calmly announced, 'into gold.'

CHAPTER 43

The faces around the table were frozen in silence as De Angelis took them through a brief history of the arcane science.

The historical evidence supported his proposition. Alchemy was indeed introduced into Europe during the Crusades. The earliest alchemical works originated in the Middle East and were written in Arabic long before they were translated into Latin.

'The alchemists' experiments were based on Aristotle's theory of earth, air, fire, and water. They believed that everything was made up from a combination of these elements. They also believed that with the right dosage and method, these elements could each be transmuted into any of the others. Water could easily be turned into air by being boiled, and so on. And since everything on the planet was believed to be made up of a combination of earth, water, air, and fire, in theory at least, it was thought possible to transmute any starting material into anything one desired to create. And topping the list of desirables was, of course, gold.'

The monsignor explained how alchemy also functioned on a physiological level. Aristotle's four elements also manifested themselves in the four humors: phlegm, blood, bile, and black bile. In a healthy human, the humors were believed to be in balance. Illness was thought to arise from a deficiency or an excess of one of the humors. Alchemy evolved beyond the search for a recipe that would turn lead into gold. It promised to uncover the secrets to physiological transformations, from sickness to health, or from old age to youth. Furthermore, many alchemists also used the search for this formula as a metaphor for seeking moral perfection, believing that what could be accomplished in nature could also be realized in the heart and mind. In its spiritual guise, the Philosopher's Stone they sought was believed to be capable of causing a spiritual conversion as well as a physical one. Alchemy promised everything to whoever unlocked its secrets: wealth, longevity, even immortality.

In the twelfth century, however, alchemy was also mysterious and frightening to those who had never experienced it. Alchemists used strange instruments and mystical incantations; they employed cryptic symbolism and suggestive colors in their art. Aristotle's works were eventually banned. At the time, any science, as it was then called, was thought to be a challenge to the authority of the Church; a science that promised spiritual purification was a direct threat to the Church. 'Which,' De Angelis continued, 'could be another explanation for the Vatican allowing the Templars' persecution to proceed unchallenged.

'The timing, the location, the origin of it all, everything fits.' The monsignor glanced around the table. 'Now don't get me wrong,' he flashed a comforting smile. 'I'm not saying such a formula exists, although to me it's certainly no more of a stretch of the imagination than the other fanciful theories of the Templars' great secret that have been discussed around this table and elsewhere. What I'm simply saying is that a man who has lost touch with reality could easily *believe* that such a formula exists.'

Tess looked briefly at Reilly and hesitated before turning to face De Angelis. 'Why would Vance want to make gold?'

'You forget, the man is not thinking with the clearest of minds. You said so yourself, Miss Chaykin. One need only look at what happened at the Met to realize that. That was not a plan drawn up by a sane man. So once you keep in mind that the man isn't behaving rationally, anything's possible. It could be a means to an end. Financing to allow him to achieve whatever demented objective he's set himself.' He shrugged. 'This man, Vance... he's clearly delusional, and he's caught in the grip of some nonsensical treasure hunt. It seems to me like you have a madman on your hands, and whatever it is he's after, sooner or later, he's going to realize that he's been chasing a ghost, and I dread to think of how he's going to react when that realization hits.'

A disconcerting quiet descended on the table as the assembled few mulled over that sobering thought.

Jansson leaned forward. 'Whatever he thinks he's after, he doesn't seem to mind how many dead bodies it takes for him to get there, and we need to stop him. But it seems to me like the only thing we have to work with right now are these damn papers.' He was holding up the copy of the manuscript. 'If we could read it, it might tell us what his next move is.' He turned to Reilly. 'What's the NSA saying?'

'It's not looking good. I spoke to Terry Kendricks before coming in, and he's not optimistic.'

'Why not?'

'They know it's a basic polyalphabetic substitution cipher. Nothing too sophisticated. The military used it for decades, but code breaking is all about frequency of occurrence, about patterns; you spot repeated words, deduce what they are, and that gives you something to work off until you ultimately manage to figure out the mnemonic key and work your way back from there. In this case, they simply don't have enough material to work with. If the document were longer, or if they had other documents written in the same code, they'd be able to deduce the key pretty easily. But six pages is just too little to go on.'

Jansson's face bent inward. 'I don't believe this. Several billion dollars of funding and they still can't crack something a bunch of monks came up with seven hundred years ago?' He shrugged, breathing out through pursed lips for a long moment. 'All right. Then we forget about the damn manuscript and concentrate elsewhere. We need to go over everything we have and find a new tack.'

*

De Angelis was watching Tess. She said nothing. She glanced over at him, and something in her eyes told De Angelis that he hadn't convinced her, and that she sensed this was about something more than just funding a personal vendetta.

Yes indeed, De Angelis mused. *This woman is decidedly dangerous.* But for the time being, her potential usefulness outweighed the danger she posed.

For just how long, though, remained to be seen.

CHAPTER 44

'What station is that?'

Tess had agreed to an offer of a lift from Reilly and sitting in the car with him now, listening to the uplifting music, the setting sun peeping out from behind a cluster of graphite clouds and painting the horizon a dark pink, she was glad she accepted his offer.

She felt relaxed, and safe. More than that, she was finding that she liked being around him. There was something about his toughness, his incisive determination, his... honesty. It was plain to see. She knew she could trust him, which was more than could be said for most men she'd come across, her ex-husband a particularly stellar example of that sub-human breed. With her house empty now that Kim and her mom had flown to Arizona, she was looking forward to a warm bath and a glass of red wine; a pill would also be drafted in to guarantee a good night's sleep.

'It's a CD. The last track was from Willie and Lobo's *Caliente*. This one's Pat Metheny. It's one of my comps.' He shook his head slightly. 'Now there's something a guy should never confess to.'

'Why not?'

He grinned. 'You kidding me? Burning compilation CDs? Come on. A sure sign of way too much free time.'

'Oh, I don't know about that. It could also be the sign of someone who's quite particular and knows exactly what he likes.'

He nodded. 'I like that interpretation.'

'I had a feeling you would.' She smiled and looked ahead for a moment, soaking in the subtle combination of the electric guitar and the complex orchestrations that were the group's trademark. 'It's good.'

'Yeah?'

'Really soothing and... inspirational. Plus we're ten min-utes into it and my ears haven't gone numb, which is a nice change from the carnage Kim normally subjects them to.'

'That bad, huh?

'Don't get me started. And the lyrics, my God... I thought I was a hip mom, but some of those "songs", if you can even call them that...'

Reilly grinned. 'What's the world coming to?'

'Hey, you're not exactly the king of hip hop either.'

'Does Steely Dan count?'

'I don't think so.'

He put on a mock dejected look. 'Bummer.'

Tess looked ahead. 'I'm telling you, it's a *New Frontier* out there,' she deadpanned, watching him from the corner of her eye, waiting for it, then grinning when she saw that it clicked with him, enjoying catching him off guard with the title of the Donald Fagen track. He gave her a small, impressed nod, and their eyes met. She felt her face warm slightly when her cellphone decided to come to life.

Annoyed by the intrusion, she fished it out of her bag and looked at it. The screen wasn't displaying the caller's number. She decided to answer it and immediately regretted it.

'Hey. It's me. Doug.'

If she wasn't normally keen to talk to her ex-husband, right now was a particularly unwelcome moment. Avoiding Reilly's eyes, she lowered her voice.

'What do you want?' she asked flatly.

'I know you were at the Met that night, and I wanted to know if there was anything –'

There it was. With Doug, there was always an angle. She cut him off. 'I can't talk about it, alright,' she lied, 'I've been specifically asked by the FBI not to talk to the press.'

'You have? That's terrific.' *Terrific? Why was that terrific?* 'No one else has been told that,' he enthused. 'So why is that, huh? What do you know that they don't?'

The lie had backfired. 'Forget it, Doug.'

'Don't be like that.' The smarmy charm reared its ugly head. 'This is me, remember.'

As if she could forget. 'No,' she repeated.

'Tess, give me a break.'

'I'm hanging up now.'

'Come on, baby –'

She snapped the phone shut, slammed it into her purse with a whole lot more force than was necessary, then exhaled heavily and stared ahead.

After a couple of minutes, she forced herself to relax her neck and shoulder muscles, and without looking at Reilly, said, 'Sorry. My ex-husband.'

'I figured. A little something I picked up in Quantico.'

She managed a small chortle. 'You don't miss a thing, do you?'

He glanced at her. 'Not usually. Unless it's about the Templars, in which case there's this really annoying archaeologist who always seems to be a couple of steps ahead of the rest of us laymen.'

She smiled. 'Don't stop on my account.'

He looked at her again, and saw that she was looking back. He held her eyes a moment longer than before.

He was definitely glad she'd accepted his offer to drive her home.

The road lights were on by the time they got to her street, and the sight of her house was enough to bring all the fears and worries of the last couple of days flooding back.

Vance was here, she shuddered. *He was in my house.*

They drove past the police cruiser parked down the road from her house. Reilly flicked a small wave to the cop sitting inside, who waved back, recognizing Tess from his briefing.

When they reached her house, Reilly pulled into the driveway and cut the engine. She glanced at the house, and felt uneasy. She wondered whether or not to ask him in for a moment before the words spilled out of her mouth. 'Do you want to come in?'

He hesitated, then said, 'Sure.' There was nothing flirtatious about his tone. 'It'd be good to take a quick look around.'

At the front door, he held out his hand for the key and went in first.

It was unnaturally quiet and Tess followed him into the living room, automatically switching on all the lights, then the television, lowering the sound. The set was tuned to the WB, Kim's favorite channel. Tess didn't bother changing it.

Reilly looked at her, somewhat surprised.

'I do it when I'm alone,' she explained. 'Creates the illusion of company.'

'You'll be fine.' His tone was comforting. 'I'll check the rooms,' he continued before hesitating, then added, 'Is that okay?'

The hesitation must be because he would be going into her bedroom, she thought. She was grateful for his concern and pleased at his sensitivity.

'Sure.'

He nodded and as he went out of the room, Tess dropped onto the couch, pulled the phone over and dialed her aunt's house in Prescott, Arizona. Hazel picked up after three rings. She had just arrived home, having collected Kim and Eileen from the airport at Phoenix and taken them out for dinner. Both of them, Hazel told her, were fine. Tess talked briefly with her mother while Hazel went to fetch Kim who was in the stables, checking out the horses. Eileen sounded a whole lot less worried than she had been. Tess guessed that it must be due to a combination of being calmed by her affable and easygoing sister and the distance the day's traveling had put between her and New York. When Kim came on, she was all lit up over the prospect of going riding tomorrow and appeared not to be missing her mother at all.

As she said goodnight and hung up the phone, Reilly came back into the room.

He looked as tired as she felt. 'It's all clear, as expected. I really don't think you have anything to worry about any more.'

'I'm sure you're right. Thanks for taking a look anyway.'

'Not a problem.' He took one last look and nodded to her, seeming to hover for the briefest of moments. Tess picked up on it.

'I'm sure we could both use a drink,' she said as she got up and led him into the kitchen. 'How about a beer, or a glass of wine, maybe?'

'No,' he smiled. 'Thanks anyway.'

'Oh, I forgot, you're on duty, right? Coffee then?'

'No, it's not that. It's just...' He seemed reticent to go on. 'What?'

He paused before adding, 'It's Lent.'

'Lent? Really?'

'Yeah.'

'And I'm guessing you're not doing it as an excuse to lose weight, are you?'

He just shook his head.

'Forty days without booze. Wow.' She blushed. 'Okay, that didn't come out right, did it? I don't want you to get the wrong idea, it's not like I'm ripe for AA or anything.'

'Too late. The image is burnt in.'

'Great.' She walked over to the fridge and poured herself a glass of white wine. 'It's funny, it's just that I didn't think anyone did that anymore. Especially not in this town.'

'Actually, it's an obvious place to live a... a spiritual life.'

'You're kidding, right? New York City?'

'No. It's the perfect place for it. Think about it. It's not like there aren't enough moral or ethical challenges to deal with here. The differences between right and wrong, between good and bad, they're pretty clear in this town. You have to make a choice.'

Tess was still processing his revelation. 'So how religious are you? If you don't mind my asking.'

'No, that's fine.'

She grinned. 'Just tell me you don't hike out to some cow-field in the middle of nowhere because someone there thinks he saw the Virgin appear up in the clouds or something?'

'No, not recently anyway. I'm guessing you're not a particularly religious person.'

'Well... let's just say I'd need to see something a bit more conclusive before you'd get me shlepping halfway across the country for something like that.'

'Something a bit more conclusive... You're saying you'd need a sign. An irrefutable, substantiated miracle?'

'Something like that.'

He didn't say anything. He just smiled.

'What?'

'See, the thing about miracles is... if you have faith, you don't need them, and if you're a doubter, well then no miracle is ever enough.'

'Oh, I can think of a few things that would convince me just fine.'

'Maybe they're there. Maybe you're just not aware of them.'

Which really threw her. 'Okay, stop. You're a badge-carrying FBI agent and you're telling me you really believe in miracles?'

He shrugged, then said, 'Let's say you're walking down the street and you're about to cross the road and suddenly, for no particular reason, right there as you're about to step off the curb, you stop. And just then, in that split second you stop, a bus or a truck zooms right past you, inches from your face, right where you would've been if you hadn't paused. You don't know why, but something made you stop. Something saved your life. And you know what? You would have probably told someone, "It's a miracle I'm still alive." To me, that's just what it is. A miracle.'

'You call it a miracle. I call it chance.'

'Faith is easy when you're standing in front of a miracle. The real test of any faith is when there aren't any signs.'

She was still thrown, not expecting this side to him. She wasn't sure how she felt about it, although she was predisposed not to be a huge fan of his line of thinking. 'You're serious.'

'Absolutely.'

She studied him as she mulled it over. 'Okay, tell me something,' she then said. 'How does faith – I mean real, sincere faith like yours – how does that sit with being an investigator?'

'What do you mean?'

She had a suspicion that he already knew what she meant; that he'd confronted it before. 'An investigator can't take anything or anyone on trust. You can't take anything for granted. You deal in facts, in proof. Beyond a reasonable doubt and all that.'

'Yes.' He didn't seem at all thrown by her question.

'So how do you reconcile that with your faith?'

'My faith is in God, not man.'

'Come on. It can't be that simple.'

'Actually,' he said with disconcerting calm, 'it is.'

She shook her head, a faint, self-deprecating smile lighting up her face. 'You know, I like to think I can scope people out pretty well, but I had you all wrong. I didn't think you would be... you know, a believer. Is that how you were brought up?'

'No, my parents weren't particularly religious. It kinda happened later.'

She waited for him to elaborate. He didn't. She suddenly felt embarrassed. 'Look, I'm sorry, this is obviously something highly personal and here I am tactlessly bombarding you with all these questions.'

'It's not a problem, really. It's just... well, my dad died when I was pretty young and I went through a tough time, and the one person who was there for me was my parish priest. He helped me find my way through it, and after that I guess it kinda stuck. That's all.'

Regardless of what he said, she sensed he didn't want to go into too much more detail, which she understood. 'Okay.'

'What about you? I take it you didn't have a particularly religious upbringing?'

'Not really. I don't know, I guess the atmosphere in the house was academic, archaeological, scientific, and it all made it hard for me to equate what I saw around me with the concept of divinity. And then I found out that Einstein didn't believe in any of it either and I thought, well, if it wasn't good enough for the smartest guy on the planet...'

'That's okay,' he deadpanned. 'Some of my best friends are atheists.'

She snapped a quick glance at him, saw that he was laughing, and said, 'Good to know,' even if he wasn't exactly right. She thought she was more agnostic than atheist. 'Most of the people I know seem to equate it with being somehow morally hollow... if not bankrupt.'

She led him back into the living room, and as they stepped in, his eyes caught a glimpse of the TV. It was showing an episode of *Smallville*, the series about Superman's travails as a teenager. Staring through the screen, he went off on a completely different tack, asking, 'I need to ask you something. About Vance.'

'Sure. What about him?'

'You know, the whole time you were talking about what happened with him, in the cemetery, the cellar, all that... I just wasn't sure how you felt about him.'

Her face clouded. 'When I knew him years ago, he was a really nice guy, normal, you know. And then, what happened with his wife and unborn child, I mean, it's pretty awful.'

Reilly looked a bit uneasy. 'You feel for him.'

She remembered feeling that confusing empathy for him before. 'In a way... yes.'

'Even after the raid, the beheading, the shootings... threatening Kim and your mom?'

Tess felt uncomfortably exposed. He was making her

aware of troubling, conflicting emotions she didn't fully understand. 'I know it sounds crazy, but, it's strange – it's like, at some level, I do. The way he talked, the way his mood swings made him act differently. He needs treatment, not hunting down. He needs help.'

'We have to catch him first. Look, Tess, I just need you to remember that regardless of what he's going through, the guy's dangerous.'

Tess remembered the calm look on Vance's face when he was sitting there, chatting with her mother. Something about him, about her perception of him, was changing. 'It's weird, but... I'm not sure they weren't hollow threats.'

'Trust me on this. There's stuff you don't know.'

She cocked her head quizzically. She thought she was ahead of the curve. 'What stuff?'

'Other deaths. The man's dangerous, period. Alright?'

His emphatic tone didn't leave much room for doubt, which confused her now. 'What do you mean, other deaths? Who?'

For a moment, he didn't answer. Not because he didn't want to. Something was distracting him. He seemed to be in a slight daze, as if he was looking beyond her. Tess was suddenly aware that he was no longer paying any attention to her. She turned, following his gaze. He seemed to be mesmerized by the TV. On the screen, the teenage Clark Kent was about to save the day yet again.

Tess grinned. 'What, did you miss that episode or something?'

But he was already heading for the door. 'I've got to go.'

'Go? Go where?'

'I've just got to go.' And in seconds, he was gone, the outer door banging shut behind him, leaving her to stare incredulously at the teenager who could see through solid walls and leap over tall buildings with a single bound.

Which really didn't explain anything at all.

CHAPTER 45

The evening traffic was still heavy as Reilly's Pontiac made its way south on the Van Wyck Expressway. Gleaming wide-bodied jets screamed overhead in a seemingly endless procession of landing runs. The airport was now less than a mile away.

Aparo, riding shotgun, rubbed his eyes as he glanced out, the crisp spring air rushing at him through the car's open window. 'What was that name again?'

Reilly was busy scanning the barrage of signs bearing down on them from every possible angle. His eyes finally settled on the one he was looking for. He pointed at it.

'That's it.'

His partner saw it too. The green sign to their right would lead the way to Airport Cargo Building 7. Underneath the main signage, and lost among the smaller logos of airlines, was the one Reilly was particularly interested in.

Alitalia Cargo Services.

Shortly after the 9/11 terrorist attacks, Congress had enacted the Aviation and Transportation Security Act. Under this act, the responsibility for inspecting persons and property carried by airlines was transferred to a newly formed agency, the Transportation Security Administration. Anyone, and anything, coming into the US would now be undergoing far more rigorous checks. Computerized tomography machines that detected explosive materials in passenger and checked luggage were deployed across the country. Travellers were even briefly X-rayed themselves, until the practice was suspended following an uproar caused not by fears of unhealthy radiation exposure, but rather by the simple fact that nothing, however private, escaped the Rapiscan machines' scanners: they showed everything.

An area of particular concern to the TSA was that of global cargo; it was potentially an even bigger threat to domestic security, albeit a less publicized one. Tens of thousands of containers, pallets, and crates poured into the US every day, coming from all corners of the world. And thus, in this new age of heightened security measures, the new scanning directives weren't limited to the luggage of travelers. They would also cover cargo shipments entering the country by air, land, or sea with large-scale cargo X-raying systems now deployed at virtually all ports of entry.

And at this very moment, as he sat down in the operations room of the Italian national airline's cargo terminal at JFK, Reilly was feeling particularly grateful for it.

A data technician was efficiently calling up the images on his monitor. 'Better make yourselves comfortable, guys. It's a pretty big shipment.'

Reilly settled into the worn chair. 'The box we're interested in should be pretty distinctive. You can just zoom through them, I'll let you know when we get a hit.'

'You got it.' The man nodded as he started scrolling through his databank.

Images unfurled on his screen, side- and top-view X-rays of crates of various sizes. In them, one could clearly make out the skeletal images of the objects the curators at the Vatican had shipped over for the Met exhibit. Reilly, still annoyed with himself at not having thought of this before, fixed his concentration on the monitor, as did Aparo. His heartbeat raced as blue and gray ghosts of ornate frames, crucifixes, and statuettes cascaded before them. The resolution was surprisingly good, much better than he'd anticipated: he could even make out small details like encrusted jewels or moldings.

And then, out of the deluge of dizzying images, it appeared.

'Hold it.' A rush of excitement surged through Reilly.

There, in high-resolution clarity, stripped of its cloaking carcass and displaying its glorious innards, was the encoder.

CHAPTER 46

Tess stopped in her tracks the second she stepped into the meeting room.

She'd been happy enough to hear from Reilly after three days of frustrating silence, three days during which she was finding it increasingly difficult to dodge her mother's insistent calls for her to join them in Arizona. She had also started to feel antsy; she realized that the investigation had taken over her life, and that, regardless of what Reilly advised, this wasn't something she could walk away from.

And now, seeing what was sitting on the conference table, any notion of her walking away from this was dead and buried.

There, built of solid, transparent plastic, was an exact replica of the multigeared rotor encoder.

She could barely manage to bring out the words. 'How...?'

She looked up at Reilly in utter amazement. He had obviously planned it that way; his call, asking her to come down to Federal Plaza, had mentioned nothing other than a mundane 'going over a couple of things with you.'

She was suddenly aware of all the other faces in the room. Jansson, Aparo, Gaines, a few others she didn't recognize – and the monsignor. She looked again at Reilly.

He just flashed a restrained, brief smile. 'I thought you might want to be here for this.' He pointed at one of the men she hadn't met before. The man was distributing a stapled printout to everyone in the room. 'That's Terry Kendricks. He built it.'

'Well, my team and I,' Kendricks quickly interjected, smiling effusively at Tess. 'Good to meet you.'

Tess was finding it difficult to tear her eyes away from the machine. She perused the printout in her hands, which confirmed her hopes. She looked up at Kendricks.

'It works?'

'Oh yes. It all fell into place perfectly. In Latin, of course. At least, that's what I'm told by the team of linguists who translated it.'

Tess still didn't get it. She turned imploringly to Reilly. 'But... How?'

'Everything gets X-rayed when it goes through customs,' he explained. 'Even when it's on loan from the Holy See.'

Tess had to sit down. Her knees felt like they were about to cave in under her. With slightly trembling hands, she studied the document he'd handed her. Eagerly, she concentrated on the neatly printed words.

It was a letter, dated in May of 1291.

'That's the time of the fall of Acre,' she exclaimed. 'The last city the Crusaders held.'

She turned her attention back to the letter and began to read, feeling the thrill of connecting directly over the centuries with men whose exploits had become the stuff of legend.

'It is with great sadness,' the letter began, 'that I inform you that Acre is no longer under our protection. We departed the city as darkness fell, our hearts heavy as we watched it burn...'

CHAPTER 47

Eastern Mediterranean – May 1291

They had sailed north along the coast all night and, when dawn broke, the galley turned west and headed toward Cyprus and the safety of their preceptory there.

After the devastating blow of those last hours at Acre, Martin had gone below to try and rest, but the movement of the ship made that hard, and images of the dying Master and of the harried escape remained locked in his mind. When he came back on deck at first light, he was shocked by what he saw. Ahead of them, bright streaks of lightning were breaking the darkness of a fast approaching storm head, and the dim rumble of thunder could be heard over the keening of the wind in the rigging. Behind them, to the east, a strip of angry, purple clouds hid the rising sun, its rays stabbing upward in a desperate attempt to lighten the grim sky.

How is it possible, Martin thought. *Two storms, one ahead of us, the other chasing us.* A quick word with Hugh confirmed that the shipmaster hadn't seen anything like it before either.

They were boxed in.

The wind speed quickened, and with it came sudden spurts of cold, stinging rain. The sail was being whipped violently against its yard, the crewmen struggling to keep its braces under control, the mast groaning in protest. The horses in the hold neighed and pawed restlessly at the planking. Martin watched as the shipmaster feverishly consulted his chart and marked their present position before ordering the overseer to hasten the pace of the galley slaves and shouting out new headings to the steersman in a desperate effort to break away from the storms.

Martin joined Aimard at the forecastle. The older knight

was also watching the approaching storms with mounting concern. 'It's as if God himself were willing the sea to swallow us,' he said to Martin, his eyes laced with deep-seated unease. Before long, the storm erupted around them with a savage ferocity. The sky darkened into an impenetrable black, turning the day into night, and the wind rose to a full gale. All around the ship, the roiling surface of the water suddenly broke into massive whitecaps that raced toward them, battering their starboard stern. Lightning exploded in tandem with ear-splitting thunder cracks, and heavy rain lashed down at the ship in a thick veil of water that cut off the outside world.

Hugh ordered a man aloft to scan the horizon for a possible landfall. Martin watched as the reluctant man braved the torrential rain and scrambled up to the crow's nest. The ship plowed on as massive waves hammered against it, some of them rising high over the stern before smashing down onto the deck. The oars took on a life of their own, some of them snapping against the hull, others slamming brutally into the shackled slaves wrestling with them, injuring several and prompting Hugh to call for the oars to be pulled in.

The ship had been tossed helplessly through mountainous waves for hours when, over the almost deafening uproar, Martin heard a splintering crack as the aft hatch covers split open and dark blue water poured into the holds. Almost at once, the ship was wallowing dangerously when from above came the wrenching sound of timber being ripped apart. The mast had snapped, and Martin looked up in time to see it crashing down onto three crewmen while catapulting the hapless observer in the crow's nest into the churning sea.

Without sail or oars, the galley was at the mercy of the storm and the currents, pushed and pulled aimlessly by the angry sea. For three days and three nights, the storm didn't let up, the *Falcon Temple* bending to its rampaging will, somehow managing to stay afloat and in one piece. Then on the fourth day, with the winds still not letting up, a lone voice cried out, 'Land! Land!' Martin peered out and saw a man pointing dead ahead, but he couldn't see anything apart from the rising sea. Then he spotted it: a distant, dark mass on the horizon, barely discernible.

And then it happened.

Cruelly, and within sight of land, the ship started to break up. The carvel-built, even planking had taken a ferocious beating, and now it was giving up. Deafening groans were followed by what sounded like explosions as the entire hull came apart. Panic erupted among the chained oarsmen, while the horses below reared and whickered furiously.

'The slaves,' Hugh roared. 'Unshackle them before they drown!' His men scrambled to release them from their chains, but their freedom was short-lived as bursts of water thundered into the hull and swept them away.

Hugh could no longer forestall the inevitable. 'Put the longboat to sea,' he bellowed, 'and abandon ship.' Martin rushed to help secure their only means for survival and saw Aimard emerge, carrying a bulky leather pouch, and head in the opposite direction, toward the forecastle. Martin yelled out to him just as another massive wave struck, and Aimard was hurled helplessly across the bridge and slammed against the chart table, impaling the side of his chest on its corner. He cried out in pain but then gritted his teeth and braced himself upright, one hand clasped against his ribs. Aimard pushed aside Martin's offer of help and wouldn't release the pouch, even though it was clear that its bulk and weight were adding greatly to his discomfort.

They barely managed to climb into the longboat, which was now level with the galley's deck, and the last glimpse Martin of Carmaux had of the *Falcon Temple* came as the battered vessel was finally consumed by the raging sea. The huge balk of timber that ended in the carved figurehead snapped like a twig before the awful might of the storm, any sound it made overwhelmed by the demonic shrieking of the wind and the hideous screams of the drowning horses. Looking at the eight other men in the longboat, Martin saw his dread mirrored in their desolate stares as, piece by piece, the ship disappeared beneath the mountainous waves.

It was the waves as much as the wind that drove them on, tossing the longboat as if it were made of paper, but the shipmaster soon had six of the nine survivors manning oars and dampening the wildest swings. As he rowed, Martin just looked ahead blankly, fatigue and despair dragging him down. They had been chased out of the Holy Land, and now the *Falcon Temple* was lost. He wondered how long they would survive, even if they did reach land. Wherever they were, they were far from home, deep in enemy territory, and barely equipped to defend themselves against the poorest foe.

The longboat plunged on for what seemed like hours before the height of the waves lessened and, at last, they saw the land that the lookout had spied. Soon, they were dragging the longboat through the surf and onto the safety of a sandy beach. The storm still howled and the cold rain still stung them, but at least they had land beneath their feet.

After hacking out the bottom of the longboat with their swords, they pushed it back into the sea which was still rough despite the passing of the eye of the storm. Anyone wandering the shoreline should not be made aware of their presence. Hugh told them that they were already on a northerly heading when the storm had struck, and he believed that the *Falcon Temple* had been swept around the island of Cyprus and then pushed headlong northward. Acting upon the seaman's knowledge and expertise, Aimard took the decision to avoid the exposed shore and march inland before heading west in search of a port.

The low hills soon gave them some shelter from the wind and, more importantly, from the eyes of any inhabitants. Not that this appeared to be a danger; they had seen no one, heard nothing but the shrieking of the storm. Even wildlife was absent, cowed no doubt by the violent weather. During the long and exhausting march, Martin could see that Aimard's condition was worsening. The blow to his ribcage was a heavy one, and the serious damage it caused was starting to take its toll. Seemingly impervious to the pain coursing through him, Aimard pressed on bravely, always clinging to the bulky pouch while clutching his painful side.

When they first came upon a town, there was a momentary flare of fear that they might have to fight in their current state. Not only were they injured and weary, they also had few arms between them. That fear was tempered by the hope that they could find food there. Both their fear and their hope proved unfounded. The town was deserted, its houses empty. At its center stood the remains of a church. Its walls were intact, but its roof was a charred skeleton of burnt timbers held aloft on high stone columns. It was hard to tell how long ago this desecration had taken place. Certainly more than a few weeks or even months; years maybe.

Across from the church, a huge old willow drooped its leafy branches over a well.

Cautiously, the survivors dropped to the ground and rested. Of all of them, Aimard of Villiers was in the worst condition. Martin was getting him some water from the well when he heard a sound, the gently melodic ringing of bells. The battered men rushed for cover and watched as a small herd of goats came through the narrow street. Soon, they were crowding around the well head, vainly scavenging for food, some dragging down the branches of the willow and gnawing at them. A goatherd appeared, a stooped and crippled old man, accompanied by a young boy.

Glancing at Aimard who gave a brief nod of acquiescence, Martin took command. Using hand signals, he sent their small band fanning outward to keep watch, while he and Hugh approached the old man who promptly fell to his knees, imploring them not to kill him and to spare his grandson. Like some of their Brothers, Martin and Aimard could speak some Arabic. Even so, it took a while to pacify the old man and assure him that his life was safe. It took even longer to explain that they wanted to buy a goat and not simply take it by force. Not that they had money or valuables of any kind, but they managed to gather between them a few oddments of clothing that, while not adding up to the value of the goat, did at least make a bargain of sorts. While the goatherd and his young helper hauled water from the well for their animals, the knights slaughtered the goat and, with a flint, lit a fire and roasted the carcass. They invited the goatherd and the boy to share in the meal.

That act of kindness probably saved their lives.

The old man, from whom they learned the name of the town, *Fonsalis,* was grateful to be alive. Late in the afternoon, he resumed his wanderings with his herd and helper. Well-fed and strengthened, the knights and crewmen rested once more, comfortable in the knowledge that they could resume their journey in the morning.

But their rest was short-lived.

The knight standing watch heard the sound first and alerted Martin. Someone was running, coming their way. It was the goatherd's grandson. Out of breath and visibly scared, he informed them that a band of Mamelukes was heading their way. The old man had seen them before, had been robbed by them, and knew that they would be coming here for water.

They had no choice but to fight them.

With Aimard's support, Martin quickly formulated a plan for an ambush. Spaced well apart, the men would form a loose V formation, the open arms facing toward the approaching enemy, the point at the well.

They salvaged pieces of wrought iron from the ruined church to supplement their meager supply of weapons and unwound the rope from the wellhead. Hugh and one of the seamen pulled it to their positions at the open end of the V. They kicked dirt over the rope where it lay across the path of the approaching horsemen, and the men all took their places. Once he was certain they hadn't missed anything that could betray their plan, Martin slipped behind the well, crouched low, and waited.

They didn't have long to wait. They heard the Mamelukes long before they saw them, their laughter loud in the still air. Clearly, their acts in this region had given them an undoubted sense of invulnerability. The Mamelukes were rightly feared. Some fifty years ago, many thousands of young men from these parts had been sold into the servitude of the Sultan of Egypt. The ruler, never imagining what would be the result of his action, formed these young men into his National Guard and called them Mamelukes, the Arabic word for 'owned.' A few years later, the Mamelukes instigated a revolution and were soon in control of Egypt. They became even more feared than the men who had originally sold them into captivity.

Decked in leather and iron body armor and breeches, each horseman carried a scabbarded long sword and a dagger in his belt. Across the pommels of each of their horses rested a large circular metal shield, and pennants that hung colorfully from their spears fluttered in the dusty air around them.

Martin counted them. The boy's estimate was accurate. There were twenty-one warriors. He knew that either all of them had to die, or their own fate would be sealed. Should one of them escape, many more would return.

When the last of the Mamelukes had passed the position taken by Hugh and his companion, Martin heard the leader of the band reach the well and dismount. Launching himself upward, Martin bolted out from behind the well as if discharged from a cannon and quickly cut down two men with savage sweeps of his broadsword. More men were in the process of dismounting when the rest of the survivors rushed out of their hiding places, screaming war cries and hacking away at the surprised horsemen with whatever weapons they held. The surprise was complete, its effect devastating.

The men that remained on horseback wheeled their mounts around and kicked them into a gallop, back the way that they had come. As they drew level with Hugh, the shipmaster heaved on the rope, drawing it tight. The horsemen never saw it. The first horses fell, the others colliding into them, sending the riders hurtling helplessly through the air. The knights were already racing toward the men and before long, no Mameluke remained alive at either end of the small battlefield.

But it was a small victory. In the dust of the entanglement, two seamen and two knights were dead. Five men, including the injured Aimard, remained.

But they now had horses, and weapons.

That night, after burying their dead, the survivors slept by the walls of the ruined church, taking turns at watch. Martin, though, couldn't sleep. His mind was still in turmoil, and he had gone into a state of extreme awareness of sounds and movements.

He heard a rustle coming from inside the church, where Aimard had been laid to rest. He knew that the older man was in great pain and he had heard him repeatedly cough up blood. He got up and walked in through the church's charred portal. Aimard wasn't where he'd left him. Martin scanned the darkness and spotted the old knight sitting up, the flames from a small fire dipping and flickering as wisps of wind curled in through the damaged roof. Approaching him, he saw that Aimard was busy writing something. It was a letter. By his side was a strange geared device, which Martin had never seen before.

Aimard raised his head, and his eyes glinted at Martin in the firelight. 'I need your help with this,' he said, his voice hoarse and raspy.

Martin approached hesitantly, feeling his muscles tighten. 'What can I do for you?' he asked.

'It seems my strength has deserted me,' Aimard coughed. 'Come.' He pulled himself off the floor and, lifting the leather pouch with great pain, led Martin deeper into the church to an area where the ground was made up of paving stones, some of them marked with names and dates. Martin realized they were grave markers.

'This one,' Aimard said as he stopped over a stone that bore the word, *Romiti*.

Martin stared at him quizzically, not sure of what was expected of him. Aimard managed a smile. 'I need you to open it up.'

Without any more explanation, Martin retrieved his sword and used it to prize up the flagstone.

'Keep it open for me,' Aimard asked as he got down on his knees and slipped the leather pouch into the dark opening. Once he was done, he nodded to the younger knight. 'That will do.' Martin carefully lowered the slab. Aimard examined it, making sure their intrusion wasn't noticeable, then got up and shuffled back to his small encampment and lowered himself painfully to the ground.

Martin looked into the darkness, his head a whirlwind of confused thoughts. When Aimard of Villiers had first encouraged him to join the Order, he had felt honored and excited. For the first three years, that honour was shown to be justified – the Knights Templar were indeed a noble group of extremely brave men, dedicated to God, to mankind, to the Church. But now that the Holy Land was lost, what was to become of them? He no longer had a clear vision of their objectives.

Other things that bothered him were now resurfacing. Over the years, he had become aware of unspoken apprehensions within the Order. He knew, from snatches of conversations accidentally overheard, that there was friction between the Order and the Church. Where he thought there should be close bonds and trust, he sensed dissent and suspicion. So much so that the Church had not cooperated with recent requests for additional men. By the Church's refusal to help, the fate of the garrison at Acre had been sealed. Had the

Church deliberately placed the Temple in jeopardy?

He shook the thought away. Surely not.

Then there were the secret meetings William of Beaujeu had held with just a few senior members of the Order. Meetings from which they returned grim faced and taciturn. Senior members like Aimard of Villiers, whose openness and honesty were among the qualities that so endeared him to Martin. There was the ornate chest, the cryptic words between Aimard and the Grand Master just before they boarded the *Falcon Temple*. And now this.

Was he not to be trusted?

'Martin.'

Startled, he turned to face Aimard, whose face was contorted with pain, his tone lowered to a guttural grumble.

'I know what you must be thinking. But believe me, when I tell you... There are things you must know, things you need to know, if our Order is to survive. William entrusted me with the knowledge and the task, but...' He broke off, coughing, then wiped his mouth before resuming, slowly. 'My journey ends here, we both know that.' He raised a hand to fend off Martin's protests. 'I must entrust this knowledge to you. You need to complete the task that I have barely begun.'

Martin felt a rush of guilt at his own unjust thoughts.

'Sit with me,' Aimard said. And after a few moments during which the older man caught his breath, he began.

'For many years, a secret has been known only to a small number of our Order. In the beginning, it was known to just nine men. Never have more than that number been privy to this knowledge. It lies at the core of our Order, and it is the source of the fear and envy of the Church.'

Aimard talked through the night. At first Martin was disbelieving, then he felt a growing sense of shock, of outrage even, but given that it was Aimard telling it to him, he knew in his heart that this tale could not be fantasy. It could only be the truth.

As Aimard pressed on, his voice frail and quivering, a realization dawned on Martin. His anger turned to awe, and then to an almost overwhelming sense of nobility of purpose. Aimard was like a father to him, and the older knight's earnest dedication held a lot of weight in Martin's eyes. Gradually but surely, it was seeping into him, embedding itself into his soul with Aimard's every word.

They were still talking when the sun rose. When Aimard finished, Martin was silent for a while. Then he asked, 'What is it you want of me?'

'I've written a letter,' Aimard told him. 'A letter which must be taken to the Grand Master of the Paris Temple. No one else must see it.' He handed the letter to Martin, who couldn't read it. Aimard nodded at the geared device by his side. 'It's in code... in case it should fall into unfriendly hands.'

Aimard paused to glance out, toward the others. 'We are in enemy territory, and there are only four of you left,' he said. 'Stay together only for as long as you must, then divide into two pairs. Take different routes to Paris. I've made a copy of the letter. One for each pair of you. Impress upon the others the importance of your mission, but do not, I beg of you, reveal the truth that I have told you here unless you are convinced your own death is imminent.'

Martin studied his old friend carefully, then asked, 'What if we should all die along the way? What happens to our Order?'

'There are others,' Aimard told him. 'Some in Paris, some elsewhere. The truth will never be lost.' He paused, catching his breath. 'Some of what is in the letters is known only to me, although I think Hugh must have guessed. But he won't ask questions. He may not be a Brother, but he's a man of unshakable loyalty. You can place your trust in him, just as I place my trust in you.'

Reaching into a pocket inside his jerkin, Aimard brought out two packages, each wrapped in oiled skin. 'Take them now. And hand one to the other pair.'

'To Hugh?'

Aimard shook his head. 'No. He's not a member of our Order, and there may come a point when the Grand Master of the Paris Temple will only listen to a true Brother. In fact, I think Hugh should be the one to travel with you.'

Martin nodded thoughtfully, then asked, 'What about you?'

Aimard coughed and wiped a hand across his beard, and Martin saw more blood in his spittle. 'So far, we've been fortunate, but more dangers will come your way, without a doubt,' Aimard said. 'Your journey can't be slowed for the sick and wounded. Not later, and certainly not now. As I said, this is my journey's end.'

'We can't leave you here,' Martin protested.

Cringing with pain, Aimard touched his fingers to his ribs. 'After the accident on the ship,' he said, 'I'm lucky to have reached this far. Take the letters and go. Somehow, you must reach Paris. A lot rests on your shoulders.'

Martin of Carmaux nodded, then, reaching out, he clasped his friend and mentor in his arms. He then rose and walked away to where the others and their mounts waited.

He spoke briefly with them and they all turned to look at Aimard of Villiers who held their eyes for just a moment before rising laboriously to his feet and walking unsteadily to the well. The geared device was in his hands. Martin watched in rapt silence as his old friend smashed it against the stone wall and, piece by piece, dropped its broken fragments into the well.

'May God be with you,' Martin said softly. 'And with us all.'

Taking the bridle of one of the horses, he swung up into the foreign saddle. Soon, the line of four horsemen was filing through the ruins of the village, their spare mounts trailing behind, before they began to head northwest, uncertain of their fate, unaware of whatever dangers might lie before them on their long journey to France.

CHAPTER 48

Tess's mind was still roaming the Mameluke hinterland when Jansson's voice interrupted her medieval sojourn and yanked her right back down to earth.

'We have to assume Vance has translated this too by now,' he stated gruffly.

Reilly nodded without hesitation. 'Absolutely.'

She remembered where she was and, still clutching the printout, she studied the faces around her. They didn't seem as caught up in the sublimity of the moment as she was. It was different for her. This extraordinary and private insight into the lives, actions, thoughts, and deaths of these legendary men touched her deeply. On another level, it was also confirmation of everything her instincts had been harping at since the night of the raid. Her whole body was tingling with anticipation. This could be her Troy, her Tutankhamen. She wondered whether any of those sitting there were at all galvanized by what the printout in their hands hinted at, or whether they were simply interested in the letter because of how it might help them solve a particularly vexing case.

Jansson's expression left no doubt as to which one it was. 'Okay, so we still don't know what we're talking about here,' he went on, 'apart from the fact that whatever it is, it's small enough to be carried around in a shoulder pouch – but at least we know where he's going. *Fonsalis.*' Jansson flashed Kendricks a questioning look.

'Sorry,' Kendricks answered somberly. 'Can't help you there. I've got a bunch of guys working on it, but so far they're hitting a wall. We haven't found any records of it anywhere.'

Jansson frowned, clearly annoyed. 'Nothing?'

'No. Not yet anyway. We're talking thirteenth-century Europe here. They didn't exactly have Mapquest back then.

Map making was a very crude, primitive exercise, and, as it is, very few charts from the period have survived, to say nothing of written texts. We're working our way through whatever writings we have from then onward, everything up to this day – letters, journals, that kind of thing. It's gonna take time.'

Tess watched Jansson sink back into his seat and run a hand up the back of his head. His face clouded. The man clearly didn't take kindly to being thwarted on anything having to do with hard, researchable data.

'So maybe Vance hasn't figured it out yet either,' Aparo offered.

Tess hesitated before stepping in. 'I wouldn't count on it. It's his area of expertise. References to somewhere like that may not come up in widely published works that you might have in your database. They're more likely to be found in some obscure manuscript of the time, the kind of rare book that someone like Vance would know where to find.'

Jansson studied her, seemingly mulling it over for a moment. Seated next to him was De Angelis. His gaze was locked on her. She couldn't read him, though. Surely, of all the people in the room, he had to appreciate the value of what they'd just had the privilege of participating in. But he hadn't shown any signs of wonder and hadn't said a word throughout the meeting.

'Alright, we need to figure this one out if we want to catch this guy,' Jansson grumbled. He turned to De Angelis. 'Father, your people can probably be a big help here.'

'Absolutely. I'll make sure our best scholars work on it. We have a huge library. It's just a matter of time, I'm sure.'

'Time we may not have.' Jansson turned to Reilly. 'The guy's definitely going to be on the move, if he hasn't left the country already.'

'I'll make sure the CBP gives this top priority.' The Bureau of Customs and Borders Protection was in charge of keeping track of who, and what, entered and exited the country. 'Wherever it is, it's got to be in the Eastern Mediterranean somewhere, right?' He turned to Tess. 'Can we narrow down the possibilities of where he's headed?'

Tess cleared her throat, thinking about it. 'It could be anywhere. They were blown off course so radically... Do you have a map of the area?'

'Sure.' Kendricks leaned over, pulled the keyboard over to him, and tapped in a few keys. A world map soon appeared on the huge plasma screen facing them. He punched in a few more keys and the screen shifted, zooming in on the map several times until it displayed the Eastern Mediterranean.

Tess stood up and walked over to the map. 'According to his letter, they left Acre, which is right here in what is now Israel, just north of Haifa – and sailed for Cyprus. They would have sailed north before crossing west, but the storm hit them before they could get anywhere near it ...' She considered the map some more, and couldn't help but let her mind drift a little, conjuring up images of their perilous journey that seemed so real that, for a moment, she felt she had actually been there with them. She mustered her thoughts, concentrating on the task at hand. 'It all depends on which way the storm took them. Did it push them east of the island – in which case they could have washed up anywhere along the Syrian coast, or the southeastern Turkish coast along here...' She traced the route with her finger. 'Or did they pass to the west of Cyprus, in which case we're talking about this area here, the southwestern coast of Turkey, from the Gulf of Antalya to Rhodes.'

'That's a pretty big target area,' Jansson noted vexedly.

'The landscapes along that whole coastline are pretty much the same,' Tess said. 'There's nothing in the letter that would suggest one or the other. But I can't imagine they were that far off the coast if they managed to spot it in the middle of a huge storm.'

Reilly nodded, studying the map. 'We can start by alerting our people in Turkey and in Syria.'

Jansson's brow furrowed in apparent confusion. 'So what's this Vance thinking? That whatever they buried is still out there waiting for him? The letter eventually seems to have made it to France. How does he know the Templars didn't send people back to recover it?'

Tess thought back to Vance's story. *They say the man never smiled again.* 'The timing is key. Vance said the old man who showed the manuscript to the priest, remember, the one who turned white at the news – he said *the old man was one of the last surviving Templars.* De Molay and the others were burnt at the stake in 1314. His dying Templar had to come after that. And that's more than twenty years after the ship sank. I guess Vance is hoping that if they hadn't been able to recover it by then, there was no one else left to do it after that.'

The room fell silent. This was a lot to take in, especially for the others in the room who weren't as well-schooled as she was in making sense of the distant past. Kendricks, who was probably the closest to her in appreciating the historical value of what they were considering here, spoke up. 'We'll run some simulations of the ship's route. Factor in seasonal winds, currents, that kind of thing. See if any details in the text match up to the geography of the land and try and get you a handle on its whereabouts.'

'Might be a good idea to cross check with any wrecks found in the area. Who knows, one of them could be this *Falcon Temple*.' Jansson's impatient body language indicated the meeting was over. He turned to De Angelis. 'You'll keep us posted?'

'As soon as I hear anything.' The monsignor was as calm and unmoved as ever.

Reilly walked Tess to the foyer by the elevators. No one else was waiting there. She was about to hit the down button when she turned to face him with a curious look on her face.

'I was kind of surprised you asked me to come in for this.

After that whole "you've got to let go of this thing" speech the other day.'

Reilly grimaced, massaging his brow. It had been a long afternoon. 'Yeah, and I'll probably be kicking myself for bringing you in on it.' His face turned more serious. 'To be perfectly frank, I was in two minds about it.'

'Well I'm glad the less boring one won the toss.'

There and then, he decided he really liked that mischievous grin. Everything about her was drawing him in. He thought back to the exhilaration that beamed across her face when she saw the replica of the encoder in the conference room. It was intoxicating; this woman could still find intense, genuine, unabashed pleasure in life, something that seemed to elude most people and had certainly eluded him for as long as he could remember.

'Look, Tess, I know how big this must be for you, but –'

She pounced on the brief pause. 'What about you? What does it mean for you?'

He flinched; he wasn't used to being probed about his motives. Not when he was working a case. It was a given. At least, it usually was. 'What do you mean?'

'I mean, is locking Vance up all you want out of this?'

He thought the answer was simple. 'For the time being, I can't afford to think beyond that.'

She was on fire. 'I don't believe that for a second. Come on, Sean,' she pressed. 'You can't tell me you're not intrigued by this. They wrote a coded message, for God's sake. About something their whole future depended on. They were burned at the stake for it, wiped out, eradicated. Aren't you in any way curious to know what's buried in that grave?'

Reilly was finding it hard to resist the enthusiasm radiating from her. 'Let's get him first. Too many people have died for this already.'

'More than you think. If you include all the Templars that died back then.'

Somehow, her comment brought it all home for him in a

way he hadn't considered before. For the first time, the magnitude of what they were dealing with was dawning on him. But he knew the bigger picture would have to wait. His priority had to be to close the METRAID case file. 'See, that's why I didn't want you involved in this any more. It's just got too strong a hold over you and that worries me.'

'And yet you called.'

There it was. That playful grin again. 'Yeah, well... it does look like we could use your help right now. With a bit of luck, maybe we'll pick him up at some border crossing, but in the meantime, it would be nice to have some of our people waiting for him at *Fonsalis*, wherever it is.'

Tess hit the down button. 'I'll put my thinking cap on.'

He looked at her, standing there, the corner of her mouth curled up just a touch, her green eyes glinting mischievously. He shook his head imperceptibly and couldn't help but let out a little chuckle. 'I didn't know you ever took it off.'

'Oh, it's been known to happen.' She glanced at him, coyly. 'On rare occasions.'

Two discreet tones chimed as the elevator doors slid open. The cabin was empty. He watched her step in. 'You'll be careful?'

She turned, holding the doors open. 'No, I intend to be totally, wantonly, inexcusably reckless.'

He didn't have time to answer her as the elevator doors slid shut and she disappeared from view. He stood there for a moment, the image of her beaming face still etched in his mind, before the familiar ping of an arriving elevator snapped him back to his grinding reality.

The curl at the edge of her mouth was still there as Tess walked out of the building. She knew something was definitely going on between her and Reilly, and she liked what she felt. She hadn't danced the dance for quite a while, and the early stages of it, as in her work, had always been the most enjoyable – at least, in her experience. *Trust me to find a parallel between archaeology and men.* She frowned at the realization that, as in archaeology, the surge of anticipation early on in a relationship, the mystery, the optimism, and the hope, never quite fulfilled their promise.

Maybe this time would be different. On both fronts.

Yeah, right.

As she walked in the crisp, spring air, the one notion she couldn't beat into submission was De Angelis's suggestion that the hidden secret had to do with alchemy. It kept hounding her, and the more she considered it, the less credible it seemed. And yet, the Vatican envoy had seemed so confident about it being that. A formula to turn lead into gold. Who wouldn't go to great lengths to hide it from rapacious eyes? And yet, something about it simply didn't compute.

Most intriguing of all was that Aimard had thought that the storm had been a display of God's will. That he was willing the sea to swallow whatever it was they were carrying and bury it forever. Why would he think that? And then there was the issue of its size. A reliquary. One small chest. What could it possibly hold that men would die, and kill, for?

Fonsalis.

She had to figure it out if she was going to stay in the game.

She decided that a few sleepless nights were on the cards. And she would make sure that her passport was in order.

She knew she would also have to face a tough phone call with her mother, in which she'd tell her that it would be more than just a couple of days before she would be joining them in Arizona.

De Angelis had returned briefly to his room at the hostel. Preoccupied with the potential problems at hand, he sat on the edge of the hard bed and called Rome. He spoke directly to a colleague far removed from Cardinal Brugnone's circle. This was decidedly not the moment to be faced with probing questions.

Aware that the edge he had, when tracking down the four horsemen, was now long gone, and similarly conscious that being close to the foundering investigation no longer served any useful purpose, he knew that he would soon have to go his own way. He gave orders that would ensure that everything was in place so that when he did choose to move, he could do so swiftly.

That done, he pulled out a sheaf of photographs from his briefcase, fanned them out on the bed, and examined them, one by one. Tess coming in and out of Federal Plaza. Leaving and returning to her home in Mamaroneck. Her office at the Manoukian Institute. Long shots, mediums, close-ups. Even in two grainy dimensions, she exuded the confidence and determination she showed in real life. She had also proved herself to be imaginative and eager. Unlike the FBI, she had quickly thrown off the constraints of thinking that all of this was mere theft.

Her background knowledge, her acquaintanceship with Vance before his attack on her, all helped to make her a useful ally and a dangerous opponent.

He touched one of the photos, tapping his finger in the center of her forehead. *Clever girl. Clever, clever girl.* If anyone was going to figure this one out, his money was on her. But he also knew she wouldn't be one to share her discovery.

It would have to be prized out of her.

CHAPTER 49

Tess had lost track of time, but from the accumulation of coffee cups on her desk and the amount of caffeine rushing through her veins, she knew it must have been many hours since she had logged onto her computer at the Manoukian Institute.

The office was empty. Outside, the pigeons and sparrows were long gone, and the garden was bathed in darkness. Another long, frustrating night beckoned.

The last couple of days were a blur. She had stayed at Columbia University's Butler Library until she'd been virtually kicked out of there when they had closed at eleven. She'd made it home sometime shortly after midnight with a stack of books in tow and had worked her way through them, finally succumbing to sleep as the sun was making its appearance outside her bedroom window, only to be cruelly jolted back to consciousness ninety minutes later by her alarm clock/radio.

Now, bleary-eyed and at her desk, she was still trawling through a small mountain of books, some she'd brought in with her, others from the Institute's vast collection. Occasionally, something would jump out at her and she would excitedly fire off Internet searches, blessing Google for the hours it was saving her and cursing the search engine whenever it failed to deliver the goods.

So far, the cursing was winning hands down.

She turned away from her desk, glancing out her window, rubbing her tired eyes. The shadows in the garden blended confusingly into each other. She found she couldn't focus properly; her eyes were rebelling. She didn't mind. She could use the break. She couldn't remember the last time she'd read as much in such a short period. And one word was seared into her retinas, even though she had yet to find any reference to it:

Fonsalis.

Staring out into the night, her eyes were drawn to the big willow tree looming over the garden. It sat there, its wispy boughs swaying in the slight evening breeze, silhouetted against hints of streets lights that bounced off the towering brick party wall behind it.

She looked at the empty bench underneath the tree. It looked so out of place, here in the heart of the city; so quiet and idyllic. She wanted to step outside, curl up onto it, and sleep for days.

And that's when an image flashed across her mind.

A confusing one.

She thought of the brass plaque mounted on a small post by the base of the willow tree. A plaque she had read a hundred times.

The tree had been imported with great fanfare over fifty years ago by the Institute's Armenian benefactor. He'd had it shipped over from his ancestral village in memory of his father who, along with two hundred other Armenian intellectuals and community leaders, had been murdered in the first days of the genocide of 1915. The Turkish Interior Minister had, at the time, bragged that he would give the Armenian people 'such a staggering blow that they will not be able to get on their feet for fifty years.' His words had proven to be tragically prophetic; the nation of Armenia suffered one tragedy after another, a dark era from which it is only just starting to emerge.

The tree had been, appropriately, chosen for its tearful symbolism. Weeping willows were commonly found in burial grounds stretching from Europe to China. The association dated back to the Old Testament, in which the tree's boughs were said to have drooped from the weight of harps hung there by the exiled people of Israel. Arabian storytellers, much later, described how two angels had appeared before

David, after he had married Bathsheba, and convinced him of his sin. Racked with grief, David was to have thrown himself to the ground and lain there, weeping bitter tears of penitence for forty days and forty nights, during which time he was deemed to have wept 'as many tears as the whole human race would shed on account of their sins, from then on and until the Day of Judgment.' The two streams of his tears were said to have flowed out into the garden, where with time, two trees sprang up: the Frankincense Tree, constantly distilling tears of sorrow, and the Weeping Willow, its boughs drooping with grief.

Tess's mind raced to the writing on the brass plaque. She could visualize the inscription on it. She remembered that it described the tree as belonging to the broader genus known as *Vitisalix*.

She also remembered that the plaque further mentioned the more specific taxonomic classification for the weeping willow.

Salix Babylonica.

It was staring her in the face.

CHAPTER 50

The next morning, Reilly and Aparo were both working the phones from their desks at Federal Plaza. Reilly was getting updated by Kendricks. The news wasn't good. The brain boxes at the NSA were still stumped by the *Fonsalis* reference. Kendricks warned him that the progress from here on would be much slower. Phone calls to friendly experts around the world had failed to enlighten them, and electronic searches of relevant databases had long been exhausted. The analysts were now working their way through tomes of literature in the traditional way, physically reading through them, searching for any reference to the grave's location.

Reilly wasn't holding his breath.

From across his desk, Aparo shot him a grim nod before he ended his own conversation. Reilly could tell that whatever bad news his partner had seemed to at least have some urgency to it. Aparo soon confirmed it. The call was from Buchinski. A man's body had been found earlier that morning in an alley behind an apartment building in the Astoria section of Queens. The relevance of the find was that the dead man had traces of Lidocaine in him. He also had tell-tale puncture marks in his neck. The victim's name was Mitch Adeson.

Reilly felt a deepening unease that the case was slipping away from them. 'How'd he die?'

'Fell from the roof. Fell, jumped, got pushed – take your pick.'

Reilly leaned back, rubbing his eyes wearily. 'Three out of four. One to go. Question is, will he pop up with a needle mark in his neck... or is he already halfway to Europe?'

Glancing around the room, he noticed the monsignor emerging from the double doors that led to the elevator foyer. The fact that he was here in person could only mean that he didn't have any breaks to report.

The somber look on his face as he sat with Reilly only confirmed it.

'I'm afraid my colleagues in Rome haven't been successful yet. They're still searching, but...' He didn't seem optimistic. 'I take it...?' He didn't need to continue.

'Yeah, we're still drawing blanks here too, Father.'

'Oh, well.' Then he managed a hopeful smile. 'If neither our scholars nor your experts have been able to find it so far... perhaps he's also having a hard time figuring it out.'

Deep down, Reilly knew this was only wishful thinking. Pictures of Vance had been circulated to all the major libraries from DC to Boston, and so far none of them had reported any sightings. Vance either already knew where he was headed, or he had his own resources, which the FBI wouldn't have access to. Either way, it didn't augur well.

The monsignor was silent for a moment, then said, 'Miss Chaykin. She seems to be very... *resourceful.*'

Reilly couldn't suppress a tired grin. 'Oh, I'm sure she's racking her brains looking for it as we speak.'

This seemed to confirm De Angelis's guess. 'Have you heard from her?'

'Not yet.'

De Angelis nodded quietly. Reilly could tell something was troubling the man, that he was holding something back.

'What is it, Father?'

The monsignor looked slightly embarrassed. 'I'm not sure. I'm just a little concerned, that's all.'

'What about?'

The priest pursed his lips. 'Are you sure she would call? If she found out?'

Coming from De Angelis, this surprised Reilly. He doesn't trust her? He leaned forward. 'What makes you say that?'

'Well, she seems to be rather driven, it's her field after all. And a discovery like this... careers have been made from far less. If I were to put myself in her shoes for a moment, I wonder what my priorities would be. Catching this Vance... or discovering something any archaeologist would give his right arm for. Would I inform the authorities and risk losing the credit and the glory... or would I go after it myself?' His tone was soft-spoken, but irresistibly confident. 'She comes across as a very ambitious lady, and ambition... it can often lead one to choose the less, shall we say, magnanimous path.'

De Angelis's words stayed with Reilly long after the priest had left.

Would she call? It hadn't even crossed his mind that she wouldn't. But then, what if the Vatican envoy was right? What incentive did she have to call? If she did figure it out and gave the FBI its location, agents would be flown out to try and intercept Vance, local law enforcement agencies would be drafted in, and the situation would quickly get out of hand; there would be little room, or consideration, for her quest. The priority, as far as the authorities were concerned, was to apprehend a fugitive. The archaeological discovery was of little consequence.

Still, she wouldn't be so reckless... or would she? *What's she going to do, fly out there by herself?*

A surge of trepidation rushed over him. *No, that's insane.*

He reached for the phone and dialed her home number. There was no answer. He let it ring until her answering machine picked up, then hung up without leaving a message. He quickly tried her cellphone. It rang five times before diverting to her messaging service.

With rapidly swelling unease, Reilly hung up and called up the internal operator. Within seconds, he was patched through to the officer parked outside Tess's house. 'Have you seen her today?'

The officer's reply was stolidly assured. 'No, not since she got home late last night.'

His internal alarms were blaring. Something felt very, very wrong. 'I need you to go up to her front door and make sure she's okay. I'll hang on.'

The officer sounded like he was already getting out of his car. 'You got it.'

Reilly waited anxiously as the seconds ticked by. He visualized the officer crossing the road, walking up the path across her front yard, climbing up the three stone steps, and ringing the bell. It would take her a few more seconds to come down if she were upstairs. Right about now, she'd be opening the front door.

Nothing.

His discomfort grew alarmingly as the seconds dragged on. Then the officer's voice crackled back through his handset. 'She's not answering the door. I had a look out back and nothing's been disturbed, there's no sign of forced entry, but it doesn't look like she's around.'

Reilly was already scrambling into action. 'Okay, listen to me,' he fired back as he gestured urgently to Aparo, 'I need you to just get in there right now and confirm to me that the house is empty. Break in if you have to.'

Aparo was rising out of his seat. 'What's going on?'

Reilly was already reaching for another phone. 'Get onto Customs and Borders.' Cupping the phone with his hand, he looked at his partner, frustration and anger in his eyes. 'I think Tess might be doing a runner.'

CHAPTER 51

Standing in line at the Turkish Airlines check-in desk at JFK, Tess stared at the display on her cellphone. The screen didn't show who the caller was, and she decided not to answer it. She knew the call was probably originating from some routing switchboard, and none of the likely callers were particularly welcome right now. Not Leo from the Institute; Lizzie would have relayed the cryptic, confused explanation for her absence by now. Not Doug, calling from L.A. – no qualms there. But Reilly... that was the one that stuck in her throat. She hated doing this to him. It was one of the toughest decisions she'd ever had to take, but now that she was going through with it, she couldn't afford to talk to him. Not yet.

Not while she was still in the country.

Stuffing the phone back into her jacket pocket, she finally reached the desk and embarked on the arduous check-in procedure. Once she was done there, she trailed the signs to the departure lounge and a much needed coffee, going by way of the newsstand where she picked up a couple of paperbacks she'd been aiming to read when she had the time; whether or not she could rein in her galloping imagination enough to concentrate on even lightweight fiction, given everything that was going on, was another matter.

She went through the passenger checks and reached the departure lounge where she sank into a chair.

She couldn't believe she was actually doing it. Sitting there with nothing more to do other than wait for the flight to be called, her mind finally had a chance to wind down, take a step back, and consider the recent events more carefully. Which wasn't necessarily a good thing. The last twenty-four hours, from the time she knew she was onto something to the actual moment she made the discovery, had been an adrenaline-induced haze. Now, alone and waiting to fly off into the night, she fell prey to a litany of fears and misgivings that came crawling out from deep within.

What are you thinking? Going out there, up into the Turkish backcountry – alone? What if you bump into Vance out there? What about all the other creeps you could run into? It's not exactly the safest country in the world. An American woman, alone in the Turkish outback. Are you nuts?

The panic attack about her physical well-being soon gave way to something that troubled her even more.

Reilly.

She'd lied to him. Again. A lie of omission, maybe, but a pretty serious one nevertheless. This was different from driving off with the manuscript and not alerting him about Vance waiting for her at home. She knew something was going on between them, something she liked and wanted to nurture, even though she sensed there was something holding him back that she couldn't quite put her finger on. She'd wondered if she had ruined any chance they had of getting together. She thought she'd gotten away with it at the time; there were extenuating circumstances and he was very understanding – in fact, he'd behaved wonderfully. And now, here she was, screwing up again.

How much does this mean to you, Tess?

She snapped out of her unsettled reverie when she sensed the harsh glow of the fluorescent lighting interrupted and felt the presence of someone standing there, blocking it. She opened her eyes.

It was Reilly. He was standing there, looming over her, and he didn't look thrilled.

Hugely pissed off was probably closer to the mark.

Reilly broke the pregnant silence. 'What do you think you're doing?'

She wasn't sure about how to answer that. Just then, a nasal voice echoed down from the overhead PA system, announcing the opening of the gate for boarding. Passengers all around them rose from their seats and formed a couple of messy lines that converged on the gate's counters, buying her a welcome respite.

Reilly glanced at them and visibly mustered some self-control before plunking himself down beside her. 'When were you planning on telling me?'

She took a breath. 'Once I got there,' she said sheepishly.

'What, were you going to send me a postcard? Damn it, Tess. It's like nothing I've said meant anything to you.'

'Look, I'm –'

He shook his head, raising both hands and cutting her off. 'I know, you're sorry, this is a big deal for you, a once in a lifetime thing, a career defining moment... We've been through this before, Tess. You just seem hell bent on getting yourself killed.'

She breathed out in frustration, mulling over his words. 'I can't just sit back and let it slip away. Besides, until this thing is sorted out, one way or another, I'm not going to feel safe, Kim's not going to be safe... He was in our house, Sean. I'm part of this, whether I like it or not.' She paused, almost afraid to ask. 'You said there were things I didn't know about? Other deaths?'

Reilly nodded, then darted a discreet glance around before lowering his voice. 'The other three horsemen from that night – they're dead. And they didn't exactly die in their sleep.'

Tess edged forward. 'You think Vance killed them?'

'It was either him, or someone involved with him. Either way, whoever's doing it is still out there and the killing part doesn't seem to bother him at all.'

Tess rubbed her eyes with fingers that, she noticed, were quivering. 'What if he hasn't figured it out yet? *Fonsalis*?'

'I think you would have gotten another visit if he hadn't. My guess is, he knows.'

She let out a deep breath. 'So what do we do now?'

Reilly studied her, clearly wondering the same thing. 'You're sure you've got it right?'

She nodded. 'Yes.'

'But you're not going to tell me where it is?'

She shook her head. 'I'd rather not. Although I'm pretty sure you can make me, right?' Overhead, the nasal voice made another announcement, inviting the last passengers to board the aircraft. Tess turned to Reilly. 'That's my flight.'

He watched as the last passengers went through the gate. 'You're sure you still want to do this?'

She gave him a nervous nod. 'I'm sure.'

'Let us handle it. You'll get the full credit for any find, I'll make sure of that. Just let us get him out of the way first.'

She looked deep into his eyes. 'It's not just about the credit. It's... it's what I do. And it's what I *have* to do.' She scoured his face for signs of empathy, for clues as to what he was thinking. 'Besides, it might be out of your hands. International finds... it can get very territorial and very messy.' She managed a tentative grin. 'So can I go now, or are you gonna arrest me or something?'

His jaw tightened. 'I'm thinking about it.' His face wasn't giving away any hints that he could be joking. Far from it.

'On what charge?'

'I don't know. I'll find something. Maybe plant a couple of pouches of coke on you.' He faked patting down his pockets. 'I know I have some on me somewhere.'

Her face relaxed.

His expression turned dead serious. 'What can I say to make you change your mind?'

She loved the way it felt to hear him ask her that. *Maybe I haven't completely screwed this up yet.* She stood up. 'I'll be fine.' Not that she believed it.

He got up and for a brief moment, they just stood there. She waited for him to say something else, but he didn't. A small part of her was even hoping he would grab her and stop her from going. But he didn't do that either. She glanced toward the gate then turned to face him again. 'I'll see you soon.'

He didn't answer.

She walked off and reached the overly cheerful woman staffing the boarding pass scanner. Tess pulled out her passport and, as she handed it to her, she looked back at where she'd left Reilly. He was still standing there, watching her go. She managed a queasy half-smile before turning away and walking down the white-paneled finger.

The four turbofan engines whined to life as the flight crew up and down the aisles made their final preparations for take-off. Tess had been assigned a window seat for the ten-hour flight and was relieved to find an empty seat beside hers. As she watched the ground staff clear the last of the servicing gear from around the aircraft, Tess felt a strange mix of exhilaration and foreboding. She couldn't help but be excited by the journey ahead, and yet Reilly's news about the dead horsemen rattled her. She blocked the disturbing imagery her mind was conjuring up and tried to convince herself that as long as she took some basic precautions, she should be safe.

She hoped.

She was reaching for the in-flight magazine when she noticed some commotion coming from the front of the aircraft. Her whole body went rigid when she realized it was due to Reilly, who was making his way down the aisle to her.

Damn it. He's had a change of heart. He's coming to take me off the plane.

Staring at him with amazement, she felt a surge of anger. As he reached her row, she edged back against the window. 'Don't, okay? Don't pull me off this plane. You've got no right. I'll be fine – I mean, come on, you've got people there, right? They can keep an eye on me. I can do this.'

His face was impassive. 'I know.' He then eased his way into the seat next to hers.

Tess stared at him, stunned. Her mouth was having trouble forming any coherent words.

He matter-of-factly took the magazine from her hands as he buckled his belt. 'So,' he said, 'do they have any decent movies on?'

CHAPTER 52

The man seated six rows back from Tess was far from comfortable. He hated flying. It didn't have anything to do with an irrational fear of it, nor was he in any way claustrophobic. He simply couldn't stand being confined for hours in a tin can where he wasn't allowed to smoke. *Ten hours.* And that wasn't counting the time spent in the equally smoke-free terminal.

Nicorette country.

He'd been lucky. Tasked with keeping an eye on Tess, he'd had to make do with an uncomfortably remote viewing spot due to the police watch on her house. Had he been any closer, though, he would have probably missed her slipping away from the back of the house, across two neighboring houses' backyards, then back to the street and the cab that was waiting for her only yards from where he'd been parked.

He'd alerted De Angelis and tailed her to the airport. From his seat in the departure lounge, he'd been able to observe Tess and Reilly at ease without any risk of detection. Neither of them was aware of his existence. He had called De Angelis from his cellphone twice. The first time to let him know that Tess had been allowed to board the aircraft. The second shortly after, this time from his seat inside the plane, when he'd barely had time to inform the monsignor of Reilly's appearance before his conversation was cut short by an insistent flight attendant who made him shut off his cellphone.

Leaning out to look up the aisle, he studied his two targets as he twirled a small disc no bigger than a quarter across his fingers. He'd noticed that Reilly hadn't brought any hand luggage on board. It didn't really matter. Tess had a carry-on bag stuffed into the overhead compartment, and she was his primary target. As he watched them, he knew he didn't need to rush things. It was going to be a long flight, and most of the cabin, including his targets, would be asleep at some point. He'd have to be patient and wait for the right opportunity to plant his tracking device. At least, he mused, it would provide him with some distraction on this otherwise irksome journey.

He shifted uncomfortably in his seat, frowning as the flight attendant passed him and proceeded down the aisle, checking to make sure the seat belts were all fastened. He hated the rigidity of the whole travail. He felt like he was back in sixth grade. *Can't smoke, can't call. Can't call them stewardesses. What's next? Permission slips to use the john?*

He glared out the window and stuffed two more pieces of Nicorette into his mouth.

De Angelis was arriving at Teterboro airport in New Jersey when Plunkett called him. The small airport was a quieter and more efficient option for his hastily arranged trip; seven miles from Manhattan, it was a favored haven for celebrities, business executives, and their private jets.

Sitting in the back of the Lincoln Town Car, the monsignor was almost unrecognizable. He had discarded his austere attire for the smart black Zegna suit he was more used to, and although he always had some misgivings when he set aside his Roman collar, he had readily done so now, opting for a blue dress shirt instead. He had also done away with the dowdy, smeared glasses he had worn during his stay in Manhattan; in their place were his habitual, rimless pair. His tattered leather briefcase was gone, a slim aluminum one now sitting next to him as the dark limousine whisked him right up to the aircraft's door.

As he climbed aboard the Gulfstream IV, he glanced at his watch again and did a quick calculation. He knew he was in good shape. He would probably land in Rome slightly before Tess and Reilly reached Istanbul. The G-IV wasn't just one of the handful of private jets that had the range to reach Rome without refueling; it was also faster than the massive, four-engined Airbus in which they were flying. He would have a bit of time to collect whatever equipment he needed to complete his mission and still be able to meet them wherever they were headed.

Taking his seat, he again pondered the dilemma Tess Chaykin presented. All the FBI really cared about was locking up Vance for the attack on the Met. She, on the other hand, was after something else; he knew that long after Vance was behind bars, she would keep on searching, turning over stones, looking for it. It was in her nature.

No, he had no doubt about it; at some point, after she had outlived her current usefulness, he would probably have to deal with this problem. A problem that had just been exacerbated by Reilly and his ill-advised decision to accompany her.

He shut his eyes and leaned back against the soft headrest of his plush swivel chair. He wasn't worried in the least. It was an unfortunate complication he would simply have to deal with.

CHAPTER 53

They were at cruising altitude before Tess began to explain her findings to Reilly. 'We were looking for a place that doesn't exist, that's all.'

They had managed to get a glimpse of the Manhattan skyline, shimmering in dizzying golden-blue hues from the setting sun, the twin towers even more notable now for their absence, the full scale of the catastrophe made even more visceral from the air. Then the red-tailed aircraft had banked and powered itself skyward through thin cloud cover, effortlessly reaching the clear air at 37,000ft. Night would come quickly now as they rushed headlong into the approaching darkness.

'Aimard of Villiers was smart and he knew that the man he was writing the letter to, the master of the Paris Preceptory, was as smart as he was.' Tess was visibly excited about her discovery. 'There is no "*Fonsalis*". There never was. But in Latin, *fons* is the word for well – not as in "feeling well", but the kind with water, like a wishing well – and *salis* means willow.'

'"The well of the willow?"'

Tess nodded. 'Exactly. And then I remembered that they were in enemy territory when Aimard wrote his letter. The village had been overrun by the Muslims, and it got me thinking – why would Aimard use the Latin name for the village? How did he know it? It was more likely he'd know the Arabic name for it, the name its conquerors used. That's the name the goat herder would have given them. But Aimard wanted to disguise the name, in case the letter fell into the wrong hands and was eventually decoded.'

'So the village was called "The well of the willow?"'

'Exactly. It was common practice to name places after any geographic features they had.'

He looked at her doubtfully. Something in her reasoning seemed to bother him. 'To do that, he had to speak their language.'

'He would have known it, or if not him, one of the others with him. By the end of the Crusades, a lot of those knights were actually born out there in the Holy Land. They called them *poulains*. And the Templars had a strange affinity to some of the Muslims. I read that they traded scientific knowledge as well as mystical insights with them, and they were even said to have hired the *hashasheen* – their incredibly efficient, pot smoking assassins – on a few occasions.'

He arched his eyebrows. 'They hired their enemies' assassins? I thought they were there to fight them.'

Tess shrugged. 'You spend two hundred years in someone else's backyard, sooner or later you make friends.'

Reilly acquiesced. 'Okay, so what is it in Arabic?'

'"*Beer el Sifsaaf.*"'

'Which you found by...?'

Tess couldn't suppress a self-satisfied grin. 'The journals of Al-Idrissi. He was a famous Arab traveler, one of the great cartographers of the period, and he kept extensive, highly detailed journals of his trips across Africa and the Muslim world, many of which survive to this day.'

'In English?'

'French, actually, but it's not that much of a stretch.' Tess reached for her tote and pulled out a map and some photocopies she had made of the old book she had found. 'He mentions the town and its pillaged church in one of his journals.' She opened up a map that was marked with scribbles and notes. 'He passed through it, on his journey from Antalya, through Myra, and up the coast to Izmir. The coastal area there has an abundance of historic sites – Byzantine, Lycian... Anyway, his journal's pretty detailed. All we need to do is follow his route and we'll find the town – and the church.'

Reilly stared at the map. 'Now that you've done it... what do you think the chances are of Vance figuring it out too?'

She frowned, then looked at him with dead certain eyes. 'I'd be amazed if he isn't on his way there already.'

Reilly nodded. He was clearly of the same opinion. 'I need to use the radio.'

He got up and headed for the cockpit.

By the time Reilly got back, Tess was well settled in, sipping the last of a glass of spicy tomato juice. She'd gotten him one too. She watched him drink it, feeling a slight quiver at the idea of sitting there next to him, bound for a distant, exotic land, en route to adventure. *If someone had told me just two weeks ago that I'd be doing this...* She smiled inwardly.

He noticed. 'What is it?'

'Nothing. I'm just... I'm still stunned that you're here.'

'Not as stunned as my boss is, that's for sure.'

Her jaw dropped. 'You're not AWOL, are you?'

'Put it this way. He's not exactly thrilled about it. But since you didn't know *exactly* where it is, and since the only way to figure it out was for you to be there *physically...*'

'But you didn't know that before you got on the plane.'

He flashed her a small grin. 'Are you always such a stickler for detail or what?'

She shook her head, amused by the revelation. So they were both going out on a limb. *He wants to be here as much as I do.* Which surprised her.

Watching him, she realized that she still didn't know that much about the man behind the badge. That evening, when he had driven her home, she'd caught a few glimpses. His taste in music; his spirituality; his sense of humor, even if it was slightly silted over. She wanted to know more. Ten hours would provide ample opportunity for that – if she could manage to stay awake. Her eyelids felt like they weighed a ton. The exhaustion of the last few days was suddenly catching up on her. She shifted in her seat, nestling against the window while turning to face him.

'So how is it you can just hop on a plane at a minute's notice?' The curling smile was back. 'Isn't there anyone back home I can bust your balls about, the way you lecture me about Kim?'

Reilly knew what she meant. 'Sorry,' he teased. 'I'm not married.'

'Divorced?'

'Nope.' Her look made him feel like he needed to expand on that. 'A job like mine can be tough on partners.'

'Well, sure. If it allows you to hop on planes with girls you barely know – I wouldn't want my husband doing that every day.'

He was glad she'd provided a way for him to tack away from where that conversation was headed. 'Talking about husbands, what about you? What happened with Doug?'

Her soft features hardened, her eyes betraying some regret and a tinge of lingering anger. 'It was a mistake. I was young –' she groaned, '– *younger*, and I was working with my dad at the time, not the most exciting of careers. Archaeology's pretty insular. And when I met Doug, he was this brash, confident showbiz guy. He's a charismatic bastard, there's no denying it, and I was just carried away by it. My dad was well known and admired in his field, but he was a pretty serious guy – a bit grim, you know? And controlling. I needed to get out from under his dominance. And Doug was the way out. This in-your-face, highfalutin go-getter.'

'And you're partial to highfalutin, are you?'

Her face scrunched inward. 'No. Well, maybe I was. A bit. Anyway, when we were dating, he loved the fact that I also had a career. He was very supportive and interested. Then when we got married... he changed overnight. He became even more controlling than my dad was. It was like he owned me, like I'd been a collectible he wanted on his shelves. And once he got it... I was pregnant with Kim before I realized I'd made a mistake. I reluctantly took up my dad's offer to join him on his dig in Turkey –'

'– this is the same trip where you first met Vance?'

'Yes,' she confirmed, 'anyway, I went there thinking the time off would be good to mull things over, and when I got back I found out he'd been having an affair with the cliché of clichés.'

'The weathergirl?'

Tess let out a pained chuckle. 'Almost. His producer. Anyway, that was it. I was out of there.'

'And you went back to using your maiden name.'

'It doesn't exactly hurt in this business. Not that I wanted that creep's name associated with mine any longer than I had to.' Far from hurting, it had gone a long way in helping her get the job at the Manoukian Institute. And that was why a potential discovery of this magnitude, which owed nothing to Oliver Chaykin or to being his daughter, might be the stroke that dissolved any lingering thoughts, in her mind and the minds of others, that she was anything other than her own woman.

Provided, of course, that she was the one who made the discovery.

Her eyelids fluttered. She was weary and needed some sleep. They both did.

She looked at him warmly. After a quiet moment, she just said, 'Thanks.'

'For what?'

'For everything.' She leaned over, kissed him softly on his cheek, and pulled back. Outside, the stars felt close enough to touch, gliding by almost imperceptibly in the darkening sky. She pulled down the window shade and, turning over and closing her eyes, she felt herself drift away.

CHAPTER 54

By the time Tess and Reilly clambered down the metal steps and onto the tarmac at Dalaman airport, it was mid-afternoon and they were both feeling frazzled. The few hours of sleep they had managed on the transatlantic flight had helped, but they could have used some real bed rest before continuing their journey. There was no time for that. Instead, they had added to their weariness by waiting three hours at Istanbul airport before catching the short connecting flight to the south coast, from where they would begin their inland trek.

Reilly had spent part of the wait in Istanbul on his cellphone, briefing Aparo before having a heated conversation with Jansson, who was still unconvinced by Reilly's rash decision to accompany Tess instead of hauling her ass in to Federal Plaza. The rest of the time was spent with the Bureau's local legal liaison officer, a paunchy man called Vedat Ertugrul who had driven out to meet them and helped facilitate Reilly's passport-less entry into the country. Ertugrul had only days earlier been notified of the likelihood that Vance may be headed for his part of the world. He confirmed to Reilly that so far, none of the possible entry points had reported anything, before going over logistical arrangements and support protocols. The FBI didn't have any agents on permanent postings in Turkey. The nearest agents were currently in Athens, helping the local police investigate a recent car bombing. Relations with the Turkish government were at best strained, due to the tensions caused by the lingering turmoil in Iraq. Ertugrul assured Reilly that, if need be, he could probably arrange for a local police escort to join them in Dalaman. Reilly thanked him but declined the offer, preferring not to have to deal with language barriers and local bureaucracies. He asked Ertugrul to simply make sure they were informed of his presence on their turf. He'd keep in close contact and call in the troops if needed, although he suspected that this was something he would probably have to handle alone.

Reilly had also used the layover to pick up some more appropriate clothing. A small backpack in his hand now held his discarded work clothes and the paperwork Ertugrul gave him to use in lieu of a passport. It also carried an Iridium satellite phone he'd given him that, via the Department of Defense's dedicated EMSS gateway in Hawaii, would keep Reilly connected to the outside world from virtually anywhere on the planet.

Also in there was his Browning Hi-Power handgun, for which Ertugrul had graciously provided extra clips and cartridges.

Tess had also used the opportunity to call her aunt's house and speak to Kim and to Eileen. The call was a hard one to make. She missed Kim and felt it even more when she heard her voice on the phone, although knowing what a great time her daughter was having provided some solace. Telling her mother what she was up to, on the other hand, was a much harder exercise. Tess worked hard at reassuring her, resorting in desperation to telling her about Reilly being there with her – which only served to worry her mother even more. Why was an FBI agent accompanying her if it wasn't dangerous, she'd asked? Tess had fumbled some explanation about her being there purely as an outside expert, then used an overhead boarding announcement as an excuse to cut the conversation short. After she'd hung up, she'd felt bad about the call. But she knew there was nothing she could have told her mother, short of not telling her she was away at all, that wouldn't have alarmed her.

What Tess barely noted was the sallow-faced man who had accidentally bumped into her as she was making her way through the crowded terminal to the ladies' room in the minutes following that tough call. He'd knocked the carry-on she'd been trailing behind her right out of her hand, but had courteously retrieved it for her and made sure she was all right before moving on.

She did notice he reeked of stale cigarettes, but then from what she remembered, most of the men here smoked. What she didn't notice was the tiny black strip, roughly the size of a coin, that he had managed to stick by the small wheel well on the bottom of the bag.

With the bag now trailing safely behind her, Tess walked with Reilly as they made their way through the stifling and chaotic terminal to the car rental desk. Ertugrul had brought some hastily procured supplies, which included a crate of bottled water, two sleeping bags, and a nylon tent. A short while later, they were settled into a slightly tattered four-wheel-drive Mitsubishi Pajero, on the centuries-old trail of a handful of shipwrecked warrior knights.

Reilly drove while Tess took on the role of navigator. She was using an assortment of maps and notes to try and retrace the route Al-Idrissi mentioned in his journals while reconciling it with elements gleaned from Aimard's letter.

As the shore dropped away behind them, the densely packed houses and low-rise apartment buildings quickly gave way to a calmer landscape. Huge swathes of the Lycian coastline had been protected as conservation areas before the airport at Dalaman was built, sparing the area from the blight of mass-market resorts. Tess and Reilly quickly found themselves driving through a more pastoral setting of older properties, fronted by rough stone walls and rusty wrought-iron fences and shaded by pine trees. On both sides of the road, the land appeared rich and fertile, dense with shrubs and dotted with clusters of trees. On the higher ground to their right, the cover thickened.

It took less than an hour to reach Köycegiz, a small town resting on the edge of a large, mystical lake that once formed a natural harbor. Carian cliff tombs, intricately carved into

the rocky hills bordering the lake and strikingly well preserved, loomed down on them somberly, a reminder of one
of the many civilizations that had settled in this region.

About two miles beyond the town, Tess directed Reilly
to turn off the main road. The asphalt was cracked and
potholed; the journey from here on would be rougher, but
for the time being the Pajero's rugged suspension was
taking it in its stride.

They drove past olive and lemon groves, past corn fields
and tomato plantations on roads lined by frankincense trees,
the vibrant colors and smells helping to awaken their dulled,
jet-lagged senses. Then they were climbing again, into thickly
forested hills dotted with the occasional sleepy village.

All around them were the poor, primitive, and picturesque
reminders of a way of life that was over a thousand years old,
a living history long since gone from the more prosperous
West. Serendipitous sights emerged to greet them as they
pressed on: a girl spinning wool with a weight as she herded
her sheep; a laden wood-gatherer, dwarfed by his tall and
unwieldy load; a brace of oxen pulling a tree-trunk plow
under the setting sun.

From time to time, Tess would get very excited as she
found extracts from Al-Idrissi's journal that matched their
progress. Mostly, though, her thoughts were not so much
about that traveler's journey, but were instead drawn to the
surviving knights who had trudged desperately across these
lands all those years ago.

By now, the light had faded and the SUV's headlights
were helping guide the way. The road had degenerated into
a narrow, rock-strewn path.

'I think we should call it a day,' Reilly said.

Tess consulted her map. 'It can't be far. I'd say we're
about twenty, thirty miles away.'

'Maybe, but it's getting dark and I wouldn't want to hit a
rock or something and risk breaking an axle out here.'

She was eager to reach their destination but, as he

maneuvered the Pajero onto a fairly level patch of ground, she had to concede that he was right. Even a flat tyre would be bad news.

They both climbed out and looked around. The last, faint traces of the setting sun glowed from behind wisps of pink-gray clouds in an otherwise clear sky. Overhead, the waxing crescent of the moon seemed unnaturally close. The mountains around them were still and deserted, enshrouded by a disconcerting quiet he wasn't used to. 'Any towns nearby we can stay in?'

She checked her map again. 'Nothing close. Last one was about seven miles back.'

Reilly made a quick visual check of the area's vulnerabilities and decided it was as good as any for an overnight stop. He headed for the SUV's rear door. 'Let's see what our man in Istanbul's got for us.'

While Reilly was busy putting in the last of the aluminum struts and setting up the tent, Tess had managed to get a small fire going. They were soon working their way hungrily through the case of supplies Ertugrul had provided, washing down slices of *basterma* sausages and *kasseri* cheese *boreks* with bottled mineral water.

Reilly watched Tess's eyes beam with delight as she opened a small carton and pulled out a piece of *lokma*, wolfing it down, her fingers dripping with syrup.

'This local guy of yours is a godsend,' she managed before popping another piece into her mouth. 'Try these, they're delicious. I couldn't get enough of them the last time I was here. It didn't help that I was pregnant at the time.'

'So what brought Vance out here?' he asked as he sampled a piece.

'My dad was working on a dig not too far from the Ararat Anomaly. Vance was desperate to have a look, and my dad invited him in.' Tess explained how in 1959, a U-2 spy plane on its way back from a reconnaissance flight over the then

Soviet Union flew over Turkey and took some images that intrigued the CIA's photo analysts for years. Word eventually leaked out and, in the late 90s, the pictures were finally released, causing a small sensation. Way up in the Armenian mountains, not far below the summit, was something that looked like a ship. Close-ups revealed what appeared to be three large curved wooden beams, resembling part of the hull of a large vessel.

'Noah's Ark,' Reilly said as he flashed back to vague headlines in the press.

'A lot of people were fascinated by it, my dad included. Trouble was, even when the Cold War began to thaw, the area was still very sensitive. The mountain's only twelve miles from the Russian border, less than twenty to Iran. A few people were granted permission and tried to climb up to see what it really was. James Irwin was one. The astronaut. Walked on the moon, and later became a serious convert to Christianity. He tried to climb up for a closer look at the Anomaly.' She paused. 'On his second attempt, he fell and died.'

Reilly frowned. 'So what do you think? Is it really Noah's Ark?'

'The consensus says it isn't. Just a curious rock formation.'

'But what do you think?'

'I don't know. No one's actually reached it or touched it. What we do know is that the story of a flood and a man with a boat and with a whole bunch of animals, it's in writings going all the way back to Mesopotamia, writings that pre-date the Bible by thousands of years. Which makes me think that maybe something like that really did happen. Not that the whole world was flooded. Just a big area somewhere in this part of the world. And one man survived it and his tale passed into legend.'

Something in the way she said it seemed so definite, so final. Not that he necessarily believed in Noah's Ark, but...

'It's funny,' he said.

'What?'

'I would have thought archaeologists, of all people, would be drawn to the mysteries of the past with more of an open mind than others, with a sense of wonder about what could have happened at a time that's so distant and removed from what we have today... and yet your approach is so rational and analytical. Doesn't it take away from the, I don't know, the magic of it?'

She didn't seem to see anything paradoxical about it. 'I'm a scientist, Sean. I'm like you, I deal in hard facts. When I go out and dig, I look for evidence about how people lived and died and fought wars and built cities... myths and legends I leave to others.'

'So if it can't be scientifically explained...?'

'Then it probably didn't happen.' She set down the box of *lokmas* and wiped her face with a napkin before stretching back lazily and rolling over to face him. 'I need to ask you something.'

'Shoot.'

'Back at JFK.'

'Yeah...'

'How come you didn't pull me off that plane? You could have arrested me, right? Why didn't you?'

From the vaguest hint of a smile and the glint in her eyes, he knew what she was getting at. She was taking the lead, which was just as well given his grating hesitation to move in that direction himself. He ducked it, for now, with a non-committal 'I don't know,' before adding, 'I knew you'd be a real pain in the ass and probably scream the house down if I took you in.'

She edged closer. 'Damn right I would.'

He felt a slight quickening in his chest and shifted his position, sliding down and leaning in more to face her. 'Plus... I figured, what the hell. Let's see if she's as smart as she thinks she is.'

She leaned closer still. Her face was now hovering inches

away from his, her eyes moving over his face. The curling smile widened. 'How magnanimous of you.'

The sky, the forest, the campfire... it was perfect. He could feel the warmth of her lips radiating out, beckoning his, and for a brief moment, he felt everything else fall away. The rest of the world simply ceased to exist.

'What can I tell you, I'm a magnanimous kind of guy. Especially when someone's out on their own... *pilgrimage.*'

She held the minute gap separating their lips. 'So given that you're here protecting me,' she whispered, 'I guess that kind of makes you my own personal Knight Templar?'

'Something like that.'

'You know,' she mused, eyeing him playfully, 'according to the official Templars manual, you're supposed to stand guard all night while the pilgrims sleep.'

'You sure about that?'

'Chapter six, subsection four. Check it out.'

The feeling was unreal.

'You think you can handle that?' she asked.

'No sweat. It's what we Templars do.'

She smiled. And with that, he leaned in and kissed her.

He moved in closer and the kiss turned more urgent. They melted into each other, lost in the moment, their minds free from thought, consumed by a sublime rush of feel, smell, and taste – and then something intruded, a familiar undertow nagging at him, pulling his mind to a darker place, to the face of his devastated mother and to a man in an armchair, his arms hanging lifelessly to his side, a gun lying innocently on the carpet, the wall behind him splattered with blood.

He pulled back.

'What?' Tess said dreamily.

He frowned inwardly as he sat up. His eyes had taken on a haunting, distant glaze. 'This... this isn't a good idea.'

She raised herself and snaked a hand through his hair, pulling his mouth closer to her. 'Oh, I beg to differ. I think it's a great idea.' She kissed him again, but just as their lips touched, he drew back again.

'Seriously.'

Tess pulled herself up on her elbow, momentarily dumbfounded. He was just looking at her, dejected.

'Oh my God. You are serious.' She looked at him askance and flashed him a cheeky grin. 'This isn't some Lent celibacy thing, is it?'

'Hardly.'

'Okay, so what then? You're not married. I'm pretty sure you're not gay, although...' She made a 'maybe' gesture. 'And last time I checked, I thought I looked pretty damn good. So what is it?'

He was struggling to put it into words. It wasn't the first time these feelings had sneaked up on him, but it had been a while. He hadn't felt this way about someone for a long time. 'It's hard to explain.'

'Try.'

It wasn't easy. 'I know we hardly know each other, and maybe I'm jumping the gun here, but I really like you, and... there are things about me I think you need to know, even if...' He didn't continue, but the implication was clear. *Even if I end up losing you because of it.* 'It's about my dad.'

Which completely threw her.

'What does this have to do with us? You said you were young when he died, that it hit you hard.' She saw Reilly wince. From the first time he mentioned it back at her house that evening, she knew she was trespassing on difficult ground, but she needed to know. 'What happened?'

'He shot himself. For no reason.'

Deep down, Tess felt a knot unwind. Her imagination had taken her to some even darker places. 'What do you mean, for no reason? There had to be a reason.'

Reilly shook his head, and his face clouded. 'That's the thing. There just wasn't. I mean, none that made sense. He was never outwardly gloomy or moody. We eventually found out he was sick, he was suffering from depression, but there wasn't any reason for it. He had a good job, he liked his work, we were comfortable, he had a loving wife. By all outward indications, he had a great life. It didn't stop him from blowing his brains out.'

Tess leaned into him. 'It's an illness, Sean. A medical condition, a chemical imbalance, whatever you want to call it. You said it yourself, he was sick.'

'I know. The thing is, it's also genetic. There's a one in four chance that I'll get it.'

'And a three in four chance that you won't.' She smiled supportively. He didn't seem convinced. 'Was he getting treated for it?'

'No. This was before Prozac became the new Aspirin.'

She paused, mulling it over. 'Have you had yourself checked?'

'We have routine psych evaluations at work.'

'And...?'

'They haven't found anything wrong.'

She nodded. 'Good. I don't see it either.'

'See it?'

Her voice softened. 'In your eyes. I could see something, a bit of distance, like you're walled off, always holding something back. At first I thought it might be your M.O., you know, the badge talking, the strong, silent type.' She was beaming with conviction and reassurance. 'It doesn't have to happen to you.'

'What if it does? I've been through it, I saw what it did to my mom. I wouldn't want to put you, or anyone I care about, through it.'

'So you're going to shut yourself off from the rest of the world? Come on, Sean. It's like telling me we shouldn't be together just because, I don't know, your dad died of cancer. Who really knows what's going to happen to any of us? You just live your life and hope for the best.'

'Not everybody wakes up one morning and decides to ride

a bullet out of this world. The thing is, I recognize a part of him in me. He wasn't that much older than I am now when he did it. I look in the mirror sometimes and I see him, I see his look and his stance, and it scares me.'

She shook her head with obvious frustration. 'You said your priest helped you through it?'

He nodded absently. 'My dad wasn't into religion. He questioned faith out of existence, and my mom, well, she kind of toed the line, she wasn't particularly spiritual anyway. After he died, I just shut down completely. I couldn't understand why he did it, why we didn't see it coming, why we didn't stop it from happening. My mom was a total wreck. She ended up spending more and more time with our priest who, in turn, started talking to me about it. He helped me understand why neither of us was to blame and showed me another side of life. The church became my sanctuary, and I never forgot it.'

Tess visibly rallied herself, speaking now with renewed determination. 'Well, you know what? I appreciate the concern and the warning, it's very gentlemanly of you, but it doesn't scare me in the least. You needed me to know, and now I do, okay? But I don't think you can go on like that, you can't let something that'll probably never happen ruin your life. You're only helping turn it into a self-fulfilling prophecy. You're not him, okay? You've got to let go, live your own life, and if that's not working, well then maybe something's fundamentally wrong in the way you live your life. You're alone, which isn't a great start, and God knows you haven't exactly chosen a bright and merry line of work.'

'It's what I do.'

'Well maybe you need to do something else.' The grin made a timely, and welcome, reappearance. 'Like shutting up and kissing me.'

Reilly's eyes moved over her face. She was trying to make sense of his life, drumming heartfelt optimism into him, and yet he hardly knew her. He felt something familiar, something that he was starting to recognize only happened when he was around her: in a word, alive.

He leaned into her and pulled her onto him, tightly.

As the two figures on the screen drew closer, their gray-blue heat signatures merged into one misshaped lump. The muted voices were now gone too, replaced by the muffled sounds of clothes being discarded and of bodies moving against each other.

De Angelis cradled a warm cup of coffee as he watched the screen with disinterest. They were parked on a ridge that overlooked the depression where Tess and Reilly had set up camp. The tailgate of the beige Landcruiser was open, revealing two screens that glowed in the darkness. One was a laptop, from which a lead snaked out to a Raytheon Thermal-Eye infrared surveillance camera that sat on a tripod, dominating the landscape before it. A parabolic directional microphone nested on a second tripod. The other screen belonged to a small, handheld PDA. It blinked with the position of the GPS tracker that clung clandestinely onto the underside of Tess's travel bag.

The monsignor turned and looked down on the dark valley below. He was quietly pleased. Things were under control, and that was how he liked it. They were close and, with a bit of luck, they would beat Vance to it. He still didn't know exactly where they were heading; he would have preferred to have audio capability inside their car, but the opportunity to plant a bug there hadn't presented itself. Not that it mattered. Whatever they found, he would be right behind them, waiting to scoop it up.

That was the easy part.

More difficult was the question of what to do with them once that was achieved.

De Angelis took one last lingering look at the screen before flicking the last of his coffee into the bushes.

He wouldn't be losing sleep over it.

CHAPTER 55

When Tess woke up, daylight was filtering in from outside. She drowsily reached over, but her hand only found empty padding. She was alone in the sleeping bags, which had been zipped together. Sitting up, she remembered that she was naked and found the clothes that had been hurriedly discarded the night before.

Outside, the sun was higher than she expected and on checking her watch, she saw why. It was almost nine, and the sun was already halfway up a strikingly blue sky that was clear and unblemished. She squinted as she looked around, finding Reilly standing by the Pajero with his shirt off. He was shaving, using hot water from an immersion coil water heater plugged into the lighter socket.

As she walked up to him, he turned and said, 'Coffee's ready.'

'I love this Ertugrul guy of yours,' she marveled as she checked out a smoking thermos. The rich smell of the velvety black coffee roused her senses. 'You guys really do travel in style.'

'And you thought your tax dollars were being wasted.'

He wiped his shaving foam off and kissed her, and, as he did, she again saw the small, discreet silver crucifix on the thin chain around his neck that she had noticed the night before. It wasn't something people wore much these days, she thought, not in her neck of the woods anyway, and it had an old-world charm to it that threw her. She didn't think it would be something she'd find remotely attractive, and yet, on him, it was somehow different. It seemed to fit; it was part of who he was.

A short while later, they were back on the road, the Pajero eating up the bumps and potholes of the pitted tarmac as they ventured further inland. They passed a few deserted houses and a small farmhouse before leaving the narrow road they were following to take an even narrower forest track that climbed steeply.

As they drove past a copse of balsam trees from which a young villager was tapping the fragrant resinous storax, Tess now saw the mountains looming ahead and felt a surge of excitement.

'Over there. See that?' Her pulse quickened as she pointed at a hill in the distance. Its peak had a distinctive, symmetrical profile. 'That's it,' she exclaimed. 'The double humpback of the Kenjik ridge.' Her eyes ate up the notes and the map in her hand as she reconciled them with the landscape before them. 'We're there. The village should be in the valley just on the other side of those mountains.'

The track cut through a thick cluster of pine trees and as they emerged out of it and back into the light, they rounded a hillock and, with the Pajero now making use of the full might of its four wheel drive, kept climbing up until they crested the ridge.

It wasn't what she expected. The sight hit her like a sledgehammer.

There, before them, nested in the valley between two ranges of lush, pine-covered mountains, stretched a huge lake.

CHAPTER 56

Tess's entire body froze as she stared out in bewilderment, then her hand clawed at the door latch and she was out of the car before it had come to a complete stop. She stormed over to the edge of the ridge and looked around in utter incomprehension. The dark, shimmering lake just lay there peacefully, stretching from one end of the valley to the other.

'I don't get it,' she blurted. 'It should be right there.'

Reilly was now standing next to her. 'We must have made a wrong turn somewhere.'

'No way.' Tess was all flustered, her mind racing, poring over the details of the journey they had taken, revisiting every marker along the way. 'Everything fitted perfectly. We followed his journey to the letter. It should be here. It should be right here.' Refusing to accept the glaring mistake, she scrambled down through the trees and walked a little further forward to get a better view. Reilly followed her.

The lake extended to the farthest reaches of the valley to their right. Its opposite end was obscured by the forest.

Tess stared at the placid water in disbelief. 'I don't get it.'

Reilly took in their surroundings. 'Look, we can't be that far off. It's got to be around here someplace. We just screwed up somewhere on the way up.'

'Yes, but where?' she said irritably. 'We followed what he wrote, right down to the double ridge. It should be right here.' She studied the map intently. 'The map doesn't even show a lake.'

She looked at him and heaved a sigh of sheer frustration.

He put his arm around her. 'Look, we're close, I'm sure of it. We've been on the road for hours. Let's find a town, somewhere to eat. We can go over your notes there.'

*

The village was small, the only *lokanta* tiny, a strictly local affair. An old man with a seamed face and dark, pebble eyes took their order, which basically involved their acquiescing to whatever he said was available. Two bottles of Efes beer and a plate of stuffed vine leaves quickly followed.

Tess was immersed in her notes. She had calmed down but was still disconsolate, visibly and justifiably mired in a deep funk.

'Eat,' he told her. 'You'll sulk better.'

'I'm not sulking,' she murmured as she glanced up at him, annoyed.

'Let me have a look.'

'What?' The glare intensified.

'Your notes. Let's go over them together, step by step.'

She pushed them away and leaned back, tightening her fists, squeezing the air out of them. 'We're so close, I can feel it.'

The old man came back with two plates of cabbage dolmas and skewers of grilled lamb. Reilly watched him as he placed them on the table, then nodded his gratitude before looking at Tess. 'Maybe we should ask him?'

'*Beer el Sifsaaf* hasn't been on any map for hundreds of years,' she grumbled. 'I mean come on, Sean. He's old, but he's not that old.'

Reilly wasn't listening to her. His eyes were on the old man, who broke into a gap-toothed smile and nodded sheepishly at him. Reilly felt a sudden tingle of anticipation. '*Beer el Sifsaaf?*' he asked the old man hesitantly, then, slowly: 'Do you know where it is?'

The old man smiled as he nodded his head vigorously. '*Beer el Sifsaaf,*' he said. '*Evet.*'

Tess's eyes lit up and she rose from her seat. 'What?' The man nodded again. 'Where?' she snapped excitedly. 'Where is it?' The man was still clearly agreeing, but now looked slightly confused. She frowned, then tried again. '*Nerede?*'

The old man pointed up the hill they had just descended. Tess lifted her gaze and followed his outstretched finger. He was waving his pointing hand to the north, and Tess was already heading for the car.

Minutes later, the Pajero was roaring back up the hill. The old man, riding shotgun, was hanging onto the handle above his window, in a state of perspiring terror as he watched the mountain tear past him, the wind whipping in through the open windows, his cries of, '*Yavas, yavas*' merely spicing Reilly's grinning abandon as they plowed ahead. Tess was leaning forward from the back seat, her eyes scanning the rushing landscape for clues.

Just before the ridge where they had seen the lake, the old man pointed, '*Göl, göl,*' and Reilly swung the wheel to take them along an even narrower track they hadn't spotted before. With tree branches whipping its sides, the SUV charged ahead. Another kilometer or so and the trees cleared, and they mounted another ridge.

The old man was grinning excitedly, pointing at the valley. '*Orada, orada! Shte!*'

As the valley opened up before them, Tess couldn't believe her eyes.

It was the lake.

Again.

She shot him a glance of utter dejection as Reilly ground the big car to a halt, and they all disembarked. They walked over to the edge of the small clearing, the old man still nodding with self-satisfaction. Tess watched him and shook her head, turning to Reilly. 'Of course, we had to find the senile one.' She looked at the old man again, imploring him. '*Beer el Sifsaaf? Nerede?*'

The old man's brow furrowed in apparent confusion. '*Orada,*' he insisted, pointing down at the lake.

Reilly took a few more steps forward and took another look. From this vantage point, he could see the whole lake, including its western edge, which had been obscured by the forest at their earlier viewing point.

He turned to Tess, a small smirk breaking across his face. 'Oh, ye of little faith,' he said.

'What's that supposed to mean?' she blurted. His fingers were calmly inviting her to join him. She looked at the old man who nodded in eager agreement, then, confused, clambered over to Reilly and saw it too.

From this new angle, Tess could see, a mile or more away and cutting across the edge of the lake, a concrete causeway that stretched from one hilltop to another. The top of a dam.

'Oh my God,' she said.

Reilly had taken a notebook from his pocket and was now sketching a cross section view of the hills with a line stretching between them for the surface of the lake. He then drew the rough outline of some houses at the bottom of the lake and showed the sketch to the old man, who took the ballpoint pen and made a large X at the bottom of the lake and said, '*Köy suyun altinda. Beer el Sifsaaf.*'

Tess looked at Reilly and he showed her his rickety drawing. 'It's down there,' he confirmed. 'Underwater. This dam flooded the whole valley, the remains of the village with it. It's at the bottom of the lake.'

CHAPTER 57

With the old man sitting more comfortably now, Reilly guided the Pajero carefully down the bumpy and rock-strewn track until they reached the edge of the lake.

It was massive, the surface of its water as smooth and silky as glass. On the opposite shore was a line of posts, incoming power and telephone lines, he guessed, and probably a road in. From the dam itself, he could see a line of pylons striding northward over a range of hills and heading toward civilization. The dam and its artificial lake apart, civilization had not impacted this place. The surrounding woodlands and higher up bleaker mountain tops, none of it especially hospitable terrain, looked to him much as it must have looked to the Knights Templar who had passed this way seven hundred years ago.

They reached the dam and, relieved to be off the rough track and as eager now as Tess was to reach their destination, Reilly sped along the concrete roadway that ran across the top of the massive concrete structure. To their left, he saw a drop of at least two hundred feet. At the far end was a maintenance station, which was where the old man was guiding them.

As they drove across the causeway, Reilly's eyes scanned the edges of the lake and the ground above them. There was no sign of life, though he couldn't be sure; the tree cover was dense, the shadows providing ample cover for anyone who didn't want to be seen. He had been careful to keep an eye out for any signs of Vance since they had entered the final stages of their journey, and hadn't seen anything that suggested any outside visitors in the area. The situation would probably have been different in the height of the summer tourist season, but right now, they seemed to be alone.

Not that any of that made Reilly feel any more comfortable. Vance had shown himself to be adept at staying one step ahead of them, and he'd shown a headstrong determination and resilience in pursuing his objective.

He was out there. Somewhere.

Reilly had used the time during the drive down to ask the old man if anyone else had asked about the village recently. Some awkward language acrobatics later, he understood from the old man that no one had asked about it, as far as he knew. *Maybe we are running ahead of him,* Reilly thought as he scanned the immediate grounds of the dam, looking for anything out of place before bringing the SUV to a halt alongside what appeared to be a small maintenance office.

A rusty white Fiat was parked outside. From here, he could see what appeared to be a road coming in from the other side. It appeared to be smooth and fairly new. 'If that's what I think it is,' he told Tess, 'we could've had a comfortable ride here in half the time.'

'Well, when we're done here,' she grinned, 'maybe we can have a smooth, fast ride out.' Her mood had changed immeasurably as she beamed at him before jumping out of the car to follow the old man, who was now greeting a younger man who had emerged from the small shed.

Reilly waited for a moment, watching her long-legged stride toward the two local men. She was incorrigible. *What,* he wondered, *am I getting myself into with this woman?* He had suggested they call in their discovery and await the arrival of a team of specialists to handle the matter, assuring Tess he would do his utmost to make sure the find was hers. She hadn't batted an eyelid before summarily dismissing his suggestion and imploring him to hold off. Despite his better judgment, he had relented, bowing to the sheer force of her enthusiasm. She was going all the way on this, and even went so far as to insist he stayed off the satphone for now, at least until she'd had a chance to take a look herself.

Tess was already in earnest conversation with the young

man, an engineer whose name was Okan. He was small and slender with dense black hair and an overgrown mustache, and from the grin plastered on his face, Reilly could see that Tess's charms were already overwhelming any reluctance the man might have to helping them. Okan spoke some English, which also helped. Reilly watched with interest as Tess explained that they were archaeologists with an interest in old churches, specifically the one beneath the surface of the lake. The engineer had explained that the valley had been flooded in 1973 – two years after Tess's map was drafted. The dam now provided most of the electric power for the thriving coastal region to the south.

Her next question to the engineer stopped Reilly in his tracks. 'You must have diving equipment here, right? For checking the dam.'

Okan appeared to be as surprised as Reilly. 'Yes, we do,' he stammered. 'Why?'

She brushed any doubt aside. 'We'd like to borrow some.'

'You wish to dive and look for this church?' he asked, his face shrouded in confusion.

'Yes,' Tess replied sprightly, raising her hands expansively. 'It's a perfect day for it, isn't it?'

The engineer glanced at Reilly and at the old man, unsure of what to make of this. 'We have some equipment, yes, but it is used only once or twice a year,' he said hesitantly. 'It will need checking, I don't know if –'

She jumped right in. 'My colleague and I can check them out. We do it all the time. Shall we follow you?' Reilly looked at her uncertainly. She shot him back a look of utter confidence. He was still pondering her wild suggestion that they were both trained divers. He didn't know about her, but he had nothing more than the most rudimentary basic training underwater. Still, he wasn't about to put a damper on her parade – not here, not in front of the two strangers. He was curious to see where her determination would lead.

Okan was decidedly uncomfortable with the idea. 'I'm not

sure, I – I'm not authorized to do anything like that.'

'Oh, I'm sure it'll be fine.' She flashed that smile again. 'We'll sign a waiver, of course,' she assured him. 'It'll be entirely our responsibility. And, obviously, we're very happy to pay a fee to... the company – for the use of the equipment.' The pause before she said 'the company' was perfectly timed. Any shorter and Okan could've missed it; any longer and he might've been insulted at such a clumsily implied bribe.

The little man studied her for a moment, then his mustache twitched and he shrugged. 'Okay. Come with me. Let me show you what we have.'

A narrow staircase led down from the office into a dusty storeroom that was haphazardly piled with equipment and hazily lit by a fluorescent lamp that flickered and buzzed. In the blue glow, Reilly could discern an arc-welding set, butane gas bottles, an oxy-acetylene burning rig, and, in the far corner, a heap of diving gear.

He left it to Tess to sort through them, and as she hefted each piece of equipment, it seemed like she knew what she was doing.

'It's not state of the art, but it'll do,' she shrugged.

She hadn't been able to find a dive computer, though, which they'd have to manage without. She saw a dive chart on the wall and asked Okan how deep the lake was. He told her he thought it was a hundred, maybe a hundred and twenty feet deep. She consulted the chart and frowned. 'We won't have that much time at the bottom. We'll need to start our dive right on top of the village.' Turning to Okan again, she asked him if he had anything that showed its location.

The little man's brow furrowed, pondering the matter. 'You must talk to Rüstem,' he finally said. 'He lived in the village before it was flooded, and he never left the area. If anyone knows where the church is, he will.'

Reilly waited for Okan to step outside the room for a

moment before turning to Tess. 'This is crazy. We should bring in some pros.'

'You're forgetting something. I am a professional,' she insisted. 'I've done this a hundred times.'

'Yes, but not like this. Besides, I'm not too happy about having both of us down there without anyone keeping an eye topside.'

'We've got to give it a shot. Come on, you said it yourself. There's no one around. We've beaten Vance to it.' She leaned into him, her face alight with anticipation. 'We can't stop now. Not when we're this close.'

'One dive,' he relented. 'Then we make the call.'

She was already heading for the door. 'Let's make it count.'

They carried the gear up the staircase and piled everything into the back of the Pajero. Okan invited Tess into his rusty white Fiat, asking Reilly to follow him with the old man. Reilly looked at Tess, who winked conspiringly before folding her legs into the small car, to the obvious delight of the engineer.

The Pajero followed Okan's car along an asphalt service road for about half a mile until the engineer pulled off and stopped beside a chain-link compound inside which were piled concrete blocks, drainage pipes and dozens of empty oil drums; all the usual clutter left over at the end of any building project. Inside the compound, an old man in traditional headdress and robe was pottering around. Reilly guessed that a little bit of private enterprise was in operation here, and wasn't at all surprised when Okan introduced the recycler, Rüstem, as his uncle.

Rüstem smiled toothlessly at them, then listened intently as his nephew rattled off some questions before answering with lots of arm waving and enthusiastic nodding.

Okan turned to Tess and Reilly. 'My uncle remembers the remains of the village very well. For many years, he brought his goats to this place. He says only parts of the church still stand.' He shrugged, interpolating a comment of his own, 'At least, that's how it was before the valley was flooded. There was a well close to the church, and he remembers a...' Okan frowned, searching for the words. 'The dead root of a very big tree.'

'A tree stump,' Tess said.

'Stump, yes, that's it. The stump of a willow tree.'

Tess turned to Reilly, her eyes blazing with anticipation.

'So, what do you think? Is it worth a look?' he dead-panned.

'If you insist,' she grinned.

They thanked Okan and the old man who drove off, the engineer flashing a reluctant last glance at Tess and, before long, she and Reilly had pulled on their wetsuits and lugged their gear to the water's edge, where Rüstem kept a couple of small rowboats. They clambered aboard, then Rüstem pushed them off and scrambled in himself. Picking up the oars, he began to row with the easy movements of someone for whom this had been a lifelong practice.

Tess used the ride out to remind Reilly of the routine pro-cedures he vaguely recalled from his only previous diving experience, during a short holiday in the Cayman Islands four years earlier. Rüstem stopped rowing when they were roughly halfway between the east and west shorelines, and about three-quarters of a mile from the dam. Muttering to himself as he squinted first at one nearby hilltop, then at another and another, he used one of the oars as a paddle to make a succession of careful positioning movements. As he did this, Reilly reached over the side and swirled both of the masks in the water.

'What do you think is down there?' he asked.

'I don't know.' She looked solemnly at the water. 'Right now, I'm just hoping it's there.'

They stared at one another in silence, then realized that the old man had stopped and was displaying his gums in a triumphant beam. He pointed downward. '*Kilise suyun altinda,*' he told them. The words sounded similar to those used by the frail man from the restaurant.

'*Sükran,*' Tess said.

'What did he say?'

'Damned if I know,' she replied as she climbed onto the edge of the boat before adding, 'but I'm pretty sure *kilise* means church, so I guess this must be it.' She cocked her head at him. 'You coming or what?'

And before he could answer, she had pulled down her mask and let herself roll backward into the reservoir with barely a splash. After a glance at Rüstem, who raised a thumb in a decidedly modern gesture, Reilly followed her, far less gracefully, into the dark water.

CHAPTER 58

As they descended into the cold gloom of the lake, Tess was overcome with a familiar rush, one that she craved badly. There was something almost mystical in knowing that she may be about to see things that had not been seen by human eyes for many years. It was already a heady feeling on land, closing in on the remnants of long-lost civilizations that lay hidden beneath centuries of sand and earth. When the site was buried under a mountain of water, the exhilaration was even greater.

This dive, though, trumped them all as far as she was concerned. If most excavations or dives at least began with the promise of some great discovery, they more often than not proved disappointing. This one was different. The trail of clues that had brought them to this lake, the nature of the coded message, and the lengths to which people were prepared to go to get to it all pointed to her being on the verge of an archaeological discovery of far greater significance than anything she had ever realistically expected to make.

They were now twenty feet down and descending slowly. Between the cold and the anticipation, it was as if every last pore on her body had suddenly come alive. She looked up at where the sunlight dappled the surface. The bottom of the old man's boat was suspended serenely above her, the water gently lapping against it. The water clarity was good considering they were basically in a blocked-up river, but the darkness was quickly closing in around them.

There was still no sign of the bottom. Tess switched on the light rig she held, its high-intensity discharge light taking a few seconds before reaching its full output and illuminating the eerie blackness ahead of her. Small particles danced in the water before her, slowly gliding by in the current, heading for the dam. She glanced at Reilly sinking down beside her as a small school of trout weaved in curiously before darting away into the dark.

She noticed Reilly gesturing below and saw the bottom of the lake slowly coming into view. It was disconcerting at first: even with the years of silt and settlement since the dam had been built, it didn't look like the seabeds she was used to. In fact, it looked just like what it was: a submerged valley, strewn with rocks and the bare trunks of long dead trees. Thick, dark algae covered most of it.

They swam side by side, spiraling out, scanning the bottom, then her trained eyes spotted it first. The old man had been true to his word; there, barely noticeable in this otherworldly landscape, were the ghostly remains of the town.

At first, all that she could make out were clusters of eroded stone walls, then gradually she began to get some sense of shape and purpose, and could see how the stones formed uniform, linear shapes. She led Reilly down further and now she could make out a street and some houses. They glided ahead, looking down at the remains of the old village, suspended over it in the stygian darkness like explorers hovering over an alien land. It was a surreal sight, the leafless branches of dead trees swaying in the faint current like the beckoning limbs of captive souls.

A sudden movement swung her eyes to the left. A school of small fish that had been feeding off clumps of algae were scattering into the shadows. Turning back, she noticed that the houses gave way to an open space. Pushing toward it, she saw the black stump of a huge tree, the spindly remains of its rotted branches barely swaying. There it was: they had found the willow. She unconsciously let out a burst of air, a small cloud of bubbles coursing out of her regulator and racing up to the surface. Her eyes feverishly scanned the surroundings. She knew it had to be close. As Reilly joined her, she spotted it: the crumbled remains of what must have been the well, a few yards upstream from the stump. She pushed forward, the beam from her light penetrating the wall of darkness beyond the well. And there, just beyond, rising upward with a kind of melancholy grandeur, were the walls of the church.

She glanced at Reilly. He was floating beside her, taking it all in, clearly as much in awe of it as she was. She kicked ahead, swooping down on the looming structure. Silt had built up against its sides, buttressing its walls. Its roof was badly gutted. As she played the light across the walls, she could tell that the condition of the church was so bad that it was most certainly in a much worse state than it had been seven hundred years ago, when the Templars had found it.

With Reilly following her, Tess dropped down and, like a bird swooping into a barn, she swam through the church's portal, where a massive door hung lopsidedly. Inside now, hovering fifteen feet above the church's floor, they moved along an underwater gallery of columns, some of them collapsed. The walls had prevented too much silt from piling in, which bode well for finding the gravestone. They advanced in tight formation, the light creating a kaleidoscope of shadows in the deep recesses to their sides.

Tess looked around, recording every macabre shape and shadow while trying to keep her racing heartbeat under control. With the portal now swallowed by the darkness behind them, she signaled to Reilly and dropped down to bottom. He followed. A huge smashed stone slab lay there, which she guessed had been part of the altar. It was smothered with algae; tiny crawfish were skulking all over it. She checked the time and gave Reilly a ten-finger signal. They had to start their ascent in as many minutes; there hadn't been enough air in the tanks to allow a long decompression stop.

Tess knew they were now close. Gliding inches from the bottom of the church, she brushed the silt off the floor gently, trying not to create too much of a cloud. There was no sign of any flagstones. Just small debris and more silt, through which eels slithered. Then Reilly nudged her. He said something, his voice a garbled, metallic sound amidst the bubbling water that escaped from his mouthpiece. She watched him reach down and whisk away some of the silt and stones off a small alcove. The floor revealed some faded carved letters. It was a grave marker. She was breathing fast now. Tracing the lettering with her finger she made out the name: Caio. She looked at Reilly, her eyes ablaze with excitement. His eyes smiled back. Laboriously and carefully, they cleared sand away from more stones. Her heart was now hammering deafeningly in her ears as, letter by letter, more names appeared. And then, through the silt, it appeared:

Romiti.

Aimard's letter was real. The decoder built by the FBI had been accurate and, most gratifying of all, her assumptions were correct.

They had found it.

CHAPTER 59

Moving quickly now, they began clearing debris and sand from all around the gravestone.

Reilly tried to edge his fingers into the crack and pry it open, but the poor purchase and his own buoyancy prevented him from being able to apply enough leverage. Tess checked her watch; five minutes left. Looking around frantically for something to use as a tool, Tess spotted some twisted pieces of metal sticking out from one of the columns. Swimming up to it, she tugged on the protruding rod until it came loose in a cloud of tiny particles of stone. She swam back down as fast as she could and, back on the floor of the church, Reilly took it from her and slid one end into the crack around the stone. Together, they heaved downward on the free end.

Suddenly, there was a creaking sound. Not below them, but above. Looking hurriedly upward, Tess saw small pieces of debris falling from where she had dragged free the ironwork. Was it just movement of the water, or was the upper section of the column sliding off its base? She looked urgently at Reilly. He jabbed his finger at the rod, signaling another attempt to pry the stone loose. She nodded and grabbed hold of it; again, they applied all their strength to the lever. This time, the grave marker moved. Ever so slightly, but it moved, though not enough to get a hand underneath. Again, they heaved on the iron bar. Once more, the marker moved, then tilted upward, allowing a huge air bubble to burst out at them. It brushed violently past them before escaping upward and disappearing through a hole in the rotted ceiling.

From above came another creak.

Looking up, Tess saw that the upper section of the leaning column was definitely inching off its base. The iron bar she'd hastily dislodged had somehow unhinged the column and loosened the precarious structure. Above her, puffs of dust burst in the water like silent explosions. She turned back to Reilly, who was struggling with the stone marker and was pointing down. She saw that there was now enough space for her hand to sneak through. She reached down, cringing as she flashed back to an old movie where a diver's hand had been grabbed by a ferocious eel. Forcing the picture from her mind, she plunged her hand inside the grave. She felt around desperately, shutting her ears and her mind to the echoing cracks and the precariousness of the ancient walls around her. Then her fingers felt something. It felt bulky. Her eyes pleaded at Reilly, urging him to lift the marker even more to make room for it. He slid his hand around the bar for a better grip and let out a huge burst of bubbles as he strained to widen the opening. Tess tugged at the object, trying to squeeze it through the hole without damaging it.

Reilly gave it a final pull, and the stone lifted enough to allow the object to slide through. It looked like a leather pouch with a long strap, around the size of a small backpack, bulging with something that was solid and seemed heavy. As Tess pulled it through the gap, the iron bar suddenly snapped and the gravestone slid down, narrowly missing the pouch as it slammed against the cavity in a dull echo and kicked up a cloud of silt. From above, another creak was followed by the sound of stone scraping against stone as the top section of the column edged slowly off its base, the roof caving in above it as it fell. Tess and Reilly exchanged urgent glances and headed for the portal, but something pulled Tess back. The pouch was stuck, its strap caught beneath the stone.

As she desperately pulled on the strap, Reilly's eyes scoured the bottom, looking for something else to use as a lever, but found nothing. Debris was now raining down on them, floating down in an ever-thickening cloud of silt. Tess tugged on the strap some more. Reilly's alarmed eyes met hers, and she shook her head. It was useless. The church was about to collapse around them, and they had to get out of there, but that would mean leaving the pouch behind. Her fingers were still clasping the battered leather. She wasn't about to give it up.

Reilly moved quickly. He sank back down and ran his fingers along the edge of the slab, then positioned his legs on either side and pulled at it in a last ditch attempt to free the strap. A large rafter floated down, landing inches from his leg. With a supreme effort, the rock moved imperceptibly – but it was enough to free the strap. He let go, pointed at the portal, and he and Tess headed for it, kicking furiously as bits of the roof plunged down around them. Avoiding them, they weaved in and out through the pillars and falling stone until, at last, they raced through the portal and emerged into clearer water.

For a few moments, they floated there, watching as the church collapsed on itself, huge chunks of masonry and stone crashing down in a balletic flurry of cloudy, bubbling water. Tess's heart was still pounding furiously. She concentrated on slowing her breathing down, conscious of the limited supply of air they carried and of the long, slow ascent ahead of them. She glanced at the pouch, wondering what it contained, wondering if it was still intact after all these years, hoping the exposure to the water hadn't ruined it. As she took a farewell glance at the well, her mind briefly drifted to Aimard and to that fateful night. Not in his wildest dreams could he have possibly imagined, seven hundred years ago, that the valley would be flooded by a man-made barrage, and that his secret hiding place would end up submerged under a hundred feet of water.

Reilly was watching her. Their eyes met. Even through the distortion of the mask, her elation was clear. She checked her watch. Their tanks would be running out soon. She jabbed her finger upward. Reilly nodded his agreement and they began the slow ascent, making sure they rose no faster than the smallest bubbles breaking out from their regulators.

Around them, the water slowly cleared as the swirling

dust clouds were left behind. The climb seemed to take forever until finally, the light started to break through. Looking up to where the sunlight streamed downward, Tess's blood drained from her face as she suddenly noticed that something was different. Reaching out her free hand, she seized Reilly's arm but from the tension in his muscles, she realized that he had seen it, too.

Above them, instead of the shadow of one rowboat, there were now two shadows.

Someone else was there, but there wasn't much they could do as their air supply was about to run out. They had to resurface. Tess's eyes hardened. She knew who it must be. And as they broke surface, she saw that she was right.

Rüstem was still there, just as they'd left him, only he had a scared and plaintive frown on his face. Sitting in the second boat, watching them with a look of muted delight – almost like a professor acknowledging the success of a bright pupil, Tess thought – was William Vance.

He was cradling a shotgun.

CHAPTER 60

As he helped Tess clamber into Rüstem's boat, Reilly shot a quick glance toward the shore. A brown Toyota pickup truck was now parked by their SUV. Two men were standing at the edge of the lake, and neither of them was the engineer, Okan. The first was much taller and bulkier than the small engineer, and the second, although wiry and no taller than Okan, lacked his thick nest of black hair. Reilly also spotted something else: both men were holding guns. From this far out, they looked like hunting rifles, but Reilly couldn't be sure. He guessed that Vance had bought himself some local muscle along the way. He wondered if any of them had thought to check the Pajero and, if so, if they'd found the Browning he'd tucked into the stow box under the seat.

Reilly studied Vance, seeing him in the flesh for the first time. *So this is the man behind this whole mess.* He thought back to the murdered horsemen in New York, trying to reconcile the man before him with all the events that had brought them to this remote place, and gauging the professor's mindset. The threatening announcement that Reilly was in fact an FBI agent hadn't fazed Vance in the least. Watching his calm, controlled disposition, Reilly wondered how this sophisticated man, this respected academic, had evolved into the fugitive sitting across from him with a shotgun in his lap; how someone with his background had managed to put together that raiding party and, more to the point, how he had gone on to kill off his hired guns, one by one, and with such efficiency and ruthlessness at that.

Something didn't fit.

He noted that Vance was fixated on the pouch in Tess's hands.

'Careful,' Vance told her as she settled into the boat. 'We

wouldn't want to damage it. Not after all this.' His tone sounded strangely detached as he stretched his hand out. 'Please,' he beckoned.

Tess looked at Reilly, unsure of what to do. Reilly turned to Vance who, with the other hand, swung the shotgun out slowly until it was pointing in their direction. The expression on the professor's face was almost rueful, but his eyes were unflinching. Tess stood up, reached over and handed him the pouch.

Vance simply stowed it by his feet and motioned toward the shore with the shotgun. 'Let's get back on solid ground, shall we?'

As they climbed off the boats at the shore, Reilly could now see that Vance's men were indeed carrying hunting rifles. The taller of the two, a rough looking man with a neck like a tree stump and a steely stare, was pointing his rifle at them, directing them away from the boats. The rifle didn't look new, but it was threatening enough. It was an odd kind of weapon for a hired thug. It occurred to Reilly that Vance almost certainly had had to make do with whomever he'd been able to find at short notice. That could work to their advantage, he thought, especially if the Browning was still in the Pajero. For the moment, though, they were too exposed, standing there dripping in their wetsuits.

Vance found an old, rickety table in Rüstem's yard and rested his shotgun against it. He glanced at Tess, his face brightening slightly. 'I guess I'm not the only fan of Al-Idrissi. I really did want to be the first to get to it, as you can imagine, but ... ' He trailed off, placing the bulky pouch on the table. He stared at it reverentially, his mind seeming to drift away for a moment. 'Still,' he added, 'I'm glad you came. I'm not sure the local talent would have brought it up as efficiently as you did.'

His fingers reached out and settled on the pouch's bulge, feeling it gently, trying to divine what secrets it held. He started to lift its flap, then stopped, his head cocked with a sudden realization. He turned to Tess. 'You should join me for this. In many ways, it's as much your discovery as it is mine.'

Tess glanced at Reilly, clearly conflicted. Reilly nodded for her to go ahead. She took a hesitant step forward, but the wiry, balding man tensed up, raising his rifle. Vance blurted some quick words in Turkish and the man relented, stepping aside to let her through. She joined Vance by the table.

'Let's hope this wasn't all for nothing,' he said as he reached for the pouch and lifted its flap.

Slowly, and using both hands, he pulled something out from inside the pouch. It was an oiled skin. He laid it on the table. His brow furrowed in apparent confusion as he studied the shrouded shape. With hesitant fingers, he unwrapped the skin, revealing an ornate brass ring around ten inches wide.

Its rim was intricately graduated with minute, regularly spaced notches, and it had a two-pointed rotating arm in its center, with a couple of smaller, secondary hands underneath.

Reilly's eyes darted from the object to the big Turk, who was also glancing back and forth from the table to Reilly and Rüstem, struggling to keep his curiosity at bay. Reilly's muscles tensed as he saw a potential opportunity, but the big man had the same idea and stepped back, raising his rifle menacingly. Reilly pulled back, noticing that Rüstem had sensed his move and now had beads of sweat peppering his scalp.

At the table, Tess's eyes were riveted on the device. 'What is it?'

Vance was busy examining it carefully. 'It's a mariner's astrolabe,' he said with a surprised look of recognition. He looked up briefly and saw her confused expression. 'It's a navigational instrument, kind of like a primitive sextant,' he clarified. 'They didn't know about longitudes then, of course, but ...'

Known as 'the slide rule to the heavens,' the astrolabe, the earliest of all scientific instruments, had been around since 150 BC. Originally developed by Greek scholars in Alexandria, its use had eventually spread into Europe with the Muslim conquest of Spain. Widely used by Arab astronomers to help tell the time by measuring the altitude of the sun, astrolabes had evolved into a highly prized navigator's tool by the fifteenth century with Portuguese sailors using them to locate their latitude. The mariner's astrolabe was crucial in helping Prince Henry the Navigator, the son of King Joao of Portugal, earn his nickname. For many years, his fleet kept its use a closely guarded secret and was the only fleet able to navigate open waters. It proved an invaluable tool throughout the Portuguese age of discovery, which culminated in Christopher Columbus's setting foot in the New World in 1492.

It was no coincidence that Prince Henry was the Governor of the Order of Christ from 1420 until his death in 1460. A Portuguese military order, it traced its origins back to none other than the Templars.

Vance examined it further, turning it over carefully, studying the graduations on its outer ring. 'This is remarkable. If this is indeed Templar, it predates the ones we've seen by over a hundred years.' His voice trailed off. His fingers had found something else in the pouch: a leather wrap.

Unfolding it, he found a small sheet of parchment.

Reilly immediately recognized the lettering: it was identical to that on the coded manuscript that had led them here. Only there seemed to be spaces between the words.

This letter wasn't in code.

Tess spotted the similarity too. 'It's from Aimard,' she exclaimed. But Vance wasn't listening. He wandered off, engrossed in the sheet of parchment in his hands. Tense seconds passed as he read it in silence, away from them. When he finally came back, a look of resignation had clouded his features. 'It seems,' he said somberly, 'that we're not quite there yet.'

Tess fought the nausea rising in her throat. She knew she wouldn't like the answer, but still managed to ask, 'What does it say?'

CHAPTER 61

Eastern Mediterranean – May 1291

'Put the longboat to sea!'

Despite the raging maelstrom around him, the ship-master's shout echoed deafeningly inside Aimard's head. As another wall of water battered the galley, his only thoughts were for the reliquary as he rushed toward the ship's fore-castle.

I have to save it.

He flashed back to the first night of their voyage when, after making sure the crew and the rest of his Brothers were asleep, he and Hugh had quietly made their way to the fore-castle, Aimard clutching the chest entrusted to him by William of Beaujeu. The Templars had enemies everywhere, and with their defeat in Acre, they were now vulnerable. The chest had to be secured well out of sight, safe from any searches that might befall them. Aimard had shared his concerns with Hugh shortly after leaving Acre; both he and Beaujeu trusted the man implicitly. He hadn't expected the shipmaster to present him with such a perfect solution.

He remembered how when they had reached the ship's bow, Hugh had raised a flaming torch to expose a deep cavity, slightly larger than the chest, that had been hacked into the back of the bird's head. Hugh climbed up and sat astride the ship's figurehead. Aimard took one last look at the ornate chest before lifting it and handing it to the shipmaster, who carefully placed it into the opening. Close at hand, a brazier burned beneath a small vat of molten resin, the surface of which rocked slowly in keeping with the increasingly heavy swell on which the *Falcon Temple* was riding. With the chest jammed firmly into the hiding place prepared for it, Aimard carefully used a long-handled metal pot to scoop up resin that he handed up to Hugh, who then poured it into the gaps between the chest and the sides of the cavity. After a moment, a bucket of water was dashed over the hot resin, sending up a sizzling cloud of steam. Hugh nodded to Aimard, who then handed him the final stage of the reliquary's concealment. A piece of thick wood, chiseled to the curve of the figurehead, was laid over the opening. Hugh hammered it into place using wooden pegs, each thicker than a man's thumb, then all this too was sealed with molten resin that was quickly hardened with water. The task completed, Aimard watched for a moment longer until Hugh scrambled from the figurehead to the safety of the deck.

Looking around, Aimard saw that no one had observed their actions. He thought about Martin of Carmaux who was resting down below. There was no need to tell his protégé what he had done. Later, when they reached port, it might become necessary, but until then he would let the whereabouts of the reliquary remain known only to himself and Hugh. As for the contents of the chest – that was something for which the young Martin wasn't yet ready.

A lightning bolt snapped Aimard back to his present predicament. He pushed his way through the rainsqualls and almost reached the forecastle when another mountainous wave slammed into the *Falcon Temple*, its brutal force lifting him off his feet and hurling him back against the chart table, impaling him on its corner. Martin was quickly with him and, despite Aimard's garbled pleas, the young knight helped him up and dragged him over into the waiting longboat.

Aimard fell into the barge and, despite the searing pain in his side, righted himself in time to see Hugh clambering over the edge and joining them. The shipmaster was clutching a bizarre circular device, a navigational instrument that Aimard had seen him use, and was busy locking it into position. The knight pounded his fist angrily at the side of the boat and looked on, helplessly, at the figurehead, which stood proudly resisting the remorseless battering of the angry sea before snapping like a twig and disappearing under the foaming water.

CHAPTER 62

Tess's heart sank as she felt the air leave her lungs. She looked incredulous. 'So that's it? After all this, it's at the bottom of the sea?'

She felt a surge of anger. *Not again.* Her mind was a confused jumble. 'So why all the mystery,' she blurted out, grim-faced. 'Why the coded letter? Why not just let the Templars in Paris know they'd lost it irretrievably?'

'To keep up the bluff,' Vance ventured. 'As long as it was within their reach, the cause was alive. And they were safe.'

'Until their bluff was called...?'

The professor nodded. 'Exactly. Remember, this thing, whatever it is, is of paramount importance to the Templars. You wouldn't expect Aimard to just leave its position unrecorded, regardless of whether or not they could get to it during their lifetimes.'

Tess heaved a ponderous sigh and plunked herself down on one of the wooden chairs by the table. She rubbed her eyes as images of an arduous, centuries-old journey and of men being dragged to burning pyres flooded her consciousness. She opened her eyes and they settled on the astrolabe again. *All this way, all these risks,* she thought... *for this.*

'They were so close.' Vance was in his own world, examining the navigation instrument more closely. 'If the *Falcon Temple* had only held together a few hours longer, they would have made it to shore, hugged the coastline and used their oars to reach one of the nearby Greek islands, which were in friendly hands. There, they would have been able to repair the mast and sail on, free from the fear of attack, either back to Cyprus or, more likely, to France.' He paused, then added, almost to himself, 'And we'd probably be living in a very different world...'

Reilly, sitting on a small batch of concrete blocks, couldn't hold back any longer. The frustration was unbearable. He'd felt he stood a good chance of taking out the Turks and Vance if he moved fast, but he didn't want to endanger Tess or Rüstem. But there was more to it than just a bruised ego. At the back of his mind, something else was vying for attention. Somewhere, this had evolved from a straightforward manhunt into something far more insidious; he felt personally threatened, but it wasn't physical. He couldn't quite put a finger on it. Deeper, more fundamental questions had been gnawing at him ever since they had decoded the manuscript, and he suddenly felt troubled and strangely vulnerable. 'A different world?' he scoffed. 'All because of, what, a magic formula to make gold?'

Vance let out a dismissive chortle. 'Please, Agent Reilly. Don't sully the Templars' legacy with petty myths of alchemy. It's a well-documented fact that they gained their wealth from the donations of noblemen across Europe, all of it given with the full blessing of the Vatican. They threw land and money at them because they were the valiant defenders of the pilgrims... but there was more to it than that. You see, their mission was thought to be sacred. Their supporters believed that the Templars were seeking something that would be of immeasurable benefit to mankind.' A hint of a smile broke through his stern features. 'What they didn't know was that had the Templars been successful, it would have benefited *all* of mankind, not just the "chosen ones," as the Christians of Europe arrogantly deemed themselves.'

'What are you talking about?' Reilly blurted.

'Among the accusations that led to the Templars' downfall was that they had gotten close to the other inhabitants in the Holy Land – the Muslims, and the Jews. Our dear knights were said to have been seduced by their contacts with them, to have shared mystical insights with them. On that front, the accusations were actually correct, although they were quickly swept aside in favor of the more colorful ones I'm sure you're both familiar with. The pope and the king – who was, after all, anointed by God, no less, and was desperate to prove he was the most Christian of kings – were understandably keen to smother that idea out, the notion of their champions actually fraternizing with the heathens, than to use it as further ammo in bringing down the Templars, however damning it was. But it wasn't just about them all sharing mystical insights. In fact, it was far more pragmatic than that. They were planning something incredibly daring, brave and far reaching, an act of lunacy perhaps but also one of breathtaking courage and vision.' Vance paused, seemingly moved by the very notion, before his eyes settled on Reilly again and tightened.

'They were,' he announced, 'plotting to unify the three big religions.'

He looked up at the mountains framing them and waved his hands expansively. 'The unification of the three faiths,' he laughed. 'Just imagine it. Christians, Jews, and Muslims – all joined in one faith. And why not? We all worship the same God, after all. We're all the *children of Abraham*, aren't we?' he mocked. His expression hardened. 'Think about it. Imagine what a different world we'd be living in if that were the case. An infinitely better world... think of all the pain and bloodshed we would have avoided over the years – today more than ever. Millions of people, none of whom would have had to die senselessly. No inquisitions, no holocaust, no wars in the Balkans or in the Middle East, no planes plowing into skyscrapers...' A fleeting glance of mischief crossed his features. 'You'd probably be out of a job, Agent Reilly.'

Reilly's mind was racing, trying to make sense of the revelations. *Could it be possible...?* He flashed to his conversation with Tess about the nine years the Templars spent in seclusion in the Temple, their rapid rise in power and wealth, and the Latin inscription Tess had told him about.

Veritas vos liberabit.

The truth will set you free.

He looked up at Vance. 'You think they were blackmailing the Church. You think the Vatican allowed the Templars to gain power at their expense.'

'They were scared out of their wits. They had no choice.'

'But... with what?'

Vance took a step closer, reached out and fingered the crucifix that hung in the unzipped V of Reilly's wetsuit before suddenly ripping it off his neck. Holding it in his fingers, the chain dangling off the back of his hand, he looked at it with scornful eyes that turned to ice.

'With the truth about this fairy tale.'

CHAPTER 63

Vance's words hung over them like the blade of a guillotine.

His eyes took on a life of their own as they glared at the small, shiny object held in the palm of his hand. Then his expression darkened. 'It's amazing, isn't it? Here we are, two thousand years later, with everything we've accomplished, everything we know, and yet this little *talisman* still rules the way billions of people live... and die.'

Sitting in his damp wetsuit, Reilly felt a shiver of unease. He darted a glance at Tess. She was looking at Vance with a rapt expression that Reilly couldn't read.

'How do you know this?' she asked hesitantly.

Vance tore his eyes away from Reilly's cross and turned to her. 'Hughes de Payens. The founder of the Templars. When I was in the south of France, I found out something about him that surprised me.'

The French historian's derisive remarks came rushing back to her. 'That he was from there, from the Languedoc – and that he was a Cathar?'

Vance's eyebrows shot up and he tilted his head, clearly impressed. 'You've done your homework.'

'But it doesn't make sense,' she countered. 'They originally went out there to escort Christian pilgrims.'

Vance's smile remained in place, but now there was an edge to his voice. 'They went out there on a mission to retrieve something that had been lost for a thousand years, something that had been hidden by the high priests from Titus's legions. What better cover for them – and what better way for them to have access to the site they were interested in – than to claim to be diehard supporters of the pope and of his ill-conceived crusade? You see, they weren't about to try and fight the Church blindly – not before amassing enough power and wealth to be able to survive such an impossible challenge. The Vatican had a long history of ruthlessly suppressing any challenge to its one and only true faith – entire villages, women and children massacred by the pope's armies for daring to follow their own beliefs. So they hatched a plan. To bring down the Church, they had to have the weapons – and the influence – to make it happen. And they almost made it. They found what they were looking for. As the Knights Templar, they became hugely powerful militarily, and immensely influential. They were very close to coming out of their spiritual closet. What they hadn't counted on was that they – not just the Templars, but all the Christian armies – would be kicked out of the Holy Land before they'd had a chance to launch their attack on the Church. And when that happened, ending with Acre in 1291, they didn't only lose their power base – their castles, their army, their dominant position in Outremer – but they also lost their prize, the weapon that would allow them to blackmail the Vatican for two hundred years, the object that would empower them to fulfill their destiny, when the *Falcon Temple* sank. And from that point on, it was only a matter of time before they were wiped out.' He nodded slightly before framing them with a fervent stare. 'Only now, with a bit of luck, we may be in a position to finish their work.'

Suddenly, the silence was shattered by a loud and terrifying crack as the head of one of Vance's men suddenly exploded outward, the force of the impact tearing his body back off its feet and throwing him against the ground in a bloody mess.

CHAPTER 64

Instinctively, Reilly lunged toward Tess, but Vance had already seized her by the waist and was pushing her to safety behind his pickup truck. More bullets whizzed by and exploded around Reilly as he dived for cover behind the Pajero while instinctively concentrating on trying to isolate the echo of the report to get a handle on where the shooter was. Three shots blasted into their SUV, ripping through the hood and into the engine block and shredding the right front tyre while giving him a very rough angle on the sniper's position: somewhere to the south, in the tree line – and hopelessly out of pistol range.

An uneasy silence descended on the forest, and after a tense moment's respite, Reilly leaned out to survey the damage. The Pajero wasn't going anywhere. He looked over toward the upturned table, where they'd been sitting. The wiry, balding Turk was huddled behind it and looked terrified. Reilly noticed a movement to his side, by the shed, a flash of blue as Rüstem emerged with a rifle, another small caliber weapon, something he probably used for hunting rabbits. The old man stood there, scanning the distant trees, bewildered, looking for a shot. Reilly waved and yelled out to him frantically, but before the man could react, two more rounds came from the sniper, one ricocheting off the concrete pipes stacked on the ground, the other spinning into the old man's chest, slamming him back against the shed like a rag doll.

From behind his Pajero's tailgate, Reilly saw Vance reaching up to yank open the door of the pickup before pushing Tess in ahead of him and scrambling in behind her. He started up the engine and cranked the car into gear. The wiry Turk managed to clamber onto the Toyota's flat bed just as it swung around and headed for the gate of the compound.

Reilly had no choice. He also had no time to retrieve his Browning from the Pajero. Looking up at the hillside nervously, he decided to risk it. He emerged from behind the SUV and darted after the disappearing pickup.

Two more shots crunched into the side of the Toyota as Reilly caught up with it by the gate and grabbed onto its tail-gate. The pickup crashed through the side pole of the gate before lumbering on down the craggy trail. Reilly hung on with pained fingers, his legs dragging on the rough ground, then his left leg slammed against a protruding rock, pain shooting up into his spine like a white hot spike. Every muscle in his body was ablaze, and he felt he was about to let go.

But he couldn't.

Tess was in the truck. He couldn't lose her. Not here, not now.

He looked up and glimpsed a handle on the inside on the sidewall. He drew on every ounce of strength left inside him and kicked the ground with spinning legs while lunging for the handle with his left hand. His fingers flew off the tail-gate and clasped onto it, and he pulled on it, levering himself upward and dragging himself onto the flat bed.

The Turk was lying low against the sidewall, clutching his rifle, peering anxiously over the side. He turned and saw Reilly climb aboard. Alarmed, the man swung the rifle stock at him, but Reilly seized the barrel and thrust it upward, hearing the report and feeling the recoil as the man squeezed the trigger. Reilly spun his legs around and smashed his boot into the Turk's groin before lunging at him. As they struggled, Reilly spotted something and looked over the cab of the pickup. Less than a hundred yards ahead, a beige Landcruiser was parked across the dirt path, blocking their way. The Turk saw it too, and there was no fall off in the engine's whine. Vance wasn't backing off. Reilly shot a glance through the back window of the cab and his eyes met Tess's. She looked frightened as she reached forward and braced herself against the dashboard.

Reilly and the Turk both grabbed onto the top of the cab as the pickup sloped off the edge of the track, juddered on the rough, rocky soil, and squeezed through between the edge of the hillside and the parked Landcruiser, ramming the front of the big SUV. It plowed through in an eruption of glass and plastic and raced on.

Reilly glanced back at the Landcruiser, which looked like it was too heavily damaged to be of any use to the shooter, and then the Turk was pulling on the rifle again, trying to free it from Reilly's grasp. As they struggled, the pickup reached the edge of the dam and bounced onto it without slowing down.

It sped along the concrete roadway that ran across the top of the dam, racing to cross to the other end. Standing now, Reilly punched the Turk repeatedly, finally succeeding in wrenching the rifle loose, only for the man to wrap his arms around Reilly's chest and squeeze hard. Too close to effectively use his knees, Reilly lashed out with his foot, kicking the man on the inside of his right ankle. The man's grip loosened, and Reilly managed to push him off. They were up against the cab now, and Reilly caught a fleeting glimpse of Tess, who was struggling with Vance, urging him to stop. She grabbed hold of the wheel, and the pickup swerved and hit the retaining wall. Reilly lost his grip on the rifle which slithered along the bed and fell clattering onto the concrete roadway, and saw the Turk's alarmed look as it disappeared in the distance. Panicking, the man lunged recklessly at him. Reacting instinctively, Reilly rolled backward underneath the Turk's rushing body and brought up his feet to throw him over the side of the speeding pickup, which again hit the wall with a resounding crack. The man flew off the truck and went straight over the wall, hurtling down the dry side of the dam, his scream vanishing in the roar of the pickup's motor.

They had reached the end of the dam and Vance spun the wheel to send the pickup sliding onto the dirt track that Reilly and Tess had followed that morning. As they bumped down the rutted trail, Reilly knew they were now shielded from the hilltop where he reckoned the sniper was positioned. Given the road conditions, Vance was forced to slow down, but there was no need to stop him just yet.

He let him drive on for a few miles before rapping on the top of the cab. The professor nodded his acquiescence and, moments later, the pickup rolled to a halt.

CHAPTER 65

After reaching in and yanking the keys out of the ignition, Reilly walked around the truck and surveyed the damage. They had gotten off lightly. Apart from some bruising and the throbbing pain in his left leg, all three of them had nothing more than cuts and grazes, and while the Toyota was heavily dented and pockmarked, he was impressed by how well it had held up.

Vance's door creaked open and the professor and Tess emerged from the truck. Reilly could see that both she and Vance looked badly shaken. He had expected it in Tess, but not in Vance. *Was I wrong about him?* He studied the man's eyes and saw, mirrored in them, the same uncertainty that was gnawing at him. *He's as surprised as I am. He wasn't expecting this.* It confirmed something that felt wrong from the moment he'd first laid eyes on the professor, out on the lake. The first shot that had taken out the big Turk henchman had also triggered an alarm inside Reilly's mind.

Vance didn't kill the other horsemen. Someone else is after this thing.

The thought bothered Reilly. This was a complication he would have been happier without. Although the possibility of an 'overseer' had been considered when the dead horsemen started popping up, it had been discounted long ago. Everything seemed to be pointing to Vance eliminating his accomplices; he seemed to be running his own show. The shots at the lake tore right through that theory. Someone else was involved, but who? Who else knew what Vance had been after and, more to the point, was more than willing to murder several people to get to it?

Vance turned to Tess. 'The astrolabe...?'

Tess nodded as if emerging from a haze. 'It's safe,' she

assured him. She reached into the cabin and brought the instrument out. Vance stared at it and nodded his head approvingly, then lifted his gaze up at the ridge they'd just scurried down. Reilly watched him quietly contemplate the deserted mountains around them. He thought he spotted resignation in the professor's eyes, but they quickly turned insolent and blazed with unsettling determination.

'What went on back there?' Tess joined Reilly.

He glanced away from the professor. 'You okay?' he asked, checking out a small graze on her forehead.

'I'm fine,' she winced before looking up at the tree line surrounding them like a huge fence. The mountains were eerily quiet, especially after the fury that had engulfed them minutes earlier. 'What the hell's going on? Who do you think is out there?'

Reilly studied the trees. There was no sign of life. 'I don't know.'

'Oh, I can think of a lot of people who wouldn't want something like this to come out,' Vance countered. He turned to face them, a satisfied smirk crossing his lips. 'They're obviously getting nervous – which means we must be close.'

'I'll feel better once we put a few miles between us.' He gestured toward the pickup. 'Come on.' He ushered Vance and Tess into the truck.

With Tess squeezed between the two men, Reilly shoved the car into gear and the battered Toyota edged down the slope, its occupants lost in silent contemplation of what lay ahead.

The second he saw the pickup charge out of the small compound and race down the dirt track, De Angelis regretted putting the Landcruiser sideways across the dirt path to block any eventual escape. The jarring din of the truck plowing into their car didn't augur well, and now the sight of the big SUV's pulverized right fender and front grille confirmed his worst fears.

He didn't need Plunkett's confirmation to know that the car wasn't going anywhere. He yanked the rear hatch open and rummaged through their gear, retrieving the GPS monitor and angrily flicking it on. The cursor blinked, displaying no movement. The tracker was stationary. De Angelis scowled at the small screen as he recognized the coordinates as those of Rüstem's compound and realized that the tracker must still be on the bag in Reilly and Tess's stranded Pajero. He'd have to find another way of locating them, which wouldn't be easy in this forested, mountainous terrain.

The monsignor discarded the monitor and turned to face the lake, fuming at the turn of events. He knew he couldn't really blame Plunkett for their dismal situation. He realized something else was at work.

Hubris.

He had been too confident.

The sin of pride. Something else for the confessional.

'Their SUV. It's still at the compound. Maybe we can use it.' Plunkett was holding the big rifle, edging away from the Landcruiser, raring to go.

De Angelis didn't move a muscle. He just stood there calmly, staring at the glassy surface of the lake.

'First things first. Hand me the radio.'

CHAPTER 66

Reilly stared back along the track, listening intently. There was no sound other than birdsong, which in the present circumstances felt strangely disconcerting. They'd gone eight or nine miles before the encroaching darkness had forced them to make plans for the night. Reilly had chosen to veer off the dirt road and follow a side trail that brought them to a small clearing by a stream. They'd have to rough it out until daybreak before making a run for the coast.

He was pretty sure that the big Landcruiser had been crippled by Vance's spirited charge. On foot, whoever had attacked them would still be hours away; in a vehicle, they could at least be heard approaching. As he watched the last glints of sunlight melt away behind the mountains, Reilly hoped the descending darkness would provide them with some measure of cover. There would be no campfires tonight.

He'd left Vance by the side of the pickup, having tied his hands behind his back. The rope was secured to the truck. A quick search of the pickup had uncovered no hidden weapons, providing some basic comforts instead, in the form of a small gas cooker and some canned food. They found no clothes to change into. He and Tess would have to stay in their wetsuits for the time being.

Reilly joined Tess at the water's edge, kneeling down for a much needed drink before settling onto a large rock next to her. His mind was a jumble of concerns and fears, all jostling for attention. He had accomplished what he had set out to do; he just had to bring Vance safely back to the US to face justice. There was little chance his prisoner could be spirited out of the country quietly. Local crimes had been committed, people had been killed. Reilly thought ahead, irked by the prospect of inevitably messy extradition proceedings with the Turkish authorities. More pressingly, he had to get them all off the mountain and back to the coast safely. Whoever had shot at them was clearly in a shoot-first-and-ask-questions-later frame of mind, while they were unarmed, had no radio, and were out of cellphone range.

As salient as those concerns were, they quickly took a back seat to the bigger issue that was hounding him. And from the uncertain look on her face, he could see that Tess was gripped by the same concerns.

'I always wondered how Howard Carter must have felt when he found King Tut's tomb,' she finally said, somberly.

'I'm guessing he had a better time.'

'I'm not so sure. He did have a curse to contend with, remember?' A faint smile crossed her features as she brightened up a bit, momentarily lifting his spirits. But it was still there. That pile of bricks pressing down on the pit of his stomach. It wasn't about to go away, and he couldn't ignore it any more. He had to understand more clearly what they had gotten themselves into.

Steeling himself, he got up and walked over to Vance. Tess followed, close by. He knelt down by the tied man, checking the rope around his wrists. Vance just stared at him quietly. He seemed oddly at peace with his situation. Reilly frowned inwardly as he debated whether or not to go into it, but decided he couldn't avoid it.

'I need to know something,' he ventured tersely. 'When you said "the truth about this fairy tale"... what were you talking about? What do you think they hid on the *Falcon Temple*?'

Vance lifted his head, his gray eyes piercing with clarity. 'I'm not entirely sure, but whatever it is, I suspect it's something that might not be too easy for you to accept.'

'Let me worry about that,' Reilly shot back.

Vance seemed to consider his words carefully. 'The problem is that like most true believers, you've never stopped to think of the difference between faith and fact, the difference between the Jesus Christ of faith and the factual Jesus of history, between truth... and fiction.'

Reilly was unmoved by the mocking he thought he detected in Vance's tone. 'I'm not sure I've ever needed to.'

'And yet you're happy to believe everything that's in the Bible, right? I mean, you do believe in all that stuff, don't you? The miracles, the fact that He walked on water, that He cured a blind man... that He came back from the dead?'

'Of course, I do.'

A faint smile crossed Vance's lips. 'Okay. So let me ask you this. How much do you know about the origin of what you're reading? Do you know who actually wrote the Bible – the one you're familiar with, the New Testament?'

Reilly was far from certain. 'You're talking about the gospels of Matthew, Mark, Luke and John?'

'Yes. How did they come about? Let's start with something basic. When they were written, for instance?'

Reilly felt an invisible weight pressing down on him. 'I don't know... they were His disciples, so I guess shortly after His death?'

Vance glanced at Tess and let out a demeaning chortle. His discomforting gaze settled on Reilly again. 'I shouldn't really be surprised, but it's amazing, isn't it? Over a billion people out there, worshipping these writings, accepting every word as God's own wisdom, slaughtering each other over them, and all of it without having the vaguest notion of where these scriptures really come from.'

Reilly felt a rising anger. Vance's haughty tone wasn't helping either. 'It's the Bible. It's been around long enough...'

Vance pursed his lips and shook his head gently, quickly dismissing it. 'And I suppose that makes it all true, then, does it?' He leaned back, his eyes wandering off into the distance. 'I was like you, once. I didn't question things. I took them on as a matter of... *faith*. I can tell you, though... once you start digging for the truth...' His gaze settled onto Reilly again, darkening visibly. 'It's not a pretty picture.'

CHAPTER 67

'What you need to realize,' Vance explained, 'is that the early days of Christianity are just one big scholarly black spot, when it comes to verifiable, documented facts. But if there isn't much we can definitely say did happen in the Holy Land almost two thousand years ago, there's one thing we do know: none of the four gospels that make up the New Testament was written by contemporaries of Jesus. Which,' he remarked as he noted Reilly's reaction, 'never fails to take followers of the faith, like you, by surprise.

'The earliest of the four,' he clarified, 'the Gospel of Mark – or rather, the one we refer to as the Gospel of Mark, since we don't even really know who wrote it, as it was common practice at that time to attribute written works to famous people – is thought to have been written at least forty years after Jesus's death. That's forty years without CNN, without videotaped interviews, without a Google search turning up scores of eyewitness reports from those who actually knew Him. So at best, what we're talking about here are stories that were passed on by word of mouth, over forty years, without any written record. So you tell me, Agent Reilly – if you were running an investigation, how accurate would you consider such evidence, after forty years of primitive, uneducated, superstitious people telling stories around their campfires?'

Reilly didn't have time to answer, as Vance quickly continued. 'Far more troubling, if you ask me, is the story of how these particular four gospels actually came to be included in the New Testament. You see, over the two hundred years following the writing of the Gospel of Mark, we know that many other gospels were written, with all kinds of tales about Jesus's life. As the early movement grew more popular and spread among the scattered communities, stories of Jesus's life took on local flavors that were influenced by the particular circumstances of each community. Dozens of different gospels were floating around, often at odds with one another. We know this for a fact because, in December 1945, some Arab peasants were digging for fertilizer in the Jabal al-Tarif mountains of Upper Egypt, close to the town of Nag Hammadi, and they discovered an earthenware jar almost six feet high. At first, they hesitated to break it, fearful that a *djinn* – an evil spirit – could be trapped inside. But they did break into it, hoping to find gold instead, and that led to one of the most astonishing archaeological discoveries of all time: inside the jar were thirteen papyrus books, bound in tooled gazelle leather. The peasants, unfortunately, didn't realize the value of what they found, and some of the books and the loose papyrus leaves went up in flames in the ovens of their homes. Other pages were lost as the documents found their way to the Coptic Museum in Cairo. What did survive, though, were fifty-two texts that are still the subject of great controversy among Biblical scholars, as these writings – commonly referred to as the *Gnostic Gospels* – refer to sayings and beliefs of Jesus that are at odds with those of the New Testament.'

'Gnostic,' Reilly asked. 'Like the Cathars?'

Vance smiled. 'Precisely,' he nodded. 'Among the texts found at Nag Hammadi was the Gospel of Thomas, which identifies itself as a secret gospel and opens with the line: "These are the secret words which the living Jesus spoke, and which the twin, Judas Thomas, wrote down." His *twin*. And there's more. Bound in the same volume with it was the Gospel of Philip, which openly describes Jesus's relationship with Mary Magdalene as an intimate one. Mary has her own text – the Gospel of Mary, in which she is regarded as a disciple and a leader of a Christian group. There's also the Gospel of Peter, the Gospel of the Egyptians, the secret book of John. There's the Gospel of Truth, with its distinctly Buddhist undertones... the list goes on.

'A common thread in all these gospels,' he continued, 'apart from attributing acts and words to Jesus that are pretty different from those in the gospels of the New Testament, is that they considered common Christian beliefs, like the virgin birth and the resurrection, to be naïve delusions. Even worse, these writings were also uniformly gnostic, because although they refer to Jesus and His disciples, the message they conveyed was that to know oneself, at the deepest level, was also to know God – that is, by looking within oneself to find the sources of joy, sorrow, love, and hate, one would find God.

Vance explained how the early Christian movement was illegal and needed to have some kind of theological structure if it was going to survive and grow. 'The proliferation of conflicting gospels risked leading it to a potentially fatal fragmentation. It needed a leadership that was impossible to achieve if each community had its own beliefs and its own gospel. By the end of the second century, a power structure started to take shape. A three-rank hierarchy of bishops, priests, and deacons emerged in various communities, claiming to speak for the majority, believing themselves to be the guardians of the only true faith. Now I'm not saying these people were necessarily power hungry monsters,' Vance declared. 'They were actually very brave in what they were trying to do, and they were probably genuinely scared that without a set of widely accepted, rigid rules and rituals, the whole movement would wither away and die.'

He told Reilly how, at a time when being a Christian meant risking persecution and even death, the very survival of the Church became contingent on the establishment of some kind of order. This grew until, around the year 180 and under the leadership of Irenaeus, the Bishop of Lyon, a single, unified view was finally imposed. There could only be one Church with one set of beliefs and rituals. All other viewpoints were rejected as heresy. Their doctrine was straightforward: there could be no salvation outside the true

Church; its members should be *orthodox*, which meant 'straight thinking'; and the Church should be *catholic*, which meant 'universal.' This meant that the cottage industry of gospels had to be stopped. Irenaeus decided that there should be four true gospels, using the curious argument that as there were four corners to the universe and four principal winds, so there should be four gospels. He wrote five volumes entitled *The Destruction and Overthrow of Falsely So-Called Knowledge* in which he denounced most of the existing works as blasphemous, settling on the four gospels we know today as the definitive record of God's word – inerrant, infallible, and more than sufficient for the needs of the religion's adherents.

'Apart from the Gospel of Peter, none of the gnostic gospels had a Passion narrative,' Vance pointed out, 'but the four gospels Irenaeus chose did. They spoke about Jesus's death on the Cross and about His resurrection, they linked the story being promoted to the fundamental ritual of the eucharist, the last supper. And they didn't even start off that way,' he scoffed. 'In its earliest version, the first of them to be included, the Gospel of Mark, doesn't talk about a virgin birth at all, nor does it have the resurrection in it. It just ends with Jesus' empty tomb, where a mysterious young man, a transcendental being of some kind, like an angel, tells a group of women who come to the tomb that Jesus is waiting for them in Galilee. And this terrifies these women, they run off and they don't tell anyone about it – which makes you wonder how Mark or whoever wrote that gospel would have ever heard about it in the first place. But that's how Mark originally ended his gospel. It's only in Matthew – fifty years later – and then in Luke, ten years after that, that elaborate post-resurrection appearances were added to Mark's original ending, which is itself then rewritten.

'It took another two hundred years – to the year 367, in fact – for the list of twenty-seven texts that comprise what we know as the New Testament to be finally agreed upon. By the end of that century, Christianity had become the officially approved religion and possession of any of the texts considered heretical was held to be a criminal offense. All known copies of the alternate gospels were burned and destroyed. All, that is, except for the ones spirited away to the caves of Nag Hammadi, which don't show Jesus to be supernatural in any way,' Vance continued, his eyes riveted on Reilly. 'They were banned because the Jesus of these texts was just a roving wise man who preaches a life of possessionless wandering and of wholehearted acceptance of fellow human beings. He's not here to save us from sin and from eternal damnation, He's here to guide us to some kind of spiritual understanding. And once a disciple reaches enlightenment – and this notion must have given Irenaeus and his cronies a few sleepless nights – the master is no longer needed. The student and the teacher become equals. The four canon gospels, the ones in the New Testament – they see Jesus as our Savior, the Messiah, the Son of God. Orthodox Christians – and Orthodox Jews, for that matter – insist that an unbridgeable chasm separates man from his creator. The gospels that were found in Nag Hammadi contradicted this: for them, self-knowledge is the knowledge of God; the self and the divine are one and the same. Even worse, by describing Jesus as a teacher, an enlightened sage – they consider Him *a man*, someone you or I could emulate, and that wouldn't do for Irenaeus and his lot. He couldn't just be a man, He had to be much more than that. He had to be the Son of God. He had to be *unique*, because by His being *unique*, the Church becomes *unique*, the only path to salvation. By painting Him in that light, the early Church could claim that if you weren't with them, following their rules, living the way they wanted you to, you were doomed to damnation.'

Vance paused, seeming to study Reilly's face before leaning forward, his whispery voice slicing the air.

'What I'm telling you, Agent Reilly, is that basically everything Christians believe in today and have believed since the fourth century, all the rituals they observe, the Eucharist, the holy days – none of it was part of what the immediate followers of Jesus believed in. It was all made up, it was all tagged on much later – rituals and supernatural beliefs which, in many cases, were imported from other religions, from the resurrection to Christmas. But the Church's founders did a great job. It's been a runaway bestseller for almost two thousand years, but... I think the Templars were right. It had already gotten way out of hand in their days, with people getting butchered if they chose to believe in something different.

'And looking at the state of the world today,' he announced with unsettling conviction, 'I'd say it's definitely passed its sell-by date.'

CHAPTER 68

'Is that what you think they were carrying on the *Falcon Temple*?' Reilly asked pointedly. 'Proof that the gospels are, as you put it, works of fiction? Proof that Jesus wasn't a divine being? Even if that were possible,' he argued, 'I can understand how that would undermine Christianity, but how would that have helped the Templars unify the three religions – assuming that is what they were really planning?'

'They started with the one they knew,' Vance countered assuredly, 'the religion that was within their reach, the one whose excesses they had personally witnessed. Once that was... *debunked*, I imagine they had already forged alliances with insiders within the Muslim and Jewish communities, partners who would work with them to instigate similar questions about their own creeds and pave the way for a new, unified view of the world.'

'By picking up the pieces of the disillusioned masses?' It was more a statement than a question on Reilly's part.

Vance seemed unmoved. 'In the long run, I think the world would have been a better place. Don't you?'

'I doubt that very much,' Reilly fired back. 'But then, I wouldn't expect someone who places so little value on human life to understand that.'

'Oh, spare me your righteous indignation and grow up, would you? It's all so ludicrous,' Vance insisted. 'We're still in the realm of fantasy, here, today, in the twenty-first century. We're really no more advanced than those poor bastards in Troy. The whole planet's gripped by mass delusion. Christianity, Judaism, Islam... people are ready to fight to the death to defend every word in these books they hold sacred, but what are they really based on? Legends and myths going back thousands of years? Abraham, a man who, if you believe the Old Testament, fathered a child at the tender age of one hundred and lived to be one hundred and seventy-five years old? Does it make sense that people's lives should still be ruled by a collection of laughable hokum?

'Polls consistently confirm that most Christians, Jews, and Muslims today are unaware of their religions' shared roots in Abraham, the patriarch of all three religions and the founder of monotheism,' Vance explained. 'Ironically, according to the book of Genesis, God had sent Abraham on a mission to heal the divisions between men. His message was that regardless of different languages or cultures, all of mankind was to be part of one human family, before one God who sustains the whole of Creation. Somehow, this lofty message got perverted,' Vance said mockingly, 'like something out of a bad episode of *Dallas*. Abraham's wife, Sarah, couldn't have children, so he took on a second wife, his Arab maidservant Hagar, who gave him a son they called Ishmael. Thirteen years later, Sarah manages to have a son, Isaac. Abraham dies, Sarah banishes Hagar and Ishmael, and the Semitic race is split between Arab and Jew.'

Vance shook his head, laughing to himself. 'The galling thing is that all three religions claim to believe in the same God, the God of Abraham. Things only got screwed up once people started squabbling over whose words were the truest representation of God's tradition. The Jewish faith got its beliefs from its prophet, Moses, whose lineage the Jews trace back to Isaac and Abraham. A few hundred years later, Jesus – a Jewish prophet – comes up with a new set of beliefs, his version of Abraham's religion. A few hundred years later, yet another man, Mohamed, shows up claiming that he is, in fact, God's true messenger, not the first two charlatans, and he promises to bring about a return to the founding revelations of Abraham – as traced through Ishmael, this time, mind you – and Islam is born. No wonder Christian leaders at the time considered Islam a Christian heresy and not a new, or different, religion. And once Mohamed died, Islam itself split into two major sects – Shi'ites and Sunnites – because of a power struggle over who should rightly succeed him.

'So we have Christians looking down on Jews,' he proclaimed, 'considering them to be followers of an earlier, incomplete, revelation of God's wishes; Muslims deriding Christians in much the same way – although they, too, revere Jesus, but only as an outdated messenger of God, not as his son. It's so pathetic. Did you know that devout Muslims bless Abraham seventeen times a day? The *Hajj* – the pilgrimage to Mecca, every Muslim's holy duty – millions of them braving stifling heat as well as the distinct possibility of getting trampled to death – do you know what it's all about? They're there to commemorate God's sparing of Ishmael – the son of Abraham! You only need to go to Hebron to see how absurd the whole thing's become. Arabs and Jews still killing each other over the most hotly contested piece of real estate on the planet, all because it's supposedly the site of Abraham's grave, a small cave that has separate, isolated viewing areas for each group. Abraham – if he ever really existed – must be turning in his grave at the thought of his squabbling, small-minded, petty descendants. Talk about dysfunctional families ...'

Vance heaved a dire sigh. 'I know it's easy to blame all the conflicts in our history on politics and greed,' he said, 'and of course they play a role... but beneath it all, religion has always been the fuel that keeps the furnaces of intolerance and hatred burning. And it holds us back from better things, but mostly, from coming to terms with the truth about who we've become, from embracing everything science has taught us and continues to teach us, from forcing us to make ourselves accountable for our own actions. These primitive tribesmen and women, thousands of years ago – they were scared, they needed religion to try and understand the mysteries of life and death, to come to terms with the vagaries of disease, weather, unpredictable harvests and natural disasters. We don't need that anymore. We can pick up a cellphone and talk to someone on the other side of the planet. We can put a remote controlled car on Mars. We can create life in a test tube. And we could do a lot more. It's time we let go of our ancient superstitions and face who we really are, and accept that we have become what someone from just a hundred years ago would consider a God. We need to embrace what we're capable of and not rely on some arcane force from above that's going to come down from the sky and make things right for us.'

'That's a pretty myopic view you're taking, isn't it?' Reilly argued back angrily. 'What about all the good that it does? The ethical code, the moral framework it sets down. The comfort it provides, to say nothing of the charitable work, feeding the poor and looking after the less fortunate. Faith in Christ is all that a lot of people out there have, and millions of people rely on religion to give them strength, to help them through their days. But you don't see any of that, do you? You're just obsessed with one tragic event, the one that ruined your own life, the one that's jaundiced your view of the world and anything good that's in it.'

Vance's expression turned distant and haunted. 'All I see is the unnecessary pain and suffering it's caused, not just to me, but to millions of people over the centuries.' After a brief moment, his gaze settled again on Reilly, and his tone hardened. 'Christianity served a great purpose when it was conceived. It gave people hope, it provided a social support system, it helped bring down tyranny. It served the needs of a community. What needs does it serve today, apart from blocking medical research and justifying wars? We laugh when we look at the preposterous gods that the Incas or the Egyptians used to worship. Are we any better? What will people think when they look back on us in a thousand years? Will we be the subject of the same ridicule? We're still dancing to tunes created by men who thought that a thunderstorm was a sign of God's anger. And that,' he seethed, 'that all needs to change.'

Reilly turned to Tess. She hadn't said a word during Vance's diatribe. 'What about you? What do you think? Do you agree with all that?'

Tess's face clouded. She avoided his look, obviously struggling to find the right words. 'The historical facts are there, Sean. And we're talking about things that have been widely documented and accepted.'

She hesitated before continuing, 'I do believe that the Gospels were initially written to pass on a spiritual message, but that they became something else. They took on a bigger purpose, a political purpose. Jesus lived in an occupied country in a terrible time. The Roman Empire back then was a world of glaring inequalities. There was great poverty for the masses and immense wealth for the select few. It was a time of famines, of sickness and disease. It's easy to imagine how, in that unfair and violent world, the message of Christianity caught on. Its basic premise, that a merciful God asks humans to be merciful to one another, beyond their families and even their communities, was literally revolutionary. It offered its converts, regardless of where they came from, a coherent culture, a sense of equality and of belonging, without asking them to abandon their ethnic ties. It gave them dignity and equality with others, regardless of their status. The hungry knew where they would be fed, the sick and the elderly knew where they would be cared for. It offered everyone an immortal future free from poverty, sickness, and isolation. It brought a new conception of humanity, a message of love, mercy, and community to a world that was rife with cruelty and gripped by a culture of death.

'I'm not as big an expert on this as he is,' Tess continued, as she motioned toward Vance, 'but he's right. I've always had a problem with all that supernatural stuff, the divinity of Jesus, the idea of his being the Son of God, born of the

Virgin Mary. The uncomfortable truth is that none of it appeared until dozens, even hundreds of years after the Crucifixion, and it only became official church policy at the Council of Nicaea in 325 AD. It was like...' she wavered, 'they needed something special, a great hook. And in a time when the supernatural was something most people accepted, then what better than to suggest that the religion you were selling wasn't named for a humble carpenter, but for a divine being who could give you the promise of an immortal afterlife?'

'Come on, Tess,' Reilly countered indignantly, 'you're making it sound like nothing more than a cynical propaganda campaign. Do you really believe it would have carried as much power, or lasted as long as it has, if it was all based on deception? Of all the preachers and wise men roaming the land at the time, He was the one who moved people to risk their lives to follow His teachings. He was the one who most inspired those around Him, He affected people like no one else had, and they wrote and talked about what they saw.'

'But that's my point,' Vance interjected, 'there isn't a single first person account of it. Nothing that can definitively prove it.'

'Or disprove it,' Reilly shot back. 'But then you're not really considering both sides of the equation, are you?'

'Well, if the Vatican was so terrified of the Templars' discovery coming out into the open,' Vance scoffed, 'I think I can guess which way its thinking leans. And if we could only finish what the Templars set out to do,' he turned to Tess, beaming with an alarmingly infectious fervor, 'it would be the final step in something that's been brewing since the Enlightenment. It wasn't that long ago that people believed that the earth was the center of the universe and the sun revolved around us. When Galileo came along and proved that it was the other way around, the Church almost had him burnt at the stake. The same thing happened with Darwin. Think about it. Whose word is the "gospel" truth today?'

Reilly fell quiet as he weighed the information. It bothered him that everything he had heard, no matter how hard he tried to dismiss it, seemed not just possible, but uncomfortably plausible. After all, there were several major religions vying for adherents all around the planet, all claiming to be the real thing, and they couldn't all be right. He guiltily recognized that he was so ready to dismiss other religions as mass delusions... why should the one he happened to believe in be any different?

'One by one,' Vance announced, his eyes locking onto Tess, 'these falsehoods, these inventions of the early founders of the Church, they're all crumbling. This would be the final one to fall, nothing more.'

CHAPTER 69

Reilly sat alone, perched on a craggy rock face overlooking the clearing where the pickup was parked. He'd watched the sky gradually darken, unveiling countless stars and a moon that was bigger and brighter than any he'd ever seen. The sight was enough to stir the soul of even the most cynical observer, but right now, Reilly wasn't in the most inspired of moods.

Vance's words still rang loudly in his ears. The supernatural elements of the story at the heart of his faith had always sat uncomfortably with his rational, questioning mind, but he hadn't ever really felt the need to subject them to such scrutiny. Vance's disturbing, and, much as he hated to admit it, convincing arguments had opened a can of worms that would be difficult to close.

The truck was barely visible now, Vance's shadowy form beside it where he'd left him. Reilly couldn't stop running the man's tirade through his mind, looking for the crack that would cause the whole, sordid edifice to crumble, but he couldn't find one. Nothing about it was counter-intuitive. If anything, it made too much sense.

A scattering of pebbles behind him snapped him out of his reverie. He turned to see Tess clambering up the ridge to join him.

'Hey,' she said. The full beam that had entranced him was gone, replaced by a troubled expression.

He gave her a small nod. 'Hey.'

She stood at the edge of the hill, taking in the stillness around them for a few moments before settling down on the rock beside him. 'Look, I'm... I'm sorry. I know these discussions can get pretty uncomfortable.'

Reilly shrugged. 'If anything, it's disappointing.'

She looked at him uncertainly.

'I mean, you really don't get it,' he continued. 'You're taking something that's unique, something that's incredibly special, and reducing it to its crudest form.'

'You want me to ignore the evidence?'

'No, but seeing them in that light, poring over every detail, makes you miss the whole point. The thing you don't understand is that it's not about scientific evidence. It shouldn't be. It's not about facts or about analyzing and rationalizing. It's about *feeling*. It's an inspiration, a way of life, a connection –' he opened his arms expansively, '– to all this.' He looked at her intently for a moment, then asked, 'Isn't there anything you believe in?'

'What I believe in doesn't matter.'

'It does to me,' he insisted sharply. 'Seriously, I'd like to know. Don't you believe in any of it?'

She glanced away, looking down at Vance who, despite the impenetrable darkness, seemed to have his eyes settled on them both. 'I guess the easy answer is that I'm in Jefferson's camp on this.'

'Jefferson?'

Tess nodded. 'Thomas Jefferson also had problems believing what was in the Bible. Although he considered Jesus's ethical system to be the finest the world had ever seen, he became convinced that in trying to make His teachings more appealing to the pagans, His words and His story had been manipulated. So he decided to take a closer look at the Bible, and stripped out everything he considered untrue, in an attempt to dig out Jesus's true words from, as he put it, "the rubbish in which it is buried." The man in the book he came up with, *The Life and Morals of Jesus of Nazareth*, wasn't anything like the divine being in the New Testament: in Jefferson's Bible, there was no virgin birth, no miracles, and no resurrection. Just a man.'

She looked into Reilly's eyes, searching for common ground. 'Don't get me wrong, Sean. I believe that Jesus was a great man, one of the most important people who ever lived, an inspirational human being who said a lot of great things. I think his vision of a selfless society where everybody trusts and helps one another is a wonderful one. He inspired a lot of good... he still does. Even Gandhi, who wasn't a Christian, always said he was acting in the spirit of Jesus Christ. I mean, clearly, Jesus was an exceptional man, no question – but then, so were Socrates and Confucius. And I agree with you that His teachings about love and fellowship should be the basis of human relations – we should be so lucky. But was He divine? Maybe you could say He had some kind of divine vision or prophetic illumination, but I don't buy the miraculous stuff and I definitely don't buy the control freaks who pretend they're God's exclusive representatives on earth. I'm pretty sure Jesus didn't intend His revolution to become what it is today, and I can't imagine he would have liked His teachings to become the dogmatic and oppressive faith that grew up in His name. I mean, He was a freedom fighter who despised authority. How ironic is that?'

'The world's a big place,' Reilly replied. 'The Church today is what men have made it over the centuries. It's an organization because it has to be, to make it work. And organizations need a power structure – how else could its message survive and spread?'

'But look at how ridiculous it's become,' she countered. 'Have you ever watched one of those TV evangelists? It's become a Vegas act, a parade of brainwashing jokers. They'll guarantee you a place in Heaven in exchange for a cheque. How sad is that? Church attendance numbers are way down, people are turning to all kinds of alternatives from yoga to Kabbalah to all kinds of New Age books and groups for some kind of spiritual uplift, simply because the Church is so out of touch with modern life, with what people really need today –'

'Of course it is,' Reilly interjected as he stood up, 'but

that's because we're moving too fast. It was very relevant for almost two thousand years. It's only in the last few decades that that's changed, at a time when we've been evolving at a staggering pace, and yes, the Church hasn't kept pace and it's a big problem. But it doesn't mean we should dump the whole thing and move on to... what exactly?'

Tess screwed up her face. 'I don't know. But maybe we don't need a heavenly bribe or the fear of hell and damnation to make us behave decently. Maybe it would be healthier if people started believing in themselves instead.'

'Do you really think so?'

She stared into his eyes. They were earnest, but calm. 'I do. And I also know I'd much rather have my daughter grow up in a world where people aren't deceived by some historical hoax, where they're free to believe in whatever they choose to believe in based on fact, not on myth.' She looked away and shrugged. 'It doesn't matter, anyway. Not until we find the wreck and see what's in that box.'

'That's not really up to us, is it?'

It took a moment for her to answer, and when she did, her voice was incredulous. 'What do you mean?'

'I came here to find Vance and bring him back. Whatever's out there... it's not my concern.' As the words tumbled out of his mouth, he knew he wasn't being entirely honest. He smothered the thought.

'So you're just going to walk away?' she blurted, clambering angrily to her feet.

'Come on, Tess. What do you expect me to do? Put New York on hold for a few weeks while I go wreck diving with you?'

Her green eyes were boring into him with indignation. 'I can't believe you're saying this. Dammit, Sean. You know what they'll do if they find out where it is?'

'Who?'

'The Vatican,' she exclaimed. 'If they get their hands on the astrolabe and find the wreck, that's the last anyone will ever hear about it. They'll make sure it disappears again, and not just for seven hundred years, but forever.'

'It's their call.' His voice was distant. 'Sometimes, some things are better left alone.'

'You can't do that,' she insisted.

'What do you want me to do?' he fired back. 'Help you dredge something from the bottom of the ocean and hold it up proudly for everyone to choke on? He's made no bones about what he's after,' he said, jabbing an angry finger toward Vance. 'He wants to bring down the Church. Do you really expect me to help you do that?'

'No, of course not. But a billion people out there might be living a lie. Doesn't that bother you? Don't you owe them the truth?'

'Maybe we should ask them first,' he replied.

He thought that she was about to press her point further, but then she just shook her head, her expression one of acute disappointment.

'Don't you want to know?' she finally asked.

Reilly held her gaze for an uncomfortable moment before turning away, and said nothing. He needed time to think this through.

Tess nodded, then looked down toward the clearing where they'd left Vance. After a pregnant silence, she said, 'I... I need to drink something,' and headed down the ridge toward the shimmering stream.

He watched her disappear into the shadows.

A hurricane of confused thoughts battered Tess's mind as she stumbled down to the clearing where they had parked the pickup truck.

She knelt down by the stream and cupped her hands to sip the cool water, and saw that they were shivering. She shut her eyes and breathed in the crisp night air, desperately trying to slow her racing heartbeat and calm herself, but it was no use.

That's not really up to us, is it?

Reilly's words had hounded her all the way down from the rocky perch, and they weren't letting go.

She glanced up at the craggy ridge and could just about make out Reilly's distant figure, silhouetted against the night sky. She busily re-ran his take on the momentous crossroads they were now facing over and over in her mind. Given all that had happened, all the bloodshed and the unanswered questions, she knew his decision to take Vance back to New York was probably the sensible one.

But she wasn't sure she could accept it. Not given what was at stake.

She flicked a look at Vance. He was sitting exactly how they'd left him, his back to the pickup, his hands tied. From the merest glint of moonlight reflecting in his eyes, she could tell he was watching her.

And that's when it hit her.

A disturbing, reckless notion that sliced straight through the havoc that was raging inside her and came rushing out.

And hard as she tried, she couldn't shake the thought away.

Reilly knew she was right. She had gone straight to the doubt he had felt earlier, listening to Vance. Of course, he wanted to know. More than that, he *needed* to know. But regardless of his conflicted feelings, he had to go by the book. It was how he did things, and besides, he didn't really have much of a choice. It hadn't been an idle remark when he'd said that they couldn't go after the wreck themselves. How could they? He was an agent of the FBI, not a deep-sea diver. His priority was to bring Vance – and the astrolabe – back to New York.

But he knew perfectly well what the end result of that would be.

He looked out into the night and saw Tess's face again, the disappointment he had seen in her eyes, and he was painfully aware that he was just as disappointed. He had no idea what might have developed between them, given time, but right now it looked as if any relationship they might have had was foundering on the rock of his faith.

And that was when he heard the sudden sound of an engine.

Not in the distance.

Close.

Startled, he glanced down and saw the pickup moving off.

His hand went instinctively to his pocket before he realized he didn't have one. He was still in his wetsuit. He flashed back to when he'd tucked away the truck's keys under its passenger seat, remembering that Tess was next to him when he did that.

And with a reeling horror, he knew.

'Tess!' he hollered as he scrambled down the slope, kicking up debris, losing his balance, and tumbling awkwardly in the darkness. By the time he reached the clearing, the pickup was already a fast-receding dust cloud way up the trail.

Tess and Vance were gone.

Furiously angry with himself for allowing it to happen, his eyes darted around, desperate to latch onto something that could overturn this disaster. They quickly found a small piece of paper sticking out from under some food provisions and camping gear that had been left for him, close to where the pickup had been parked.

He picked it up. He immediately recognized Tess's handwriting:

> Sean,
> *People deserve to know the truth.*
> *I hope you can understand that —*
> *and that you'll forgive me...*
> *I'll send for help as soon as I can.*
> *T.*

CHAPTER 70

Reilly woke up in a daze, his mind bristling with raw emotions. He still couldn't believe Tess had left with Vance. Much as he tried to rationalize it, it still galled him – more than galled, it ate away at his every fiber. He was angry at being duped, at being left there in the middle of nowhere. He was stunned by her decision to leave, even more so at her having gone off with Vance. He was bewildered by her temerity, and concerned about her putting herself in danger – yet again. And, much as he tried to suppress it, he couldn't help feeling his pride had taken a pretty big hit too.

Straightening up, he felt the chirping of birds and the blinding morning glare assaulting his senses. It had taken him forever to fall asleep in the sleeping bag that had been left for him, his exhaustion finally overwhelming his anger into submission late in the night. Squinting, he checked his watch and saw that he'd been out for barely four hours.

It didn't matter. He had to get moving.

He drank from the stream, feeling the welcome effects of the cold mountain water. The tightness in his stomach reminded him that he hadn't eaten in almost twenty-four hours, and he quickly polished off some bread and an orange. At least they'd thought of that. He felt his body slowly come alive, and as his head cleared, angry thoughts and images flooded his consciousness.

He took in the landscape around him. There was no noticeable wind, and apart from the birdsong, which had now subsided, everything was deathly still. He decided he would follow the trail back to the dam and to Okan's office, from where he'd probably be able to contact Federal Plaza – not a call he was looking forward to.

He had barely started the long trek back when he heard a

distant sound. It was an engine. His heart skipped a beat as he imagined it was the pickup, but he quickly realized the sound wasn't that of a road vehicle. It was the throaty chatter of a helicopter, the beating of its blades echoing against the hills and growing more audible by the second.

And then he saw it, recognizing the familiar silhouette slicing across the valley. It was a Bell UH-1Y, a recent incarnation of the iconic workhorse of countless wars. Skimming the trees on the opposite ridge, it suddenly banked and was now headed straight toward him. He knew he'd been spotted. He felt his muscles tighten as he quickly ran through the possibilities of who could be on board: either Tess had done what she'd said she would do and alerted the authorities to his presence, or the shooters from the lake had found him. He sensed it was more likely to be the latter. He scanned the immediate surroundings, his mind coolly seeking out the most strategic points, but he decided against taking cover. They were armed and he wasn't, and besides, he didn't have what they were after. More to the point, he was tired, and angry. He just didn't feel like running.

He watched the helicopter circle overhead and saw the markings on its tail, a circular red and white bullseye-like insignia. He relaxed a little, realizing it was a Turkish Air Force chopper. It dropped down onto the clearing, kicking up a blinding cloud of sand and spray. Covering his eyes with his hand, Reilly approached it hesitantly. Its door slid open, and through the shroud of dust, he saw a small figure moving lithely toward him over the rough ground. As he got closer, he could see that the man wore khaki cargo pants and a dark windbreaker, and sported sunglasses. The man was almost within touching distance before Reilly recognized De Angelis.

'What are you doing here?' Reilly's eyes were darting around, taking in the helicopter, trying to make sense of the apparition. A dying gust from the rotor wash flicked back De Angelis's windbreaker, and Reilly glimpsed a holstered

Glock handgun under it. Momentarily stunned, he looked into the cabin where he spotted the sniper rifle by the feet of a man who sat huddled there, lighting up a cigarette with the insouciance of a bored tour guide. Two other men, soldiers in Turkish military fatigues, sat across from him.

Conflicting thoughts flooded his mind as he scrutinized the monsignor. He pointed at the chopper. 'What is this? What the hell's going on?'

De Angelis just stood there, impassive. As he took off his shades, Reilly noticed that the monsignor's eyes looked different. They held none of the self-effacing kindness that the priest had exuded in New York. The grimy spectacles he had always worn there had somehow concealed a menace that was now radiating unmistakably from him.

'Calm down.'

'Don't tell me to calm down,' Reilly burst out. 'I don't believe this. You damn near got us all killed. Who the hell are you and where do you come off taking potshots at us? Those men back there are dead –'

'I don't care,' De Angelis snapped, interrupting him. 'Vance needs to be stopped. At any cost. His men were armed, they had to be taken out.'

Reilly's mind was reeling in disbelief. 'And what have you got planned for him?' he fired back. 'You gonna burn him at the stake? What, are you lost in a time warp or something? The days of the Inquisition are over, *Father*. Assuming that's what you really are.' He pointed at the sniper rifle by Plunkett's feet. 'Is that standard issue in the Vatican these days?'

De Angelis fixed him with an unwavering glare. 'My orders don't just come from the Vatican.'

Reilly took in the army helicopter, the soldiers in it, and the civilian sitting with a sniper rifle by his feet. He had seen that cold, impervious look before. His mind raced through the events since the armed incursion into the Met, and suddenly the pieces fell into place.

'Langley,' he blurted out as he shook his head, staggered.

'You're a goddam spook, aren't you? This whole thing...' His voice trailed off before coming back assuredly. 'Waldron, Petrovic... The horsemen in New York. It wasn't Vance. It was you all along, wasn't it?' He suddenly lunged forward, grabbing De Angelis and pushing him back with a hard shove. He moved in, reaching for the priest's throat. 'You've been –'

He didn't have time to finish the sentence. The monsignor reacted with lightning reflexes, deflecting Reilly's hands while grabbing one of his arms and twisting it in one fluid, agonizingly painful move, bringing him down to his knees.

'I don't have time for this,' he rasped, as he held Reilly at bay for a moment before flinging him off into the ground. Reilly spat out the dirt in his mouth as the pain in his arm throbbed. The monsignor took a couple of steps, circling around the fallen agent. 'Where are they? What happened here?'

Reilly slowly pushed himself back onto his feet. He caught a glimpse of the man in the chopper, who was looking on with a mocking grin on his face. He felt a fury rising from deep within. If he had been wondering about the extent of the monsignor's personal involvement in the murders in New York, that little demonstration of the man's physical prowess quickly dispelled any doubts he might have had. He had seen it before; the man had hands that could kill.

He dusted himself before staring at De Angelis. 'So what are you exactly?' he asked bitterly. 'A man of God with a gun, or a gunman who's found God?'

De Angelis remained impassive. 'I didn't have you down for a cynic.'

'And I didn't have you down for a murderer.'

De Angelis breathed out as he seemed to mull his response. When he finally spoke his voice was laced with indifference. 'I need you to calm down. We're on the same side.'

'So what was that, back at the lake? Friendly fire?'

De Angelis studied Reilly with cool, insolent eyes. 'In this battle,' he stated flatly, '*everyone* is expendable.' He paused, seeming to wait for its significance to fully sink in with Reilly before continuing. 'You've got to understand something. We're fighting a war. A war we've been fighting for over a thousand years. This whole notion of a "clash of civilizations"... it's not just a fanciful theory coming out of some Boston think tank. It's real. It's happening as we speak, and it's growing, becoming more dangerous, more insidious, more threatening by the day, and it's not going to go away. And at its core is religion because, like it or not, religion is a phenomenal weapon, even today. It can reach into the hearts of men and make them do all kinds of unimaginable things.'

'Like murder suspects in their hospital beds?'

De Angelis let it go. 'Twenty years ago, communism was spreading like a cancer. How do you think we won the Cold War? What do you think brought it down? The SDI, Reagan's "Star Wars"? The Soviet government's stunning incompetence? Partly. But you know what really made it happen? The pope. A Polish pope, reaching out, connecting with his flock, getting them to tear down those walls with their bare hands. Khomeini did the same thing, broadcasting his speeches from Paris while he was in exile, igniting a spiritually starved population thousands of miles away, inspiring them to rise up and kick out the Shah. What a mistake that was, allowing that to happen... Look where we are today. And now, Bin Laden's using it too...' He paused, frowning inwardly, then fixed Reilly sharply. 'The right words can move mountains. Or destroy them. And more than anything in our arsenal, religion is our ultimate weapon, and we can't afford to let anyone disarm us. Our way of life, everything you've been fighting for since you joined the Bureau, hinges on it... everything. So my question to you is simple: are you, as your President once put it so eloquently, with us... or against us?'

Reilly's face hardened, and he felt his chest constrict. The wall of doubt he'd hastily erected was obliterated by the monsignor's mere presence. It was an unwelcome substantiation of everything Vance had said.

'So it's all true?' he asked, as if emerging from a fog.

The monsignor's answer came back dry and fast. 'Does it matter?'

Reilly nodded absently. He wasn't sure anymore.

De Angelis looked around, scanning the bare ground. 'I assume you don't have it anymore?'

'What?'

'The astrolabe.'

Reilly was taken aback by the question. 'How did you know about –?' he fired back, before his voice trailed off, realizing he and Tess must have been under audio surveillance the whole time. He went quiet and let his anger settle for a moment, then shook his head, dejected, and said, 'They've got it.'

'Do you know where they are?' De Angelis asked,

Reluctantly, and still deeply mistrustful of the monsignor, Reilly filled him in about what had happened the night before.

The monsignor weighed the information somberly. 'They don't have much of a head start, and we know the general area they're heading for. We'll find them.' He turned, raising a hand and twirling it around, signaling the pilot to fire up the twin turbines, before glancing again at Reilly. 'Let's go.'

Reilly just stood there and shook his head. 'No. You know what? If it's all one big lie... I hope it blows you all out of the water.'

De Angelis looked at him, thrown.

Reilly held his gaze for a moment. 'You can go to hell,' he said flatly, 'you and the rest of your CIA buddies. I'm out.' And with that, he turned and walked away.

'We need you,' the monsignor called out after him. 'You can help us find them.'

Reilly didn't bother turning around. 'Find them yourself. I'm done.'

He kept walking.

The priest's voice bellowed out after him, struggling against the growing whine of the chopper's engines. 'What about Tess? You gonna leave her with him? She could still be helpful. And if anyone can get through to her, you can.'

Reilly turned, still walking, taking a few steps backward. He saw De Angelis's knowing glare, which made it clear the monsignor knew how close he and Tess had gotten. He just shrugged. 'Not any more.'

De Angelis watched him leave. 'What are you going to do? Walk back to New York?'

Reilly didn't stop. He didn't answer either.

The monsignor called out after him one last time. His voice was now angry, and tinged with frustration.

'Reilly!'

Reilly stopped, dropped his head for a moment before deciding to turn.

De Angelis took a few steps forward and joined him. His mouth shaped a smile, but his eyes remained bleak and remote. 'If I can't convince you to work with us... maybe I can take you to someone who can.'

CHAPTER 71

Vatican or CIA, whoever made the travel arrangements had done a pretty good job. The helicopter had flown to a military air base near Karacasu, not far north from where Reilly had been picked up. Once there, he and De Angelis boarded a waiting G-IV which had flown up from Dalaman to pick them up, and made the fast journey west to Italy. Immigration and customs were swiftly bypassed in Rome, and less than three hours after the monsignor had materialized out of a dust cloud in the Turkish mountains, they were speeding through the Eternal City in the cosseted comfort of an air-conditioned, black-windowed Lexus.

Reilly needed a shower and clean clothes, but as De Angelis was in a hurry, he'd had to settle for washing on board the jet and replacing his wetsuit with BDU pants and a gray T-shirt hastily obtained from the Turkish air force base's supply center. He didn't complain. After the wetsuit, the battle dress uniform was a welcome relief, and, more to the point, he was in a hurry too. He was feeling increasingly uneasy about Tess. He wanted to find her, although he tried not to delve too deeply into his motives. He was also having second thoughts about having agreed to the monsignor's invitation; he wasn't sure what awaited him at their final destination, and the sooner he was out of there and back on the ground in Turkey, he thought, the better. But it was too late to pull out. He had clearly sensed from De Angelis's quiet insistence that this visit wasn't just an idle whim.

He had spotted St Peter's Basilica from the aircraft, and now, as the Lexus cut its way through the midday traffic, he saw it again, looming up ahead, its colossal dome soaring gloriously out of the haze and chaos of the congested city. Although the sight of such a prodigious edifice inevitably inspired feelings of awe in even the most hardened of disbelievers, Reilly felt only betrayal and anger. He didn't know much about the world's greatest church, beyond that it housed the Sistine Chapel and that it was built over the resting spot of the bones of St Peter, the Church's first pope who had died there after being crucified, upside down, for his faith. As he looked at it, he thought of all the sublime works of art and architecture the same faith had inspired, the paintings, statues, and places of worship that had been created around the world by the followers of Christ. He thought of the countless children who said their bedtime prayers every night, the millions of worshippers who attended church services every Sunday, the sick who prayed for healing, and the bereaved who prayed for the souls of the departed. Had they all been deceived too? Was it all a lie? And, even worse – had the Vatican known all along?

The Lexus made its way down the Via de Porta Angelica to the St Anne gate, where a large, cast-iron portal was opened by colorfully outfitted Swiss Guards just as the car reached it. With a quick nod from the monsignor, the Lexus was waved in, entering the smallest country on the planet and ushering Reilly into the center of his troubled spiritual world.

The car stopped outside a porticoed stone building and De Angelis promptly got out. Reilly followed him up the short steps and into the solemn hush of a double-volume vestibule. They walked briskly along stone-flagged corridors, through dim, high-ceilinged rooms, and up wide marble staircases, finally reaching an intricately carved wooden door. The monsignor put away his aviator shades and replaced them with his old tinted glasses. Reilly looked on as, with the ease of a great actor about to go on stage, De Angelis's expression morphed from that of a merciless covert operative into the gentle priest who had materialized that day in New York. To Reilly's added surprise, he took a deep breath before he rapped his knuckles firmly on the door.

The answer came back quickly, in a soft-spoken tone. *'Avanti.'*

De Angelis opened the door and led the way inside.

The walls of the cavernous room were lined with shelves from floor to ceiling, and overflowed with books. The herringbone, oak floor had no rugs. In one corner, by a stone fireplace, a large chenille sofa sat between two matching armchairs. Backing up to a towering pair of French windows was a desk, which had a heavily padded chair behind it and three wingback chairs facing it. The room's only occupant, a burly and commanding figure with grizzled gray hair, stepped around the desk to greet De Angelis and his guest. A somber severity was etched on his face.

De Angelis introduced Cardinal Brugnone to Reilly, and the men shook hands. The cardinal's grip was unexpectedly firm, and Reilly felt he was being studied with an unsettling perspicacity as the old man's eyes moved over him silently. Without taking his eyes off his guest, Brugnone exchanged a few words in Italian with the monsignor which Reilly couldn't make out.

'Please sit down, Agent Reilly,' he finally said to him, motioning toward the sofa. 'I hope you will accept my gratitude for all that you have done and continue to do in this unfortunate matter. And also for agreeing to come here today.'

As soon as Reilly had taken a seat, and with De Angelis settling into another chair, Brugnone made it clear he was in no mood for idle chatter by coming quickly to the point. 'I've been given some background information on you.' Reilly glanced at De Angelis who did not meet his gaze. 'I'm told you are a man who can be trusted and who does not compromise his integrity.' The big man paused, his intense, brown eyes bearing down on Reilly.

Reilly was more than happy to dive straight in. 'I just want the truth.'

Brugnone leaned forward, his large square hands pressed flat against each other. 'I'm afraid the truth is as you fear it.'

After a quiet moment, he pushed himself out of his chair and took a few heavy paces to the French windows. He stared out, squinting against the harsh midday glare. 'Nine men... nine devils. They showed up in Jerusalem, and Baldwin gave them everything they wanted, thinking they were on our side, thinking they were there to help us spread our message.' He chortled, a sound that in other circumstances might have been mistaken for a laugh, but which Reilly knew was an outward expression of a very painful thought. His voice lowered to a guttural grumble. 'He was a fool to believe them.'

'What did they find?'

Brugnone took a breath, a kind of inward sigh, and turned to face Reilly. 'A journal. A very detailed and personal journal, a gospel of sorts. The writings of a carpenter named Jeshua of Nazareth.' He paused, fixing Reilly with a piercing gaze before adding, 'the writings... *of a man.*'

Reilly felt the air leave his lungs. 'Just a man?'

Brugnone nodded his head somberly, his big shoulders suddenly sagging as though an impossible weight was upon them. 'According to his own gospel, Jeshua of Nazareth – Jesus – was not the Son of God.'

The words ricocheted around Reilly's mind for what seemed like an eternity before plummeting to the pit of his stomach like a ton of bricks. He lifted his hands, making a vaguely all-encompassing gesture. 'And all this...?'

'All this,' Brugnone exclaimed, 'is the best that man, that mere, mortal, frightened man, could come up with. It was all created with the most noble of intentions. This you must believe. What would you have done? What would you have us do now? For almost two thousand years, we've been entrusted with these beliefs that were so important to the men who began the Church, and which we continue to believe in. Anything that could have undermined these beliefs had to be suppressed. There was no other choice, because we could not abandon our people, not before and certainly not now. Today, it would be even more catastrophic to say to them that it is all...' He struggled with the words, unable to complete the sentence.

'A massive deception?' Reilly concluded tersely.

'But is it really? What is faith, after all, but a belief in something for which there doesn't need to be any proof, a belief in an ideal. And it's been a very worthy ideal for people to believe in. We need to believe in something. We all need faith.'

Faith.

Reilly struggled to grasp the ramifications of what Cardinal Brugnone was saying. In his case, it was faith that had helped him, at a very young age, to deal with the devastating loss of his father. It was faith that had guided him throughout his adult life. And now, of all places, here at the very heart of the Roman Catholic Church, he was being told that it was all one big sham.

'We also need honesty,' Reilly countered angrily. 'We need truth.'

'But above all, man needs his faith, now more than ever,' Brugnone insisted forcefully, 'and what we have is far better than having no faith at all.'

'Faith in a resurrection that never happened?' Reilly fired back. 'Faith in a heaven that doesn't exist?'

'Believe me, Agent Reilly, many decent men have struggled with this over the years, and all come to the same conclusion: that it must be preserved. The alternative is too horrific to contemplate.'

'But we're not talking about His words and His teachings. We're just talking about His miracles and His resurrection.'

Brugnone's tone was unflinching. 'Christianity wasn't built on the notion of a wise man's preachings. It was built on something far more resonant – the words of the Son of God. The resurrection isn't just a miracle – it's the very foundation of the Church. Take that away and it all collapses. Think of the words of St Paul, in First Corinthians: "And if

Christ has not risen, then our preaching is in vain, and your faith is also in vain."'

'The founders of the Church – they *chose* those words,' Reilly fumed. 'The whole point about religion is to help us try and understand what we're doing here, isn't it? How can we even begin to understand that if we start with a false premise? This lie has warped every single aspect of our lives.'

Brugnone exhaled deeply and nodded in quiet agreement. 'Maybe it has. Maybe, if it had all started now and not two thousand years ago, things could have been handled differently. But it isn't starting now. It already exists, it's been handed down to us and we must preserve it; to do otherwise would destroy us – and, I fear, deal a devastating blow to our fragile world.' His eyes were no longer focused on Reilly, but on something far away, something that seemed almost physically painful to him. 'We've been on the defensive ever since we started. I suppose it's natural, given our position, but it's becoming more and more difficult... modern science and philosophy don't exactly encourage faith. And we're partly to blame. Ever since the early Church was effectively hijacked by Constantine and his political acumen, there have been far too many schisms and disputes. Too much doctrinal nitpicking, too many fraudsters and degenerates running around, too much greed. Jesus's original message has been perverted by egotists and bigots, it's been undermined by petty internal rivalries and intransigent fundamentalists. And we're still making mistakes, which isn't helping our cause. Avoiding the real issues facing the people out there. Tolerating shameful abuses, horrible acts against the most innocent, even conspiring to cover them up. We've been very slow at coming to terms with our rapidly changing world, and now, at a time when we're particularly vulnerable, it's all threatened again, just as it was nine hundred years ago. Only now, this edifice that we've built is greater than anyone dreamed it would become, and its fall would be simply catastrophic.

'Maybe if we were starting the Church today, with the true story of Jeshua of Nazareth,' Brugnone added, 'maybe we could do it differently. Maybe we could avoid all the confusing dogma and just do it simply. Look at Islam. They got away with it, barely seven hundred years after the crucifixion. A man came along and said, "There is no god but God, and I am his prophet." Not the Messiah, not the son of God; no Father or Holy Spirit, no confusing Trinity – just a messenger of God. That was it. And it was enough. The simplicity of his message caught on like wildfire. His followers almost took over the world in less than a hundred years, and it pains me to think that right now, in this day and age, it's the world's fastest-growing religion... although they've been even slower than us at coming to terms with the realities and the needs of our modern times, and that will inevitably cause them problems down the road as well. But we've been very slow, slow and arrogant... and now we're paying for it, just when our people need us the most.

'Because they do,' he continued. 'They need us, they need something. Look at the anxiety around you, the anger, the greed, the corruption infecting the world from the very top down. Look at the moral vacuum, the spiritual hunger, the lack of values. The world grows more fatalistic, cynical, more disillusioned every day. Man has become more apathetic, uncaring, and selfish than ever. We steal and kill on an unprecedented scale. Corporate scandals run into billions of dollars. Wars are waged for no reason, millions are killed in genocides. Science may have allowed us to get rid of diseases like smallpox, but it has more than made up for it by devastating our planet and turning us into impatient, isolated, violent creatures. The lucky ones among us may live longer, but are our lives any more fulfilled or peaceful? Is the world really any more *civilized* than it was two thousand years ago?

'Hundreds of years ago, we didn't know better. People could barely read and write. Today, in our so-called enlightened age, what excuse do we have for such abysmal behavior? Man's mind, his intellect, may have progressed, but I fear his soul has been left behind – and, I would even argue, regressed. Man has demonstrated time and again that he is a savage beast at heart, and even with the Church telling us we're accountable to a greater power, we still manage to behave atrociously. Imagine what it would be like without the Church. But it's obvious that we're losing our ability to inspire. We're not there for the people, the Church is just not there for them any more. Even worse, we're being used as an excuse for wars and bloodshed. We're spiraling toward a terrifying spiritual crisis, Agent Reilly. This discovery could not be happening at a worse time.'

Brugnone fell silent and looked across the room at Reilly.

'Maybe it's inevitable, then,' Reilly offered in a resigned, subdued voice. 'Maybe it's a story that's run its course.'

'Perhaps the Church is dying a slow death,' Brugnone agreed. 'After all, all religions wither away and die at some point, and ours has lasted longer than most. But a sudden revelation like this... Despite its failings, the Church is still a huge part of people's lives. Millions out there rely on their faith to get them through their daily existence. It still manages to provide solace, even to its lapsed members, in their times of need. And ultimately, faith provides us all with something that's crucial to our very existence: it helps us overcome our primal fear of death and the dread of what may lie beyond the grave. Without their faith in a risen Christ, millions of souls would simply be cast adrift. Make no mistake, Agent Reilly, allowing this to come out would plunge the world into a state of despair and disillusion unlike anything we've ever seen.'

An oppressive silence descended on the room, pressing down heavily on Reilly. There was no escape from the unsettling thoughts that were blockading his mind. He thought back to where this journey had all begun for him, standing on the steps of the Met with Aparo on the night of the horsemen's rampage, and wondered how he had managed to end up here, at the very epicenter of his faith, engaged in a deeply disturbing conversation he would have much rather never had.

'How long have you known?' he finally asked the cardinal.

'Me, personally?'

'Yes.'

'Since I took my present post. Thirty years.'

Reilly nodded to himself. It seemed an awfully long time to have to labor under doubts like those that were now battering him. 'But you've come to terms with it.'

'Come to terms?'

'You accept it,' Reilly clarified.

Brugnone mulled it over for a moment, his eyes darkly troubled. 'I will never come to terms with it, in the sense that I believe you mean. But I have learned to accommodate it. That's the best that I've been able to do.'

'Who else knows?' Reilly could hear the condemnation in his own voice, and he knew that Brugnone heard it too.

'A handful of us.'

Reilly wondered about what that meant. *What about the pope? Does he know?* He felt he really wanted to know – he couldn't imagine the pope not knowing – but he held back from asking the question. Only so many blows at a time. Instead, another idea was vying for his attention. His investigative instincts were stirring, clawing their way out of the mire of his besieged mind.

'How do you know it's real?'

Brugnone's eyes brightened, and the edge of his mouth broke into a faint smile. He seemed heartened by Reilly's hopeful defense, but his dire tone quickly smothered any such hope. 'The pope sent his most eminent experts to Jerusalem when the Templars first discovered it. They confirmed it to be genuine.'

'But that was almost a thousand years ago,' Reilly argued. 'They could have easily been fooled. What if it was a forgery?

From what I've heard, it wasn't beyond the Templars' capabilities to pull off something like this. And yet you're ready to accept it as fact without even seeing it...?' The implication hit Reilly just as the words tumbled out of his mouth. 'Which can only mean you've always doubted the story in the Gospels...?'

Brugnone met Reilly's consternation with a beaming, comforting expression. 'There are those who believe the story was only ever meant to be taken metaphorically; that to truly understand Christianity is to understand the essence of the message at its heart. However, most believers take every word in the Bible as being, for want of a better term, the gospel truth. I suppose I fall somewhere in the middle. Perhaps we all walk a fine line between freeing our imaginations to the wonders of the story, and allowing our rational minds to doubt its veracity. If what the Templars found was in fact a forgery, it would certainly help make us more comfortable with spending more time on the more inspirational side of that line, but until we find what they were carrying on that ship...' He framed Reilly with an ardent stare. 'Will you help us?'

For a moment Reilly did not answer. He studied the deeply lined face of the man before him. Although he felt that the cardinal harbored a deep-seated core of honesty, he had no illusions about the motives of De Angelis, and he knew that helping them would inevitably mean working with the monsignor, a prospect that held little appeal to him. He glanced over at De Angelis. Nothing he had heard did anything to alleviate his mistrust of the duplicitous priest, nor dampen his contempt for the man's methods. He knew he would have to figure out how to deal with him at some point in the future. But there were more pressing matters at hand. Tess was somewhere out there, alone with Vance, and there was a potentially devastating discovery looming over millions of unsuspecting souls.

He turned his gaze to Brugnone. 'Yes,' was his simple reply.

CHAPTER 72

A light southeasterly wind stroked the waters around the *Savarona*, conjuring up a fine salty mist that Tess could almost taste as she stood on the aft deck of the converted trawler. She relished the freshness of the mornings out at sea, as well as the calming serenity that came with each sunset. It was the long hours in between that were proving difficult.

They'd been lucky to find the *Savarona* at such short notice. From the Caribbean to the coast of China, the demand for undersea exploration vessels had boomed in recent years, limiting availability and fueling prices. In addition to the marine biologists, oceanographers, oil companies, and documentary film makers that traditionally accounted for most of that demand, two new groups of end users were now driving the market: adventure divers, a growing legion of people who were willing to pay tens of thousands of dollars for a chance to get up close and personal with the *Titanic* or cozy up to hydrothermal vents 8,000 feet below the surface of the ocean near the Azores; and treasure hunters or, as they preferred to be known these days, 'commercial archaeologists.'

The Internet had played a crucial role in helping locate the research ship. A few phone calls and a short flight later, Vance and Tess had made their way to the port of Piraeus, in Athens, where the *Savarona* was moored. Its captain, a tall, striking Greek adventurer called George Rassoulis who sported a tan that looked like it went deep enough to reach his bones, had initially turned down Vance's proposal due to a scheduling conflict. Preparations were already underway for him to take a small group of historians and a film crew into the northern Aegean in search of a lost fleet of Persian triremes. Rassoulis could only offer his services to Vance for no more than three weeks before having to take his party north, and three weeks, he had explained, wouldn't be anywhere near enough. As it was, his ship had been booked for two months, which was in itself a relatively short window given that locating ancient shipwrecks successfully was something akin to finding a needle in a haystack. But then most expeditions lacked something Vance had at his disposal: the astrolabe, which, he hoped, would narrow the location of his quarry down to within ten square miles.

Vance had told Rassoulis that they were after a crusader vessel, hinting at the possibility of it carrying gold and other valuables that were being spirited out of the Holy Land after the fall of Acre. Intrigued, Rassoulis had reluctantly agreed to take them on, swept along by Vance's enthusiasm, the professor's infectious belief in the ancient instrument's ability to deliver them the *Falcon Temple* within that limited timeframe, as well as a tinge of greed. The captain was more than happy to indulge Vance's request for total discretion. He was used to treasure hunters – *commercial archaeologists* – and their need to avoid publicity. And given that he had negotiated a cut of the treasure's value for himself, it was also in his best interests to make sure no outsiders crashed their party. He had explained to Vance how the ship would trawl the search site from the outside in for no more than a few hours at a time before sailing away to other, 'fake' search spots in order to divert attention from their target area, a tactic that suited Vance perfectly.

What Tess was now rediscovering – the last time she'd been through it, she remembered, was off the coast of Alexandria in Egypt, the time Clive Edmondson had made his clumsy pass – was that the trawling process required a lot of patience, something she didn't exactly have in abundance right now. She was desperate to find out what secrets lay beneath the gentle swell that undulated beneath her feet, and she knew they were very close. She could feel it, and it made the long spells at the railing even harder to bear.

As the hours floated by, she would drift away into her thoughts, her eyes unconsciously riveted on the two cables that trailed behind the old ship and disappeared beneath its foamy wake. One pulled a low-frequency side-scan sonar, which mapped every noticeable protrusion on the undersea surface; the other dragged a magnetic resonance magnetometer, which would detect any residual iron in the wreck. There had been a couple of moments of excitement in the previous days. On each occasion, the sonar had detected something, and the ship's ROV – the remotely operated vehicle, affectionately named *Dori* after the absent-minded fish in *Finding Nemo* – had been sent down to investigate. Each time, Tess and Vance had rushed into the control room of the *Savarona*, hearts racing, full of hope. They had sat there, eyes glued to the monitors, watching the hazy images coming back from *Dori*'s camera, their imaginations spurred into overdrive, only to have their hopes dashed by the realization that what the sonar had found wasn't exactly what they had been hoping for: in one instance, it was a wreck-sized outcropping of rock and, in the other, the remains of a twentieth-century fishing boat.

The rest of the time was spent waiting, and hoping, at the railing. As the days drifted by, Tess's mind roamed the recent events of her life. She found herself constantly reliving the moments that had led to her being here, sixty kilometers off the coast of Turkey, on a diving ship with a man who had led an armed robbery on the Met in which people had been killed. Her decision to leave Reilly and join Vance haunted her over the first few days. She would feel pangs of guilt and remorse, and experience panic attacks, and she often had to work hard to smother an urge to leave the ship at any cost and get away. Those worries had slowly subsided with each passing day. At times, when she wondered about whether or not she should have done it all, she did her best to rationalize her decisions and push the unsettling thoughts away, convincing herself that what she was doing was important. Not just to her – although, as she'd told Reilly, a discovery like this would make a huge difference to her career and, by extension, to hers and Kim's financial security – but to millions of others around the world, a world in which Kim would grow up. A better, truer world, she hoped. Ultimately, though, she knew it was pointless to try and justify it. It was something she felt inexplicably compelled to do.

One concern she couldn't smother was about Reilly. She thought about him a lot. She wondered how he was, and where he was. She thought about the way she had abandoned him and run off like a thief in the night, and found it hard to rationalize. It had been wrong, horribly wrong, and she knew it. She had endangered his life. She'd left him out there, in the middle of nowhere – and with a sniper on the loose. How could she have done something so irresponsible? She wanted to know he was alright; she wanted to apologize to him, to try and explain why she'd done it, and it pained her to think that this was one blow for which she would never be able to make amends, at least not as far as he was concerned. But she also knew that Vance had been right when he had said that Reilly would hand their discovery over to people who would bury it forever – and that was something she couldn't live with. Either way, she realized, their relationship had been doomed – ironically, by the very thing that had brought them together.

Presently, with a six-foot swell rolling lazily under it, the *Savarona* turned to begin yet another run down the premapped grid. Tess's gaze drifted away from the cables and up to the horizon, where wisps of dark clouds were intruding on an otherwise clear sky. She felt a tightness in her chest. Something else had been nagging at her ever since the night she had driven off with Vance. It was an unsettling feeling that was always there, clawing away at her from the inside, never letting go, and with the completion of each trawling run of the *Savarona*, it got harder and harder to ignore: was she doing the right thing? Had she thought things through enough? Were certain secrets better left buried? Was pursuing the truth in this case a wise and noble quest, or was she helping unleash a terrible calamity on an unsuspecting world?

Her doubts were cut short by the appearance of Vance's tall figure. He stepped out from the wheelhouse and joined her at the railing. He seemed annoyed.

'Nothing yet?' she asked.

He shook his head. 'After this run, we'll have to clear out of here for the day.' He stared out, sucking in a chestful of ocean air. 'I'm not worried, though. Three more days and we'll have covered the entire search area.' He turned to face her and smiled. 'We'll find it. It's out there, somewhere. It's just playing hard to get, that's all.'

His gaze was distracted by a faint buzzing in the distance. His eyes narrowed as he scanned the horizon, his brow furrowing when he spotted the source of the noise. Tess followed his eye line and saw it too: a tiny dot, a helicopter, skimming the surface of the sea several miles away, on a seemingly parallel heading. Their eyes remained locked on it, tracking it as it followed a straight course before banking away. Within seconds, it was out of sight.

'That's for us, isn't it?' Tess asked. 'They're looking for us.'

'They can't do much out here,' Vance shrugged, 'we're in international waters. Then again, they haven't exactly been playing by the rules, have they?' He glanced up at the bridge, where an engineer was entering the control room. 'You know what's funny?'

'I can't imagine,' she said dryly.

'The crew. There's seven of them, and two of us, which makes nine,' he mused. 'Nine. Just like Hughes de Payens and his gang. Poetic, don't you think?'

Tess looked away, failing to find anything even remotely

poetic in what they were doing there. 'I wonder if they ever had the same doubts.'

Vance arched an eyebrow as he cocked his head and scrutinized her. 'You're not having second thoughts, are you?'

'Aren't you?' She was aware of the tremor in her voice and could see that Vance picked up on it. 'What we're doing out here, what we might find... doesn't it worry you in the least?'

'Worry?'

'You know what I mean. Haven't you stopped to think about the shock, the chaos this could bring?'

Vance scoffed dismissively. 'Man is a pitiful creature, Tess. Always desperate to find something or someone to worship, and not just by himself, no – it has to be worshipped by everybody, everywhere, at any cost. It's been the bane of man's existence since the dawn of time... Worried about it? I'm looking forward to it. I'm looking forward to liberating millions of people from an oppressive lie. What we're doing is a natural step forward in man's spiritual evolution. It'll be the beginning of a new age.'

'You talk about it as though it's going to be greeted with parades and fireworks, but it's the exact opposite, you know that. It's happened before. From the Sassanids to the Incas, history's riddled with civilizations that just collapsed after their gods were discredited.'

Vance was unmoved. 'They were civilizations built on lies, on shifting sands – just like ours. But you worry too much. Times have changed. The world today is a bit more sophisticated than that.'

'They were the most advanced civilizations of their time.'

'Give those poor souls out there some credit, Tess. I'm not saying it won't be painless, but... they can handle it.'

'What if they can't?'

He held his palms out in a mock helpless gesture, but there was nothing helpless about his tone. He was dead serious. 'So be it.'

Tess's eyes stayed locked on his for a moment before she

354

turned away. She stared out toward the horizon. Wisps of gray clouds seemed to be materializing out of nowhere, and in the distance, whitecaps were now flecking an otherwise uniformly dark sea.

Vance leaned against the railing next to her. 'I've thought about this a lot, Tess, and on balance, I have no doubt that we're doing the right thing. Deep down, you know I'm right.'

She didn't doubt he'd thought about it a lot. She knew he'd been consumed by it both academically and personally, but he'd always considered it from a distorted point of view, through a lens that was shattered by the tragic deaths of his loved ones. But had he thought deeply enough about how something like this would affect virtually every living soul on the planet? How it would put into question not just the Christian faith, but the notion of faith itself? How it would be seized upon by the enemies of the Church, how it would polarize people, and how millions of true believers would quite possibly lose the spiritual core that sustained their lives?

'They'll fight it, you know,' she declared, surprised by a hint of hope in her voice. 'They'll bring experts out of the woodwork to discredit it, they'll use everything they can think of to prove that it's just a hoax, and given your history...' She suddenly felt uncomfortable elaborating that point.

He nodded. 'I know,' he calmly agreed. 'Which is why I'd much rather you presented it to the world.'

Tess felt the blood drain from her face. She stared at him, taken aback by his suggestion. 'Me...?'

'Of course. After all, it's as much your discovery as it is mine, and, as you said, given that my recent behavior hasn't been exactly –' he paused, searching for the most appropriate term '– *praiseworthy*...'

Before she could formulate an answer, she heard the big ship's engines wind down and felt it suddenly slow to a crawl before turning into the breeze. She spotted Rassoulis emerging from the bridge and, in the swirling fog of her mind, she heard him calling out to them. Vance kept his eyes locked on her for a moment before turning to the captain, who was gesturing excitedly for them to join him and yelling what she thought sounded like, 'We've got something.'

CHAPTER 73

Standing quietly at the rear of the bridge, Reilly watched as De Angelis and the *Karadeniz*'s skipper, a stocky man by the name of Karakas who had dense black hair and a bushy mustache, leaned over the patrol boat's radar display and selected their next target.

There was no shortage of them. The dark screen was lit up with dozens of green blips. Some of them had small, digital alphanumeric codes tagged on, which indicated a ship with a modern transponder. Those were easier to identify and rule out, using Coast Guard and shipping databases, but they were few and far between. Overwhelmingly, the contacts on the screen were just anonymous blips coming from the hundreds of fishing boats and sailing craft that crowded this very popular strip of coastline. Figuring out which one of them was carrying Vance and Tess, Reilly knew, wouldn't be easy.

This was his sixth day at sea, which, as far as Reilly was concerned, was already plenty. It had become quickly obvious to him that he wasn't a sea dog, not by a long shot, but at least the sea had been reasonably well behaved since they'd started their search and, mercifully, the nights were spent on dry land. Each day, they would sail out of Marmaris at the break of dawn and work their way up and down the coastline, from the Gulf of Hisaronu to the area south of the Twelve Islands. The *Karadeniz*, a SAR-33 class patrol boat, gleaming white with a wide, slanted red stripe on its hull next to the words *Sahil Güvenlik* in bold, unmissable letters – the Turkish Coast Guard's official name – was lightning quick and reasonably comfortable, and was able to cover a surprisingly large patch of sea over the course of a day. Other boats based at Fethiye and Antalya were scouring the waters further east. Agusta A-109 helicopters were also involved, performing visual sweeps at low altitude and alerting the speedboats to promising sightings.

The coordination between the various air, sea, and land components of the search was almost flawless; the Turkish Coast Guard had extensive experience in patrolling these busy waters. Relations between Greece and Turkey were always less than cordial, and the close proximity of the former's Dodecanese islands was constantly a source of fishing and tourism disputes. In addition, the narrow strip of sea separating the two countries was favored by human traffickers of desperate migrants trying to reach Greece and the rest of the European Union from the still non-EU Turkey. Still, there was a lot of sea to cover, and with most of the traffic consisting of innocuous pleasure craft without anyone on radio watch, sifting through them was proving to be a laborious, grueling endeavor.

As the radar operator pored over some charts next to his screen and the radioman compared notes with the crew of one of the helicopters, Reilly stepped away from the screen and looked out the windshield of the *Karadeniz*. He was surprised to see some nasty weather lying to the south. A billowing wall of dark clouds lay just above the horizon, separated by a thin strip of bright yellowish light. It looked somewhat unreal.

He could almost feel Tess's presence, and knowing that she was out there somewhere, frustratingly within reach and yet beyond it at the same time, grated at him. He wondered where she was, and what she was doing at that very moment. Had she and Vance found the *Falcon Temple* already? Were they already on their way to... where? What would they do with 'it' if they found it? How would they announce their find to the world? He'd thought a lot about what he would tell her when he did catch up with her, but, surprisingly, the initial anger he had felt at being abandoned had long since abated. Tess had her reasons. He didn't agree with them, but her ambition was an intrinsic part of her and helped make her what she was.

He looked across the cockpit and out the opposite side of the boat, and what he saw unsettled him. Far to the north of their position, the sky was also darkening ominously. The sea had taken on a gray, marbled look, and whitecaps littered the distant swell. He noticed the helmsman glance across to another man on the bridge, who Reilly assumed was the first officer, and indicate the phenomenon with a nod of the head. They seemed to be sandwiched between two opposite fronts of bad weather. The storms appeared to be moving in tandem, converging on them. Again, Reilly looked at the helmsman who now appeared a bit ruffled. As did the first officer, who approached Karakas and was clearly discussing it with him.

The skipper consulted the weather radar and the barometer, and exchanged a few words with the two officers. Reilly glanced over at De Angelis, who picked up on it and translated for him.

'I think we might have to head back earlier than planned today. We seem to have not one, but two rather nasty weather fronts, both of them heading our way and fast.' The monsignor looked at Reilly uncertainly, then arched an eyebrow. 'Sound familiar?'

Reilly had already made the association before De Angelis had mentioned it. It was uncomfortably close to what Aimard had described in his letter. He noticed that Plunkett, who was out smoking a cigarette on deck, was eyeing the gathering storm with some concern. Turning to the cockpit, he saw that the two officers he'd been watching were now intent on a batch of dials and monitors. This and their frequent glances toward the converging banks of dark clouds told Reilly that the storms were making both men uneasy. Just then, the radar operator called out to the skipper and uttered something in Turkish. Karakas stepped over to the console, as did De Angelis. Reilly tore his eyes away from the storm front and joined them.

According to the skipper's clipped translation, the radar operator was walking them through a chart onto which he had plotted the movements of some vessels he had been tracking. He was particularly interested in one of the ships, which had a curious navigation pattern. It had spent a noticeable time sailing up and down a narrow corridor of sea. This, in itself, wasn't unusual. It could easily be a fishing boat, trawling an area favored by its captain. Several other blips behaved in the exact same way. But the radar operator noted that whereas over the last couple of days, a contact, which he believed could well be the same ship, would spend a couple of hours navigating up and down this particular patch of sea before heading off and trawling elsewhere, the vessel he was now watching had been stationary for the last two hours. Furthermore, of the four vessels in the area, three were now moving out, presumably because they'd spotted the approaching storms. The fourth – the contact in question – wasn't budging.

Reilly leaned in for a closer look. He could see that the three other contacts on the screen had indeed altered course. Two of them were heading for the Turkish mainland, the third toward the Greek island of Rhodes.

De Angelis's brow furrowed as he absorbed the information. 'It's them,' he said with chilling assurance as Plunkett came indoors. 'And if they're not moving, it's because they've found what they're looking for.' He turned to Karakas, his eyes hardening. 'How far are they?

Karakas scanned the screen with expert eyes. 'About forty nautical miles. In this sea, I'd say two – two and a half hours away, maybe. But it's going to get worse. We might have to turn back before we get to them. The barometer readings are falling very quickly, I've never seen anything like it.'

De Angelis didn't miss a beat. 'I don't care. Send in a chopper to have a closer look, and get us over there as fast as you can.'

CHAPTER 74

The camera glided through the forbidding darkness, past streaming galaxies of plankton that lit up the screen before quickly sailing out of the glare of its spotlight.

The images from the ROV unfurled before a breathless audience in the control room of the *Savarona*, a cramped space situated behind the vessel's bridge. Vance and Tess were standing, leaning over the shoulders of Rassoulis and two technicians who were seated before a small bank of monitors. To the left of the monitor showing the images from *Dori*'s camera, a smaller GPS positioning monitor displayed the current location of the ship as it circled and doubled back on its course, trying to hold its position against a surprisingly strong current. A smaller screen on the right showed a computerized representation of the sonar scan, a big circle with concentric bands of blue, green, and yellow; another, a pixeled compass, showed their heading as just off due south. But no one was giving those monitors more than a fleeting, occasional glance. Their eyes were all riveted onto the central monitor, the one showing the images from the ROV's camera. They watched in rapt silence as the bottom came rushing up, the pixeled reading in the corner of the screen quickly closing in on the 173 meters that the depth sounder of the mother ship was showing.

At 168m, the starry flecks grew thicker. At 171m, a couple of jerking crayfish scurried out of the light, and then, at 173m, the screen was suddenly flooded by a silent burst of yellow light. The ROV had landed.

Dori's highly protective guardian, a Corsican engineer by the name of Pierre Attal, was locked in concentration as he used a joystick and a small keyboard to manipulate his robotic ward. He reached for a small trackball at the edge of the keyboard and, responding to his fingers' orders, the camera rotated on itself, panning across the seabed. Like the images from a Mars probe, the pictures showed an eerie, inviolate world. All around the robotic visitor was nothing but a flat expanse of sand that disappeared into a stygian darkness.

Tess's skin was tingling with guarded anticipation. She couldn't help but feel excited, although she knew they weren't necessarily there yet, not by any means. The low-frequency, side-scan sonar only provided the rough position of any promising target; the ROV then had to be deployed, its high-frequency sonar allowing the eventual pinpointing, and examination, of those sites. She knew the ocean floor underneath the *Savarona* dropped as deep as 250m in places and was covered with scattered coral reefs, many the size they'd expect the *Falcon Temple* to be. The sonar scans weren't enough to distinguish the wreck from these natural mounds, which was where the magnetometers came into play. Their readings would help detect the wreck's residual iron, and although they were carefully calibrated – Rassoulis and his team had calculated that after 700 years of saltwater corrosion, there would be, at most, a thousand pounds of iron left in the *Falcon Temple*'s remains – they still carried the risk of triggering false alarms due to natural pockets of geomagnetism or, more commonly, from more recent wrecks.

She watched as the procedure she had witnessed twice in recent days unfurled again. Using the most minute of tugs on the joystick, Attal confidently guided the ROV across the sea floor. Every minute or so, he would set it down in another cloudburst of sand. He would then hit a button that would cause its pinger to initiate a 360-degree sweep of its immediate surroundings. The team would carefully study the resulting scan before Attal would be back at the controls, firing the small robot's hydraulic thrusters and propelling it forward on its silent quest.

Attal had repeated the exercise over half a dozen times

before an inchoate patch appeared in the corner of the screen. Guiding the ROV to the spot, he initiated another sonar scan. The screen took a couple of seconds to record the results before Tess saw the patch coalesce into an oblong pinkish shape, beckoning to her from its blue surroundings.

Tess glanced at Vance, who met her eyes calmly.

Without looking up at them, Rassoulis said to Attal, 'Let's get a closer look.'

The ROV was on the move again, skimming the bottom of the sea floor like an undersea hovercraft as Attal guided it expertly to its target. At the next ping, the pink shape grew more distinct along its edges.

'What do you think?' Vance asked.

Rassoulis glanced up at Vance and at Tess. 'The magnetometer reading's a bit high, but...' He pointed a finger at the image on the scan. 'You see how it's squared off at this end, and pinched in over here, at the other end?' He raised a hopeful eyebrow. 'It doesn't look like a rock to me.'

The room fell silent as the ROV moved in. Tess's eyes were locked on the screen as the camera floated over a cloud of sea plants that swayed almost imperceptibly in the desolate waters. As it dropped back down and hugged the sand again, Tess felt her pulse quicken. At the edge of the ROV's beam, something was coming into view. Its edges were too angular, its curves too regular. It looked man-made.

Within seconds, the unmistakable remains of a ship became discernible. The robot banked over the site, revealing the skeleton of a ship, its wooden ribs hollowed out by teredo worms.

Tess thought she spotted something. She pointed excitedly at the corner of the screen. 'What's that? Can you get a tighter shot of that?'

Attal guided his robot as directed. Tess leaned in for a better look. In the bright glow of its spotlights, she could make out something rounded, barrel-like. It looked like it was made of rusted metal. It was hard to tell the relative scale of the objects on the screen, and for a moment she wondered if what she was seeing was a cannon. The thought triggered a sudden ripple of concern inside her – she knew a ship from the late crusades wouldn't have been carrying one. But as the ROV swung closer, the curved metallic shape appeared different. It looked flatter and wider. From the corner of her eye, Tess saw an unhappy grimace break across Rassoulis's face.

'That's steel plating,' he shrugged. She knew what he meant before he said it. 'It's not the *Falcon*.'

The ROV banked around it, showing it from another angle. Attal nodded in grim confirmation. 'And look, over here. That's paint.' He looked up at Tess and shook his head with dismay. As the robot nosed around the sunken vessel's hull, it was pretty clear that what they had found were the remains of a far more recent ship.

'Mid-nineteenth century,' Rassoulis confirmed. 'Sorry.' He shot a glance out the window. The sea was getting increasingly restless, and dark-bellied clouds were rolling in from two fronts with alarming speed. 'We'd better get out of here and head back anyway. This doesn't look good.' He turned to Attal. 'Bring *Dori* up. We're done here.'

Tess nodded slowly, heaving a dejected sigh. She was about to turn and leave the room when something at the edge of the screen caught her eye. She felt a sudden shiver of excitement and stared at it, wide-eyed, before jabbing a finger at the monitor's left side. 'What's this? Right here? You see that?'

Rassoulis craned his neck in, staring intently at the screen while Attal maneuvered the robot toward the spot Tess had pointed out. Peering between the two men, Tess studied the screen intently. At the edge of the ROV's frail light, a protrusion was coming into view. It looked like a leaning tree stump, rising out of a small mound. As the robot edged nearer, she could see that the mound was composed of what appeared to be spars, some of them trailing strands of seaweed, but which her imagination hoped were actually remnants of rigging. Some of the pieces were curved, like the ribs of an ancient carcass. Centuries of marine growth covered the ghostly remains.

Her heart was racing. It had to be a ship. Another one, an older one, partially obscured by the more recent wreck lying on top of it.

The ROV moved in closer, gliding over the disintegrating, coral-encrusted wreckage, its lights bathing the protrusion in their whitish glow.

Tess suddenly felt the air being sucked out of the room around her.

There, basking in the otherworldly glare of the spotlight and jutting out of the ocean floor in fierce defiance, stood the falcon figurehead.

CHAPTER 75

In the heaving wheelhouse, Rassoulis, Vance, and Tess stared out with growing concern at the approaching storm fronts. The wind had climbed to thirty knots, and the swell around the *Savarona* had grown into breaking waves, the churning water now matching the roiling black clouds in their threat.

Below the bridge, a small crane was settling the ROV down onto the main deck. Attal and two other crewmen stood there, braving the weather as they waited to fasten it down.

Tess pulled the windblown hair out of her face. 'Shouldn't we be heading back?' she asked Rassoulis.

Vance jumped in, unhesitant. 'Nonsense. It's not that bad. I'm sure we have time to send the ROV down for one more look,' he smiled assertively to Rassoulis, 'don't you agree?'

Tess watched the captain as he studied the bruised, angry skies bearing down on them. To their south, lightning tore at the clouds, and even from this distance, they could see that thick veils of rain were now sweeping across the sea. 'I don't like it. One front we can handle, but two... We can slip through them if we leave now.' He turned to Vance. 'Don't worry. Storms out here don't last too long, and our GPS locator's accurate to within a meter. We'll come back once it's passed, probably by morning.'

Vance scowled inwardly. 'I'd really rather not leave here without something,' he said calmly. 'The falcon figurehead, for instance. Surely, we have time to recover that before we have to get out of here, don't we?' From Rassoulis's concerned frown, it was clear he wasn't exactly thrilled with the idea. 'I'm just worried that the storm will last longer than you expect,' Vance pressed on, 'and then, what with your other charter already booked, it could be months before we can get back and who knows what can happen in the meantime.'

Rassoulis scowled at the converging weather fronts, clearly evaluating whether or not the *Savarona* could afford to hang around the wreck site.

'I'll make it worth your while,' Vance persisted. 'Bring up the falcon and I'm done here. You can have anything else that's down there.'

Rassoulis cocked a curious eyebrow. 'That's all you want? The falcon?' He paused, scrutinizing Vance. Tess watched him and felt like she was intruding on a major poker game. 'Why?'

Vance shrugged, and his expression became distant. 'It's personal. Call it a matter of... closure.' His eyes hardened, settling back on Rassoulis. 'We're wasting time. I'm sure we can do it if we move quickly. And after that, it's all yours.'

The captain seemed to consider his options for a few seconds, then nodded and stepped away, hollering orders at Attal and the other crewmen.

Vance turned to Tess, his face jittery with nervous energy. 'Almost there,' he murmured, his voice crackling. 'We're almost there.'

'How much further?' De Angelis yelled to the captain.

Reilly could feel the bridge of the *Karadeniz* reverberating heavily, much more so than it had before. For over an hour, they'd been cutting diagonally through waves that were stampeding toward their starboard side and pummeling the patrol boat's hull with increasing ferocity. With the wind shrieking in and the engines straining against the swell, they were having to shout to make themselves heard.

'Just under twenty nautical miles,' Karakas replied.

'What about the chopper?'

The skipper consulted his radar operator, then shouted back, 'Contact estimated in just under five minutes.'

De Angelis breathed out heavily, stewing with impatience. 'Can't this damn thing go any faster?'

'Not in this sea,' Karakas answered tersely.

Reilly stepped closer to the skipper. 'How bad will it be by the time we reach them?'

Karakas shook his head, his expression grim. He didn't shout his answer, but Reilly heard it anyway.

'God knows,' he shrugged.

Tess watched through rapt eyes as Attal's fingers coaxed *Dori*'s manipulator arm to attach the last of the harnesses to the falcon figurehead. Despite the difficult conditions, the crew had worked fast and with military precision in equipping the ROV with the necessary recovery equipment before sending it back into the churning water. Attal had performed his magic at the joystick, guiding the ROV down and positioning the retrieval netting with disarming efficiency. All that remained was to pull it back, use the remote control to trigger the simultaneous inflation of the three lifting bags, and watch as the figurehead floated gently up to the surface.

Attal nodded his readiness. 'We can bring it up, but ...' He let out a Gallic shrug, his eyes glancing toward the windshield which was buffeted by the howling wind.

Rassoulis frowned, staring out at the maelstrom raging around them. 'I know. Getting it on board once it surfaces won't be easy.' He turned to Vance, his expression dour. 'We can't put a Zodiac down in this sea, and I don't want to risk sending divers in either. It's going to be hard enough getting the ROV back, but at least it's tethered and mobile.' He paused, evaluating the rapidly deteriorating conditions, before seemingly making up his mind. 'We won't be able to bring it up today. We'll leave the floats down there and come back for it when the storm clears.'

Vance looked incredulous. 'We have to bring it up now,' he insisted. 'We might not get another chance.'

'What are you talking about?' Rassoulis shot back. 'No

one's going to come out here and steal it from under us in this weather. We'll come back for it as soon as the weather allows it.'

'No!' Vance burst out angrily. 'We have to do it now!'

Rassoulis cocked his head back, surprised by the tone of Vance's outburst. 'Look, I'm not risking anyone's life over this. We're heading back, and that's it.' His eyes bored sharply into Vance's for a second before he turned to Attal. 'Bring *Dori* up as quickly as you can,' he snapped. But before he could issue any more orders, something attracted his attention. It was the familiar, guttural thumping of helicopter blades. Tess heard it too, and from Vance's scowl, it was obvious he had as well.

They grabbed some windbreakers and stepped out onto the narrow deck outside the bridge. The wind had risen to a full gale, and sheets of rain were now sweeping in with it. Tess shielded her eyes with her hand as she scanned the turbulent sky, and she soon spotted it.

'There,' she yelled, pointing at it.

It was skimming the water, heading straight for them. Within seconds, it was on them, bathtub white and with a wide diagonal red stripe, thundering over their heads before arcing up and banking for another pass. It slowed as it neared the ship, then hovered in place alongside the *Savarona*'s port side, fighting the wind, its rotor wash blasting the sea and kicking up a swirling plume of water off the crests of the foaming waves. Tess could clearly make out the Turkish Coast Guard markings on its fuselage, and could see the pilot talking into his microphone as his eyes moved over the vessel.

He then pointed at his headset, gesturing vigorously for them to pick up their radio.

On the *Karadeniz*'s bridge, Reilly saw De Angelis's face light up. The report from the helicopter confirmed the contact to be a diving ship. Despite the gravely worsening conditions, it was holding position. The pilot could see activity on the deck around the crane, indicating the imminent recovery of a submersible of some sort. He had also spotted the two target figures on its deck, and their descriptions clearly left no doubt in the monsignor's mind.

'I've asked him to establish radio contact with them,' Karakas told De Angelis. 'What do you want me to tell them?'

De Angelis didn't hesitate. 'Tell them they're about to get hit by a storm of Biblical proportions,' he answered flatly. 'Tell them they should get out of there if they want to live.'

Reilly studied De Angelis's face, and it only confirmed the uncompromising threat he had read into the monsignor's reply. The man was determined not to let them escape with what they had come for, at any cost. He'd already shown his callous disregard for human life when it came to protecting the Church's big secret. *Everyone's expendable,* he had stated in no uncertain terms, back in Turkey.

Reilly had to step in. 'Our first priority should be their safety,' he countered. 'There's a whole diving crew out there.'

'My point, exactly,' De Angelis calmly replied.

'They don't have too many options,' Karakas pointed out. He studied the radar screen, which showed the numerous blips clearing out of the area. 'The storms have them boxed in from the north and the south. They can either head east, where we've got two patrol boats waiting to pick them up, or they can come west toward us. Either way, we've got them. I doubt they'd have much luck trying to outrun us in that.' His smile wasn't particularly humorous. It occurred to Reilly that Karakas might actually relish a chase which, combined with De Angelis's sanguine predisposition, didn't bode well.

He glanced toward the foredeck and the 23mm automatic cannon mounted there and felt a surge of unease. He had to alert Tess and those with her as to what they were up against.

'Let me talk to them,' Reilly blurted out.

De Angelis glanced at him, nonplussed by his request.

'You wanted me to help,' Reilly pressed on. 'They don't know we're out here. They also might not be aware of the full scale of the storm that's about to hit them. Let me talk to them, convince them to follow us to shore.'

Karakas didn't look like he cared, either way. He looked at De Angelis for guidance.

The monsignor held Reilly's gaze with cold, calculating eyes, then nodded his acquiescence. 'Give him a mike,' he ordered.

Tess's heart leapt into her throat when she heard Reilly's voice on the ship's radio. She grabbed the microphone from Rassoulis.

'Sean, it's Tess.' She was breathless, her pulse pounding in her temples. 'Where are you?'

The helicopter had long since peeled off and headed back, disappearing quickly into the dark, rainswept sky.

'We're not far,' Reilly's voice came crackling back. 'I'm on a patrol boat, about fifteen nautical miles west of you. We have two other boats to your east. Listen to me, Tess. You need to drop whatever you're doing and get the hell out of there. The two storm fronts are about to collide right on top of you. You need to head west right now, on a course of,' he paused, seemingly waiting for the information before coming back with, 'two seven zero. That's two, seven, zero. We'll meet you and escort you back to Marmaris.'

Tess noticed Rassoulis looking uncertainly at Vance, who grew visibly riled. Before she could answer Reilly, the captain took the mike from her. 'This is George Rassoulis, the captain of the *Savarona*. Who am I talking to?'

Some static followed, then Reilly's voice came back. 'My name's Sean Reilly. I'm with the FBI.'

Tess saw Rassoulis's expression darken as he shot a dubious look at the professor. Vance just stood there, immobile, before turning away and taking a few steps toward the back of the bridge.

Without taking his eyes off Vance, the captain asked, 'What's the FBI doing warning a Greek diving ship about a storm in the middle of the Mediterranean?'

Vance answered for him, his back still turned. 'They're here for me,' he said with surprising indifference. When he turned, Tess saw that he was holding a handgun aimed at Rassoulis. 'I think we've heard enough from our friends at the FBI.' And with that, he fired two shots into the radio. Tess screamed as sparks and debris came arcing out of it. The static coming from the speaker instantly died out.

'Now,' he hissed, his eyes seething with barely contained rage, 'can we all get back to the business at hand?'

CHAPTER 76

Tess's entire body went rigid. She felt as if her legs were nailed to the floor of the cockpit, and could only stand quietly in her corner and watch as Vance took a few menacing steps toward Rassoulis and ordered him to initiate the recovery sequence for the figurehead.

'It's pointless,' the captain argued, 'I'm telling you we can't get it on board, not in these conditions.'

'Hit the damn button,' Vance insisted, 'or I'll do it for you.' He glowered at Attal, who was still sitting at the command console of the ROV, his fingers frozen against the joystick.

The engineer glanced at his captain, and Rassoulis relented, nodding slightly. Attal nudged the controls. On the monitor, the image from *Dori*'s camera grew smaller as the ROV receded, then, one after another, the orange lift bags started to inflate, blowing up to full girth within seconds. At first, the falcon didn't seem to move, stubbornly resisting the upward pull of the large floats. Then all of a sudden, in a burst of sand, it rose up like an uprooted tree trunk, trailing a swirling cloud of the sediment that had settled around it over the centuries. Attal guided the ROV up in a parallel climb, keeping the hazy, otherworldly image of the rising figurehead on screen.

Tess heard the door to the pilothouse rattle as a crewman stepped in from the gangway. She noticed Vance break his concentration and tear his entranced eyes away from the screen to glance over at the commotion. Abruptly, Rassoulis lunged at Vance and began wrestling with him for the gun. Tess stepped backward, screaming, 'No!' Attal and another engineer rose to their feet to help the captain when, deafeningly loud in the enclosed space, the gun went off.

For a moment, Vance and Rassoulis stood, locked together and immobile, before Vance pulled away and the captain slumped to the floor, blood spilling from his mouth as his eyes rolled upward and out of sight.

Horrified, Tess stared down at the captain's body, which convulsed slightly before going limp. She glared at Vance. 'What have you done?' she yelled as she sank to her knees by Rassoulis, unsure of what to do, then listening for a breath, feeling for a pulse.

She found none.

'He's dead,' she cried. 'You've killed him.'

Attal and the other crewmen were frozen in disbelief. Then the helmsman snapped into reflex action, hurling himself at Vance, clawing for the gun. With surprising speed, Vance clubbed him across the face with a blow from the butt of his handgun, sending him crashing to the floor. For a brief moment, Vance appeared to be in a daze, then his eyes focused and his expression hardened.

'Get me the falcon and we can all go home,' he ordered. 'Now.'

Hesitantly, the first mate and Attal went about the recovery preparations, blurting orders out to the other crewmen, but the words blew by Tess in an indecipherable haze. She couldn't stop staring at Vance, whose eyes had taken on a life of their own. They didn't belong to the erudite professor she'd first met all those years ago, nor to the driven, broken man with whom she'd embarked on this misguided journey. She recognized the cold, detached, harshness she saw in them. She'd first seen it at the Met, on the night of the raid. It had scared her then, and right now, with a dead man on the floor beside her, it terrified her.

Looking again at Rassoulis's body, a sudden realization hit her: that she might very well die here. And in that instant, she thought of her daughter, and wondered if she would ever see her again.

*

Reilly snapped backward as Rassoulis's voice disappeared and the radio's speaker erupted into a loud, static hiss. A shiver of dread raced down his spine. He thought he'd heard what sounded like a gunshot through the radio, but he couldn't be sure.

'Captain? Tess? Anyone?'

There was no answer.

He turned to the radioman beside him, who was already fiddling with the console's controls, shaking his head and reporting back to the skipper in Turkish.

'The signal's gone,' Karakas confirmed. 'It looks like they've heard all they want to hear.'

Reilly stared ahead angrily out through the whirling windscreen wipers that did nothing to improve the visibility. The *Karadeniz* was straining hard, battling the increasingly ferocious waves. All of the chatter on the bridge was in Turkish, but Reilly picked up that the gunboat crew seemed to be more focused on the raging sea than on the other boat, which still appeared to be stationary. Although the *Savarona* was now theoretically in visual range, the lashing rain and the high seas meant that it came into view only every now and again, as the surging swell beneath both boats peaked simultaneously. As Reilly caught a glimpse of it, all that he could make out was a blurred distant shape. He felt a fist swell in his throat as he thought of Tess being out there on the battered vessel.

Reilly saw Karakas and the first officer exchange a few clipped words, then the skipper turned to De Angelis, deep ridges of concern lining his leathery forehead. 'This is getting out of hand. The wind's almost at fifty knots, and in these conditions, there isn't much we can do about forcing them to follow us.'

De Angelis seemed strangely unfazed. 'As long as they're out there, we keep going.'

The skipper breathed heavily. His eyes darted to Reilly, looking for some insight into De Angelis's state of mind but not finding any. 'I don't think we should stay out here much longer,' he stated flatly. 'It isn't safe anymore.'

De Angelis turned to face him. 'What's the matter,' he said indignantly, 'can't you handle a few waves?' He jabbed an angry finger toward the *Savarona*. 'I don't see them turning tail and running. They're clearly not afraid to be out here.' His mouth twisted oddly. 'Are you?'

Reilly watched as Karakas stood there, his pulse visibly quickening at the taunt. The skipper glowered at the monsignor before barking some orders at his nervous first officer. De Angelis nodded, shot a quick glance at Plunkett and turned to stare ahead, and just from his profile, Reilly could tell that the monsignor was grimly pleased.

Tess stood next to Vance, staring out, the spray raking the windshield like buckshot as rainsqualls hurled themselves at the wheelhouse from all directions. Great patches of foam were blowing in dense white streaks all around them, and the *Savarona*'s decks were awash with water.

And then they appeared.

Three orange lift bags, off to the boat's starboard side, thrusting out of the water like breaching whales.

Tess's eyes strained, trying to cut through the lashings of rain, and then she spotted it, a large, dark balk of rounded timber bobbing between the floaters. Despite the wear of centuries, it was unmistakably carved in the shape of a bird, and strongly evocative of its former glory.

She glanced at Vance and saw his face light up. For the briefest of moments, she felt a sudden thrill, a surge of excitement that eclipsed all the dread and horror she'd been feeling.

And then it all came rushing back.

'Get the divers in,' Vance yelled at the first mate, who was tending to the helmsman's bloodied cheek. Seeing the hesitation in the man's eyes, Vance extended his arm and thrust his handgun into the terrified man's face. 'Do it. We're not leaving here without it.'

Just then, a large wave slammed into the ship's stern. With the *Savarona* slewing heavily to one side, the helmsman staggered up to his feet and took over from the overwhelmed crewman, fighting the wheel to keep the ship from broaching and rolling over as he maneuvered it out of danger and closer to the floating lift bags. Expertly defying the waves, he maintained the battered vessel's position while two other crewmen got into gear and reluctantly dived off the deck, heavy recovery cables in their clutches.

Tess watched nervously as the divers struck their way to the rig, tense minutes ticking by agonizingly before a glimpse of a thumbs-up signaled their success. The first mate then hit a switch, and out on deck, the winch cranked noisily to life, straining against the roll of the ship and the pounding of the waves. The figurehead, still harnessed to the lift bags, rose out of the foaming water and swung over, headed for the ship's waiting deck.

Vance suddenly frowned, his attention gripped by something beyond the suspended rig. Attal's face brightened as he gripped Tess's arm and nodded in the same direction, toward the west. She glanced beyond the bow and saw a ghostly shape in the distance. It was the *Karadeniz*, straining against the crushing waves and bearing down on them.

Vance spun angrily to the helmsman. 'Get us out of here,' he ordered, waving his handgun furiously.

Streaks of sweat tinged with blood streaked down the helmsman's face as he struggled to keep the ship from turning broadside to the waves. 'We have to recover the divers first,' he protested.

'Leave them,' Vance roared. 'The patrol boat will pick them up. It'll help delay them.'

The helmsman's eyes were darting around, taking in the wind readings on the weather radar. He pointed toward the *Karadeniz*. 'The only way out of this storm is toward them.'

'No. We can't go that way,' Vance shouted.

Tess watched the *Karadeniz* inch closer, and turned to

Vance. 'Please, Bill. It's over. They have us surrounded, and if we don't get out of here now, the storm's going to kill us all.'

Vance flashed her a silencing glare, then shot anxious glances out the windshield and down at the weather radar. His eyes turned to ice. 'South,' he barked to the helmsman. 'Take us south.'

The helmsman's eyes rocketed wide, as if he'd been punched in the gut. 'South? That's right into the storm,' he countered. 'You're insane.'

Vance shoved his gun into the face of the hesitating man and, without warning, squeezed the trigger, nudging the gun slightly off to one side just as it erupted. The bullet just missed the helmsman and smashed into a bulkhead behind him. Vance shot a quick, threatening glance at the others on the bridge before shoving his handgun back into the shell-shocked man's face. 'You can take your chances with the waves ... or with a bullet. It's your call.'

The helmsman just stared back at him for a moment, flicked a quick eye over his instruments, then spun the wheel and pushed forward on the throttles. The boat churned ahead, leaving the divers floundering helplessly in its wake, and plunged head-on into the wrath of the storm.

It was only when Vance finally took his eyes off the helmsman that he noticed Tess was gone.

CHAPTER 77

On the bridge of the *Karadeniz*, De Angelis stared through the Fujinon marine binoculars in furious disbelief.

'They've got it,' he said through clenched teeth. 'I don't believe it. They've managed to bring it up.'

Reilly had also spotted it, and a ripple of concern raced down his spine. *So it was all true after all.* There it was, plucked out of the abyss after hundreds of years by one man's unwavering tenacity.

Tess. What have you done?

And with a reeling horror, he knew De Angelis would stop at nothing now.

The first officer, standing next to them, also had his eyes peeled on the dive boat, but had other concerns. 'They're heading south. They're abandoning the divers.'

As soon as he heard that, Karakas began snapping orders. Instantly, a siren blasted, followed by rapid-fire commands over the gunboat's loudspeakers. Divers began suiting up immediately, while out on deck, crewmen hastily readied one of the patrol boat's inflatable craft.

De Angelis watched the frenzied activity with utter disbelief. 'Forget the damn divers,' he barked, pointing frantically at the *Savarona*. 'They're getting away. We need to stop them.'

'We can't leave them here,' Karakas shot back, the scorn in his eyes barely disguised. 'Besides, that ship will never make it through this storm. The waves are too big. We need to get out of here as soon as we've recovered the divers.'

'No,' the monsignor snapped back firmly. 'Even if there's just one chance in a million that they'll make it out in one piece, we can't allow it to happen.' He stared sharply out the windshield, then turned back to face the stocky captain, his eyes gleaming with menace. 'Sink them.'

Reilly couldn't stand back any longer. He lunged at De Angelis, grabbing him and spinning him around heavily to face him. 'You can't do that, there's no –'

He stopped in his tracks.

The monsignor had pulled out a big automatic and shoved its muzzle into Reilly's face. 'Stay out of this,' he shouted, nudging Reilly back toward the rear of the cockpit.

Reilly stared beyond the cold steel barrel hovering millimeters from him and into De Angelis's eyes. They blazed with murderous fury.

'You're outlived your purpose here,' the monsignor rasped. 'Do you understand me?'

There was such implacability in De Angelis's expression that Reilly believed he would pull the trigger without the slightest hesitation. He also knew that if he made a move on him, he would be dead long before he even reached him.

He nodded and eased back, steadying himself against the motion of the boat. 'Easy, now,' he said calmly. 'Easy.'

De Angelis kept his eyes locked firmly on Reilly. 'Use the cannon,' he ordered the skipper. 'Before they get out of range.'

Reilly could tell that Karakas was hugely uncomfortable with what was taking place on his ship. 'We're in international waters,' he objected, 'and if that's not enough for you, that's a Greek ship we're talking about. We already have enough trouble with –'

'– I don't care,' De Angelis raged, turning to face Karakas and waving his handgun furiously. 'This ship is operating under NATO command and as the ranking officer, I'm giving you a direct order, Captain –'

This time, it was Karakas who interrupted. 'No,' he stated flatly, staring down De Angelis. 'I'll take my chances with a military tribunal.'

The two men squared off for a tense moment, the monsignor's right arm fully extended, his handgun squarely in the captain's face. To Karakas's credit, he didn't flinch. He just stood his ground until the monsignor thrust him aside, turned to Plunkett and ordered him to watch them and charged for the door to the gangway. 'The hell with you,' he seethed. 'I'll do it myself.'

Plunkett moved into position, pulling out his own holstered handgun as the monsignor slid the door open. The gale force wind blasted into the bridge. De Angelis steeled himself and stepped out into the raging storm.

Reilly darted an incredulous glance at Karakas just as a big wave slammed into the cutter broadside, rocking the bridge and forcing everyone on it to grab a handhold. Reilly saw the opportunity and took it. He bolted at Plunkett, getting to him just as the CIA operative was reaching out to steady himself against the console beside him. Reilly managed to block the hand that held the gun against the counter while delivering a jarring uppercut that loosened Plunkett's grip enough for Reilly to wrangle the gun off him. Plunkett came back with a furious, wild swing, but Reilly blocked it and, without hesitating, swung the handgun at the killer, connecting with a savage blow across his forehead. Plunkett slumped to the floor, unconscious.

Reilly tucked the handgun under his belt, stepped past the captain, grabbed a life vest and frantically strapped it on, and followed De Angelis out.

The wind pounded him immediately, slamming him back against the pilothouse's wall like a rag doll. Reilly steadied himself and, pulling himself along the railing hand over hand, spotted the rain-lashed silhouette of the monsignor inching his way forward along the bulwark and heading inexorably for the foredeck, where the automatic cannon was mounted.

Shielding his eyes as he advanced, he glanced beyond the bow and glimpsed the *Savarona*. It was lurching heavily, only a couple of hundred yards away now but separated from the patrol boat by a mountainous sea.

Reilly suddenly froze. On the deck below the diving ship's wheelhouse, a small figure appeared to be moving, battered by torrents of water, clinging desperately to the rigging.

He felt the air leave his lungs.

He was sure it was Tess.

Tess hastened down the companionway, her thoughts a blur and her heartbeat throbbing deafeningly in her ears. She scanned the walls, desperately trying to remember where she'd seen the axe.

She finally found it, mounted on a bulkhead just outside the galley. Within seconds, she'd also found a life jacket and strapped it on. Sucking in a deep breath and rallying herself for what she was about to do, she yanked open the watertight door, stepped over the coaming and threw herself into the fury that was raging outside.

Tess knew Vance wouldn't risk moving from the cockpit. Clutching the axe with one hand and using the other to steady herself, she moved carefully across the main deck, releasing lifebelts as she went, hoping they might be of some use to the stranded divers.

She saw a huge wave crest over the bow and locked her arms around a railing, bracing herself as a wall of water hit her head-on and buried the deck. She then felt the deck slide away from under her as the *Savarona* flew off the top of the wave and rocketed down its steep back before landing heavily in its trough. She pulled herself up and, through the tangle of hair that whipped stingingly across her face, she spotted the falcon, dangling in mid-air several feet above the deck, swaying wildly. She scrambled toward the base of the crane and the wire rope emerging from its reel.

Reaching it, she glanced up at the window of the cockpit. Through the veils of spray, she saw Vance's alarmed face. She steeled herself, raised the axe and swung it with all her might. She almost lost her grip as it bounced off the taut cable, and looked up to see Vance rushing out of the wheel-house and fighting the wind that plowed into him. He was gesturing wildly and screaming what looked like a continuous, 'No!' from the top of his lungs, but with the howling of the wind, Tess couldn't hear it. Undeterred, she swung again, steadied herself, and then swung yet again. A strand snapped, then another as she smashed the axe down repeatedly in a frenzied flurry of blows.

She wasn't going to let Vance have it. Not this way. Not at this cost. She'd been a fool to give him the benefit of any doubt, and it was time to start making amends.

The last strand finally gave way, and as the *Savarona* rolled to port, the falcon suddenly dropped, crashing down heavily into the sea.

Tess clutched her way along the sloping deck, away from the pilothouse, ducking to avoid Vance's sight line instinctively. Darting a quick backward glance, she glimpsed the flotation bags emerge from the foaming water. Her heart stopped as she waited to see if they still held the falcon, then she let out a heavy breath when she spotted its dark brown, rounded shape sticking out from between the inflated balloons.

Her elation at succeeding was short-lived as, at that very moment, a staccato of small explosions rocked the *Savarona*. Diving for cover, Tess glanced back at the patrol boat pursuing them and was amazed to see the cannon at its bow spitting out a deadly fire.

Lashed by the driving spray and the ferocious wind, Reilly raced after De Angelis.

The *Karadeniz* strained to hold its position, its rescue divers hauling one of the stranded divers onto a rigid inflatable boat while the other man clung desperately to a lifebelt until he too could be hauled aboard.

The monsignor finally reached the foredeck. Within seconds, he had positioned himself firmly between the gun's semi-circular, padded shoulder mounts. Unlocking the fearsome weapon and swinging it around with expert ease, he quickly found the escaping dive boat and unleashed a ferocious burst of incendiary 23mm shells.

'No!' Reilly yelled, climbing over the railing and onto the cannon's deck. Even with the wind screaming past his ears, the noise from the cannon was deafening.

He lunged at De Angelis, jolting the gun off course and sending the tracers arcing away from the *Savarona* and disappearing harmlessly into the sea. The monsignor slid one of his shoulders out from the gun's mount and grabbed Reilly's hand, twisting his fingers back to an unnatural angle before swinging a savage blow that caught Reilly in midcheek and sent him stumbling backward across the tilting, waterswept deck.

Unable to regain his feet, Reilly was swept across the deck and carried away from De Angelis. He tried desperately to grab something to arrest his slide. His hand caught a piece of rope and he held on. He managed to pick himself up but could only hang on as the patrol boat lurched heavily up a mountain of water. By the time it crested the wave, De Angelis had pulled himself back into position, and the diving boat came back into view. The monsignor let rip with another volley. Horrified, Reilly stared helplessly as dozens of shells traced their brilliant, deadly paths through the near darkness to rain down on the dive boat. Flames and puffs of smoke leapt into the air as most of the shells impacted on the *Savarona*'s unprotected stern.

Crouching low behind a steel boxing, Tess's heart was beating its way out of her chest as the *Savarona* shuddered under the remorseless pounding from the rapid-firing chain gun. At 1000 rounds per minute, even a short burst packed a devastating punch.

The shells were chewing up the deck all around her when a muffled explosion from deep inside the vessel rocked her, causing her to scream. Almost immediately, a cloud of black smoke billowed from the stern and out of the smokestacks on the whaledeck. The ship lurched sideways, almost as if someone had hit the brakes. Tess knew the engine had been hit. She guessed – hoped – that the fuel tank itself had been spared, as the ship hadn't exploded from under her. She counted down each passing second, waiting for it to happen, but it didn't.

But this was just as bad.

Without power, the crippled dive boat was helpless against the confused sea. Waves were coming in from all directions, pummeling the ship and causing it to lurch and spin like a bumper car in a fairground.

Tess stared in horror as a huge mountain of sea rose up behind the *Savarona*, caught up with it and broke over the pilothouse. She barely managed to clip on a lifeline to the railing and clasp her arms around it before the water avalanched over the ship, inundating the entire deck and causing the half-inch Lexan windows of the cockpit to implode.

She wiped the wet hair off her face and glanced up at the ravaged wheelhouse. There was no sign of Vance or of the others. She felt the onset of tears and crumpled herself up into a ball, hanging on for dear life. She looked to where she had last seen the patrol boat, expecting it to be even nearer now, but it was nowhere in sight.

And then she saw it. A huge, sixty-foot wave. So steep it was almost vertical, with a massive trough in front of it that seemed to be sucking the *Savarona* in.

It was bearing down on the stricken ship across its port side.

Tess shut her eyes, tight. Without power, there was no way to turn the dive boat to either face the wave, or run from it – not that there was anyone left at the helm. Either maneuver would have caused the ship to take a big hit and be engulfed by water, but it would have still come out right side up.

This monster was about to slam into them broadside.

And when it did, it lifted the 130-ton steel ship effortlessly and rolled it over like a child's toy.

*

Reilly watched the shells erupting across the dive boat's stern and the black smoke spewing out from it, and yelled at De Angelis as loudly as he could, but he knew there was no way the monsignor was going to hear him over the screaming wind and the clamor of the gunfire.

He suddenly felt exhausted and totally depleted, and at that very moment, he realized what he had to do.

Bracing himself against the railing, he pulled out the automatic, steadied its muzzle against the onslaught of the wind as best he could, and pulled the trigger repeatedly. Red puffs erupted from the monsignor's back and he arced backward, then fell forward against the machine gun, tilting its barrel toward the angry sky.

Reilly tossed the Glock aside and peered out from the patrol boat's deck. Eyes straining against the squall, he searched for the *Savarona*, but all he could see through the sheets of rain were rampaging mountains and valleys of foaming, white-streaked water.

The rescue divers had somehow managed to make it back on board with the men they had pulled out of the sea, and Reilly felt the patrol boat turning away from its previous heading, the engines surging in an effort to hasten the turn and limit the time it would sit 'beam-to' to the waves and be exposed to broaching. A sense of panic gripped him as he realized they were heading back, away from the storm.

Just then, the waves cleared for a few seconds and his eyes rocketed wide at the sight of the capsized dive boat, its filthy hull slipping below the converging waves.

There was no sign of survivors.

He looked back toward the bridge and saw the skipper motioning to him frantically to get back inside. Reilly shielded his face and pointed toward where he'd seen the *Savarona*, but Karakas waved his hands in a *No* gesture and pointed away, indicating they had to get out while they still could.

Reilly gripped the railing with white knuckles, his mind feverishly sifting through his options, but there was really only one thing he could contemplate doing.

He scrambled toward the gunboat's rigid inflatable boat, which the divers had left tethered off its starboard side. Dredging everything in his memory that he could recall from a routine FBI training course with the US Coast Guard, he leapt into the motorized lifeboat, pulled the release lever, and, hanging onto its handles, held his breath as it jettisoned off the patrol boat and into the raging sea.

CHAPTER 78

Reilly managed to fire up the inflatable's motor and, peering into the blinding curtain of rain and spray, he steered toward where he thought he'd last seen the capsized *Savarona*. He was winging it as best he could in the constantly shifting landscape around him, riding on instinct and on hope, as he'd lost all sense of direction. The water was so frothy and the air so wet that it was almost impossible to tell where the sea ended and the sky began.

The sea rose and fell in vertiginous swells, one wave breaking over him and flooding the small craft just as quickly as another would rock the water out of it. He hung on as it climbed up and down the walls of water, its motor rising to a hellish scream every time it was thrown over a wave and its propeller spun free.

Interminable minutes later, he spotted it, a dark brown angular shape jutting out of a trough that looked like a hole in the sea. Muscles straining, he pointed the small outboard toward it, but kept getting thrown off course by uncooperative, battling waves. He had to constantly adjust his heading as he caught glimpses of the overturned trawler between the mountains of water.

There was still no sign of Tess.

The closer he got to it, the more horrific the sight became. Debris was scattered around the hull, floating alongside it in an eerily synchronized dance of death. The aft section of the ship was now completely submerged, and its prow, pointing out of the sea like an angled iceberg, was slowly sliding beneath the waves that washed over it.

Desperately, he searched for survivors and for Tess, his hope fading, then surging when, to the far side of the hull, he spotted her, bobbing in an orange life jacket, thrashing her arms wildly.

Steering the inflatable toward her, he maneuvered around the massive, barnacle-encrusted hull and edged closer to her, his eyes darting from her to the treacherous waves that were hammering them without remorse. When he was near enough, he reached out with one hand and grabbed at her outstretched arm, missed, then desperately reached out again and this time, their fingers locked and he managed to hang on.

Dragging her into the boat, a faint, desperate smile crept across his face and he saw her face light up with relief that, suddenly, turned to fear. She was looking behind him. He spun around, just in time to see a large chunk of debris from the *Savarona* being hurled by a breaking wave and heading straight for him.

And then his world went black.

Disorientated and utterly bewildered, Tess was certain that she was going to die and could hardly believe her eyes when she saw Reilly coming toward her in the inflatable lifeboat.

Using every ounce of strength she had left, she managed to grab his outstretched hand and lift herself half into the tiny craft when she saw the piece of wooden planking spinning over a wave and smashing into him. It struck him squarely on the head and sent him flying off the edge of the lifeboat.

She slid back into the water and reached out and grabbed him, hanging onto him while struggling to keep her other hand gripped on one of the inflatable's handles. Through the thrashing water, she saw that his eyelids were shut, his head bouncing listlessly against the neck support of the life jacket. Blood streaked from a big gash across his forehead, disappearing and reappearing as each surge of water washed over the wound.

She tried to push him into the lifeboat but quickly realized that it was an impossible task. Worse, it was sapping the little energy she had left. The lifeboat was becoming more of a liability than a lifesaver, filling with water and threatening to ram into them with every resurgence of the swell. With a heavy heart, she let go of the handle to which she was clinging, and seized hold of Reilly instead.

Watching as the inflatable was swept away, she struggled to keep Reilly's head above the surface. For what felt like forever, it took all of her determination just to stay conscious. The storm showed no signs of abating, and Tess knew that she had to stay alert, but it was a losing battle. Her strength was quickly fading.

That was when she saw a large piece of timber, a hatch-cover of some sort, she guessed. Desperately, she struck out toward it, one arm clasping Reilly to her until, at last, she managed to reach out with her other arm and grasp a rope trailing from it. Laboriously, painfully, she dragged herself and Reilly onto the flat platform, then used the rope to tie them both to it as best she could. She also hooked the belts of her life jacket into his. Whatever else happened, they wouldn't be separated. In some strange way, that thought triggered a small stirring of hope inside her.

As the storm continued to explode its might around her, Tess closed her eyes and sucked long draws of air into her lungs, trying to calm her fears. Whatever else, she could not afford to panic. She had to find the strength she would need to keep herself and Reilly from losing their tenuous grip on this frail scrap of timber. Other than that, she was helpless. All she could do was lie back and let the elements take them wherever they wanted them to go.

The makeshift raft seemed to settle for a moment, and Tess opened her eyes, wondering if the respite was a sign of better things to come. She couldn't have been further from the truth. Towering over them was a gargantuan wave, one that completely dwarfed the one that had capsized the *Savarona*. It appeared to hang there, motionless, almost taunting her.

Holding desperately onto Reilly, Tess shut her eyes and awaited the onslaught, and then it came, smashing down on them like a falling cliff and swallowing them up as effortlessly as if they were dead leaves.

CHAPTER 79

Tuscany – January 1293

His back to the bitter wind that swept down from the north, Martin of Carmaux crouched low by the small fire. The howling of the wind was compounded by the roar from a waterfall that plunged down into the shadowy depths of a narrow ravine. Beside Martin, wrapped in the tattered remnants of a cloak taken many months ago from one of the Mamelukes slain at *Beer el Sifsaaf*, Hugh moaned softly in a fitful sleep.

In the course of their long journey since washing ashore after the sinking of the *Falcon Temple*, Martin had developed much affection for the old sailor. Aimard of Villiers apart, he'd never met anyone with a greater sense of devotion and determination, to say nothing of Hugh's stoic acceptance of all that had befallen them. In the long, arduous days of their travels, the seaman had sustained several injuries in fights and accidental falls, yet he still covered mile after brutal mile without a word of complaint.

At least he had until the last few days. The harsh winter now had them firmly in its deathly grasp, and the icy blasts from the mountain range that separated them from France were starting to take their toll on the weakened man.

For the first few weeks after leaving *Beer el Sifsaaf*, Martin had kept the four survivors together, believing that as long as they were within easy reach of their Muslim enemies, they needed the strength this gave them. After they left Mameluke territory, however, he decided that the time had come to follow Aimard's plan and split into two pairs. The dangers they still faced, in particular from roaming bandits in the foothills of the Stara Planina and for much of the thousand and more miles that would follow before they reached the Venetian states, were very real.

He had decided on a simple plan. After they had divided into two pairs, they would follow a predetermined route, about half a day apart. This way, those ahead could give warning to those that followed of any dangers; and those behind could help out the leaders should any harm befall them. 'At no time,' he had urged, 'must the safety of the letters be compromised. Even if it means abandoning any one of us to his fate.'

No one had argued.

He hadn't allowed for the savagery of the terrain. Barring their way were mountains and chasms, fast-flowing rivers and dense forests. They had been obliged to make many detours from their planned path. After they had separated, with him and Hugh leading, only once had he seen signs of their comrades. That had been many months ago.

Along the way, they had lost their horses, through death or trading or for food, and had been reduced to walking weeks ago. Many a night, as he lay exhausted by a campfire but unable to sleep, Martin wondered if the others had been more fortunate, if they had perhaps found an easier and safer route and had already reached Paris.

It made no difference to his plans. He could not give up. He had to go on.

Looking now at Hugh's sleeping figure, a dispiriting thought hit him. He thought it unlikely that the old sailor would reach Paris with him. The winter weather would get harsher, the terrain more difficult, and his companion's wheezing cough was getting much worse. Earlier that night, Hugh had been gripped by a violent fever, and his coughing had produced blood for the first time. Reluctant though he was, Martin knew that the time was fast approaching when he would have to leave Hugh and press on alone. But he couldn't leave him helpless here in the foothills of the mountains. Hugh would surely freeze to death. He had to find shelter, somewhere to leave his friend, before carrying on.

They had glimpsed a small town the day before, across the mountain range. The town was close to a quarry they had skirted, where they had seen distant tiny figures toiling amidst clouds of dust and huge slabs of marble. Perhaps he could find someone in the town in whose care he could leave Hugh.

When Hugh emerged from his troubled sleep, Martin told him his thoughts. The shipmaster shook his head emphatically. 'No,' he protested, 'you have to continue on to France. I will follow as best I can. We can't rely on these strangers.'

That much was true. The people of this land were known and mistrusted for their dealings and here, in the far north, bands of robbers and slave traders added to the area's notoriety.

Heedless of his companion's protests, Martin clambered down the rocks that lined the edge of the waterfall. A light snow had fallen overnight, enshrouding the mountain in a ghostly blanket. As he made his way through a narrow crevice, Martin paused to take a breath and noticed that one of the rocks had fissures that resembled a splayed cross, much like that which the Knights Templar had made their symbol. He contemplated the strange cracks for a moment, seeing in them a hopeful portent. Perhaps Hugh would find a peaceful end to his days in this quiet, desolate valley after all.

Once in the town, Martin was soon at the door of the local healer, a portly man whose eyes watered in the cold that was snapping at them. The knight told him the tale he had concocted during his descent to the town: that he and a companion were travelers headed for the Holy Land.

'My companion is sick and needs your help,' he pleaded.

The older man eyed him warily. Martin knew he undoubtedly looked like a penniless vagabond. 'You can pay?' the man asked gruffly.

'We have little money,' he nodded, 'but it should be enough to pay for some food and shelter for a few days.'

'Very well.' The man's eyes softened. 'You look like you're about to collapse yourself. Come in and eat something, and tell me where you've left your friend. I'll find some men to help bring him down from the mountain.'

Comforted by this sudden change in the man's demeanor, Martin entered the low-ceilinged room and accepted some bread and cheese willingly. He had indeed been close to collapse, and the food and drink were a welcome tonic to his battered body. In between greedy mouthfuls, he pointed out the ridge where he'd left Hugh, and the stocky man left.

As Martin emptied his plate, a sudden sense of unease grew inside him. As though emerging from a fog, he padded to the window and peered cautiously from it. A little way down the muddied street, the doctor was talking to two men, his hands gesturing back toward the house. Martin pulled away from the window. When he looked again, the doctor was gone, but the two men were now coming toward him.

He felt his muscles tighten. There could be, he knew, any number of reasons for this, but he feared the worst. And then he risked another look and saw one of them pulling out a large dagger.

Moving quickly across the house in search of a weapon, he heard some whispering from outside the back door. He slid silently across the floor, and pressed his ear to the door and listened. He saw the iron fastener on the door lift, and hugged the wall as the door slowly creaked open.

As the first of the men edged cautiously in, Martin reached out and grabbed the man, knocking the dagger out of his hand and sending him crashing heavily into the stone wall. He kicked the door back squarely onto the second intruder, slamming him against the wooden jamb. Retrieving the dagger with lightning speed, Martin leapt at the dazed man, grabbing him around the neck and driving the blade into his side.

He pulled the dagger free and let the man's body slump to the ground, then turned quickly to where the first man was pulling himself up from the floor. Striding across the room, Martin kicked him down before raising the dagger and burying it into the man's back.

Quickly, Martin snatched whatever food he could find and piled it into a pouch, reckoning this might be of greatest help to Hugh. Slipping out through the back door, he circled the town stealthily until he found the path that led up the mountain.

It didn't take long for them to come after him. Four, possibly five men, judging by the angry voices echoing up through the bleak woodland.

Snowflakes were drifting down from the overcast sky as Martin reached the rockface where he had rested earlier. His eyes settled on the evocative cracks and he stopped, flashing back to the instructions he had given to his brothers-in-arms all those months ago. *At no time must the safety of Aimard's letter be jeopardized.* His mind racing, he studied the fissures forming the splayed cross.

He knew he could never forget this place.

Using the dagger, he scraped at the base of the rock, freeing some stones the size of a man's fist, then thrust the pouched letter far into the hole he had made before replacing the stones and hammering them home with his booted heel. Then he continued his climb, making no attempt to conceal his passage.

Before long, the shouts of the men behind him were fading beneath the dull thunderous drumming of the waterfall. But when he reached the campsite, there was no sign of Hugh. Looking back, he saw his pursuers, now in plain sight. Five men in all. At the back of the pack was the doctor who had betrayed him.

Grabbing his broadsword, Martin resumed his climb toward the rim of the hill over which the force of water plunged. This, he decided, was where he would make his stand.

The first of the men, younger and stronger than the others, was some distance ahead of them, and he leapt forward with only a long-tined pitchfork in his grasp. Martin leaned back, then swung his broadsword, slicing through the pitchfork's handle as if it were a piece of kindling. The man fell forward, still moving fast through his own momentum. Martin stooped, thrust his shoulder into the man's gut, lifted him and threw him over and down into the chasm beneath the falls.

The man's scream was still echoing in Martin's ears when two of the others reached him. Although they were older and warier, they were better armed. The first one carried a short sword with which he flailed the air in front of Martin. For a trained knight like Martin, it was almost like dealing with a child. A simple parry followed by an upward flick, and the man's sword was also disappearing down the waterfall. With the return swing, Martin slashed through the man's shoulder, almost severing the arm. Then he stepped aside to avoid the third man's rush, reaching out a foot to trip him. The man fell to his knees, and Martin slammed down the handle of his sword, clubbing his head to the ground. Then he reversed the sword and with an executioner's swing, split the man's spine high on his neck.

Looking downward, he saw the doctor who was stumbling back the way he had come, and then he suddenly felt an agonizing pain in his back. He turned to see that the man he had disarmed was back on his feet, a trembling hand gripping the younger man's pitchfork. Blood was dripping from its tines. Martin stumbled forward, the burning pain in his back forcing an involuntary gasp from his lips. Summoning what strength he had left, he swung at the man with a forward slash of his sword, ripping out his throat.

For a moment Martin stood motionless, a thickening shroud of fatigue settling over him, then above the thunder of the torrent he heard a sound and spun around, gasping in pain as he did so. The last of his pursuers was rushing toward him, an old and rusting sword grasped in his hand. Martin was too slow to react, but before the man reached him, Hugh came staggering out of the undergrowth. The man spotted him and turned away from Martin, gripping his sword with both hands and driving it straight through the old sailor's torso.

Blood seeped out of Hugh's mouth, but somehow, he not only managed to remain upright, he staggered forward, pushing the sword further into his chest as he clasped his hands tightly around his stunned attacker. Slowly and agonizingly, Hugh kept going, pushing the man backward, step by step, never easing up on his iron grip despite the man's attempts to free himself, until they reached the lip of the ravine overlooking the waterfall. The man saw what was about to happen and screamed, still struggling in Hugh's grasp.

Momentarily heedless of his own fate, Martin looked up to where Hugh stood poised on the brink of the waterfall, the other man helpless in his grim embrace. His eyes met Hugh's, and he saw something like a smile tugging at the old sailor's lips, and with a final, brotherly nod, the master of the lost *Falcon Temple* stepped over the edge, taking the struggling man and himself into eternity.

A sudden, violent blow struck the back of Martin's head, and he felt a nausea rising in his throat. Twisting around in pain and barely conscious, he saw the hazy figure of the doctor standing over him, a rock in his hands.

'A man as strong as you will fetch a very good price indeed at the quarry, and thanks to you, I won't have to share it with the others,' the doctor sneered. 'And you might want to know that some of the men you killed today are kin to the overseers at the quarry.'

The doctor raised the rock high, and Martin knew that there was nothing he could do to avert the coming blow, to prevent his capture and ensuing enslavement, to recover the letter and resume his journey to Paris. Lying there in the fresh snow, images of Aimard of Villiers and William of Beaujeu swam into his mind before the rock came down and their faces faded to black.

CHAPTER 80

A hammering boom of thunder rolled over Tess, jolting her out of her sleep. She stirred, drifting in and out of consciousness, unsure of where she was. She could feel the rain pelting the back of her head. Every inch of her body ached, and she felt like she'd been trampled by an elephant. As her senses slowly awakened, she could hear the wind whistling past her and the waves crashing around her, and it unnerved her. The last thing she remembered was a wall of water that was about to bury her. She was gripped by a sudden surge of dread as she wondered if she was still at sea, lost in the storm, getting battered by waves, and yet... something felt wrong. It all felt different to her. And then she realized why that was.

She wasn't moving anymore. She was on land.

The dread gave way to relief and she tried opening her eyes, but they stung fiercely and she quickly decided to take it slowly. The images around her were blurry and faint. She panicked for the briefest moment before realizing that something was blocking her view. Reaching up with a trembling finger, she brushed away the wet mat of hair that covered her face, and she gently felt her eyelids. They were all puffed up, as were her lips. She tried to swallow, but couldn't. She felt like she had a ball of thorns stuck in her throat. She needed water, the unsalted kind.

Slowly, the hazy images drifted into focus. The sky still looked dull and gray, but she felt the sun coming up behind her, and judging from the roar of the breaking surf, that was also where the sea was. She tried to sit up, but her other arm was pinned down by something and wouldn't move. Pulling on it caused a rippling pain to shoot through her. Reaching across with her free hand, she saw that it was tied down with a rope that had eaten its way into her flesh. Lying back down, she remembered strapping herself and Reilly to the wooden hatchcover.

Reilly. Where was he?

She realized he wasn't next to her on the platform, and the dread came thundering back. She sat up and struggled to free her arm, and managed to slip it out from under the rope. She pushed herself to her knees and slowly stood up, taking in the surroundings. She could make out a long expanse of sand that stretched away from her, up and down the coast, sweeping across to a rocky headland at each end. She took a few hesitant steps, scanning the deserted, desolate beach through half-shut eyes, but saw nothing. She wanted to shout out his name, but her burning throat wouldn't allow it. And then she felt a wave of nausea and light-headedness wash over her. She weaved slightly, then sank back to her knees, feeling any lingering energy slip away. She wanted to cry, but no tears came.

Unable to find any more strength, she flopped forward onto the sand, unconscious.

When she woke up again, things were very different. For one thing, it was quiet. No howling wind. No pounding surf. Although she could hear the beating rain in the background, it was heavenly quiet around her. And then there was the bedding. Not a plank of wood, nor a cushion of sand. This was an actual, bonafide bed.

She swallowed and immediately sensed the improvement in her throat, and as she looked around, she understood why. Looming over her was an IV drip, hanging off a small chrome stem by the bed, its tube taped to the inside of her arm. Her eyes darted around. She was in a small, simply furnished room. Next to her bed was a simple chair of turned wood, and a side table. A small carafe of water and a glass sat on the table, on a lacy, white mat whose edges were slightly frayed. The walls were whitewashed and unadorned, except for a small, wooden cross on the wall by her side.

She tried to sit up, but her head was swimming. The bed creaked under her shifting weight, the noise echoing out of the room. She heard footsteps and some garbled words, a female voice, urgent, and then a woman appeared, smiling at her as she studied her with concern. She was a large woman, in her late forties, and had olive skin and curly brown hair that was tied under a white scarf, bandana-style. Her eyes sparkled with kindness and warmth.

'*Doxa to Theo. Pos esthaneste?*'

Before Tess could answer, a man hurried in, looking delighted to see her. He had wire-rimmed glasses, a coppery tan and gelled, rat pack hair that gleamed like black enamel. He blurted out some hurried words in the same foreign language to the woman before smiling at Tess and asking her something else that she found incomprehensible.

'I'm sorry,' she mumbled, her voice quavering. She cleared her throat. 'I don't understand...'

The man looked stumped and exchanged a quizzical glance with his companion before turning to Tess. 'I apologize, I thought you were – you're American?' he asked in a heavily accented English as he reached over and handed her the glass of water.

Tess took a sip and nodded. 'Yes.'

'What happened to you?'

She searched for the words. 'I was on a boat, we hit a storm, and...' Her voice trailed off. Clarity was fighting its way through the fog of her mind, and questions were forming. 'Where am I? How did I get here?'

The man leaned in and felt her forehead as he spoke. 'My name is Costa Mavromaras. I'm the local doctor, and this is my wife Eleni. Some fishermen found you on the beach at Marathounda and brought you here to us.'

The names and the accent threw Tess. 'Where is... *here*?'

Mavromaras smiled at his assumption. 'Our house. In Yialos.'

Her face must have still been mired in confusion, because the doctor's brow furrowed, mirroring her look. 'Yialos, in Symi,' he explained, then paused, studying her. 'Where did you think you were?'

Tess's mind blurred.

Symi?

What was she doing on a Greek island? A rush of questions flooded her mind. She knew Symi was in the Dodecanese Islands, somewhere close to the Turkish coast, but she wanted to know exactly where it was and how she'd gotten here. She wanted to know what day it was, how long it had been since the storm had struck the *Savarona*, how long she'd been drifting at sea – but that could all wait. There was something else she desperately had to know.

'There was a man with me,' she asked, her voice rising in urgent quivers. 'Did the fishermen find anyone else...?' She stopped when she saw the doctor's expression turn guarded, and watched with rising concern as he glanced at his wife. He looked back at her and nodded, and there was an unmistakable sadness in his expression that strafed her heart.

'Yes, they found someone, on the same beach as you, but I'm afraid his situation is a little bit more serious than yours.'

Tess was already pulling her legs off the bed.

'I need to see him,' she urged them. 'Please.'

Tess's legs, already weakened and barely able to support her for the short walk down the corridor to the adjacent room, almost gave way from under her when she saw Reilly. The top of his head was wrapped in a big, neat dressing, and there was no sign of blood. There was a dark, yellow bruise around his left eye and cheek, and both his eyelids were swollen shut. His lips were cracked and bruised. An IV drip like hers snaked down into his arm, but he also had a respirator mask strapped to his face, the machine pumping away noisily nearby. Worst of all was the color of his skin. It had a blue-ish, deathly pallor to it.

Tess felt a great tearing inside as Mavromaras helped her into a chair by Reilly's bed. Outside, the rain hadn't stopped. The doctor explained that the fishermen had found them when they'd been out checking on their boats on a beach on the island's east coast. They had rushed them over to him in treacherous weather, braving the rain-soaked roads of the island to reach the town and his clinic.

That was two days ago.

Her condition hadn't really worried him, as her pulse had responded quickly to the IV solution and, although she didn't remember it, she had been drifting in and out of consciousness the whole time. Reilly, however, was in worse shape. He'd lost a lot of blood, his lungs were weak, but they could deal with all that. The blow he'd clearly taken to the head was the main problem. Mavromaras didn't think it had cracked his skull, although he couldn't tell for sure as there weren't any X-ray facilities on the island. Either way, he'd suffered a major trauma to the head, and hadn't regained consciousness at all since he'd been found, half-drowned on the beach.

Tess felt the blood drain from her face. 'What are you saying?'

'His vital signs are steady, his blood pressure is better, his breathing is weak but at least he's doing it himself, unaided – the respirator is only there to keep him hyperventilated, to make sure his brain gets enough blood while he's unconscious. Beyond that...'

Her face clouded as she fought off the terrifying thought. 'You're saying he's in a coma?'

Mavromaras looked at her, somberly. 'Yes.'

'Do you have everything you need to treat him here? I mean, shouldn't we get him to a hospital?'

'This is a small island, and I'm afraid we don't have one here. The nearest one is on the island of *Rodos* – Rhodes. I've been in contact with them, but unfortunately the air ambulance helicopter was damaged three days ago when trying to land in the storm, and they're waiting to fly in some spare parts from Athens to fix it. It wouldn't have been able to fly here anyway, because of the storm. They're hoping the weather will improve tomorrow, but to be frank with you, I'm not sure moving him is a good idea, and besides, he won't be any better off over there, there's not much they can do either aside from hooking him up to some more advanced monitors that we don't have here.'

Tess felt the fog that shrouded the room growing thicker. 'There's got to be something you can do?' she stammered.

'I'm afraid not, not with comas. I can keep an eye on his blood pressure, on the oxygenation of the blood, but there's no way of,' he paused, searching for the appropriate term, '*waking* someone out of it. We just have to wait.'

She was almost afraid to ask. 'How long?' she finally managed.

He opened his hands outward, uncertainly. 'It could be hours, days, weeks... There's no real way of knowing...' His voice trailed off, his eyes conveying the rest. It obviously wasn't just a question of 'when'.

Tess nodded, grateful not to hear him verbalize the horrible possibility that had already entrenched itself firmly in her mind the instant she had walked into the room.

CHAPTER 81

Tess hovered between her room and Reilly's for the rest of the day, anxiously looking in on him and finding Eleni there each time. The nurse had kept on gently herding her back to her bed, reassuring her in broken English that Reilly would be fine.

She'd given the doctor and his wife a rather different version of the events that brought her and Reilly to the island, omitting any mention of why they were out here in the first place or of the Turkish gunship opening fire on them. She'd been careful to mention that there were other people on the dive boat, in case any of the others had been found, alive or otherwise, but Mavromaras had somberly informed her that although some debris, presumably from their dive boat, had washed up on the island, he hadn't heard of any other survivors, or bodies, being found.

She'd used the phone to call Arizona, getting straight through to her aunt's house and finding Kim and Eileen there, worried at not having heard from her for several days. Their surprise at her telling them she was on a tiny Greek island was palpable even across the crackling, echoey phone line. She'd been careful not to mention the name of the island, although she later wondered why she had bothered doing that before realizing she wasn't ready to face the outside world and its questions just yet. After hanging up, she thought she had done a reasonable job at calming their concerns over her safety, telling them she was just exploring an unexpected work opportunity in the area and would be in touch again soon.

Around sunset, two local women had appeared at the doctor's house and had been shown to Tess's room. Although they spoke little English, she eventually understood that they were the wives of some of the fishermen who had found her on the beach. They had brought her some clothes; a pair of cotton pants, a nightdress, a couple of white blouses and a thick cotton cardigan into which she happily wrapped herself. They had also brought a large, piping-hot clay pot of *giouvetsi* with them, which Eleni explained was a lamb and rice pasta stew. Tess had dug into it gratefully, surprising herself by wolfing down a large plateful with newfound appetite.

Later, a hot bath had worked wonders for her general stiffness, and Mavromaras had changed the dressing on her arm, the purple bruising from the rope looking to her as though it would be with her forever. Then, and despite her hosts' gentle objections, she'd spent most of the rest of the evening sitting at Reilly's bedside, although she'd found it hard to talk to him the way, she knew, some people did to loved ones who were also comatose. She had doubts about whether or not it would actually help him, and she wasn't sure if, given everything that had happened, hers was the voice he'd most want to hear. She blamed herself for what they'd been through, and although there was so much she wanted to tell him, she wanted to say it when he was in a position to respond, favorably or not. She didn't want to force herself on him when he was, at best, a captive listener, and at worst, not listening at all.

Close to midnight, she'd eventually succumbed to exhaustion, physical as much as emotional, and gone back to her room. She'd dropped off to sleep effortlessly, her head nestling between two musty pillows.

By the next morning, Tess felt strong enough to venture out of the house and walk off her stiffness. The wind was still blowing, although the rain had petered out, and she felt a short walk would probably do her a lot of good.

She slipped into her clothes and looked in on Reilly. Eleni was there, as always, and was gently massaging his leg. Mavromaras soon appeared and examined him. Reilly's condition was stable, he told her, but not markedly improved. He explained that in these situations, any improvement wouldn't be gradual. It would happen more or less at once. Reilly would be unconscious one moment and, if he were to emerge from his coma, he would simply awaken without any physiological warning.

Mavromaras had to check on another patient across the island, and said he'd be back in a couple of hours. Tess asked if she could walk him out to his car.

'The air ambulance service in Rodos called me this morning,' he told her as they stepped outside the house. 'They should be able to fly in sometime tomorrow.'

Although Tess had been anxious earlier to get Sean to a proper hospital, she wasn't so sure anymore. 'I've been thinking about what you said. Do you really think we should take him there?'

A gracious smile crossed the doctor's face before he answered. 'Frankly, it's up to you. It's a very good hospital and I know the man in charge there, they'll look after him well, I can assure you.' The uncertainty must have been etched clearly all over her face, because he then added, 'We don't need to make any decisions now. Let's see how he is in the morning, and we can decide then.'

They walked across the street, skirting a couple of big puddles of water, and reached a slightly rusting old Peugeot. Mavromaras opened its door which, Tess noticed, wasn't locked.

She glanced up and down the narrow street. Even in these overcast conditions, the town was breathtaking. Tier upon tier of neat, neo-classical houses painted in warm pastel colors straddled the steep hill all the way down to the small harbor below. Many of them had triangular pediments and red tile roofs and were of a pleasing, subtle uniformity of style. Water spilled down overwhelmed gutters at the sides of the road and tumbled down the steep flight of steps cutting up the hill. Overhead, the bruised sky still looked poised for another onslaught.

'That was one hell of a storm,' Tess observed.

Mavromaras eyed the clouds, nodding. 'It was far worse than anything anyone can recall, even the oldest people in town. And especially for this time of year...'

Tess flashed back to the storm that had hit the *Falcon Temple* all those years ago and, almost to herself, she murmured, 'An act of God.'

The doctor cocked a curious eyebrow, surprised by the comment. 'Maybe. But if you want to think in those terms, think of it more as a miracle.'

'A miracle?'

'Of course. A miracle that you and your friend were washed ashore on our island. It's a big sea out there. A little bit further north and you would have landed on the Turkish coast which, in this area, is rocky and completely deserted. The towns are all on the other side of the peninsula. A bit further south and you would have missed the island entirely and been carried out into the Aegean and...' He raised his eyebrows and nodded knowingly, leaving the rest for her to fill in, then shrugged and threw his medical bag into the passenger seat. 'I have to go. I'll be back this afternoon.'

Tess didn't want him to leave just yet. There was something comforting about his presence. 'Isn't there anything I can do to help him?'

'Your friend is in good hands. My wife is an excellent nurse, and although this isn't anything like the hospitals you're used to in America, trust me when I tell you we've had a lot of experience dealing with all kinds of injuries. Even on small islands like this, people do get hurt.' He paused, thought about it for a moment as he studied her, then added, 'Have you talked to him yet?'

Tess was taken aback by the question. 'Talked to him?'

'You should do that. Talk to him. Inspire him, give him strength.' His tone was almost fatherly, and then he smiled, shaking his head slightly. 'You must think you've fallen on some small town witch doctor. I promise you that's not the case. Many studies by prominent physicians support the idea. Just because he's in a coma, doesn't mean he can't hear. It just means he can't respond... yet.' He paused, his eyes beaming with hope and empathy. 'Talk to him... and pray for the best.'

Tess let out a small chuckle and looked away wistfully. 'I'm not very good at that.'

Mavromaras didn't look convinced. 'In your own way, although you don't realize it, you're already doing it. You're praying for him just by wishing he would recover. A lot of prayers are being said for him.' The doctor pointed across the way toward a small chapel. She could see a few locals greeting each other at its door, some of them leaving while others were heading in. 'Many of the men on this island earn their living from the sea. There were four fishing boats out at sea the night the storm hit. Their families prayed to God and to the Archangel Michael, the patron saint of sea-farers, for their safe return, and those prayers were answered. All of them managed to come back to us unharmed. Now, more prayers are being said, prayers of thanks. And prayers for your friend's recovery.'

'They're all praying for his recovery?'

The doctor nodded. 'We all are.'

'But you don't even know him.'

'It doesn't matter. The sea brought him here to us, and it's our duty to nurse him back to health so he can go on with his life.' He climbed into the car. 'Now I really must go.' And with a small wave and a parting glance, he drove off through pools of muddy rainwater and disappeared down the hill.

For a moment, Tess watched him go. She turned to walk back into the house, then hesitated. She couldn't remember the last time that she had been inside any chapel or church or religious building of any kind, except for her work and, of course, during the brief episode in the burnt-out remains of the church in Manhattan. Splashing her way across the soaked road, she crossed the small pebble courtyard, pushed the door open and stepped inside.

The small chapel was half full, with people huddled in earnest prayer on pews that were old and worn smooth through many years of use. Tess stood at the back, looking around. The chapel was simple, its whitewashed walls covered in eighteenth-century frescoes, and lit by the glow of scores of candles. Moving around the chapel, she noticed an alcove that held silver icons of St Gabriel and St Michael, which were adorned in precious stones. Swept away by the flickering candlelight and the hushed tones of prayer, a strange sensation came over her. She suddenly felt like she wanted to pray. She felt uncomfortable with the notion and shook the unsettling thought away, convinced that to do so would be hypocritical.

She was turning to leave when she spotted the two women who had brought over the food and clothing the day before. They had two men with them. The women saw her and hastened over, fussing all over her with unabashed delight at her recovery. They kept repeating the same phrase, '*Doxa to Theo*,' and although she couldn't understand what they were saying, she smiled back and nodded, moved by their genuine concern. Tess understood that the men were their husbands, the fishermen who had also escaped the storm's wrath. They greeted her warmly. One of the women pointed at a small cluster of candles in a niche at the rear of the chapel and said something Tess didn't catch at first, but gradually became clear. She was telling Tess that both women had lit candles for Reilly.

Tess thanked them and glanced down the nave of the chapel, at the clusters of townspeople who were sitting there, joined in prayer in the dipping candlelight. She stood there quietly for a moment before turning and heading back to the house.

Tess spent the rest of the morning at Reilly's bedside, and after a hesitant start, she found that she was able to talk to him after all. She avoided talking about the recent events, and knowing so little about his life, she decided to stick to her own past, telling him stories about her adventures in the field, her successes and her embarrassments, anecdotes about Kim, whatever crossed her mind.

Eleni came into the room at around midday, inviting Tess downstairs to have lunch. The timing couldn't have been better, as Tess was running out of things to say and was headed ever more perilously toward having to actually face and talk about what she and Reilly had lived through together. She still wasn't comfortable with the idea of discussing anything meaty with him while he was still unconscious.

Mavromaras had returned from his consultation, and Tess informed him that she had thought about the idea of moving him to Rhodes, but preferred to keep Reilly where he was, as long as the doctor and his wife were still happy to have them there. Her decision seemed to please them, and she was relieved to hear, in no uncertain terms, that she and Reilly could stay until such a time when a major decision regarding his condition needed to be taken.

Tess spent the rest of the day and most of the next morning at Reilly's bedside, and after lunch, felt she needed to get some air. Noticing how much the storm had abated, she decided to venture out a little further.

The wind was now nothing more than a strong breeze and at long last the rain had completely died out. Despite the dark-bellied clouds still crowding the skies over the island, she decided she rather liked the town. It wasn't blighted by the slightest modern development and had kept the charm of its simple past intact. She found the narrow lanes and the picturesque houses calming, the smiles from passing strangers comforting. Mavromaras had told her that hard times had befallen Symi after the Second World War, when a large part of the population had packed up and left after the island was bombed by both the Allied and Axis powers, who had traded roles as occupiers. Happily, the recent years had seen a marked improvement in the island's fortunes. It was thriving again now that Athenians and foreigners were cottoning on to its appeal, buying up the old houses and caringly bringing them back to their former glory.

She climbed up the stone steps of the Kali Strata, past the old museum and reached the remains of a castle, which had been built by the Knights of St John in the early fifteenth century on the site of a much older fortification, only to be blown up while housing a Nazi munitions dump during the war. Tess meandered through the ancient site, stopping at a plaque commemorating Filibert de Niallac, the Knights' French Grand Master. *More knights, even here in this lost little corner of the world*, she mused as she thought back to the Templars and stared out at the spectacular views over the harbor and the whitecapped sea beyond. She watched as swallows darted in and out of the trees by the old windmills, and saw a lone ship, a trawler, venturing out from the sleepy port. Seeing the wide blue expanse that surrounded the island triggered an unsettling feeling in her. Smothering her discomfort, she felt an urge to see the beach where she and Reilly had been found.

She headed for the main square where she found a driver who was headed for the monastery at Panormitis, beyond the small settlement at Marathounda. A short, bumpy ride later, he dropped her off at the entrance of the town. As she made her way through the small cluster of houses, she ran into the two fishermen who had found her and Reilly. Their faces lit up at seeing her, and they insisted on having her join them for a cup of coffee at the small local taverna, and Tess happily agreed.

Although the conversation was severely limited due to the language barrier between them, Tess understood that more debris from the dive boat had been found. They led her to a small dump just beyond the taverna, and showed her the bits and pieces of timber and fiberglass that had been picked up from the beaches on either side of the bay. The storm and the sinking came rushing back to Tess, and she felt saddened at the thought of the men who had lost their lives on the *Savarona*, and whose bodies would never be recovered.

She thanked them and was soon walking on the deserted, windswept beach. The breeze carried the fresh smell of the churned sea, and she was relieved to see that the sun was hinting through the clouds, prying its way through them after a long absence. She moved slowly along the edge of the tideline, scuffing her feet in the sand, the hazy images of that fateful morning flooding her consciousness.

At the far end of the beach, well out of sight of the small settlement at the mouth of the bay, she reached an outcropping of black rocks. She climbed onto it, found a flat patch, and sat down, hugging her knees and staring out at the sea. A long way out, a large rock jutted out from the water, small white topped breakers surging around it. It looked menacing, yet another danger she and Reilly had escaped. She became aware of the wails of the sea gulls, and looking up she saw two of them swooping down playfully and tussling over a dead fish.

All at once she realized that tears were rolling down her cheeks. She wasn't sobbing, or even crying, really. They were just tears, welling up out of nowhere. And just as suddenly as they had started, they dried up, and she realized that she was shivering, but not with cold. It was something more primal, rising up from deep inside her. Feeling a need to shake it off, she rose to her feet and continued her walk, climbing across the rocks and finding a small pathway that snaked its way along the shore.

She followed it, past three more rocky inlets, and reached another, more remote, bay at the southern tip of the island.

There didn't seem to be any roads leading down to it. A crescent of virgin sand arced away from her, ending with another headland that rose into a towering, jagged overhang.

She looked down the beach in the diffused twilight, and an odd shape attracted her attention. It lay on the far end of the bay, at the edge of the rocks. She squinted, willing her eyes to pull it into focus, and she was aware that her breathing was quickening, her mouth suddenly dry. Her heartbeat raced ahead.

It can't be, she thought. *It isn't possible.*

And then she was running along the sand until, gasping for breath, she came to within a few feet of it and stopped, her mind reeling at the possibility.

It was the falcon figurehead, all tangled up in the harness of its rig, the orange floaters wrapped, half deflated, around it.

It looked intact.

CHAPTER 82

Tentatively, Tess reached out and touched it. She ran her hands over it, her eyes ratcheted wide, her imagination propelling her back through time to the days of the Knights Templar, to Aimard and his men and their final, fateful voyage on the *Falcon Temple*.

A tangle of images flooded her mind as she tried to remember Aimard's words. *What had he said exactly?* The chest was placed into a cavity that had been carved out of the back of the falcon's head. The remaining void had been filled with resin, then covered with a matching piece of wood that was hammered into place with pegs. That, too, had been sealed with resin.

She examined the back of the falcon's head closely. She could just about discern the marks of where resin had been packed in, and, feeling around carefully with trained fingers, she found the edges of the lid and the pegs that had held it in place. The seals all looked unscathed, and no water seemed to have seeped into the resin-covered cavities. From what she could see, it was highly likely that whatever had been locked away inside the chest was still safe and undamaged.

Looking around, she found two chunks of rock and used them as a hammer and chisel to break into the cavity. The first few layers of wood flaked off easily, but the rest proved to be stubbornly solid. Searching around the beach, she came across a piece of rusted steel rebar and used its sharp, broken edge to scrape through the resin. Working feverishly and with total disregard for any concerns of conservation the archaeologist in her would have insisted upon only weeks ago, she was able to claw her way under the timber lid and into the cavity. She could now see the edge of the chest, small and ornate. Wiping her sweaty brow, she scraped off enough of the resin from around the chest, and used the rod to dislodge it. Sinking her fingers around it, she finally managed to lift the small box out.

All of her excitement came surging back and she tried to control it, but it was next to impossible. She actually had it, in her hands. Although the chest was intricately decorated with silver carvings, it was surprisingly light. She carried it into the lee of a large rock where she could examine it closely. There was an iron hasp with, not a lock, but a wrought-iron ring. She used the rock to hammer at the hasp until, finally, it came away from the wood and she was able to lift the lid of the chest and peer inside.

Carefully, she lifted out the chest's contents. It was a package, wrapped in what appeared to be an oiled animal skin much like the one Aimard had used to protect the astrolabe, and tied with leather thongs. Very slowly, she unfolded the skin. Nestling in it was a book, a leather-bound codex.

The instant she saw it, she knew what it was.

It was inexplicably familiar, its humble simplicity belying its prodigious contents. With trembling fingers, she lifted up the cover slightly and peered at the writing on the first sheet of parchment inside it. The lettering on it was faded but readable, and as far as she could tell, the codex's contents were undamaged. She knew, with absolute certainty, that she was the first person to see it, the mythical treasure of the Knights Templar, ever since it was put into the chest seven hundred years ago by William of Beaujeu and entrusted to Aimard of Villiers.

Except that it was no longer a myth.

It was real.

Cautiously, aware that this should be done in a laboratory, or at the very least indoors, but unable to resist the urge to get a better look, Tess opened the codex a bit wider and lifted up a sheet of parchment. She recognized the familiar, brownish tint of the ink used at the time, made from a mixture of carbon soot, resin, wine dregs, and cuttlefish ink.

The handwriting was difficult to decipher, but she recognized a couple of words, enough to know that it was written in Aramaic. She had encountered it occasionally in the past, enough to be able to identify it.

She paused, her eyes riveted on the simple manuscript in her hands.

Aramaic.

The language spoken by Jesus.

Her heart pounding noisily in her ears, she stared at parchment, recognizing more words here and there.

Very slowly, almost unwillingly, she began to fathom just what she held in her hands. And to realize who had first touched these sheets of parchment; whose hand had written these words.

They were the writings of Jeshua of Nazareth.

The writings of the man the entire world knew as Jesus Christ.

CHAPTER 83

Gripping the leathery skin that held the codex, Tess walked back slowly, along the beach. The sun was setting, the last glimmer of light poking through the gray wall of cloud that lingered on the horizon.

She had decided against carrying the chest back, choosing to hide it behind a large rock instead, in order not to attract unwanted attention. She would come back for it later. Her mind was still floundering with the implications of what she believed she held in her hands. This wasn't a shard of pottery, it wasn't Troy or Tutankhamen. This was something that could change the world. It had to be handled, to say the least, with extreme care.

As she approached the small cluster of houses at Marathounda, she took off her cardigan and wrapped it around the small pouch. The two fishermen had already left the taverna, but she got one of the men there who recognized her from earlier that day to drive her back to the doctor's house.

As she stepped inside, Mavromaras greeted her with a big smile. 'Where have you been? We've been looking for you.' Before she could rattle off some lie, he was herding her deeper into the house, toward the bedrooms. 'Come, quickly. Someone wants to see you.'

Reilly was looking at her, his breathing mask gone, a valiant attempt at a smile on his dried lips. He was sitting up at a slight angle, propped up against three large pillows. She felt something shift inside her.

'Hey,' Reilly said, weakly.

'Hey yourself,' she answered, relief breaking across her face. She felt uplifted in a way she'd never experienced before.

She turned and, trying not to attract Eleni or the doctor's attention to it, laid the bundled cardigan casually on a small cabinet facing the bed, before approaching Reilly and stroking his forehead softly. Her eyes moved over his bruised face and she caught her lower lip with her teeth, feeling some tears welling up.

'It's great to have you back,' she managed in a small voice.

He shrugged, his face brightening slowly. 'From now on, I choose where we go on vacation, alright?'

Her face lit up, and she was unable to stop a tear from trickling down. 'You got it.' She turned, her moist eyes beaming at the doctor and his wife. 'Thank you,' she mouthed. They just smiled and nodded. 'I – we both owe you our lives. How can I ever repay you?'

'Nonsense,' Mavromaras replied. 'We have a saying in Greek. *Den hriazete euharisto, kathikon mou.* It means there's no thanks necessary for what is a duty.' He glanced at Eleni, exchanging an unspoken signal. 'We'll leave you,' he said softly, 'I'm sure you have a lot to talk about.'

Tess watched them turn to leave, then hurried up to the doctor and gave him a hug, kissing him on both cheeks. Blushing through his tan, Mavromaras smiled modestly and stepped out of the room, leaving them alone.

As she turned to move back to Reilly's bedside, she spotted the bundled cardigan that sat there on the cabinet like an unexploded bomb. She felt awful at being deceitful, both to the generous couple who had saved her life, and to Reilly. She desperately wanted to tell him about it, but she knew the timing wasn't right.

Soon, though.

With a heavy heart, she summoned up a smile and joined him at his bedside.

Reilly felt like he'd been away for weeks. He felt an odd, stinging numbness in his muscles, and there was a dizziness in his head that just hung there. One of his eyelids was still partially shut, and the uneven depth perception wasn't helping either.

He didn't remember much, beyond shooting De Angelis and hurling himself into the sea. He'd asked Mavromaras how he'd gotten there, and the doctor could only give him the sketchy details he had heard from Tess. Still, waking up and finding out that she was there, and in one piece, was a huge relief.

He tried raising himself carefully into a sitting position, and it brought a slight wince of pain onto his face. He settled back against the pillows.

'So how did we end up here?' he asked.

He listened as Tess told him what she remembered. She also had a black hole in her memory, from the freak wave to waking up on the beach. She told him about the hit he took to the head, how she'd strapped their life jackets together, and about the wave. She told him about the hatchcover and showed him the deep cut on her arm. She wanted to know why the Coast Guard vessel fired on them, and Reilly told her about his journey, from the moment De Angelis had stepped out of the helicopter in Turkey.

'I'm sorry,' she said contritely when it finally came up. 'I don't know what came over me. I don't know, it was just – I must have been out of my mind, leaving you there like that. This whole mess, it's just...' She couldn't find the words to express her remorse.

'It's okay,' he countered, a faint smile crossing his cracked lips. 'Let's not talk about it now. We both made it, and that's the main thing, isn't it?'

She nodded reluctantly, beaming her appreciation, and he continued, explaining how it had been the monsignor all along, killing the horsemen in New York, even manning the gun himself on board the *Karadeniz*. He told her how he had shot De Angelis.

And then he told her about Cardinal Brugnone's revelations.

Tess felt a huge pang of guilt when Reilly took her through what had been revealed to him at the Vatican. The monumental truth about what she had found on the beach, confirmed to him by the very people it stood to harm the most, had electrified every pore on her body, but she couldn't show it. She did her best to appear stunned, asking questions, hating herself more and more with every fake reaction. She wanted to whip out the codex and share it with him right there and then. But she couldn't do it. A deep-set unease was etched across his face, and she knew that what Brugnone had told him, the lie at the heart of the Church, was a wound that had to be hurting. There was no way she was going to inflict the finality of its physical proof on him this soon. Right now, she wasn't even sure if or when she could ever do it. He needed time. She needed time, too, to think things through.

'Are you gonna be okay?' she asked hesitantly.

He stared into the distance for a moment, his face clouding as he obviously struggled to put his feelings into words.

'It's weird, but this whole thing, Turkey, the Vatican, the storm... it just feels like a bad dream. Maybe I'm too drugged up or something, but... I'm sure it'll hit home at some point. Right now, I'm so tired, I just feel completely drained, but I don't know how much of it is physical and how much of it is something else.'

Tess scrutinized his weary face. No, now was definitely not the right time to tell him about it. 'Vance and De Angelis got what they deserved,' she said instead, brightening, 'and you're alive. There's cause for faith in that, isn't there?'

'Maybe,' he half-smiled, unconvincingly.

Reilly's eyes moved over her face, and, although nodding off to sleep, he found himself thinking about the future. It wasn't something he had ever really thought about, and it surprised him to have it cross his mind now, here, barely alive on this distant shore.

For a fleeting moment, he questioned whether or not he wanted to go on being an FBI agent. He had always liked being with the Bureau, but this case had cut deep. For the first time ever, he felt tired of the life he had chosen, tired of spending his days thrashing around inside the heads of demented lowlifes, tired of experiencing the worst the planet had to offer. He wondered idly if a career change might help restore his appreciation for life – maybe even his faith in mankind.

He felt his eyelids drooping.

'Sorry,' he barely managed, 'I think we'll have to save this till later.'

Tess watched Reilly sink into a deep sleep, and felt exhausted herself.

She thought about what he had joked about, about choosing vacations. It brought a smile to her face, and she shook her head lightly. She mused that a vacation was just what she needed, and she knew exactly where she would take it. All at once, Arizona seemed like heaven. She decided she would go straight there. She couldn't even conceive of going back to the office. Just change planes in New York, and go see her daughter. And if Guiragossian and anyone else at the Institute didn't like it, then to hell with them.

It suddenly occurred to her that there were lots of interesting things for an archaeologist to do in the southwestern states, and she remembered that Phoenix had a world-class museum. Then she glanced at Reilly. Chicago born and raised, New Yorker by adoption, obviously addicted to being right in the thick of it. She wondered if he could ever give it all up and trade it in for a quiet life in a desert state. And somehow, quite suddenly, that seemed to matter. A lot. Maybe more than anything else.

Stepping out onto the balcony of his room, Tess looked up at the stars in the sky, remembering the night that she and Reilly had been alone at the campsite on the way to the lake. The island was quiet even during the daytime, but at night it became ethereally peaceful. She was acutely aware of the stillness and quiet. There might be nights like this in Arizona, but not in New York. She thought about Reilly, wondering what he would say and do if she did quit the Manoukian Institute and move to Arizona. Maybe she would ask him sometime.

Looking out over the glimmering sea, she considered what to do about the codex. It was undoubtedly one of the most important archaeological and religious finds of all time, and one with staggering ramifications for hundreds of millions of people. To announce the find would make her the most famous member of her profession since the discoveries at the Great Pyramids in Egypt almost eighty years ago. But what would it do to the rest of the world?

She wanted to talk to someone about it.

She *needed* to talk to Reilly about it.

She frowned inwardly, realizing that she had to do it, and soon. But right now, he needed rest, and so did she. She thought of going to her own bed, but went back inside and curled up beside Reilly. She closed her eyes and very soon, she too was drifting off to sleep.

CHAPTER 84

The next few days drifted by in a daze. Tess would spend time with Reilly in the morning before going out for long walks, returning by lunchtime. Late in the afternoon, she would venture out again, usually up to the castle ruins from where she would watch the sun melt into the shimmering Aegean waters. She loved that part of her day the most. Sitting there in quiet reflection, with the scent of sage and chamomile wafting down from the hillside, she found the idyllic setting among the rocks somewhat reassuring, a bit of respite from the small bundle in her room that was preying on her mind at all times.

She'd met a lot of people during her walks, locals who were never short of a smile for her and always had enough time for a small chat, and by the third day, she had explored most of the small streets and pathways of the town and had started venturing further. To the pastoral soundtrack of donkey guffaws and goat bells, she would explore the hidden corners of the island. She had taken a long walk to the tiny islet of San Emilianos, where she'd meandered among the icons of its whitewashed church and wandered along the pebbly beach, gazing forlornly at the sea urchins that lined the rocks below its waterline. She'd also visited the sprawling monastery at Panormitis where, to her surprise, she'd met three Athenian businessmen in their early forties who were staying in its stark guest rooms and who had told her they were there for a few days of rest and contemplation and what they had intriguingly termed 'renewal.' In fact, it was virtually impossible to get away from the Church's presence on the island. The churches were the focal point of its villages, and like all Greek islands, Symi had dozens of tiny chapels scattered across virtually every hilltop. No matter where you were, there was always a reminder of the Church's influence within sight, and yet, oddly, it didn't feel oppressive to Tess. Far from it. It seemed an organic, intrinsic part of the island's life, a magnet that drew its inhabitants closer and gave them comfort and strength.

Reilly's condition was improving all the time. His breathing was much less strained, the puffiness in his lips and around his eyes had subsided, and the waxy pallor had gone from his cheeks. He was now walking around the house, and that morning he had said they couldn't stay hidden away from the rest of the world forever. Now that he was up to it, he would need to make arrangements for their return. Leaving the house with what felt like the weight of the world on her shoulders, Tess knew that she would soon have to confront the issue and discuss what she'd found with him.

She had spent the rest of the morning back at Marathounda, where she'd retrieved the chest that had held the codex, and was presently walking up to the doctor's house when she bumped into the two women who had brought her the food and clothing. They were coming out of the small church and were clearly delighted to see her. They told her they had heard the news about Reilly's recovery, and hugged her warmly, gesticulating and nodding in unison to express their heartfelt relief. Their husbands were also with them. The men shook hands with her, their faces beaming with sympathy and relief, before the foursome trundled off, waving back with bright smiles and leaving Tess standing there, watching them, lost in her thoughts.

And that's when it finally sank in. The realization that had been clamoring at her from deep within for days, the confusing feeling that had overcome the instincts of a cynical lifetime, but that she was still denying. Until now.

I can't do it to them.

Not to them, not to millions of others like them. The thought had been preying on her mind, day and night, since she'd found the codex. Everyone she had met in the last few days, all the people who had been nothing but unreservedly kind and generous to her. This was about them. All of them, and countless others throughout the world.

This could wreck their lives.

The thought suddenly made her sick to her stomach. If the Church can inspire people to live like that, to give like that, particularly in this day and age, she thought, then it must be doing something right. It has to be worth preserving. What did it matter if it was based on a story that embellished the truth? Is it even possible to create something with such a phenomenal power to inspire, she wondered, without straying outside the strict confines of the real world?

Standing there, watching the two couples walk away and melt back into their lives, she couldn't believe she'd even contemplated any other option.

She knew she couldn't do it.

But she also knew she couldn't avoid telling Reilly any longer.

That evening, after avoiding him for most of the afternoon, she led him up to the castle ruins. She held onto his hand with a sweaty palm, her other arm tightly gripped around a small bundle that was wrapped in the cardigan. The sun was almost gone, and the sky was now gleaming with a light, pinkish haze as it held the last of the day's light.

She placed the bundle on a partially collapsed wall and turned to Reilly. She found it hard to meet his look, and her mouth felt dry.

'I...' All of a sudden, she wasn't sure anymore. What if she just hid it, ignored it, and never mentioned it to him. Wouldn't he be better off not knowing, especially given what happened to his father? Wouldn't she be doing him a favor by never bringing up the fact that she had found it, seen it, touched it?

No. Much as she would have liked to do that, she knew it would be a mistake. She didn't ever want to be less than truthful with him again. She'd already done enough of that for a lifetime. Deep down, she was hoping that, despite everything, she and Reilly could have a future together, and she knew it would be impossible for them to grow closer with such a huge unspoken lie between them.

She was suddenly aware of the intense stillness around her. The sparrows she had heard earlier were silent now, as if in sympathy with the moment. She steeled herself and tried again. 'I've been wanting to tell you something for a few days, I really wanted to, but I needed to wait until you were well enough.'

Reilly looked at her uncertainly. She knew her unease was obvious. 'What is it?'

Tess felt her insides seizing into a tight knot and simply said, 'I need to show you something.' She then turned and peeled off the layers of the cardigan, exposing the codex tucked inside its folds.

A fleeting glance of surprise crossed Reilly's features before he lifted his gaze and studied her. After what felt like an eternity to her, he asked, 'Where'd you find it?'

She couldn't say the words fast enough, relieved to get it all off her chest at last. 'The falcon was washed up on a beach a couple of bays down from where we were found. The lifting bags were still attached to it.'

She watched as Reilly examined its leathery cover before taking it carefully into his hands and glancing at one of the pages inside. 'It's amazing. It just looks so... basic.' He turned to Tess. 'The language. Can you read it?'

'No. I can just tell that it's Aramaic.'

'Which I'm guessing is the right language, the one it should be in.'

She nodded uneasily. 'It is.'

He just stared absently at the ancient binder, his mind locked in thought, his eyes surveying every inch of its cover. 'So what do you think? Is it real?'

'I don't know. It definitely looks the part, but you can't

really tell without sending it to a lab – there are many tests we'd have to run on it: carbon dating, analyzing the composition of the paper and the ink, checking for calligraphic consistency...' She paused and drew a nervous breath. 'Only here's the thing, Sean. I don't think we should send it to a lab. I don't think we should have anyone run tests on it.'

He cocked his head, thrown. 'What do you mean?'

'I mean I think we should just forget we ever found it,' she stated emphatically. 'We should burn the damn thing and just –'

'– and just what?' he countered. 'Act like it never existed? We can't do that. If it's not real, if this is some Templar forgery or some other hoax, then there's nothing to worry about. If it is real, well then...' He frowned, his voice trailing off.

'Then no one should ever know about it,' she insisted. 'God, I wish I hadn't told you about this.'

Reilly looked at her, perplexed. 'Am I missing something here? Whatever happened to "the people deserve to know?"'

'I was wrong. I don't think it matters anymore.' Tess heaved a ponderous sigh. 'You know, for as long as I can remember, I could only see what was wrong with the Church. The bloody history, the greed, the archaic dogma, the intolerance, the scandals of abuse... So much of it has become such a joke. I still think a lot of it could use one hell of an overhaul, without a doubt. But then, nothing's perfect, is it? And if you look at what it does when it works, when you think about the compassion and the generosity it inspires... That's where the real miracle lies.'

A slow, rhythmic clapping of hands suddenly echoed across the deserted ruins around Tess, startling her.

Turning to where the sound was coming from, she saw Vance stepping out from behind a stone wall. He kept on clapping, each slow clap distinct from the next, his eyes riveted on hers, his mouth twisted in an unsettling grin.

CHAPTER 85

'So you've seen the light. I'm really moved, Tess. Our infallible Church has got itself another convert.' Vance's tone couldn't have been more mocking or more quietly threatening. 'Hallelujah! Praise the Lord!'

Reilly watched him draw nearer and felt his muscles tighten. Vance was bedraggled and looked thinner, more gaunt than he had before. He wore simple clothes, no doubt also a gift from another charitable islander. More importantly, he wasn't carrying a weapon, which was a relief. Reilly didn't exactly relish the idea of trying to disarm the professor, not in his current weakened condition. Without a gun, though, and no doubt as worn out from getting thrashed around by the storm as he and Tess were, the professor didn't pose too much of a threat.

Vance kept approaching Tess, only now he was focusing on the codex in Reilly's hands. 'It's as if it just wants to be found, isn't it? If I were a religious man,' he scoffed, 'I'd be tempted to think we were destined to find it.'

Tess looked incredulous. 'How did you –'

'Oh, much like you, I guess,' Vance shrugged. 'I woke up with my face in the sand and a couple of crabs eyeing me curiously, and just about managed to get myself to the monastery at Panormitis. Father Spiros took me into their alms house. He didn't ask any questions, and I didn't feel any need to elaborate either. And that's where I saw you. I was delighted you had made it out too, which was more than I could have hoped for, but this...' His eyes moved over the codex. It was as if he was entranced by it. 'This is a real gift. May I?'

Reilly raised his hand in a halting manner. 'No. That's close enough.'

Vance stopped advancing. His face took on a bemused expression. 'Come on. Look at us. By any measure, we should all be dead. Doesn't that tell you something?'

Reilly was unmoved. 'It tells me you're going to be able to stand trial and spend a few years as a guest of our prison service.'

Vance seemed to drift away in a disappointed, almost hurt look, then in one unhesitant move, he rushed at Tess, grabbing her with one arm around her neck, the other now holding a large diving knife inches from her throat.

'I'm sorry, Tess,' he said, 'but I'm with Agent Reilly on this. We can't just ignore what fate has gone out of its way to hand us. You were right the first time. The world does deserve to know.' His eyes were blazing wildly, darting back and forth, keeping Reilly in check. 'Give it to me,' Vance ordered. 'Quickly.'

Reilly made a rapid study of the situation, but the knife was too close to Tess's throat for him to make a move, especially in his weakened state. It was safer to give Vance the codex and deal with him once Tess was out of harm's way. He made a calming gesture toward Vance with one hand. 'Just take it easy, alright? You can have the damn thing.' He reached out with the other hand, the one holding the manuscript. 'Here. Take it.'

'No,' Tess interjected angrily, 'don't give it to him. We can't let him go public with it. It's our responsibility now. It's my responsibility.'

Reilly shook his head. 'It's not worth your life.'

'Sean –'

'It's not worth it,' he insisted, flashing her a look of hard resolve.

Vance smiled thinly. 'Put it on the wall and back up. Slowly.'

Reilly set it down on the rough stones and took a few steps back. Vance inched forward, awkwardly maneuvering Tess closer to the wall.

He stood over the codex for a few seconds, almost scared

of touching it, before reaching out with trembling fingers and carefully lifting the cover open. He studied it in enraptured silence, turning over the sheets of parchment and mumbling '*Veritas vos liberabit*' to himself, a blissful calm now radiating from his weary features.

'I really would have liked you to be a part of this, Tess,' he said softly to her. 'You'll see. It's going to be wonderful.'

And at that moment, Tess decided to make her move. She shoved his arm violently off her shoulder and darted away from him. Vance briefly lost his footing, and as he reached out to balance himself, he lost his grip on the knife which fell from his hand onto the low stone wall and clattered out of view, disappearing into the dry bushes behind it.

He straightened up, flipping the codex shut and grabbing it with both hands, and saw that Reilly had positioned himself between him and the pathway leading out of the castle ruins, effectively blocking him. Tess was at his side.

'It's over,' Reilly stated flatly.

Vance's eyes rocketed wide as if he'd been punched in the gut. He shot quick glances around him, hesitated briefly, then leapt over the low wall and bolted into the maze of ruins.

Reilly was quick to react, clambering over the wall and rushing after him. Within seconds, they had both disappeared behind the ancient stones.

'Come back!' Tess yelled out. 'To hell with him, Sean! You're not well yet. Don't do this.'

Although he heard her screams, Reilly didn't stop. Instead, struggling over the soft ground, he was already climbing steadfastly upward, breathing heavily, hot on Vance's heels.

CHAPTER 86

Vance was moving fast, across a steep trail that cut into the side of the mountain. The scattered trees and the olive groves soon gave way to a harsher terrain of rocks and dried out bushes. Glancing back, he saw Reilly coming after him, and cursed inwardly. He scanned the surrounding area. The town was nowhere in sight, and even the castle ruins and the disused windmills had now disappeared from view. The hillside rose in a steep incline to his right, and to his left, the rocky ground seemed to curve sharply down into the sea below. There was no other choice. It was either confront Reilly or keep moving. He chose the latter.

Behind him, Reilly was breathing heavily as he tried to keep Vance within reach. His legs felt rubbery, the muscles in his thighs already burning despite the relatively short distance he had covered. He faltered on a small outcropping but managed to keep his balance and narrowly avoided injuring his ankle. Straightening himself up, he suddenly felt dizzy and took a few deep breaths, shutting his eyes and concentrating, trying to summon up any reserves of energy he could draw on. He glanced toward Vance and saw his receding silhouette clambering out of view. Rallying himself, he willed his legs forward and resumed his pursuit.

Driving himself further along the slippery surface of the rocks, Vance finally reached the top of a crag only to realize that he was trapped. Before him was an almost vertical drop down to jagged rocks far below. A sliding sea was crashing against them in rhythmic bursts of white foam.

Turning urgently, he saw Reilly who was climbing into view.

Reilly reached the rockface and clambered onto a large rock. He was now level with Vance, less than ten yards away from him. The two men stared at one another.

Vance was taking big gulps of air, catching his breath. He scanned the surroundings angrily, left then right. Seeing that the ground was firmer to the right, he decided to head that way.

Reilly shot after him.

Vance raced along the stepped bluff, but was barely twenty yards away when he stumbled in a small fissure, his foot caught between two rocks. He recovered his footing and pushed himself forward.

Painfully aware that he had little strength left in his legs, Reilly saw his opportunity and threw himself forward in a dive, his fingers reaching for Vance's ankles. He barely made contact, but it was enough. Vance lost his precarious balance again and fell. Scrambling forward on his hands and knees, Reilly lunged at Vance's legs, but his arms were as weakened as his legs. Vance rolled over and scuttled backward, the codex still gripped tightly in his hands. He kicked at Reilly, his foot smashing into his face and sending him careening a couple of yards down the slope. Vance then pulled back and hauled himself to his feet.

Reilly's mind was a blur, and his head felt like it weighed a ton. He tried to shake the daze away and rose up, only to hear Tess's voice echoing from behind.

'Sean,' she was yelling to him. 'Just let him go. You're just going to get yourself killed.'

Reilly saw her climbing up and looked at Vance, who was barely making progress and was still within reach. He turned back toward Tess, gesturing wildly. 'Go back. Go back and get some help.'

But Tess was already with him. She was also out of breath and held onto him. 'Please. It isn't safe up here. You said it yourself. It's not worth either of our lives.'

Reilly looked at her and smiled, and at that very moment, he knew with utter certainty that he would spend the rest of his life with this woman. In that instant, he heard a panicked scream from Vance's direction. He turned in time to see Vance slipping down the smooth, steep outcropping he was climbing across, his fingers clawing for purchase but finding none in the polished surface of the black rocks.

Vance's feet finally caught onto a small ledge just as Reilly started forward, hastening across the rockface. He got to the overhang and looked down. Vance was hugging the wall of stone with one shivering hand, the other still locked around the codex.

'Take my hand,' he bellowed as he reached down, stretching his arm as far as it would go.

Vance glanced up, a look of sheer terror in his eyes. He inched the arm with the codex upward, but they were still a few inches apart. 'I can't,' he stammered.

Just then, the ledge under his feet crumbled away, removing the support from under his left leg. He reached out to hang on, and his fingers instinctively let go of their hold. The codex flew from his outstretched hand, opening as it bounced off an outcropping of rock. Pages of the diary spun into the air, floating in the salty air, spiraling downward toward the crashing water below.

Reilly didn't even have time finish his 'Don't –'

Vance's voice erupted into a tortured 'No!' as he grabbed hopelessly for the papers. Then he was falling fast, outstretched arms flailing at the fluttering pages that looked like they were goading him. He tumbled helplessly into the void before smashing onto the rocks below.

Tess reached Reilly and hung onto him. They edged outward, peering down the vertiginous drop. Vance's body lay there, bent at unnatural angles. Waves crashed around him, lifting him up and moving him around like a rag doll. And all around his crumpled body, pages of the ancient document were gliding down into the sea, its swell swallowing up the ink that was washing off the parchment as well as the blood seeping from Vance's open wounds.

Reilly held firmly onto Tess. He stared down wistfully as

the last of the pages were sucked out to sea. *I guess we'll never know,* he thought somberly, grinding his teeth at the thought.

And then he spotted something.

Letting go of Tess, he quickly backed up over the edge and climbed down the rockface.

'What are you doing?' she yelled, leaning over to see where he was going, her voice sick with worry.

Moments later, he reappeared over the lip of the rock. Tess reached down and helped him up, and saw that he was clutching something between his teeth.

It was a piece of parchment.

A lone page from the codex.

Tess stared at it in disbelief as Reilly handed it to her. He watched her. 'At least we have something to prove we didn't just imagine it all,' he managed, still breathless with the effort of retrieving it.

Tess studied the page in her hand for a long moment. Everything she'd lived through since that night at the Met, all the bloodshed and the fear and the turmoil inside her came rushing back at her. And in that moment, she knew. She knew, without a shadow of a doubt, what she would do with it. And without hesitation, she smiled at Reilly, crumpled up the sheet of parchment, and sent it spinning over the bluff.

She watched it fall into the sea, then turned to Reilly, and wrapped her arms around him.

'I've got all I need,' she told him, before taking his hand and leading him away from the ledge.

EPILOGUE

Paris – March 1314

The sumptuously decorated wooden grandstand stood close to the edge of a field on the Île de la Cité. Brightly colored pennants rippled in the light breeze, the thin sunshine reflected in the gaudy accoutrements of the king's courtiers and henchmen who were already assembled there.

At the back of an excited and chattering crowd of commoners, Martin of Carmaux stood, stooped and weary. He wore a shabby brown robe, the gift of a friar he had met a few weeks earlier.

Although he was only a few years past forty, Martin had aged grievously. For almost two decades, he had labored in the Tuscan quarry under a brutal sun and the merciless lashes of the overseers. He had all but abandoned hope of escape when one of many rock slides, this one worse than most, killed a dozen of the men who slaved there, as well as some of the guards. By a stroke of luck, Martin and the man to whom he was shackled had been able to use the confusion and the swirling clouds of dust to make their escape.

Undeterred by the long years spent in virtual slavery and completely cut off from any news from beyond that accursed valley, Martin had only one thing in mind. He headed straight for the waterfall and found the rock with the fissures that resembled the Templars' splayed cross, recovered Aimard's letter, and began the long journey through the mountains and into France.

The journey had taken several months, but his long-delayed return to his homeland had only brought him crushing disappointment. He had learned of the disasters that had befallen the Knights Templar and as he drew ever closer to

Paris, he knew that he was too late to do anything that would alter the Order's fate.

He had searched and asked, as discreetly as he could, but had found nothing. All of his Brothers were gone, either dead or in hiding. The king's flag flew over the great Paris Temple.

He was alone.

Presently, standing there and waiting among the gossiping crowd, Martin identified the gray-clad figure of Pope Clement, who was climbing the steps of the grandstand and taking his place amidst the peacock-bright courtiers.

As Martin watched, the pope's attention turned toward the center of the field where two stakes had been surrounded by brushwood. Movement caught Martin's eye as the emaciated and shattered bodies of two men he knew to be Jacques de Molay, the Grand Master of the Order, and Geoffroi de Charnay, the Preceptor of Normandy, were being dragged onto the field.

With neither of the condemned men possessing any lingering capacity for physical resistance, they were quickly bound to the stakes. A heavy set man stepped forward with a lighted brand, then looked to the king for instructions.

A sudden stillness fell over the crowd, and Martin saw the king raise a hand in a careless gesture.

The brush was lit.

Smoke began to rise, and soon, flames licked through, twigs popping and crackling as the heat built up. Sickened and utterly helpless to intervene, Martin wanted to turn and walk away, but he felt the need to observe, to bear witness to this depraved act. Unwilling though he was, he pushed through to the front of the crowd. It was then, to his astonishment, that he saw the Grand Master raise his head and look directly at the king and the pope.

Even from this distance, the sight unsettled Martin. De Molay's eyes were blazing with a fire more fierce than the one that would soon consume him.

Despite his frail and broken appearance, the Grand Master's voice was strong and steady. 'In the name of the Order of the Knights of the Temple,' he rasped, 'I curse you, Philippe le Bel, and your buffoon pope, and I call on God Almighty to have you both join me before his seat within the year, to suffer his judgment and burn forever in the furnaces of hell...'

If de Molay said anything else, Martin didn't hear it, as the fire roared upward, obliterating any screams of the dying men. Then the breeze turned, and smoke swept over the grandstand and the crowd, carrying with it the sickening stench of burning flesh. Coughing and spluttering, the king stumbled down the steps, the pope trailing behind him, his eyes streaming from the smoke. As they passed close to where Martin stood, the old Templar watched the pope. He felt the bile of anger rising and burning in his throat, and at that moment, he realized that his task was still not over.

Perhaps not in his lifetime. But one day, maybe, things would be different.

That night, he set off, leaving the city and heading south to the land of his forefathers, to Carmaux. He would settle there, or elsewhere in the Languedoc, and live out his days. But before he died, he would ensure that the letter did not vanish forever. Somehow, he would find the means for it to survive.

It had to survive.

It had to fulfill its destiny.

He owed it to those who had died, to Hugh and to William of Beaujeu and above all to his friend Aimard of Villiers, to ensure that their sacrifices had not been worthless.

It was all down to him now. He thought back to Aimard's final revelation that night, deep inside the church by the willow tree. About the painstaking efforts of their predecessors, who had first concocted the deception. About the nine years of meticulous crafting. About the careful planning that had taken almost two hundred years to bear fruit.

We came close, he thought, *so close. It was a noble goal. It was worth all the hard work, all the sacrifices, all the pain.*

He knew what he had to do.

He had to make sure the illusion was kept alive. The illusion that it was still out there, waiting.

The illusion that it was real.

And at the right time, certainly not during his lifetime, maybe, just maybe, someone would be able to use their lost masterpiece to achieve what they had all set out to do.

And then, a bittersweet smile broke across his face as a hopeful thought drifted into his mind. *Maybe one day*, he mused, *it would be obsolete.* Maybe the plan would no longer be necessary. Maybe people would learn to overcome their petty differences, and rise above murderous squabbles over personal faith.

He shook the thought away, chiding himself for his wistful naïveté, and kept on walking.

ACKNOWLEDGMENTS

Many people generously contributed their knowledge, expertise and support to this book, and I'd like to start off by thanking my great friend Carlos Heneine, for introducing me to the Templars and, as always, having fun batting ideas back and forth with me; Bruce Crowther, who helped usher me into this new realm; and Franc Roddam, who swooped in and gave it wings.

I'd also like to personally thank Jon Wood and Susan Lamb for their enthusiasm and support, along with Juliet Ewers, Jenny Page, and everyone at Orion. It's been a real treat.

A humongous thank you, too, to my agent Eugenie Furniss, without whose passion, years of relentless prodding, and support this book would never have materialized. Also thanks to Jay Mandel, Tracy Fisher, Lauren Heller Whitney, Lucinda Prain, Rowan Lawton, and everyone at the William Morris Agency.

Warm nods of gratitude are also due to Olivier Granier, Simon Oakes, Cephas Howard, Eric Fellner, Leon Friedman, Maître François Serres, Howard Ellis, Adam Goodman and everyone at Mid-Atlantic Films in Budapest for their continued support, Dotti Irving and Ruth Cairns at Colman Getty, Samantha Hill, Kevin and Linda Adeson (sorry about roughing up Mitch), Chris and Roberta Hanley, Dr Philip Saba, Matt Filosa, Carolyn Whitaker, Dr Amin Milki, Bashar Chalabi, Patty Fanouraki, and Barbara Roddam.

Last, but galaxies away from least, I'd like to thank my wife Suellen, who's lived with this project for so long; a man couldn't ask for a greater supporter, friend and soulmate.